Peter James was educated at Charterhouse and then at film school. He lived in North America for a number of years, working as a screen writer and film producer (his projects included the award-winning *Dead of Night*) before returning to England. His previous novels, including the number-one bestseller *Possession*, have been translated into twenty-eight languages. All his novels reflect his deep interest in medicine, science and the paranormal. He has recently produced several films including the BAFTA-nominated *The Merchant of Venice*, starring Al Pacino, Jeremy Irons and Joseph Fiennes, and *The Bridge of San Luis Rey*, starring Robert De Niro, Kathy Bates and Harvey Keitel. He also co-created the hit Channel 4 series *Bedsitcom*, which was nominated for a Rose d'Or. His first crime novel, *Dead Simple*, won the German Krimi-Blitz 2005 prize for crime fiction, the 2006 French Prix Polar International, and the French 2007 Prix Coeur Noir. His second, *Looking Good Dead*, was shortlisted for the 2007 British Galaxy Book Awards Crime Thriller of the Year and the French 2007 Prix SNCF Du Polar. He is currently adapting *Dead Simple* and *Looking Good Dead* for television. Peter James lives near Brighton, in Sussex, and in Notting Hill, London. Visit his website at www.peterjames.com.

DENIAL

Peter James

An Orion paperback

First published in Great Britain in 1998
by Orion
This paperback edition published in 1999
by Orion Books Ltd,
Orion House, 5 Upper St Martin's Lane,
London WC2H 9EA

An Hachette Livre UK company

Reissued 2006

A CIP catalogue record for this book is available
from the British Library.

Printed and bound in Great Britain by
Clays Ltd, St Ives plc

The Orion Publishing Group's policy is to use papers that
are natural, renewable and recyclable products and
made from wood grown in sustainable forests. The logging
and manufacturing processes are expected to conform to
the environmental regulations of the country of origin.

www.orionbooks.co.uk

'A man who has not passed through the inferno of his passions has never overcome them.'

Carl Jung

ACKNOWLEDGMENTS

I've been incredibly lucky to have had the support and enthusiasm of some truly wonderful people in my research for this novel. The input of Dr David Veale, Dr Celia Taylor, Detective Chief Inspector David Gaylor and Detective Constable Mick Harris in particular, who were so much more generous with their time and their thoughts and their creative ideas than I had any right to expect, helped to shape and underpin the whole novel.

The friendliness and enthusiasm with which the Sussex Police helped me was quite overwhelming. Without being able to name every single one of the many officers I spent time with in Brighton, Hove, Haywards Heath, Crawley and Hampstead police stations and out on patrol, I owe a huge debt of thanks to the Chief Constable, Paul Whitehouse, QPM, who made it possible for me. I also owe very special thanks to Chief Superintendent Mike Lewis, Detective Chief Inspector George A Smith, WPC Ren Harris, PC Nick Dimmer, PC Glen Douglas, PC Nick Bokor-Ingram of Brighton Police. Chief Superintendent David K Ashley, Sergeant Phil Herring, DS Bill Warner and Tony Howard, of Hove Police. Acting Inspector Ian Jeffrey, PC Brian Seamons and PC Gary Pearson of the Haywards Heath Traffic Division. Ross Parsons of the Sussex Ambulance Service. And to the staff of the National Missing Persons Helpline.

Very deep thanks also to Dr Dennis Friedman, Roy Shuttleworth, Julie Carlstrom MFCC, Dr M Anton, Richard Blacklock, Elizabeth Veale, Dr Nigel Kirkham, Veronica Hamilton Deeley – Coroner for Brighton and Hove – Nigel McMillan, Indra Sinha, Spink & Son Ltd, Chris Wellings of Graves, Son & Pilcher, Lyall Watson, from whose marvellous book *Lifetide* I gleaned the information on the bower-bird, and Dr Roderick Main for his knowledge of Carl Jung and his excellent book *Jung on Synchronicity and the Paranormal*.

As ever, deep thanks also to my indispensable unofficial editor Sue Ansell, to Patricia Preece and to my UK agent Jon Thurley for his immense contribution and patience. And, of course, thanks to my wife Georgina, and to my hairy friend Bertie who after five years has at last learned not to chew floppy disks that fall on the floor . . .

Peter James, Sussex, England, 1998
scary@pavilion.co.uk

Prologue

In the aloof, detached house in Holland Park, which, like its equally smart neighbours, rose four storeys high and was fronted by a gravel drive and iron railings, Thomas Lamark brought breakfast up to his mother, as he did every morning, on the absolute dot – the nanosecond – of ten thirty.

Standing six foot six inches tall, with sleek good looks and a charmer's smile, Thomas was an alluring man of thirty-seven. Attired in a Liberty silk dressing gown, leather slippers from Gucci, a gold Rolex wristwatch, and Givenchy cologne, he wore nothing under the dressing gown; his mother liked to know that he was naked beneath that fine silk.

On the silver tray was an exquisite Herend teapot containing Fortnum and Mason Breakfast Tea, and a matching bone china cup and saucer. Alongside them lay a copy of *The Times*, and a single white rose he had just picked from the garden and which was still moist from the dew – she always loved his little surprises and this morning Thomas was in the mood for a reward. He hoped she would be too.

He stopped outside her bedroom. All the interior doors of the house were stately, with panelling and beading, satin white paintwork and crystal handles; but this door on the second floor, standing plumb centre across the landing from the carved staircase, with a bronze bust of his mother's head on a pedestal outside, seemed somehow more imperious than the rest. Even after all these years it continued both to awe him and attract him.

There were days when he felt like throwing the tray over

her and screaming, *Let me be free!* – but this was not one of them.

He checked his watch, waited for the second hand to complete the sweep on its circuit. At precisely ten thirty, he entered his mother's bedroom.

Thomas had been awake throughout the night in front of his computer; a cybertraveller of the world, he rested but seldom slept. Nights passed in games of chess with a man called Jurgen Jurgens in Clearwater Springs, Florida, or in speculation on extra-terrestrial life with a chat-line group in San Francisco, or in discussing recent gruesome deaths with a contributor to the *Fortean Times*. He checked e-mail from several medical newsgroups to which he subscribed, traded recipes with a woman in Chesapeake bay, and monitored the movements of stock markets around the world, charting the progress of the shares in his mother's portfolio and studying the websites of the companies behind them. Each morning he fed her stockbroker with fresh information.

He had an IQ of 178.

Walking in silent footfalls across the carpet, unable to take his eyes from his mother's face, his heart filled with adoration – and another, conflicting emotion with which he had struggled all his life, he placed the tray on the table at the foot of the two-poster canopied bed, opened the white lace and damask curtains by pulling their cords, then secured them with tasselled ropes. The room smelt of Chanel perfume and his mother's clothes. The smells of his childhood. The smells of his life.

Aroused, he stared at her.

Her blonde hair, which had tumbled across the pillow, glowed as if the rays of sunshine were a theatrical spotlight. He knew that she was not going to open her eyes or move until he had kissed her, although she was awake now, for sure. This was her tease.

And these precious seconds each morning, when she lay looking so gentle, so sweet, so pretty, as he stood adoring her in silence, these moments were the pearls of his life.

He was rapt. She was beautiful, fifty-nine years old, an

2

angelic vision. Her face was white, it was always white in the morning, but today it seemed even whiter, her beauty even purer. She was beyond perfection; she was the state of grace to which his existence was rooted.

'Good morning, Mummy,' he said, and walked over to kiss her. She never opened her eyes until that kiss. This morning her eyes stayed shut.

He noticed now, for the first time, the popped blister packs of capsules littering the floor beside the bed. The empty tumbler.

There was a tightening inside him. Even as he bent, he knew something had changed in this room. She had come home in distress yesterday. She'd had a headache and gone to bed early.

Her cheek was cold against his lips. It felt inert. Like soft putty, it yielded but did not spring back.

'Mummy?' His voice came out sounding all wrong.

A bottle sat on the floor beside the bed: the cap was off, the contents had gone.

'Mummy?'

Panic blurred his vision; the floor rose, the room shifted as if it was being rocked by an ocean swell. He threw his arms around her, tried to move her, to lift her up, but she was rigid, like a slab of meat from the freezer.

He screamed out to her, grabbed an empty blister pack from the floor, tried to read the label but he couldn't focus. He seized the bottle but could not read its label either. Then he lunged for the phone, stumbled, grabbed the receiver and dialled 999.

'Ambulance,' he blurted, then the address and phone number, and then in deep, sobbing gulps the words, 'Please, my mother, Gloria Lamark, the actress! Gloria Lamark! *Gloria Lamark!* Please, please come. She's taken an overdose.'

He dropped the receiver. It bounced on the carpet then dangled.

The operator talked back to him calmly. 'The ambulance is on its way. Please stay on the line, sir. Can you feel a pulse? Is she breathing normally? Do you know what she has taken? How long ago she took them? Is she on her back? If so, please lay her on her side. Do you know if the tablets were taken with alcohol? All the time I'm speaking to you an ambulance is on the way. Could you please get together the tablets that you think she's taken to show the paramedics, sir? Please ensure her airways are clear.'

He had his arms around his mother's neck and was hugging her to him, choking on his sobs, haemorrhaging tears. She had no pulse, she wasn't breathing, she was hours past that. He heard the ambulance-service operator's voice, a distant tinny echo, and in fury he snatched up the phone. 'I went to fucking medical school, you stupid bitch!'

He threw the phone down and clutched his mother to him again. 'Mummy, don't do this to me. Don't leave me! You promised you'd never leave me. Come back, please come back, you *must* come back!'

He pressed his lips to her mouth, tried to open it, but it stayed shut, tight shut. Locked.

She had thrown away the key.

Chapter One

She was smiling at Michael through the wide rectangle of soundproofed glass that separated the cramped radio studio from the cramped control room.

Her name was Amanda Capstick. She worked as a producer for an independent television company that was making a documentary on psychiatrists. Twenty-nine, blonde hair that touched her shoulders and a smile that touched his heart; a smile as cheeky as her face was pretty.

She was the first woman Michael Tennent had looked at twice in the three years since his wife, Katy, had died.

And he knew why: it was because in some way she reminded him of Katy, although she was really quite different. At five foot nine, Katy had been a slender, classical beauty. Amanda was a good six inches shorter and had more of a tomboy figure. And yet when she had called and asked for half an hour of his time, and the following day had walked into his office, just three weeks ago, she had reignited a spark in him that he had thought was dead.

She made him smile. And Katy had made him smile – once, at any rate; the Katy he wanted to remember. He tried to ignore Amanda Capstick, concentrate on his caller, but he couldn't. Normally he did his weekly one-hour radio show for the benefit of his callers, but tonight he was aware that he was doing it for the benefit of Amanda Capstick, sitting behind that glass window in her denim suit and her white T-shirt with her classy wristwatch.

She was his audience. She had been inside his head for the past three weeks, although this was the first time he had seen her since that first brief meeting. And it was only her presence, and nothing else today, that had enabled him to forget, if only for a short while, the nightmare that had begun when he had received the phone call from the City of Westminster Coroner's officer.

Amanda Capstick watched the psychiatrist hunched over the console, oversized headphones clamped to his ears, his face partially obscured by the bulb of grey foam rubber that encased the mike, deep in concentration, and serious, soooo seeeeerious. He was interesting-looking, a mixture of maturity and wisdom coupled with distinct flashes of a little boy lost. And at forty, he was on that attractive cusp between youth and middle age.

He dressed on the cusp, too: a quiet navy suit, but with a fashionably high-cut collar, and a bold tie. His dark brown hair was gelled back, and he wore small oval tortoiseshell glasses that on some people would merely have been a fashion statement, but which gave him the air of an intellectual, and something beyond that. She felt she was looking at an adventurer.

You'd be good in my documentary, she thought. He had a natural air of authority, of commitment. But what she liked most about him was his openness, his lack of arrogance. So many medics, particularly psychiatrists, seemed to have become jaded by their profession. They had lost their inquisitiveness, seemed to have reached a point at which they were satisfied with what they understood.

This guy was different. And there was a touching sadness about him. When he smiled, it seemed he was struggling against some inner conflict that forbade him to smile. She knew, from her research, that he had lost his wife three years ago in a car smash – maybe he was still grieving.

She knew also that he did this programme every Wednesday between seven and eight p.m. for Talk Radio. He wrote a weekly column for the *Daily Mail* on psychiatry. He had a special interest in obsessive compulsive disorder and body dysmorphic disorder – the official name for what the media called 'imagined ugliness syndrome' – and he appeared

6

regularly in the press or on television, either giving opinions or as an expert witness in criminal proceedings.

Three days a week he saw mostly private patients at the Sheen Park Hospital, near Putney, and a further two days a week saw research patients at the Princess Royal Hospital Medical School, where he was honorary senior lecturer. He had a reputation as a philanthropist, giving donations to establish new self-help organisations for phobia sufferers and for those with his speciality disorders, and he was always prepared to waive his charges if a patient had a problem getting either the National Health Service or private insurance to pay.

Michael had never found the secret of getting comfortable in this studio. It smelt of stale air. It was either so hot that he ran with perspiration, or there was such a cold blast that his eyes watered. The cans were clumsy and always slipping down over his ears. The coffee seemed to get weaker and the flavour of the Styrofoam cup stronger each week. And he always had to be careful: he must resist the temptation to slide one of the control knobs up or down, avoid being distracted by the swinging arms on the level dials or touching the mike or the battery of switches with hand-written notices that said DO NOT SWITCH OFF!

Normally he never suffered from nerves on this show, he just relaxed, got on with it and did his best to help distressed people who did not know where else to turn for help. But tonight he had the distraction of Amanda. And he had that news on his mind. That terrible, terrible news that one of his patients, an actress, had committed suicide, and that he was to blame. He usually found that the hour flew by, but tonight it had crawled. He'd had difficult callers, and in trying to play to Amanda – his gallery – he'd lost the spontaneity and warmth that normally came out of the intimacy of his one-to-ones with his callers.

Now it was nearly over, thank God. And on the end of the line for the past ten minutes he had had Marj, from Essex. Right now he could have cheerfully strangled her. She was talking to him in the same tone she might have used to a supermarket checkout girl who'd overcharged her for an avocado.

Doing his best to remain calm, he said, 'I think you ought to read that book on Freud again, Marj. It was Carl Jung who believed in the collective unconscious, not Sigmund Freud.'

'I don't think so, Dr Tennent. And you still haven't explained my dream,' she said petulantly. 'My teeth falling out. What does that mean?'

Through the cans, the producer said, 'Wind it up, Michael, news in sixty.'

Michael glanced up at the clock above Amanda Capstick's face. Its hands were closing on seven p.m.

'It's a very common dream, Marj. I explained it in detail to a caller a couple of weeks back. There are two periods in life when your teeth fall out: the loss of milk teeth, which means all the problems relating to maturing, in particular that of taking on responsibility. And the other period,' he said, with perhaps more malice than he had intended, 'is where you are now, from the sound of your voice. Fear of old age, and all the baggage that comes with it, becoming undesirable, ineffectual, impotent. *Toothless*, effectively.'

'But that's what *Freud* said,' the woman retorted.

The producer's voice in his ear said, 'Ten seconds!'

'We have to end it there, I'm afraid, Marj,' Michael said. 'I hope I've helped you a little.' He clicked the switch, tugged off his cans and felt a trickle of sweat scurry down the back of his neck. Amanda Capstick smiled at him again from behind the window and gave him a thumbs-up.

He grimaced back at her and shrugged, then sipped the last tepid half-inch of his coffee. The studio door opened, and the producer, Chris Beamish, six foot tall, bearded, eyes wary and birdlike, came in, nodding solemnly.

'How was it?' Michael asked the same question every week.

And Beamish gave him the same reply each week, 'Good, good programme, I think they liked it.'

'I was off-key,' Michael said. 'I was toast.'

'No, they liked it,' Beamish repeated, speaking by some

8

kind of proxy on behalf of the show's alleged 382,000 listeners.

'You're very good,' Amanda told Michael, a few minutes later, as they walked past the security guard in the deserted lobby. 'You have a very comfortable way with the callers.'

He smiled. 'Thanks, but I wasn't on the ball tonight.'

'I'd like to use a segment of your show in my programme.'

'Sure.'

'We could try to do it live and get that spontaneity.' She paused and then said, 'Ever thought of having your own television show? Something like Anthony Clare's *In The Psychiatrist's Chair*?'

'I'm not convinced that media psychiatry is the right thing for people,' he said. 'I'm having a lot of doubts about this. Ten minutes isn't enough. Nor is half an hour. I'm beginning to think I might be doing more harm than good. Doing this without being able to see faces, body language, is difficult. I thought originally it might encourage people to see the benefits of psychiatry. Now I'm not sure.'

They reached the doors. Michael smelt her perfume: it was subtle, a faint muskiness, and he liked it. In a moment she would be gone and he'd be heading home to another evening on his own, defrosting something from Marks and Spencer, then scanning the television guides or trying to get stuck into a book, or catching up on some paperwork, or –

– writing the report the Coroner's officer had requested.

He wanted desperately to stop her from disappearing. But it had been so long since he had chatted up a woman that whatever apology for a technique he'd once had was now long gone. Also he had no idea whether she was single or married, and glanced surreptitiously down at her hands.

She wore no rings. Her hands were surprisingly small and bony and the varnish on the nails was chipped, as if she was a grafter who didn't give a toss about appearances, and he found this endearing. He didn't like perfection. Too many of his patients were perfectionists. He liked to see a bit of slack in life.

'Do you have time for a quick drink?' he asked, surprising himself by how nonchalant he sounded.

Their eyes met and held. She had beautiful eyes, cobalt blue, bright, intensely alive. She smiled, glanced down at her watch, then looked away evasively. 'Actually, thanks, but I – I have to get to a meeting at eight.'

'Sure,' Michael said, masking his disappointment with a cheery smile, and wondering what kind of a good-looking hunk this meeting was with.

He thought about her as he drove home, steering the Volvo in the slow crawl south over Putney Bridge and up the high street. He thought about her smile through the glass window of the control room. He thought about that look she had given him in the doorway as they were leaving. There had been some kind of attraction, definitely.

She had turned down his offer of a drink.

But hadn't he detected some hint of reluctance in the way she'd turned it down?

There would be other chances. They'd be meeting again. Or . . . hell, he could call her tomorrow and try his luck. Why not?

Oh, yes, Dr Michael Tennent, and what exactly would she see in you? You're a decade older than her. She's a young, bright, hip girl with the world at her feet. You're an old fart in a Volvo.

You're not even any good at your job any more. The proof of that is in this morning's paper. You'd better hope Amanda Capstick doesn't get to see it.

But she liked me. She did. She really did. So she had a date, so what?

He would call her in the morning, he decided.

She could always say no.

Chapter Two

No one ever prepares us for death. It ought to be on the school curriculum. Instead, teachers make us learn that in a right-angled triangle, the square on the hypotenuse is equal to the sum of the squares on the two remaining sides. I've carried that nugget in my head for twenty-five years and never yet had any use for it. They make us learn how to ask the way to the town hall in French. I've got through thirty-seven years of my life without ever needing to do this.

But they don't ever teach you how you are going to feel when someone close to you dies. And that is going to happen to all of us. It has just happened to me, and I'm all alone here, having to work this out for myself.

It seems there's a whole sequence of emotions you go through. Shock. Denial. Anger. Guilt. Depression.

I've been through shock, ticked that one off. I've been through refusal to accept. Ticked that box, too. Now I'm at the anger stage.

I'm angry with a whole lot of people. But, most of all, I'm angry with you, Dr Michael Tennent.

You killed my mother.

Chapter Three

'Wednesday 9 July 1997. Report to Dr Gordon Sampson, Coroner, City of Westminster. From Dr Michael Tennent MD, MRC Psych. *Subject:* Gloria Daphne Ruth Lamark, deceased.

'I had been seeing the deceased as a patient since March 1990. Prior to that she was a patient of my colleague, Dr Marcus Rennie, at the Sheen Park Hospital, intermittently from 1969 to his retirement in 1990. Her records show that she was under psychiatric care and on anti-depressant medications continually since 1959. (See attached schedule.)

'My last interview with her, on Monday 7 July, was particularly unproductive. In recent months I had felt she was making some progress towards realisation of her difficulties, and towards acceptance that she was temperamentally unsuited to the disciplines required in the acting profession, and I was trying to encourage her to find other interests, particularly in the field of charity, where she could make a useful contribution to society and in so doing lead a more fulfilled existence.

'In my opinion she was a deeply troubled woman, suffering from a personality disorder that prevented her from living an ordinary, socially interactive life, and led to her turning into a virtual recluse. This personality disorder was developmental from childhood or adolescence and the collapse of her promising career as a film actress during the mid 1960s was almost certainly a trigger for deterioration.'

In his den at home, Michael rewound the tape on his dictating machine, listened to the beginning of his report, then continued. 'She had major roles, including some as leading lady, in several films during the late 1950s and the early 1960s but these rapidly petered out while she was still only in her twenties. She blamed the collapse of her career on a combination of factors. The birth of her son, Thomas. The breakdown of her marriage. Underhand behaviour by some of her rivals, in particular the actress Cora Burstridge, whom she believed, obsessively, went out of her way to destroy her career for motives of jealousy and self-advancement.

'In my opinion the root cause of the demise of the deceased's career was her personality disorder. She was unable to accept or face any of the realities of life. She had a massive ego, which needed constant feeding, and would lapse into bouts of violent, uncontrollable rage when any aspects of her talents or abilities were questioned, frequently causing actual bodily harm to others.

'She displayed manic depressive symptoms in characteristic mood swings, during which she would veer between a severely exaggerated opinion of her own talents, and extreme depression. To this end she maintained a large retinue of staff, whose principal role, in my judgement, was to pander to her ego and maintain her delusion that she was still a grand star (there are certain parallels that may be drawn here with the character in the film *Sunset Boulevard*).

'On a number of occasions during consultations the deceased broached the subject of suicide, although my records show that she had not mentioned it for two years. It is recorded that she attempted to take her own life in 1967, and again in 1986, following the failure of a theatrical play in which she was attempting an acting comeback. Previous attempts are a known high-risk factor and I was aware of this throughout my dealings with her. However, from the relatively low dosages of pills taken on these previous occasions, the wording of the notes, and the general circumstances, it has been my opinion that these attempts were more a cry for help than serious intent to take her own life.

'She was able to maintain her lavish lifestyle due to inheriting a substantial part of the estate of her estranged husband, the German industrialist Dieter Buch, who died in a skiing accident before any divorce arrangements had been finalised.

'Since the mid 1960s the deceased's life had revolved totally around her son, Thomas, who has lived at home with her for most of his life, and upon whom she has been utterly – and abnormally – dependent, emotionally and socially.'

Michael stopped dictating. His report would almost certainly be read out in court at the inquest. He needed to consider her son's feelings carefully. Gloria Lamark's relationship with the son she rarely spoke about, and whom he had never met, had always bothered him, but he'd never succeeded in drawing out of her the full truth of it.

He gathered that the boy had been expelled from school for some reason she would not talk about, and had spent years of his childhood undergoing psychiatry. He had the feeling Gloria knew something was wrong with him, and had been shielding him, but whether it was for the boy's sake, or to protect her own image, he had never been able to ascertain.

At fifty-nine she had still been a beautiful woman. After her husband had left her, she'd had a series of sexual relationships, but they had never lasted, and from the time her son had reached his early teens, she had stopped seeing other men.

He sensed that she was desperately protective of Thomas, and knew that for most of his childhood he had been educated at home. She had told Michael that Thomas had wanted to be a doctor but again, for some reason he could never elicit from her, the young man had dropped out of medical school and returned home. He appeared to have no friends.

Michael was pretty sure that this was due to the control she exerted over him. An overbearing possessiveness was not uncommon in mother-son relationships, although, he suspected, in Gloria Lamark's case it might have gone further than that.

Gloria had always told him that Thomas was perfect in

every way. It was inevitable she should think that. It would have been inconceivable to her that she might have produced a son who was less than perfect. In his mind Michael had an image of a meek, inadequate, brow-beaten weakling.

He wondered how the poor man was coping now.

Chapter Four

This place. The stairwell. The multi-storey car park. Grey precast concrete. Used syringes and torn burger wrappers. The smell of urine. Ceiling lamps squeezing out feeble haloes of light through filters of dead flies and dust.

Tina Mackay did not have a problem with this place in the mornings when there were always people around and daylight enough to read the graffiti, but at night, in dusk or darkness, it hot-wired her imagination, firing up all kinds of thoughts that she really did not want to be having.

The door slammed behind her, silencing the snarled traffic on High Holborn and replacing it with a hollow reverberating boom as if she was standing inside a vast drum. Then, shadows jumping around her, and newspaper headlines of dismembered torsos on her mind, she began to make her way up the five flights of steps. This was the one part of her journey home that she hated. But tonight she was distracted.

Tonight she had a date!

Her mind was on what she was going to wear, whether she should wash her hair (not enough time, so not an option). Shoes. Lipstick. Perfume.

Handbag?

Shit, I forgot to collect my shoes from the repairer! Black suede. They would have gone perfectly with her outfit, and now she would have to do a fast rethink. *Damn. Damn. Damn.*

Someone had pulled the day away from beneath her like it was some big rug. Happened most days, time just ran out on her, work piles got bigger, lists grew longer, more and more phone calls did not get returned. But tonight she was going to forget all that. Tonight she almost wasn't afraid of the echoes of her footsteps that taunted her up the stairwell. Tonight she was thinking about Tony (*the Hon. Anthony!*) Rennison. Hunk, serious intellectual, shy, funny.

And he liked her.

And she liked him, big-time.

Suddenly Tina, who had always acted old for her years, was a kid again. Two weeks ago, before she'd met Tony, before he'd asked her out that first time, she had been thirty-two going on forty-two or maybe even fifty-two.

Short, with boyish brown hair, she had a pleasant face, plain but not unattractive, but in the way she dressed and carried herself, she exuded an aura of confidence. It made people instinctively trust her, had seen her rise to head girl at school and now editorial director of Pelham House, one of London's most aggressive publishers, where she had transformed the fiction list and was in the process of turning round the once-ailing non-fiction.

But tonight she was a schoolgirl, with butterflies in her stomach that were fluttering harder with every step she took nearer her car, nearer home.

Nearer her date.

Her Golf GTI, exhaust broken, was in its bay in the far corner, rear end sticking out beneath the giant heating duct that in the darkness looked like some lurking prehensile beast. The Golf welcomed her arrival with a sharp beep, a wink of its lights and the sound of its locks thudding open. She was a little surprised when she opened her door and the interior light failed to come on.

Inside, she clunked her seat-belt buckle home. Then, as she put her key in the ignition, the passenger door opened and a massively tall figure slid into the seat beside her.

A male voice, laconic and confident, right next to her, inches from her face, said, 'Remember me?'

She froze.

'Thomas Lamark.' He sounded as if he was rolling an ice-cube around in his mouth. 'Remember me?'

Oh, Jesus, she thought, her brain cells colliding inside her head. The car reeked of cologne. Givenchy. It was the same perfume her date wore. Was this him, playing some joke? Except the voice was different. This was a calm, deep, controlled voice. There was a cold beauty in it. Chilling. An almost poetic resonance. Her hand scrabbled for the door handle.

'No,' she said. 'I don't remember you.'

'You should remember my name. *Thomas Lamark*. You turned down my book.'

There were no people around up here. It was nearly eight o'clock. The attendant was in his booth, five storeys below.

'Your book?' She couldn't see his face: she was talking to a silhouette, a tall, lean silhouette.

'You turned it down.'

'I'm sorry,' she said. 'I – it – your name doesn't ring a bell. Thomas Lamark?'

'You wrote me a letter. I have it here.'

She heard a rustle of paper. Then she heard him say, ' "Dear Mr Lamark, Thank you for sending your manuscript, *The Authorised Biography of Gloria Lamark*, to us. After careful reading, we regret we are unable to consider this for publication on our lists. We hope you will be successful with it elsewhere. Yours sincerely, Tina Mackay, Editorial Director." '

There was a silence. Tina wondered what chance she had of opening the door and making a run for it.

'This regret, Tina. Is this real? Do you really regret this?' Then he added, 'I need to know. It's very important to me.'

There were other cars up here. Someone must appear soon, she thought, hoped. Just play for time. He was a crank, that was all, just a crank.

'Would you like me to take another look at it?' Her voice came out small and crushed.

'It's a bit late for that now, Tina.'

'We use outside readers. I – we get so many manuscripts, it's impossible to read every one myself. I get sent two hundred manuscripts some weeks.'

'This wasn't important enough for you to read, Tina?'

'No, that's not what I meant.'

'Oh, I think it is, Tina. What you are saying is it might

18

have been important enough for me to write it, but it wasn't important enough for you to read it. It's the biography of my mother – Gloria Lamark.'

'*Gloria Lamark?*' she echoed, her throat constricted with fear.

'You're never heard of her?' His scorn was corrosive.

'I – look – why don't you let me have it back, and I – I will read it.'

Then his tone changed, suddenly, into utter charm and, for a brief moment, her hopes rose. 'You know something, Tina? I wish I could do that. I really do. You have to believe me that I'm sincere about this.'

Tina saw a glint of something metallic. She heard a click and a slap. Then silence. 'What was that?' she said.

'It was a coin. A very special coin that belonged to my late father. A gold twenty-mark coin from the state of Hesse-Darmstadt, minted in the year 1892, the last year of the reign of King Ludwig the Fourth. I just tossed this coin. Heads and tails. One and zero. Binary. You can put the whole of life in a binary code. That's how computers work, you know that, Tina? On and off. Everything on this planet is as black and white as that. There is a great beauty in simplicity. If you'd read my book you'd know that.'

'I – I'll read it.'

'No, the moment's gone. Everything in life has a moment. Did you ever think about that?'

'Nothing's ever too late.'

'No, you're wrong. This conversation. This is all much too late.' He tossed the coin again. 'Heads,' he said. 'Do you have any idea what *heads* means?'

'No.'

'You would have if you'd read my book.'

19

Chapter Five

What on earth did I ever see in you?

Once Amanda would have died for him, but now, to-night, she was staring across the restaurant table at a virtual stranger.

His name was Brian Trussler; he was forty-six. He had a lean, hard, street-wise face, and thin fair hair cropped short, except for a handful of strands left long to cover his bald dome. He was wearing a tired-looking grey Armani jacket over a black shirt, and a loud tie. He had a wife, Linda, two young sons, Adam and Oliver, three smart cars and a Harley Davidson motorcycle.

Although he was not handsome in any conventional sense, Amanda had always been jealously aware of his ability to attract women. When she had first met him, seven years back, he exuded a sense of energy she had never felt from any human being before. He gave the impression that, if he wanted, he could move mountains. It had been that energy, together with a degree of starstruck awe, that had instantly attracted her to him.

They had begun an affair, in a room at the Halcyon Hotel after lunch at the Caprice, on their first date. She had ended it in the Caprice seven years later. Two months ago. Almost to the day.

He seemed to have aged since then. His hair had lost its lustre, his face had grown florid and was lined with broken veins, as if years of heavy boozing had taken their toll. He looked like he was going to seed.

She was aware that if she had still been in love with him she probably wouldn't have noticed. There had been a time when she had loved every hair on his body, and couldn't imagine life without him. And she would still have been in love with him if he hadn't let her down.

If he had been honest with her . . . if he had kept his word . . .

Not a million ifs, only a few, just the ones that mattered.

She was surprised at her lack of feelings for him now. She'd been dreading this meeting, and wasn't even sure why she had agreed to come. Perhaps because she felt sorry for him – he'd been distraught, phoning her incessantly, bombarding her with e-mails, faxes and flowers, pleading with her to change her mind. Or perhaps it was because she needed to see him one more time to be *absolutely* sure.

And now she *was* absolutely sure. It was a huge relief. Finally, after seven years, she was free of the feelings that had enslaved her. She could pass the Caprice without any sudden pang. She could listen to 'Lady in Red', without being paralysed by an intense yearning for him. She could wake up in the morning without a deep pain inside her because it was Saturday morning and she wouldn't be seeing him until Monday evening. And instead of his phone calls being the highlight of her days, they were now an intrusion.

And, seven years on, the message that her mother, her sister, Lara, and her best friend, Roxy, had all been trying to drum into her head had got through.

Brian Trussler, you are a complete fucking shit.

He pulled out his cigarettes and lit one. 'Amanda, don't do this to me,' he said. 'I love you so much. I totally and utterly adore you.'

'I know,' she said flatly.

He stared at her and drummed his free hand on the tablecloth. His eyes were bloodshot, and she wondered whether he looked so bad because he wasn't sleeping. He'd told her he couldn't sleep for thinking of her, and that had made her feel bad. She didn't want to hurt him.

He was breathing heavily. 'I'm prepared to leave Linda.'

Linda was pretty, with short dark hair and a sad expression, as if she had known something was wrong in their

21

marriage. Amanda had never felt malice towards her, only envy and, at times, a terrible guilt.

She shook her head. 'No, you're not prepared to leave her, Brian. I've heard you say that so many times.'

'This time I am.'

Was he capable of distinguishing the truth, any more, from the web of lies in which he lived? Amanda asked herself. She had met him when she was a twenty-two-year-old fresh-faced graduate from film school, and had applied for a job as an assistant at his production company. At the interview she'd been awed to meet the man in person – she'd seen his credits, sometimes as director, sometimes as producer on countless successful television dramas, *The Bill*, *London's Burning*, *Cracker*, *Frost*, *Casualty*. But she'd not seen his true face.

He was a crook. On his company's own series, he ripped off everyone with whom he came into contact. If the BBC gave him £250,000 an episode, he would make it for less and creatively account the difference. He bribed people and took backhanders.

He wasn't interested in making anything of quality or winning awards, or prestige, he was interested solely in milking the system of as much money as he could. He had a reputation for churning out safe, reliable police procedurals and hospital dramas. It didn't bother him a whit that, creatively, American imports like *ER* and *NYPD Blue* kicked them into touch.

And in those early, heady days, it didn't bother Amanda either. She was meeting stars, she was involved in making prime-time dramas with good ratings, she was twenty-two, she was madly in love with one of the gods of television, and she had a career break to die for! Brian had told her that his marriage had been over effectively for years, he was going to leave his wife, and – huge carrot – he was on the verge of giving Amanda her very own series to produce.

Four years later he had not left his wife, and had not given Amanda her own series, so she dumped his job, and took a more challenging one at 20–20 Vision. Yet she had found it impossible to break with Brian. Determined to try, she had spent a miserable three months without him, but after a boozy lunch they had ended up back in bed together.

She watched him now, sucking hungrily and edgily on his cigarette. 'You've had seven of the best years of my life, Brian. I'm twenty-nine, OK? My biological clock's ticking. I want a life, and you have to be fair to me. I want a husband. I want children. I want to spend my weekends with the man I love.'

'Let's start a family right away,' he said.

The waiter brought their coffee. Brian ordered a brandy. She waited until the waiter was out of earshot.

'Great,' she said, reproachfully. 'Your wife's seven months pregnant and now you want your mistress pregnant as well. What planet are you on, Brian?'

He looked at her balefully. 'Are you seeing someone else?'

'No.'

He looked relieved. 'So – is there hope for us?'

'No,' she said. 'I'm sorry, Brian, there isn't.'

Chapter Six

thursday, 10 july 1997. 3.12 a.m.
from: tlamark@easynet.co.uk
Usenet Newsgroups.
Fan Clubs.

Posting to alt.fan.Gloria_Lamark.

I am deeply sad to announce the death of my mother, Gloria Lamark, on Tuesday 8 July, at her home in London.

The funeral will take place at Mill Hill Cemetery next Wednesday, 16 July at 12.00. This will be followed by refreshments at 47 Holland Park Villas, London W14.

All her friends and fans are welcome.

It is recommended you arrive early to avoid disappointment.

Details of a memorial service to accommodate those unable to fit into the church will be announced later.

Don't forget to check out the Gloria Lamark Website!
http://www.gloria_lamark.com

Chapter Seven

'I have a secret,' the old man said, then fell silent.

There were often long gaps between his sentences, and Michael Tennent was used to this; he sat in his comfortable chair, holding his patient's file and straightened his back a little. Katy used to tell him his posture was lousy.

Katy.

Her photograph was still on his desk and she was still in his mind, part of her in his every thought. He wanted her out of it, and yet at the same time, perversely, he did not. What he really wanted was to be free of the pain, to be able to move forward. But always the guilt stopped that.

The office was a long, narrow, attic room in the elegant Palladian mansion that had once been the London home of a tea-importing tycoon, and was now the Sheen Park Hospital. It housed the consulting rooms of six psychiatrists and four psychotherapists, as well as thirty private bedrooms for in-patients. It was approached via a rhododendron-lined driveway that wound for a quarter of a mile through well-kept parkland that stretched right down to the Thames. The view was denied to Michael and his patients. His office had just one small round window, like a naval porthole, set above head height, just below the eaves.

The office was a tip. His desk, a couple of tables and a row of filing cabinets were pushed up against the walls, and almost every inch of their surfaces was covered in files, letters, medical magazines or books waiting for his review. Even the computer monitor had a pile of stuff on top of it that had been there so long Michael didn't even notice it any more.

He needed therapy himself, he knew, and that was ironic. He ought to be able to handle his grief. But the fact that he still had Katy's photograph on his desk told him otherwise. One moment they'd been driving along a road, Katy crying, himself feeling a shit, and the next moment –

Blank.

Amnesia. The same defence mechanism that protected some murderers. You could do the most appalling thing to another human being, and when you woke up the next day, hey, you'd forgotten all about it.

The notes on the index card were a blur. He lowered his head a fraction, hit the bottom sector of his varifocal lenses and the words sharpened.

On the front page of the file was typed: *Dortmund*, Herman Baruch. b. 07–02–1907. Dortmund was dying of terminal cancer, colon cancer originally, but now his body was riddled with secondaries. Somehow he kept going: inside his skeletal body was an inner strength, some residue from the demons that had once driven him and which he was trying now to exorcise. He got through his daily life having retained a fragile sanity. It was all he could hope for. And, Michael thought, more than he deserved.

But Michael was too much of a professional to let Dortmund's past affect his judgement or his treatment. The man had been prosecuted at Nuremberg, but had escaped the gallows. Since then, tormented with post-traumatic stress disorder and guilt, every night for fifty-four years Dortmund had travelled to hell and back.

Sometimes just looking at this man made Michael shiver. He tried to imagine what it might have been like to have been in Belsen in 1943, with Katy, but separated from her by a twenty-foot-high chain-link fence, women and children one side, men the other, smelling the death and decay, seeing the smoke rise from the ovens.

These thoughts *were* unprofessional, Michael reminded himself, but how could anyone detach that from his mind? He looked back at Dortmund and revulsion squirmed through him. Even so a part of him felt sorry for the man. There were even moments when Michael liked him: in the presence of this former Nazi, he was reminded that we all have the potential to do evil, and that sometimes, although we condemn a man's behaviour, we can still accept him as an individual. And this particular individual intrigued Michael.

Dortmund was ninety. Liver spots stained his face, and his mouth curled down at the corners. His shiny pate pushed up through thin strands of hair, like a porcelain bowl nestling in straw. He never smiled.

'I need to ask you . . .' Dortmund said.

'Yes?' Michael replied, gently, encouraging him.

'Can you keep a secret?'

'Of course.'

'Patient confidentiality? The Hippocratic oath, yes?'

Michael hesitated. Not all doctors took that, these days, but he was too tired to go into details: Dortmund was an early bird. He liked to come in at seven thirty in the morning, almost as though he could retreat back to his lair before the rest of the world was up and about and avoid facing the world. Michael didn't mind coming in early once a fortnight like this. It enabled him to get some paperwork done in the hour after Dortmund had left. 'Correct,' he said.

Dortmund stared at him as if uncertain whether he was taking the mickey. Even after all these years in England, Dortmund's grasp of the language was limited. Michael had found on many occasions that it had been dangerous to attempt to crack a joke. Jokes depended so often on subtleties of language. These eluded Dortmund.

'Yes.' The old man nodded. 'You know, it's a long time I have this secret – since I am small boy, since maybe I was seven, eight years old.' He got up from the sofa, tottered across the room and stopped beneath the porthole window. Morning sunlight illuminated him like a relic in a display case. 'I know things that are going to happen, Dr Tennent. I see things, sometimes. Always bad things.'

Michael watched him, waiting to see if he was going to continue, then said, in a neutral voice, 'You are psychic? Is that what you are saying? Is that your secret?'

27

Dortmund walked towards him, stopped, placed his bony fingers on the polished mahogany handle of his walking stick, and stared at him with rheumy eyes.

'I do not have very much in my life to be proud of,' he said. 'And I'm not proud of this.'

'Tell me what kind of things you see.'

'I know when a tragedy is to happen to someone. I made the decision to undergo analysis because I wanted to find redemption before I die. I am not finding that, not yet, but I am seeing something, and perhaps this is why I am here with you. Perhaps destiny sent me, to try to warn you.'

'To warn me of what?'

'That you are going to lose a woman whom you love.'

Michael was tempted to say, *You are three years too late*, but he didn't. The man's stare was making him uncomfortable. He glanced away. When he looked back Dortmund was still gazing at him, with a strange desperation. Michael did not want this. He did not want to legitimise the man's fantasies by asking him for details. He needed time to think about it, to come back with a measured reply. Anyhow, what other woman did he love? Only his mother, and she was seventy-nine and in rude health. If he was about to lose her, he did not want to know – and not from this man.

Michael looked at his watch and, to his relief, the fifty minutes were up. 'I think we'd better stop there for today,' he said.

After Dortmund had departed, Michael added to the man's notes, 'Suicide risk'.

His next patient was late, and he had a gap of a few minutes. Despite himself, he used it to phone his mother. She sounded fine; his father was down at Lymington harbour, pottering around with his boat. She was going with a friend to see a local flower show.

He felt cheered by her voice. Unlike his patients, and himself, his parents at least had found contentment and peace in their life.

Chapter Eight

Sodden with perspiration, trapped on a hard metal surface, her arms, midriff, legs and ankles bound tightly, her head crushed in a vice, Tina Mackay could move her eyes but nothing else. She was dimly aware that she had a catheter in her urethra. She had no idea of the time, nor of where she was.

'You want to know something?'

She stared at the man, fearfully, trying to keep thinking straight despite the agony in her mouth.

Thomas Lamark, holding bloodstained tooth forceps in his rubber-gloved hand, stood over her, looking down with gentle grey eyes. 'Relax, Tina, not all knowledge is painful. This could be useful knowledge for you. My mother has always taught me the value of good manners, OK? Life is a learning curve. You learn things, you become a better person. Don't you want to be a better *person*, Tina?' His voice was deep and absurdly genial.

She said nothing. She had come to realise some hours back, that down here in this place, with its bare concrete walls, sound was not going to get out. Screaming had ceased to be an option.

Somehow she had to try to reason with the man, and she sensed that somewhere inside him was a humanity she could reach if she could establish a rapport with him.

'Good manners means apologising when you are in the wrong. It takes a big person to apologise – are you big enough, Tina? I mean to *really* apologise for turning down my book?'

It was hard for her to speak now, but she tried once more, to plead with him through her broken mouth, her voice a

29

ragged, bloodied mumble. 'Yssshhh. Can you ftchh yrrr brrrook. Trrrgettterh. Shweee can wrrkkkk on it trrgtrrrher.'

He shook his head. 'Tina, I'm sorry, you saw with your own eyes what happened when I tossed the coin. I have to do what the coin tells me. You have to make rules in life and stick by them. Both our lives are out of control, right?'

She acknowledged this with her eyes.

'But you could have done something to prevent this, Tina. I couldn't, and that's the difference between us. I was born the way I am. I never asked to be this way. All my life people have told me I'm not right in the head. I have to accept that. I really hate being this way, but I can't fight it. I have to accept that I do things differently.'

He took a couple of steps back, smiled, removed his surgical scrubs, and raised his massive hands expansively. 'Do you like what I'm wearing?'

She looked as if she had not understood the question, so he repeated it. 'My clothes? Do you like my clothes?'

She stared through a mist of tears at his face. At his frame. He was exceptionally tall, at least six foot six. Oh, God, who the hell *was* this madman? He was good-looking – and there was something wrong about this – he was almost impossibly good looking, with black swept-back hair, and wearing an open-necked white shirt, navy slacks, black suede loafers. Elegant, but dated, he resembled some louche character in a Noël Coward play.

'Nicesshh,' she mumbled, approvingly. 'Shhlelegant.'

'You're not just saying that, are you, Tina?'

'Nrrrrrrrrr.'

He smiled such a warm smile that just then she believed everything was going to be all right. 'The shirt is from Sulka,' he said. 'They make a beautiful lawn cotton, it's really comfortable. My mother always chooses my clothes. This is the way she likes me to look. Do you like my shoes?'

She grunted assent.

'Gucci. They're hard to get – this style's been really popular. If you want some, you'll have to order them now, otherwise when the next shipment comes in, they'll all be gone.'

He turned and walked out of sight. 'OK, now let's have some music. All set?'

The room erupted with a Gregorian chant that seemed to Tina to explode upwards through the floor, down from the ceiling, and out from all four walls. Thomas Lamark came back, wearing his blue surgical scrubs once more. He smiled and his eyes rolled dreamily. He was away, lifted high up by the stark chords, the falsetto voices, the pitch, wailing then falling.

He danced, to his own private rhythm, sweeping the forceps through the air with his gloved hand, like a conductor with his baton. Then he leaned over the terror-stricken publisher, seized one of her front teeth with the forceps, gripped it hard and levered the handle sharply upwards. There was a sharp snap as the tooth came away with part of the root.

The music absorbed her scream, like a swab.

Chapter Nine

thursday, 10 july 1997
There's this thing about friends that has always bothered me. People have friends, it's a normal thing to have friends.

Everything I watch on television, movies, comedies, dramas, all the people have friends they can phone, chat to, visit.

How do you get friends?

Seems to me from my experience that if you surf the Net for friends, all you get is people wanting to sell you sex. I go into a pub and start talking and people think I'm trying to pick them up.

I'm aware there's something inside me that makes me different from everyone else. I'm not sure what it is, a lack of patience, perhaps, or I'm badly adjusted in some other way.

My mother always told me she was the only friend I needed. I never really believed that, but now she's gone, even after just forty-eight hours, I'm beginning to realise she was right.

I see the world my way, my mother's way. She said that the world is forever out to screw you. You have to hit back in any way you can.

Otherwise the world has won.

When in doubt, toss the coin. The coin is guided by a Higher Authority. When in doubt, He will make that decision for you.

There's only so much responsibility that any human being can bear.

Chapter Ten

Gloria Lamark had been attracted to 47 Holland Park Villas by its grandeur and its theatrical atmosphere. Square, detached and classically proportioned, it was large enough to have been the manor house of a rural community, although here in Holland Park, in London, it was just one of a row of similar-sized houses, some with Georgian or Regency façades, others, like number 47, with a Victorian Gothic frontage, crenellated parapet, high, narrow windows and arched lintels that gave it a secretive and even faintly surreal air.

In a quiet avenue only a short distance from the hurly-burly of Kensington High Street, set back from the road behind a circular gravel driveway, the house was concealed from prying eyes by a high wall, electric wrought-iron gates, and a riot of foliage from trees, mature shrubs and the heavy cladding of ivy on the walls.

In 1955, with visions of becoming a society hostess as her acting career rose to meteoric heights, Gloria Lamark had moved here.

The interior of the house had the feel of a stage set, with a flagstone floor in the huge hall, wide corridors and stair-cases, and décor that was entirely black, grey and white. Almost every inch of wall space was hung with framed photographs, again mostly black and white, of the actress.

Gloria Lamark had wanted to be the only colour in the house, and was insistent that nothing should compete with her. She had never once, in forty-two years, permitted any other than white flowers in the house or the garden, which was planted almost entirely with evergreens. Koi carp were allowed in the pond, which had been designed with classical columns and arches like a miniature Italian lagoon, but only because, being underwater, they would not overshadow her with their colouring. Visitors who outshone her were never invited back.

In the beginning there had been a few lavish parties, but within a decade, along with her circle of friends, they had petered out. Subsequently there had been a trickle of dinner parties, absurdly formal and stultifyingly dull for all present, except Thomas. He loved watching his mother at the head of the table, dressed in her finery, listening to her holding court with stories he had heard a thousand times before and of which he never tired.

He was thinking about one of those dinner parties now as he sat in front of his computer in his den on the first floor, directly below his mother's bedroom where he would ordinarily have heard her if she had called out to him. The heavy charcoal drapes – blackout curtains from the Second World War – kept out all but a few slivers of light from the morning sun. He had drawn the curtains throughout the house.

At this moment he wished he could gouge the sun out of the sky and blind the world. Light was for the living, darkness for the dead. This was now the house of the dead.

It was ten thirty-five on Thursday morning and he had been up, as usual, all night. Although it wasn't quite as usual because his mother was no longer here, and therefore it would never be *as usual*. Everything had changed. The past was another country where they did things differently. But it wasn't as simple as crossing a frontier to move into the new country. First there was unfinished business. All travellers had to pack before they left. Completing unfinished business was like packing.

He considered the metaphor, and liked it. You could use a suitcase, or you could use –

He lifted the Elastoplast on his wrist and looked at the row of punctures where the bitch editor had bitten him in the multi-storey car park last night. Human bites were dangerous, worse than a dog's, worse than a rusty nail. He

34

should have a tetanus jab, but he was so busy. How could he fit one in with everything else that had to be done?

Through sodden eyes, he looked up from his diary entry on the computer screen to the poster of his mother on the wall above his desk. She was all around him in this room, framed photographs, posters and poems she had written to him. But this one, above his desk, was his favourite. Her face peeked sulkily through a cascade of wavy blonde hair; her lips pouted as she stared with disdain at something beyond the camera. One black-lace-stockinged leg reached out of the open passenger door of a sports car, an XK120 Jaguar, and her skirt was drawn provocatively high, revealing, or almost revealing (he could never quite make up his mind), an inch of bare white thigh.

The caption beneath read: LAURENCE HARVEY/GLORIA LAMARK . . . IN . . . RACE OF THE DEVILS!

She had been the leading lady. Her name was *above the titles*! She had starred with one of the greatest male leads of the twentieth century. His mother!

And now she was dead, her career ruined by evil, scheming people, her worth trashed by rinky-dink little nobodies like scumbag bitch Tina Mackay, and then, finally, murdered by Dr Michael Tennent.

His mother was lying in a fridge in a funeral home. He knew about post-mortems, he knew about the indignity. He thought of his mother, the beautiful, incredible, lovely creature, lying there, naked, her brain lifted out of her skull by some pathologist, then chopped up and wrapped in a white plastic bag along with the rest of her internal organs, and stuffed back inside her like giblets in a supermarket chicken.

He wept silently at the thought. Dignity had meant so much to her, and now she'd been hacked open by saws and carving knives and scalpels on a steel mortuary table.

He looked down at his desk. At Tina Mackay's teeth. He had washed the blood off them and neatly arranged them in their correct order, to make sure he hadn't overlooked any. A full set. In pretty good condition – she must have taken good care of them.

Then he felt a sudden pang of guilt at the pain he had caused her. He raised the Elastoplast and inspected the row of punctures on his wrist. Then he looked at the words he had just typed on the screen.

You have to hit back in any way that you can.

You have to.

They made him feel better. *Cause and effect.* That was the way the world worked. Tina Mackay had bitten him and now she wouldn't bite him again.

No need for guilt.

Her rejection of the manuscript had caused her to be here in the first place. This was all entirely her fault.

The human will to live is a strange thing, he thought. People will do anything to stay alive, say *anything*. Even when, like Tina Mackay, all you are staying alive for is more pain and the hope of death.

His conscience clear now, he leaned across to his Bang and Olufsen stack and pressed PLAY. Immediately the psychiatrist's voice filled the room. Thomas knew by heart every one of the words on the tape.

He rewound it, sat back, and listened again, for the hundredth, or maybe the thousandth, or maybe the millionth time to Dr Michael Tennent's anxious voice.

'This is Dr Tennent speaking. Gloria, would you please give me a call as soon as you get this message? I'm rather afraid I upset you this morning. It might be helpful if we had a quick chat on the phone.'

He pressed STOP, looked back at the screen, and tried to continue writing up his diary. But the words were just a blur as now, alone in his den, he wept for all that he had lost.

Chapter Eleven

His session with Herman Dortmund had left Michael
Tennent's mind in an even more turbulent state than when
he had arrived that morning. He hadn't been able to
concentrate at all on his next patient, a forty-two-year-old
woman suffering from body dysmorphic disorder, who'd
had cosmetic plastic surgery on her face and body eleven
times in the past five years. And the tragedy was that she'd
been a beautiful woman to start with and was incapable of
believing it. Unlike Gloria Lamark, who had been incapable
of believing she might ever lose her looks.

His head ached like hell. In spite of the cool beige linen
suit he was wearing, he felt clammy. He ought to go home,
gulp down a couple of paracetamol, sit in a darkened room.
But he had a full list today, and a few were totally
dependent on him. The newspaper obituary on his desk
was proof of that.

An overdose of drugs.

He knew exactly why she had done it, that was the worst
part. She had done it because –

His phone buzzed. His secretary, Thelma, announced the
arrival of his eleven o'clock appointment. Michael asked
her to have the patient wait a few moments.

'Yes, Dr Tennent,' she said, then added nervously, 'I
listened to the programme last night. I thought it went very
well. If you don't mind me saying, you sounded much
more confident than usual.'

Michael had inherited Thelma from his predecessor, and
reckoned she had a bullying husband and almost certainly
a bullying father. A small, trim, grey-haired woman, nervy,
servile and anxious to please, she looked older than she

was. He guessed she had probably learned to get through life by avoiding confrontation. She just steered a course through the rocks and stuck rigidly to it. Few highs but few lows. Existence at its baldest. That was all far too many people had to hope for.

She rarely expressed opinions to him, which made her remark now all the more surprising.

'Really?' he probed. 'I didn't think I'd done a very good job last night.'

She hesitated. 'It seemed as if you were speaking much more from the heart than usual. I – I don't mean that you aren't usually good, but there was definitely something different.'

Amanda? he wondered. He said, 'Thanks. I'm not at all sure I'm going to continue doing it, though.'

'You *should*, Dr Tennent,' she said emphatically. 'I think you help people.'

'I'm not so sure.' He paused. 'Give me a couple of minutes, I have to make a call.'

He replaced the receiver and stared at the framed photograph of Katy, a head and shoulders shot. Their last holiday together. They were on a boat going down the Nile, and she was leaning against a deck rail, grinning, looking at him with those trusting blue eyes. The wind had twisted her blonde hair around her neck, and strands of it lay across her pink cashmere jumper. She had a healthy tan and those three colours, the brown skin, the blonde hair, the pink jumper against the clear rich blue of the Nile sky seemed perfection. Exquisite.

So why had he done what he had?

Why?

She *was* beautiful. An English rose. A princess. His brain was a kaleidoscope of memories. She could eat anything and she never put on weight. She loved food. Grilled Dover soles a yard long. Hunks of rare steak smothered in onions. Great big sticky doughnuts filled with custard cream. He remembered on their honeymoon when she'd rammed a massive doughnut into his mouth, then licked the sugar off his lips, all the time laughing and scolding him as if he were a child.

Dead.

Trapped beside him in the wreckage of the car, broken and bleeding and inanimate. The airbag lying limp like some grotesque parody of a spent condom. The bloodied face of the dead man in the van that they had hit head on, staring accusingly out through the crazed glass of the windscreen, while the firemen sawed their way in and the crowd stood around gawping.

yourfault . . . yourfault . . . yourfault

Memories he did not want to have, but which he needed to confront.

Every day, every night, his mind returned to that accident. A safe door had locked shut in his brain. Inside it were a few seconds of his life, twenty, maybe thirty, in which his whole world had changed. He could not get to them, could not find the key, or the combination, that would unlock that door.

Once, when things had been good, they used to have those intense conversations lovers have over a bottle of wine or curled up in bed, and often they'd talk about death and how they'd cope if one of them lost the other. Katy always said it would make her sad to think that if she died he might never be happy again, and she'd made him promise faithfully that he would move on, find someone else, start a new life.

Now that generosity of spirit was twisting him up inside as he looked at Amanda Capstick's business card lying on his desk: 20-20 Vision Productions Ltd. Amanda Capstick. Producer.

Then he looked again at the *Times* obituary. Gloria Lamark.

An overdose of drugs . . .

He almost knew it by heart now.

Gloria Lamark, movie actress, died from an overdose of drugs in London on 9 July, aged 69. She was born in Nottingham on 8 August, 1928.

A leading actress in the 1950s, hailed by critics as Britain's Brigitte Bardot, although in many respects a far more accomplished actress, her numerous roles included *The Arbuthnot File*, directed by Orson Welles, *Race of The Devils*, directed by Basil Reardon, *Storm Warning*, directed by Carol Reed, and her most successful film, *Wings of the Wild* opposite Ben Gazzara. Her first stage appearance was aged three at the Nottingham Playhouse in *Mother Goose*. Her husband, German industrialist Dieter Buch, died in 1967. She is survived by her son, Thomas.

Then, as if it would ease his guilt not to have the paper in front of him, he slipped it into a drawer. This was behaviour wholly contrary to the advice he gave his patients. Confront your problems, your inadequacies, your fears, your demons, your monsters. *Don't file them away in a drawer.*

An overdose of drugs.

It happened to every psychiatrist, although that knowledge did not make it any easier. And he'd never particularly liked the woman, but that made no difference to his distress. His job was to help people, not to sit in judgement of them. And he had failed.

And the worst of it was that he knew exactly why he had failed. He'd taken a gamble he should never have taken. Gloria Lamark had not been up to it.

He removed his glasses and buried his head in his hands. *Oh, God, how the hell could I have been so stupid?*

His phone rasped. He picked it up and heard Thelma's voice.

'Shall I send Mrs Kazan in now?'

'A couple more minutes,' he said.

He looked again at Amanda Capstick's card, and thought of her smiling at him through the glass control-room window. The warmth she had radiated.

Keeping his eyes well clear of Katy's photograph, he dialled the number. A telephonist put him on hold, then Amanda was on the line. She sounded pleased to hear him. 'You were great,' she said. 'Last night, on the programme. I was *so impressed*!'

'Oh – uh – right – thanks!'

'No, really, you were *so* good! We're going to include a segment for sure.'

'I'm delighted,' he said. 'Uh – look – um – listen,' he was feeling swelteringly hot suddenly, 'I – I was given two tickets for the Globe Theatre, next Thursday evening. To see *Measure for Measure*. I – I just wondered if you'd been there? Whether it would interest you?'

She hadn't been there, she told him. And yes, it would interest her hugely. She sounded genuinely delighted to have been asked. And she'd seen a televised version, she said, but she'd never seen the play performed live.

Michael replaced the receiver, elated. He'd done it. They had a date!

Seven whole days away, but that didn't matter. For the first time in three years he had something to look forward to.

Thelma buzzed him again, the phone rasping away urgently.

But now not even Thelma mattered.

Chapter Twelve

'Tina, look, I want to show you! You're in the *Evening Standard*!'

Thomas Lamark leaned over the operating table and held the front page in front of Tina Mackay's closed eyes.

Her face was pale. Dark rings around her eyes. Blood dribbled from her mouth. She didn't look good.

She hadn't made the front-page splash, Ulster was the lead story, but the only photograph was Tina Mackay's face.

EDITOR – KIDNAP FEARS GROW.

'I'm the only person in the world who knows where you are, Tina. How do you feel about that?'

There was no reply.

He checked her blood pressure: it was very low. Her pulse was racing: 120. There was still only a small amount of urine in the catheter bag. He hadn't given her fluids or food since she had been here.

How did I forget to do that?

This worried him. He'd always had bad memory lapses but now they were getting worse. He looked down at her with remorse, trying to remember how long she had been here. Almost a week. 'You poor thing, you must be thirsty, hungry, I didn't mean to make your life hell. I wanted to hurt you, to punish you, I wanted you to understand pain, Tina, because you gave my mother so much pain. I wanted to educate you, but I didn't mean to be cruel by depriving you of food and water. Do you understand that?'

He searched for a flicker of response in her face, but saw none.

Raising his voice, he said, 'I'm saying sorry, Tina. I'm

apologising, I really do want to apologise. Can you forgive me?'

No response.

He put down the *Evening Standard* on the metal table where he laid his instruments, then opened the *Daily Mail*, and held that up above her face. 'You're in the *Mail* too. Page five. It's a nice-sized piece, a good photograph.' He looked at it. Her brown hair was cut short, the way it was now; she was neatly dressed, smiling pleasantly, she looked a responsible person, in a school prefect way. She could never, ever, have been beautiful in the way that his mother had been, and this made him sorry for her.

Trying to cheer her up, he said, 'They say nice things about you, Tina. That you rose from being a secretary to a senior fiction editor, and now you're in charge of the entire non-fiction list.'

He put down the *Mail*, opened the *Mirror* and held that up for her to see. 'Tina, take a look at this. Here's a photograph of your boyfriend. The Honourable Anthony Rennison. He's saying he can't understand what has happened to you, he's at his wit's end.'

Thomas studied the man's face more closely, then looked down at Tina. Here were two people and they had a relationship. How had they met each other? How had they become boyfriend and girlfriend?

'Tell me, Tina, why do you like this man? He's really not very good-looking – he's a chinless wonder. Why would someone want to go out with a man like this, but not with me?'

Still no response.

He turned away and put down the newspaper.

What have I done to this woman?

A tear rolled down his cheek.

What have I done?

Have to snap out of this.

'Tina, you kept on saying to me how sorry you were about not publishing my mother's book. You have to understand that I'm sorry too. I'm sorry my mother had to go to her grave without her biography being published.'

43

Then he turned away and paced up and down the concrete chamber, churning a question over and over in his mind. *Do I keep her or let her go?*

Finally he pulled his coin out of his pocket, tossed it in the air and palmed it.

Tails.

'Tina, I'm letting you go.'

Chapter Thirteen

tuesday, 15 july 1997. 4 a.m.
The caterers are coming to day, to get everything organised for tomorrow, and I need to keep my mind clear. Lots to think about.

I go to see Tina and find she's already gone. No pulse at all. It only took a small dose of curare, which paralysed her lungs. The end would have been quick for her, in her state.

On the whole I think she made some good progress here, she got well beyond the apex of the learning curve I set for her. I told her what Socrates said, that the greatest pain is that which is self-inflicted, and she was intelligent enough to understand this. I'm glad for her that she did.

I feel that with the benefit of what she's learned, next time she wouldn't make the same mistake. But that's for the Higher Authority to decide.

God can flip his own coin.

Chapter Fourteen

Nobody came.

Thomas sat in the back of the black Daimler limousine, trying to work this one out. Some part of London he did not know was sliding past outside, distorted by the refractions of a million prisms. Maybe it was raining outside, maybe he was crying, maybe both, who cares?

He lashed out with his foot and kicked the upright seat in front of him, the one beneath the glass that partitioned off the driver. He saw the driver turn his head slightly to observe him in the mirror. So what?

His mother was dead, nothing mattered any more.

Except this.

Nobody had come! Just the people from the funeral directors' – the drivers, the pall-bearers, Mr Smyte, the dapper man who had made all the arrangements. A locum clergyman, who ignored eighty per cent of the information Thomas had briefed him with on his mother. And some brain-dead kid reporter from a local rag, carrying a cheap camera, who had had the gall to ask him who Gloria Lamark was.

Jesus!

Maybe they had misunderstood the directions and were waiting at home now. There had been an obituary in *The Times* – OK, he'd written it for them, they hadn't had one in stock, but that was irrelevant. He'd put the posting out to the newsgroup fan club. He'd put the information up on his mother's website. Blanked from his mind was the knowledge that no one ever corresponded with the newsgroup, and no one ever visited the website.

The driver, a little man in black in a peaked cap, was

ogling women. Thomas could see his head turn, constantly, in the direction of attractive girls.

He could scarcely believe this. They were driving home from his mother's funeral and here was this man, this creep employee of the undertakers', who should have been thinking respectful thoughts, instead thinking about doing things with his penis.

Thomas leaned forward and hammered on the glass partition. 'Stop that at once!'

The driver turned his head, startled and confused. 'Sir?'

But Thomas had already settled back in his seat. He wagged his index finger backwards and forwards like a metronome. The driver, even more puzzled, turned his attention back to the road.

No one was at the house, either. Thomas paced up the marquee, his shiny black lace-ups from Lobb sinking into the matting that had been laid on the lawn. He was wearing a black Boss suit, summer weight, a mohair and silk blend that had a slight sheen. Beneath he wore a crisp white mandarin-collared shirt from Favourbrook, with a single black diamond stud closing the neck.

He'd bought the clothes specially for the funeral. He needed to show his mother he was all right, he was coping. The outfit was more modern than she would have chosen, but this was the image he wanted to portray to the press, that she was a modern woman, in every sense, they were modern people, children of the nineties, they were millennium people.

It was muggy inside the marquee, but he was comfortable; the heat wasn't a problem. He was cool.

He was powerful.

He could feel the power swinging through his body as he walked. It swung through his arms, through his legs; he swaggered up the length of the marquee then down it again.

Six barmen stood to attention behind the champagne bar. Fifteen waitresses were ranked behind the tables laden with food. Half lobsters. Dublin Bay prawns. Stone-crab

47

claws. Loch Fine oysters. Platters of whole roast snipe. Couscous. Mangoes, guavas, passion fruit, lychees. His mother's favourite foods. A feast. He had catered for three hundred. There was a podium with a microphone where Thomas had planned to make a speech, to welcome everyone, to thank them all for attending.

There was even a fucking liveried Master of Ceremonies.

The marquee had a ruched ceiling. That had cost extra. Green-striped walls. The rain was making its own rhythm on the roof, and in the far corner some had found a way in and was dribbling down.

Just as well no one's here, the fucking marquee leaks.

Thomas paced up and down again. Just himself, the six barmen, the fifteen waitresses, the Master of Ceremonies.

That reporter from the local rag in Mill Hill, who had come to the burial, was sticking in his gullet. A gormless creep in white socks and a cheap suit, hair cut like a lavatory brush – and wearing a candy-striped tie, a pink, yellow, white and magenta striped tie, with small orange globes sprinkled around it – at his mother's funeral!

I'm sorry, my editor sent me here. I'm afraid I hadn't heard of Gloria Lamark before today.

What kind of a jerk reporter goes to a funeral of someone he hasn't even heard of? And who then stands there smirking because no one else bothered to come? And who didn't have enough respect to put on a black tie?

He had the youth's card in his pocket. Justin F. Flowering. The youth had even written his home number on the reverse. He hadn't even had the decency to come back to the house.

I don't like you, Justin F. Flowering. I don't even like your name. You and I are going to become very bad friends.

The waitresses were all watching him. So were the barmen. They didn't know yet that no one had turned up to Gloria Lamark's funeral.

Not even any of the faithful old retainers had come. Not one. He guessed that they were upset because they'd been sacked. In the past couple of years his mother had had some strange moods. One by one she'd fallen out with her staff, some of whom had been with her for thirty years, and fired them. Most recent of all she'd sacked their cleaning lady. Now there was no one. She'd told Thomas she just wanted it to be the two of them together, no outsiders, no interruptions to their happiness in the house.

All the same, he'd thought some of them might have come today, out of respect. Couldn't they have found it in their hearts to forgive her? At least Irma Valuzzi, her dresser. Or Enid Deterding, her secretary. But they had not shown up. The only apology for absence had been from Joel Harriman, her publicist, who was recovering from a heart-bypass operation. All the same, he could have sent some-one from his office, couldn't he? Instead, he'd sent a fucking telegram.

And what about Dr Michael Tennent? No, he wouldn't have come. He wouldn't have had the nerve to show his face.

Thomas marched through the house and into his mother's study, closing the door so no one could hear him. Like her bedroom, this room smelt of her. Chanel No. 5. It was in the wallpaper, in the curtains, in the cushions on the divan, it was in her handwriting on the sheets of notepaper that lay on the desk, her lists that she wrote out for him daily.

Separate headings on separate sheets. Daily shopping lists headed Cosmetics, Vitamins, Homeopathic Remedies, Chinese Herbs, Additional Medications, Food, Hardware, Miscellaneous. Daily Phone Call lists. Correspondence lists. There was a stack of bills and invoices. On the top was an invoice for Durrant's, the press-cutting service.

He sat down in the massively ornate chair at the desk, suddenly overwhelmingly tired as he stared at the tiny pile of condolence letters. He avoided his mother's eyes. They were everywhere he looked in the room, staring out at him from frames. Accusing him.

You fool.

You've let me down.

You've made a complete fool of me.

And he had. He knew that. The barmen out there would

be smirking in another ten minutes, when they realised the truth of the situation. So would the waitresses. It was probably best to stay in this room now, let the funeral directors deal with everything. He'd done his bit, strutted his stuff. Now they could all go to hell.

He looked at the one tiny framed photograph his mother had kept of his father, whom he had barely known – he had left when Thomas was three. He was standing in front of an aircraft propeller in a greatcoat; his own plane, his mother had told him once. A tall man, with Teutonic good looks, sharp dark hair and a stiff, unsmiling expression. Thomas liked this photograph. The man had a coldness, an arrogance, the kind of man no one *ever* makes a fool of.

He was his father's son.

He picked up the phone. It was old-fashioned, with a dial rather than numbers. His mother had preferred that: she thought it more elegant to dial than to press buttons. He dialled Joel Harriman's home number.

The publicist answered, his voice instantly recognisable, the squeaky, creepy voice of the school fat boy. 'Thomas, hi, sport, how's it going?'

Thomas reckoned Joel Harriman had lost the plot two decades ago, but his mother had insisted on keeping him on, and Thomas knew why: it was because the creep knew how to work flattery. Strands of hair carefully parted over his bald dome, designer warm-up suits, trainers, perma-tan, he kept up a prodigious, relentless bombardment of badly typed, badly photocopied press releases about Gloria Lamark to the press and media.

To his credit, Joel Harriman managed to get her birthday listed in several national papers and magazines, as well as occasional down-the-line local radio interviews when one of her old films reappeared on television, and he briefed people well.

'Did you tell anyone? What did you say to people?' Thomas asked, choking with anger.

The tone of the man's voice changed. 'Hey, sport! What's up?'

'Tell me what the hell you said to everyone?'

50

'We sent out the press release with the wording you gave us.'

'Who did you send it to?'

'Everyone! And we rang all the people we thought might want to know personally. Huh? Michael Grade, Dickie Attenborough, Christopher Lee, Leslie Phillips, Nigel Davenport, Dulcie Grey, Michael Denison, John Gielgud, Michael Winner, Barry Norman, Ray Cooney, Michael Codron, Tony Hopkins, Sean Connery – hey, come on! I mean, you have to remember a lot of the people who were her friends are dead now or infirm.'

'We only had one obituary. In *The Times*. The one I wrote,' Thomas said.

'Oh – uh, you didn't see the one in *Screen International*? There should be one in *Variety* next week. So anyhow, sport, tell me, how's it going?'

'Good,' Thomas said quietly.

'So – she's having a good send-off? Big turnout?'

'Huge.'

'Great, that's great. She was a great lady. You know something? Today's actresses, not one of them's got her class.'

'I have to get back now,' Thomas said. 'Got a lot of people on my hands here.'

'Sorry not to be with you. I'm glad there's been a good turnout. Listen, chin up, you've been a great son to her. She was a very lucky lady to have had you. We're all going to miss her.'

Thomas replaced the receiver. The anger inside him felt like something had broken loose, had got out of its cage and was rampaging around inside his head.

He looked up at the walls, at the photographs. His mother was angry, too, she had a real rage on. That was the thing in this world: there were so many different ways you could be angered. No sooner did you start to square off one set than another came out of midfield.

You had to organise yourself. Or else, as Pope said, 'Lo! thy dread empire! Chaos is restored!'

Chaos.

The Butterfly Effect would get you. One tiny beat of wings on the far side of existence . . . you had to stop that from happening, you had to catch the butterfly and tear off its wings.

He flipped the business card of the young smug reporter, Justin F. Flowering, out of his wallet and let it fall onto the desk. It landed face up, and that was a good sign.

He pulled a coin out of his pocket and flipped it.

Heads. Good. *Bad friends!*

He dialled 141, followed by the number on the business card. Justin F. Flowering was back at his desk and answered.

Thomas altered his voice just enough so that the reporter would not recognise it. 'Someone told me you were at Gloria Lamark's funeral today. You're writing a piece?'

'The big no-show. Yes.'

'When are you writing it?'

'For tomorrow's paper.'

'You want some scandal about her? To juice the piece up?'

'What do you have?'

'We need to meet. I can't do this over a phone.'

'Who are you?'

'I can't tell you that. Just be where I tell you. Six o'clock this evening. Then you can go back, write your piece. You're going to like this, Justin. You're going to like that we spoke. You're about to hit an enormous learning curve.'

Chapter Fifteen

'I'm much clearer in my mind now,' Amanda said. 'I'm feeling more confident. I really do feel I'm getting my life sorted out.'

'It's always hard to face reality. Much easier to ignore it or to reinvent it in a way that suits us.'

Amanda nodded. She knew the problem. She hadn't needed three years of therapy at sixty-five pounds a session to understand the reality; it had been there all the time during the whole seven years. Finally, she had faced it.

And now, in the large room with pale turquoise walls and big wicker furniture, wooden floor covered in scattered Afghan rugs and a plump crimson Buddha on the mantelpiece, Amanda Capstick told her therapist this.

Her therapist's name was Maxine Bentham, and she was a distant descendant of the philosopher Dr Jeremy Bentham. Jeremy Bentham had been a passionate advocate of the right to happiness, and believed people should be free to live unhindered by restrictive legislation. Following his beliefs, Maxine believed that too many people spent their lives choking on guilt. People should be freed of the restrictive baggage with which life saddled them.

She was a solid woman, not fat, not matronly, just snug, and had a warm, attractive face with fair hair cropped boyishly short, and a sharp, alert expression. She was dressed as usual in a black ankle-length designer smock that fitted like a sack, her fingers were crusted with chunky rings, and a lump of quartz crystal the size of a small planet hung from her neck.

Amanda sat in a wicker armchair, and sipped her mint tea, which had gone tepid. It always gave her a boost to be here. Therapists weren't supposed to give opinions unless specifically asked, but Amanda had told her she *wanted* opinions. Maxine was like a wise aunt and she made Amanda feel comfortable and secure. She wished she were able to talk to her mother the way she talked to Maxine. Her best friend, Roxy, had a great relationship with her own mother, they were like mates, and Amanda had always envied that. She and her mother got on fine, but they were not *mates*, and probably never would be.

Her mother was a sixties flower-child who had never really moved on, never fully got her life together. She was much closer to her sister, Lara, although she found her husband, a workaholic investment banker, tedious. And she adored their three young children, her nephew and nieces.

Maxine squatted cosily on the floor, leaning against a sofa, calmly looking up at her, waiting for her to continue.

'*Brian!*' Amanda said. 'You know, I don't even like the name! I can't believe I ever even went out with someone called *Brian!*'

Maxine smiled. Her voice had a transatlantic tinge from ten years in San Francisco. 'This is interesting, Amanda. Can you remember when you first started to dislike his name?'

'I don't like anything about him!'

'I'm not buying into that. I don't think you're ready to dislike everything about him yet. I'm still not sure you're ready to let go. I think you've got to the top of one hill, which is great, but there's a higher one in front of you.'

'I'm there!' Amanda said, determinedly. 'I really am.'

'Why do you think that?'

Amanda stared at the lines of grey daylight she could see through the slats of the Venetian blinds. Down in the street below, a trendy terrace a few blocks from Portobello Road, some driver of a car or a van or a truck was thunking his horn; it was an ugly sound, jarring.

'Because . . .' Amanda said. She waited for another blast of the horn to stop, wriggled in her chair, crossed her legs, then uncrossed them again. It was a grey, muggy day. Even in a T-shirt and lightweight jeans she was too warm in this normally cool, airy room. The horn stopped but immediately it started again. An alarm, she realised. Then, mercifully, it ceased. 'I have a date!'

Perspiration was running down her. *Christ I hope I'm not going down with some lurgy! And, if I am, I hope to hell it's better by tomorrow!*

Maxine looked pleased, not thrilled but pleased. 'You have?'

'I haven't accepted an offer of a date since . . .'

Maxine gave her the space to think.

Finally Amanda smiled. 'I guess for seven years.'

'Since you first slept with Brian?'

'Yes.' Amanda blushed and grinned like a schoolkid. She always felt like a kid in here.

'OK, Amanda, all this is good. What is not so good is the way you are handling Brian right now. What I want to see from you is *rejection*. What I'm actually seeing is *denial*. You hadn't been taking his calls, you hadn't been responding to his e-mails, you have been *denying* his existence, OK? You had dinner with him, but did you really tell him the truth?'

'Yes, I did.'

'Did you say, "*Listen*, Brian, you've let me down. When we got into this whole thing together it was because you had told me your marriage was over. A month after we had started sleeping together, you dropped the bombshell that your wife was pregnant with your second child. OK, she was four months pregnant and she'd kept it from you because she'd had so many miscarriages she was nervous to talk about it, but that was some bombshell!"' She watched Amanda's face. 'Sure, you had to wait. He couldn't leave his wife while she was pregnant, he had to wait until she was back home, the baby was fine, she was settled.' Maxine shrugged. 'Then his wife had post-natal depression, so again he couldn't leave her. For seven years you had one excuse after the other. He was always going to leave her and he never did. And then, two months ago, after telling you he hasn't made love to her for six years, he breaks the news that she is pregnant again. And suddenly he's run out of road, and you wake up and you realise where you have been for seven years. Did you just *think* that during your dinner or did you actually *tell* him?'

'I – I told him.' She thought for a moment. 'Yes, I did.'

'Were you angry with him or calm?'

'I was calm. I tried to help him understand how I felt.'

'Because you still love him.' Maxine said, bluntly.

'I don't.' Amanda was emphatic. 'No. Not any more. I – I sat there across the table and I felt nothing.'

'You didn't feel *nothing*, Amanda. You must have felt *something*. Tell me what you felt.'

Amanda was silent. Then she said, 'I thought how *middle-aged* he looked. I felt sorry for him. I was pitying him. And I thought of some of the things I used to do to his body and I felt really, really – yuk!'

The therapist's face was impassive. 'This date you have accepted, is this man different?'

'Very.'

'Married?'

'No, his wife is dead.'

'And are you excited about seeing him or are you just using this date as some kind of a test to see what it would feel like to be out with another man? You need to be honest with this answer, Amanda.'

'A test, I guess, in part. He's taking me to the Globe Theatre tomorrow, and I haven't been there. And it's a play I want to see.'

'People go on dates because they want to be with each other, Amanda. This doesn't sound like a *date*, it sounds like an *evening out*. You haven't mentioned one thing about this man you are going with. Don't you think that's a little strange?'

'He's a very interesting guy.'

'Does he turn you on? Do you want to sleep with him? Do you want to have his children?'

Amanda grinned and reddened again. 'Hey, slow down! I –'

'You what?'

'I haven't thought about those things.'

'You did with Brian. You told me you went to bed with him on your first date.'

'Yes. I couldn't keep my hands off him. I just fancied him to death the moment I saw him.'

'And this new man? You don't fancy him to death?'

Amanda shook her head. 'No, I just like him. I hardly know him. Anyhow, I have a hidden agenda with him. I need him to be in my programme. It's not a romance thing.'

'What did you say his name was? Michael? So poor Michael is just an unwitting volunteer in your experiment, he's your control sample, right? To see what it feels like being out with another man?'

'No! It's not as simple as that!'

'Explain what you mean.'

'Where's this going, Maxine?'

'You tell me.'

'I don't know. I have no idea. Probably nowhere.'

'Are you sure you're not attracted to him?'

'You're putting me under pressure!'

'Uh-huh!' Maxine nodded vigorously and good-humouredly. 'I want an answer. Are you sure you're not attracted to him?'

'I'll tell you next week.'

Chapter Sixteen

At a quarter to six Justin Flowering left his desk at the *Mill Hill Messenger*, saying nothing to his news editor, hoping that he would be able to surprise him with a scandalous story about the actress Gloria Lamark in his overnight basket.

He popped a piece of gum in his mouth and headed in the direction in which the stranger on the phone had instructed him earlier. His route took him along a street filled with dilapidated light-industrial units, the largest of which was a repair depot for London taxis, and then straight through into the long, dark archway beneath the railway line.

Half-way along, as instructed, he waited, lolling against the wall, chewing his gum, thinking about his job. He was nineteen and on a one-year work experience with the paper. His dream was to become a sports writer, and maybe one day a commentator, like his hero Des Lynam. He was tall, wiry and athletic, and hoped he'd get through this interview with the mysterious caller, get back to the office, finish his article and still have time to catch the last half-hour or so of his club's football practice tonight.

A car was approaching, followed by a van. He looked at the van, but it was red, and it drove on past. More vehicles followed, but no white van.

He thought again about the strange, very tall man, Gloria Lamark's son, who had been so angry with him at the funeral this afternoon; the way the man had screamed at him when he'd tried to ask him a few questions about his mother, as if he should have had her entire biography printed in his brain.

Maybe he should have. He had tried his best to find out a bit about the actress before going to the funeral and had even checked out her website.

Another van was approaching now. This was white. He stiffened and moved to the kerb. The van indicated and pulled over. The driver was wearing a baseball cap and sunglasses. In the darkness of his cab, it was impossible to make out his face.

Justin climbed in and pulled the door shut. The driver held out his hand. 'Hallo,' he said, in a voice that sounded familiar.

As their hands met, Justin felt a slight prick, like an insect bite, in his palm. The driver held his hand, clamped tight. As Justin tried to free it, the driver's face blurred.

The driver's face was still a blur, but now Justin Flowering was watching him through a steamed-up window, the smell of pine in his nostrils.

Drenched in sweat, he was spreadeagled in a sauna cabin, with his back propped up, his legs splayed out in front of him and strapped firmly to the slats, his arms pulled out either side of him and also strapped to slats. The heat was agonising. He was still in his suit and he was desperately thirsty.

The driver was looking at him through the glass window in the door, through the cloud of searing steam, and Justin knew his face now. It was Gloria Lamark's son, Thomas.

The man was playing some kind of ridiculous practical joke on him, keeping him here in the sauna, accompanied by a television set and a video-recorder placed on a chair in front of him, both wrapped in plastic to protect them from the steam, playing one of his mother's old films for him. On the screen a biplane was being flown by a woman, while a man, an actor Justin did not recognise, was clinging desperately to a wing strut.

Justin was angry, but at the same time he was wary of the man. There was an air of darkness about him, as if he could kill someone without any trouble at all. He needed to

59

handle this carefully. Then the door opened and Justin was grateful for the blast of cool air that accompanied it.

Thomas Lamark came in and nodded at the television set. '*Wings of the Wild*, Justin F. Flowering. Her best film. Are you enjoying it?'

To appease the man, Justin nodded.

'I really don't like your tie, Justin F. Flowering. Didn't anyone ever tell you that you should wear a *black* tie to a funeral? A plain black tie?'

'No, no one told me.' Something Justin saw in the man's eyes frightened him even more.

'You don't look comfortable, Justin F. Flowering. I thought you were a hard-boiled newspaperman, I thought you could take heat. So, now, tell me the names of the actor and the actress on the screen?'

'Gloria Lamark,' the young reporter said.

'Very good. And now the man?'

The reporter stared at him blankly.

'I did tell you,' Thomas said. 'I told you the names of all her films, and all the stars. You probably have your head filled with art-house junk, don't you? You like Fellini? Jean-Luc Godard? *Robbe-Grillet*?'

'I don't go to the films much.'

'You have to understand, Justin F. Flowering, that the plots of my mother's films weren't complex. That's not to say they weren't clever, but they were straightforward. No art-house crap. None of that boring *nouvelle vague* crap. But I tell you something, Justin, she made *great* movies. And that's why her career was destroyed. By jealous people. I want you to remember this for your article, OK?'

Justin nodded.

'They don't make those kinds of films any more. They'll never make them like that any more. They can't because she is dead. And they killed her. *They*!'

In a sudden squall of rage, Thomas stepped forward, emptied the bucket of water over the coals, stepped back as the steam exploded, refilled the bucket, and emptied that over them, too. The heat was incredible. Justin screamed.

Thomas Lamark stepped out of the cabin and closed the door.

Justin lay there, twisting his head to the right, then to the left, trying to find some pocket of cool air in the searing, claustrophobic steam. It burned his lungs as he breathed it in. Burned his nostrils, his eyes, crackled his hair. It was so hot that his brain tricked him into thinking he'd been plunged into ice. Then it returned him again to the heat.

A short while later, the door opened. Thomas Lamark stood in the entrance, holding an unlit blowtorch in one hand and a rotary band-saw, attached to a flex, in the other.

'Justin F. Flowering, we're going to play a little game to help you remember my mother's films. I'm going to tell you them all once again. When I've finished, you are going to repeat them back to me. Just the titles, OK?'

'Yes.' The reporter's voice sounded unstable.

'Good, this is going to be fun, Justin. Just one thing I want you to remember. Each time you make a mistake, I'm going to cut off one of your limbs. OK?'

The reporter stared back at him in bald terror.

Thomas recited the list, all twenty-five films. Then he said, 'Your turn now, Justin.'

'Could you repeat the list?'

'I'll repeat it if you make a mistake, but not until then, Justin. In your own time, just go ahead.'

'*W-Wings of the Wild*.' Justin Flowering said.

Thomas nodded, approvingly.

'*The – The – The Argossy File*.'

Thomas smiled. 'Close, Justin, but not quite right. It's *The* Arbuthnot *File*! But you were close enough, I'll give you the benefit of the doubt.' He smiled back so warmly that now Justin knew he was only joking about cutting off his limbs.

He smiled back. 'Thank you.'

'You're very welcome,' Thomas said. 'Now, in your own time again.'

'*Race of The Devils*.'

'Yes. Only twenty-two to go now, Justin!'

'*Storm Warning*.'

'Twenty-one!'

'Um – um – something *Monaco*?'

'I can't help you, Justin. You have to do this by yourself.'
He stared with hatred at the youth, stared at the fair hair
matted on his head, the sweat guttering down his face.

The reporter had run out of names. He stared back
helplessly at Thomas.

'Twenty and a half, that's not very good, Justin F.
Flowering. I think I'd better give your memory a jolt.'

Thomas switched on the rotary saw and stepped forward.

Justin screamed. He thrashed against his bonds in desperation, but he was locked solidly in place. He saw the
blade of the saw come down towards his wrist, lower,
closer.

The man would stop. He was teasing now he would stop.

He felt a sharp sting along the top of his wrist. Saw a red
ribbon of blood appear. He heard the grind of the blade and
with it, simultaneously, his mind numbed by shock but his
body screaming out, he felt excruciating pain, as if his hand
was being crushed in a vice. He closed his eyes, his scream
coming out as a gurgling drool, and when he opened them,
the man was holding up his severed hand.

'Silly boy, Justin. Don't ever make the mistake again of
not taking me seriously.'

Justin stared, thinking through his pain and shock that
this must be a dream, he would wake up in a moment. And
then he saw the flame shooting from the nozzle of the
blowtorch. Heard its furnace roar. Saw the man pick it up
and move it towards the end of his arm.

He bellowed, his lungs at breaking point inside his chest.

Then the pain exploded through his body. His brain felt
as if it was twisting inside his skull.

Then darkness.

Chapter Seventeen

thursday, 16 july 1997. 3 a.m.
Buy a white van.

Honestly, that's my best advice. Nothing new or too shiny, nothing that is going to attract attention. Just a plain white van, a Ford Transit is fine. Or a Hiace. Doesn't matter. Just make sure it's mechanically sound, that it has good wiring and a decent battery. People will think you're a workman on call, a plumber or something. They won't notice you. If you have a white van you become invisible.

You do.

And if you're invisible, you're in a smart space.

I've been trying to teach Justin F. Flowering about Heisenberg's Uncertainty Principle. But he's really not in much of a mood for learning – certainly not more than one thing at a time.

I've been trying to explain to him that Heisenberg believed that the very act of observing a scientific experiment changed the behaviour of the objects under scrutiny. So I tried to point out to Justin F. Flowering that the mere act of my watching him in the sauna in turn watching the motion pictures starring my late mother was affecting him in some subtle ways – ways that were probably too subtle even to measure.

He couldn't get his head around that at all.

He's going to be in that sauna a long time. I'm keeping an eye on the clock. He's watching Race of The Devils *right now. It lasts exactly ninety-eight minutes. I'll go down in a minute and see what he'd like to watch next. There's a huge choice, she made so many great movies. I think that if he watches every one of her films a few times over, it will help his memory a lot.*

Actually, you don't just need a white van. You need a white van and a drawing pin – a thumbtack.
I will explain about the thumbtack.

Chapter Eighteen

'If I must die,
  I will encounter darkness as a bride,
  And hug it in my arms.'

The player exited, stage left. Another entered, stage right.
Michael had no idea who either of them was. His body was
in the front row of the dress circle of the Globe Theatre. His
mind was elsewhere, surfing the ether, but mostly thinking
about Amanda.

The mention of death brought it back to the play.

It hadn't been such a smart idea to come to the theatre.
They should have just gone for a drink, or a meal, somewhere they could have talked. Now he had to sit next to her
for three interminable hours, unable to talk, unable to
concentrate on the play, and unable to get comfortable on
his hard seat.

His mind veered from Amanda to Gloria Lamark. He felt
guilty that he hadn't gone to her funeral yesterday, yet how
could he? How could he have looked at her son, her friends,
knowing he had been responsible for her death? Yet in not
going he had been running away. Again, he had done what
he always told his patients not to do.

Michael had problems with Shakespeare. He liked the
tragedies because he knew them all pretty well, in particular *Lear*, but he didn't know *Measure for Measure* at all. He
should have boned up on it, and had intended to, but had
not got round to it. Now he had lost track of who was who.

One of the characters was the Duke of Vienna. Another,
called Angelo, was a kind of born-again Puritan who had
sentenced to death someone called Claudio for sleeping
with his fiancée. A woman called Isabella (Claudio's sister?

65

Michael thought that was a possibility) was doing a lot of talking.

There is a smell peculiar to all theatres. It comes with the eddies of cold air from somewhere deep beyond the stage. It's a smell of wigs and old clothes and make-up and nervous human beings. Michael had been aware of it since he was a small child, going to pantomimes, and it excited him. Even in the open air the smell was here, but above it, tonight, he was even more aware of Amanda's perfume. The same perfume she had been wearing last week, faintly musky, incredibly sensual.

She was concentrating on the play with the rapture of a child at a magic show. She was really enjoying this! She was laughing at jokes that eluded him, clapping after speeches, deliciously uninhibited in her enthusiasm, and almost scarily knowledgeable. He felt ignorant.

An ignorant, boring old fart. With a dull car. Who no longer knew how to chat up birds.

And she looked lovely. Lovelier than he had remembered, although she was being more distant than he had hoped. The evening had started coolly, a formal handshake when he had gone to her flat to collect her. With equal formality she had invited him in for a drink. There hadn't really been time but he had said yes anyway, partly out of politeness, but more out of curiosity to see her lair.

The place had surprised him. He had supposed, for no particular reason, that she had a poky ground-floor or basement bedsit, dark, dingy, the kind he and most of his friends had lived in when he'd been a medical student. Instead he was led up into a large, airy loft, with a magnificent view east across Hampstead, St John's Wood and the whole of the West End of London.

The flat was minimally furnished, with a polished oak floor and limed wood skirtings, doors, dados and furniture, and the walls were hung with a small number of fine original modern paintings, elegant and witty neo-classical scenes; one he particularly admired was a parody of Botticelli's *Birth of Venus* set in a car park, with Venus emerging from a beat-up Cadillac. Her kitchen was a stainless-steel high-tech playground, and she served him ice-cold Chilean sauvignon in a tall, fine glass.

She had a standard of elegance far and above the denim-clad rough-and-tumble tomboy that he had met in his office and in the radio studio. And tonight, to match the flat, she looked demure, intensely feminine, drop-dead gorgeous.

He hadn't known what to expect, but whatever had been in his mind, it was not this. Often people look different the second time you meet them. They look different in different environments; but he could never, ever remember such a change in anyone.

She was one very smart, very together young lady.

And she was making him feel extremely *un*together. His confidence had taken the evening off, and he was stricken by a fear of rejection, by a fear of losing her that was alien to him.

During the past three years there had been no shortage of colleagues and friends trying to fix him up with women, but he hadn't wanted to know. After a series of embarrassing dinner parties where he had been fixed up with blind dates – *Mike, you'll adore her, you'll get on so well together!* – he had stopped accepting the invitations. The entire world seemed peopled with screwed-up divorcées who'd turn to him at the dinner table and say crass things like, 'How do I know you're not analysing me now?'

Katy had been special. Beautiful, warm, caring, balanced, a terrific companion, a wonderful hostess, and a hugely talented designer who had made the interior of their modest little house in Putney into a beautiful space, and had worked a miracle in the garden. They had shared so much together, they had been more than lovers, more than great friends, they had been soul-mates.

Why the hell had he fouled it up?

In Amanda, for the first time, he had encountered some-one who seemed to have some of Katy's qualities. But instead of rising to the occasion, he found his tongue tied in a granny knot, a double reef, a round turn and two half hitches, a figure of eight, a bowline and a whole raft of others all at once. And his brain mushed.

He had stood in her stunning flat, mumbling about the weather, the traffic, the problems of parking in London. If she'd had any suspicions that he might be a sad old Volvo-driving fart last week, that ten minutes in her flat confirmed it. With knobs on.

He wished he'd come on his motorbike. But the red Ducati had stood at the back of his garage under a dust sheet for the past three years. He simply hadn't felt like riding it any more.

They'd talked about London's changing architecture in the car all the way to the theatre. They both liked the Lloyds Building and hated Canary Wharf. It had been an improvement, but damage limitation rather than progress.

She had terrific legs. And he wasn't sure whether her skirt was simply a fashionable length, or whether it was deliberately provocative. That showed how far out of touch with fashion he was.

Sad bastard.

On stage, a man was proclaiming,

'Ay but to die, and go we know not where;
To lie in cold obstruction, and to rot;
This sensible warm motion to become
A kneaded clod, and the delighted spirit
To bathe in fiery floods, or to reside
In thrilling region of thick-ribbèd ice;
To be imprisoned in the viewless winds,
And blown with restless violence about
The pendent world; . . .'

His chance for redemption came during the first interval. They fought their way through the crowd at the bar and found the drinks he had ordered. They clinked glasses and Amanda's eyes were alight.

'So,' she said, brightly, 'how was your day? What did you do?'

He nearly blew this chance, big-time. 'I was out early this

morning collecting dog faeces.' Instantly he regretted telling her this: it was not the stuff of romance.

'I used to have a dog,' she said, with a vehemence that startled him. 'And I always used a pooper-scooper.'

'I didn't mean I object to dog faeces,' aware he was digging himself in deeper. 'I was collecting them for a patient.'

She gave him a seriously strange look.

'An OCD sufferer,' he added hastily.

'OCD?'

Someone jostled him, spilling beer over the top of his glass and down inside his shirt cuff. He pretended to ignore it. 'Obsessive compulsive disorder. She's panicked by dirt – uh – by the thought of dirt. I was collecting dog faeces in specimen bottles to bring into the room as part of her therapy.'

Amanda lightened up. With a startling burst of enthusiasm she asked, 'Could we include this in the film segment?'

'I'd have to ask my patient, I don't know if she'd agree.'

'We could use an actress.'

He nodded.

'So what kind of things do you make her do with these faeces?'

'Exposure is the conventional treatment. Facing up to fear. She's obsessed with contamination – she's frightened to touch door handles, taps, public telephones, and she's a compulsive handwasher, gets through several bars of soap a week. And one of her problems is that she's incapable of walking down a street past dog faeces. She has to turn back. So we start with easy things, like getting her to touch the door handle. I have to try to get her to recognise this is a *thinking* problem rather than contamination.'

Amanda grinned and drank some of her lager. 'I love the idea of dog turds in glass jars.'

And Michael liked how she drank the beer, how she swigged it with gusto; there was something about the way she enjoyed this simple pleasure that turned him on even more. Katy had loathed beer.

I'm comparing them.

There was an earthiness he really liked about Amanda. She was elegant, pretty, yet he could sense a wild streak in her, and, not for the first time tonight, he found himself wondering what it would be like to make love to her.

He was getting a hard-on standing here at the bar. He wished he had the courage to put his arm around her, but right now he was so nervous she might think he was being forward that he kept moving away every time their bodies touched.

He wanted so much to give her a signal, to touch her hand, or just stroke back the cluster of blonde hair that had tumbled down over her forehead. Her face and arms and legs were lightly tanned. A few freckles nestled in the soft-looking golden down on her arms and he found the colour of those hairs deeply sensual.

You are gorgeous, you are seriously, seriously, gorgeous. I love the way you look, I love where you live. I want to know you better. I am smitten, I really am!

'I can draw you a habituation curve,' he said.

'A what?'

'It's a graph. We measure *anxiety* and *time*. The first time I introduce her to the glass jar, we'll see the highest curve, the second time, it will be less, and so on.'

God I'm hopeless, he thought, suddenly. *The great seducer. Talking to my date about dog turds in jam jars.*

Later, as they left the theatre, Michael told her he had booked a table at the Ivy, in Covent Garden.

'Hey!' she said. 'That is one of my *favourite* restaurants. How did you know? Are you psychic?' It was a coincidence, also, she thought. The Ivy was the sister restaurant to the Caprice where Brian took her. The Ivy was more low-key, less brash. And Michael was far more low key and less brash than Brian.

'I'm a shrink,' he said, deadpan. 'I know everything.'

She grinned, threw a glance straight into his eyes, and said nothing. Michael was fleetingly distracted by a drop-head Ferrari revving noisily and beautifully in the jam of cars.

Neither of them noticed the white van parked directly across the street from the restaurant's main entrance.

Chapter Nineteen

The elegantly dressed old lady did not notice the white van either.

The taxi pulled up outside her handsome white Regency mansion block facing the Hove seafront promenade, swinging into a gap almost directly in front of the van. It was four o'clock in the afternoon.

With blue cotton-gloved fingers, she handed a five-pound note to the taxi driver and smiled sweetly, but with some difficulty, through skin that was drum-tight from her fifth face-lift. 'Keep the change.'

'Ten pence, thanks darling.'

Still smiling sweetly, a Hannington's department store carrier bag suspended from her arm, she walked in small, carefully articulated steps, but with fine deportment, her head held proudly high, a silk scarf fluttering in the sea breeze from her broad-brimmed hat, towards the entrance portico.

There was a sharp *ping* as the ten-pence coin hit the pavement right beside her. 'Have it back, you old bat! You obviously need it more than I do!'

She turned towards the taxi, raised a hand in the air and gave him two fingers. Just in case he hadn't got the signal clearly enough, she jigged her arm up and down to emphasise it.

Horrible, ignorant man. Didn't he know who she was? Did he live down a hole in the ground or what? Hadn't he watched television last night? Read today's newspapers? The BAFTA awards!

She had been given a *Lifetime Achievement Award*! Last night!

And this little cretin hansom cab driver hadn't recognised her. And he expected a tip! It was bad enough having newsagents run by foreigners, but now to have to put up with cab drivers who didn't recognise you, and who didn't have the manners to offer to carry your shopping at least to the front door!

She let herself into the building, took the painfully slow, rattly lift up to the third floor and walked down the corridor to her apartment. She was surprised when the door opened on the first turn of her Banham key: she always double-locked it. Must have forgotten today, she thought, painfully aware that her memory was becoming increasingly erratic.

There were several new congratulatory cards lying on the floor, and she was greeted by the scents of the dozens of fresh flowers that had been arriving all morning.

'Cora Burstridge!'

The joy at hearing the sound of her own name, and uttered in such a very charming way, was somewhat reduced by the fact that it came from inside her flat, and some moments after she had locked the door from the inside, and secured it with the safety chain.

She turned and saw a tall, fine-looking man with his hand outstretched in greeting. He looked so charming, so at ease, that in spite of all her anxieties, she meekly held out her hand and shook it.

Through her glove she felt a tiny prick in her palm.

The man kept hold of her hand, kept smiling. She began to feel a little dizzy. She heard him say, 'My name's Thomas Lamark. I wanted to have a chat with you about a film role you stole from my mother.'

He kept hold of her hand as she sank, gently, to the floor.

Then, from his pocket, Thomas produced a small tin that he had bought an hour earlier from a fishing-tackle shop near Brighton seafront. He opened it and peered in, wrinkling his nose against the sour smell and the solid mass of small, white, writhing maggots.

He blew them a kiss, then closed the lid.

Chapter Twenty

'So?'

'So?'

'Come on! How was it?'

'What?'

'Your date. Your *second* date!'

The Orange signal died. Amanda, in a yellow satin jacket and black T-shirt, heard a couple of shrill beeps, then her cellular phone was silent. She hit the SEND button and, almost instantly, her assistant, Lulu, answered.

The traffic inched forward, stopped. She wasn't going to make the next green light. A lorry halted alongside her, the thunking of its engine making it hard to hear Lulu's voice. Diesel exhaust billowed in her face. She raised her voice. 'I'll be there in about ten minutes, Lulu. Anyone show up yet?'

'No.'

Relief!

'Apologise to them when they do.'

'Want me to explain you had a heavy date which is why –'

'I did *not* have a heavy date, OK?'

'OK, OK! Relax! Chill out! This is not a good way to start your day, Amanda. You do not want to start off stressed. Stress will find you, you don't have to go looking for it.'

'Jesus, Lulu, what the hell have you been reading now?'

'George Jean Nathan. He said, "no man can think clearly when his fists are clenched." Are your fists clenched, Amanda?'

'They're going to be in a minute,' she said.

Again, the connection failed. And Amanda's temper

74

nearly did too. Lulu was small, bug-eyed, big-hearted, but she could be dementing too. The lights changed.

She drove on in silence. Nine twenty-five a.m. was a bad time to be in a hurry across London. Superbad. She had wanted to be in early today: she needed to get prepared for a pitch meeting at Anglia Television with two writers whose series idea she had optioned. Instead she was embarrassingly late.

It was Michael Tennent's fault.

Fifteen minutes later, puffed and flustered after running a good half-mile from the Poland Street multi-storey where she had parked her car, she let herself in through the front door of the building in Maddox Street, a few yards up from New Bond Street, and stepped into the narrow entranceway where the sign, 20–20 Vision Productions (black on clear Perspex, hip, high-tech lettering), was squeezed into a row containing several others that looked distinctly less smart. One was for a recruitment agency, one for a firm that imported Italian belts, and one, in Arabic, for an outfit run by a plump, rather shabby-looking Middle Eastern man out of a tiny office on the attic floor.

The door swung shut behind her, closing out the fumes of the cars, taxis and vans stretched back from the traffic lights at Bond Street, and she hauled herself up the two flights of stairs that were steeper than the north face of Everest.

Your fault that I'm late, Michael Tennent!

They had been the last diners to leave Aubergine. She could barely remember what she'd eaten. They had just talked.

She had invited him up to her flat for coffee and they were still talking when the windows started to lighten. Michael had left then, first with a stiff, rather clumsy handshake, then with an equally clumsy kiss. At twenty to five in the morning.

Her alarm was set permanently for seven during the week. After Michael had left, she had changed it to seven thirty to give herself an extra half-hour. Fatal error. It was always dangerous to reset her alarm clock when she was tired, because she invariably did it wrong. This morning, she had crashed into panicky consciousness at a quarter to nine when the phone rang.

It had been Brian. He had just hoped to catch her before she left for the office. He wanted to see her, he was finding life hell without her.

She thanked him for waking her. Then she told him to strap himself to a Scud missile and launch himself off a cliff.

As she walked in the door Lulu thrust a mug of coffee into her hand. She sipped it gratefully, then mouthed, silently, 'Are they here?'

'They just phoned. They're stuck on the M4. A jackknifed lorry, won't be here for at least half an hour. God likes you today.'

Lulu had round glasses, which emphasised her bug eyes. Her hair was black and spiky, and so heavily gelled it looked like a dead hedgehog. At four foot nine, she bordered on being vertically challenged. She was dressed in army fatigues and clumpy black boots, which gave her a seriously butch appearance, although in fact she was man crazy and had made more conquests than Amanda could keep count of. 'Oh,' she added, 'Chris Pye at the BBC called. He won't be around until this afternoon. Arch Dyson at Flextech wants to speak to you as soon as poss. And Brian just rang.'

Ten people worked at 20–20 Vision, but this morning the place felt quiet. The two partners who owned the business, and the rest of the staff, were on a shoot, and it was just Amanda and Lulu holding the fort. Lulu held the whole place together. Technically, she was Amanda's production assistant; in reality, she was telephonist, dogsbody, senior researcher and script-reader too.

20–20 Vision specialised in hard-edged documentaries – corruption in the building industry, armaments manufacturers breaking embargoes, government cover-ups over nuclear waste. It had collected a whole raft of awards, and three years back had had an Oscar nomination for a short on Russian nuclear trade with terrorist organisations.

She hadn't told Michael Tennent the truth about the

documentary they were making on psychiatry. She'd told him it was a straightforward look at modern psychiatry and psychotherapy methods. It wasn't. It was an attack on the profession. They wanted to show how people's lives could be messed up by therapy; that the whole world had become therapy obsessed – and that practitioners held a dangerous amount of power over their patients. The power, even, of life and death.

Amanda walked through into her own office and stood on the wrong side of her desk, scanning the pile of fresh envelopes. It wasn't much of an office: a cramped room, with a crummy little window that looked out onto a metal fire escape, but she had brightened it up with a couple of erotic Egon Schiele prints and framed press flyers of the two previous productions for which she'd been responsible – one on the pharmaceutical industry's attempts to block fast cures for stomach ulcers, the other on artificial intelligence.

Lulu followed her in. 'So, the second date. How did it go?'

The question hung in the air while Amanda squeezed behind her desk and sat down. Her chair, which had a wonky spring, went *boink*. 'Wasn't a date.' She tapped her keyboard, logging on to her e-mail.

Lulu stood defiantly in front of the desk, hands on hips. 'Wasn't a date, huh?'

'It was a working supper.'

'That's what your voice is telling me. It's not what your face is telling me. You go out with a guy for a working supper once, and it's a working supper. You go out twice with him and that's a *date*!'

'The first time was the theatre. I went with him because I wanted to see the Globe,' Amanda said.

'And last night you went to Aubergine because you wanted to see the restaurant?'

Among the raft of new e-mails on her screen, Amanda noticed one from Michael Tennent. She was keen to open it right away and wished Lulu would leave her alone.

'And,' Lulu added, 'he's your type.'

'How do you know? You've never met him.' Lulu was really irritating her now. The e-mail was tantalising her.

'He's older than you. You lost your father when you were a kid, your mother never remarried. You go for a father figure.'

'Lulu, give me some space, will you? I've got to get myself sorted out before the others tip up.'

'This is real stop-out week for you, Amanda. Monday night, the BAFTA awards. Tuesday night . . . hunt-the-shrink! I'm going to run you an eye-bath. You don't want the Anglia bigwigs to think you had a sleepless night because you were worried about the pitch, do you?' And Lulu marched out of the room with a cheeky grin.

Amanda pulled out the pilot script and the series proposal. It was for a documentary series on how pesticides in farming were threatening the whole world's ecosystem. She read the first paragraph.

Then she read Michael Tennent's e-mail. It had been sent half an hour ago. It said, simply: 'Four hours since I saw you. I'm missing you.'

Chapter Twenty-one

Sometimes in his den, late at night, Thomas Lamark basked in the glow of his computer screen, imagining he was basking in tropical sunlight.

He wondered what it would be like to visit his friend, Jurgen Jurgens, in Clearwater Springs, Florida, with whom he played chess over the Internet but whom he had never met. He did not even know what Jurgen Jurgens looked like.

Tonight he was sending him an e-mail.

Jurgen,

Thanks for your kind words about my mother, they were of much comfort to me. I hadn't realised how terrible it would be without her. I was always afraid that if she died I would miss her, but it is much more than that: it is like she was a buffer zone between myself and oblivion – that there was a generation between myself and extinction – or the abyss. Now there is nothing.

And I have all kinds of guilt going on inside me about whether I was a good son to her. In my heart I know the truth is that I wasn't. I could have done so much more to make her happy. All I can do now is try to make up for that in all the ways I can. I guess it's not going to help her – but at least it will help me come to terms with my grief.

Actually, I am really angry today. I am angry at the state of Mother's grave. I went to the cemetery this evening, to give her some good news, and I was not at all pleased with the condition of her grave. This is no way to treat someone just because they are dead.

For a start, still no headstone – I'm told that is going to

take months – but, really, does the grave have to look that awful? This great ugly mound? It doesn't look like a grave at all, it looks like an allotment, just a mess of turned-over earth. I'm going to speak to someone about this, I just do not find this acceptable. It isn't dignified.

I'm not letting Mummy lie looking like some root crop that's just been planted.

I met a bearded nerd in the graveyard (you know the type I mean – anorak, knapsack, socks, sandals, hostile personality) who started telling me the reason they dig graves so deep is that a decomposing human body is dangerously infectious. All the chemicals and gases and bacteria. It can take over a hundred years, in some soil conditions, before a human corpse ceases to be a health threat.

I really don't like this idea at all. She's my mother. I want to think of her as a dignified human being, not some decomposing fucking health threat.

It's probably politically incorrect to be dead now, anyway. You're bound to be offending some minority group by being dead.

We live in a weird world.

Your friend.

Thomas

Chapter Twenty-two

wednesday, 23 july, 1997
The only real friend I ever had is dead. It feels as if the lights in this house have gone out for ever.

Justin Flowering, down in the sauna, is still alive. At least, he still has vital signs, if you can call that being alive. He was whimpering earlier but he isn't whimpering any more now. I don't feel remorse for him the way I feel it for Tina Mackay. Am I becoming hardened?

It feels cold in this room. The cold has its own beauty, and there is such beauty in front of me. Such power. Such knowledge. Such wisdom. This machine is so smart. You have to respect computers, you really do. I do, and mine responds to this. It repays me handsomely. It gives me anything I want. And tonight it gives me a doctor in Cheltenham and one of his patients.

The doctor's name is Dr Shyam Sundaralingham and his patient is called Dr Terence Goel. Sundaralingham is a great name! Tamil, common in the south of India, not unknown but less common in England.

I don't think I mentioned before that I am a great mimic. I used to entertain Mummy for hours mimicking voices of characters in films and on television. She loved it. I hear a voice just once and that's it, I have it. I wouldn't mind a career as a mimic. I like that guy on television who's so good at voices. Can't remember his name right now. It's late.

Actually, I have a problem with my memory and I can't blame it on tiredness, because it isn't only when I'm tired. I just keep forgetting things, lists, names, events. Sometimes it feels as though whole blocks of time have been removed from inside my memory. Other times, I'm fine.

Zippidy-do-dah.

The thing about this electronic world is that it creates new reality. If a computer record says that we exist, then we do exist! We exist through our birth records, our banking records, our credit records, our driving records, our postal codes. Our biological bodies, these days, are merely hard copies of these electronic records. We are moving from the era of Biological Man into a new era of Digital Man.

It is very easy to use this new technology to create new people. Almost too easy. Just a rudimentary ability to hack computers is really the only requirement. Just insert the new character into the digital records. Ensure that you fill in a little credit history, a little academic history, a little medical history, perhaps even the occasional motoring misdemeanour to add a touch of authenticity, and there you have it. A human being able to come and go as he pleases, able to operate a bank account, to have a driving licence, a passport, credit cards, a telephone.

Anything at all.

For instance, just a few days ago, there was no such person as this doctor, Shyam Sundaralingham of Cheltenham, or his patient, Dr Terence Goel.

Now, at 3.30 a.m., Wednesday 23 July, Dr Terence Goel is an impressive character. A cousin of the famous British astronomer Sir Bernard Lovell, Dr Terence Goel, 38, is a member of the Scripps Research Institute, prior to which, from 1986 to 1995 he was a junior professor of astronomy at the Massachusetts Institute of Technology and a member of the Select Presidential Advisory Committee on the Search for Extra-terrestrial Intelligence for Ronald Reagan.

In 1993 he had a paper published in Nature *magazine, arguing that there was incontrovertible proof showing the existence of extra-terrestrial life.*

His last car in the US was a '94 Infinity. He made one parking violation, in January 1995, which he paid promptly. In June 1995 he moved to Britain to take up an advisory post at the secretive government listening and monitoring installation GCHQ.

In 1993, his wife, Leah, died in car crash when he was driving.

Dr Terence Goel now resides in Cheltenham. In December 1995, he made a five-year deed of covenant for £600 to the

Imperial Cancer Research Foundation. He's a pretty caring guy.

He has joined a local chess club. He drives a Ford Mondeo 16 valve – it's a bit of a comedown from an Infinity, but he finds it suitable for the narrow Gloucestershire roads.

He has just applied to join Mensa and taken the home test. His IQ was 175. (I've been modest there, mine is higher.)

His e-mail address is tgoel@aol.com

He has a neat website.

Terence Goel is the kind of guy I could become really good friends with. I am confident he will serve me well. But first, I must make absolutely sure that he is the right man for me. I'm going to submit him to the most important test.

I'm going to flip a coin.

Chapter Twenty-three

'Georgia On My Mind' was playing on the Volvo's radio as Michael drove up the rhododendron-lined drive of the Sheen Park Hospital. He mouthed the words and turned it up loud.

It was coming up to eight thirty. The song was still playing when he pulled into the car park and he kept the ignition on, listening to it, not wanting it to end, shutting his window in case his colleagues wondered if he had finally flipped.

And he was wondering whether Amanda had got his e-mail. He was thinking hard about whether he should have sent it.

It had been an impulse. That was how he had felt. And still felt. He was missing her. Badly.

And Georgia was on his mind. In his heart, his soul, the beat of the song was the beat of his heart. The slow, husky voice of Ray Charles was making his heart ache.

It was a fine morning. Amanda had played this song, it had been on a CD some time during the hours they had sat talking. He hadn't heard it in maybe twenty years and now he was hearing it twice within a few hours. Some kind of omen?

He didn't believe in omens, but he didn't disbelieve in them either. It was just that if there was a God, Michael thought He had better things to do than fart around arranging crows into strange patterns in the sky, or sending black cats scurrying across roads in front of people to spook them, or fixing ladybirds to land on people's bare arms so they'd think they were going to win the lottery. Or maybe that was what God got his kicks doing. Just farting around, messing with people. He had taken Katy away and now maybe He was going to give Michael Amanda instead. Or maybe He wasn't.

As flies to wanton boys are we to the gods; they kill us for their sport.

He entered the front of the building and immediately got jumped on by one of his colleagues, Paul Straddley, who had a patient suffering from a fear of vomiting. He wanted Michael's advice.

'He has anxiety or a real vomit phobia?' Michael asked, barely making any attempt to conceal his irritation. All he wanted right now was to get to his office, to see whether Amanda had replied to his e-mail and have some strong coffee.

Paul Straddley was a neurotic little man with a permanently anxious face and ragged hair. Dressed today in a brown polyester suit that was too short in the sleeves and legs, he looked more like a 1950s back-room boffin than an eminent psychiatrist with an impressive list of publications to his name.

'He's frightened to eat – he's afraid that food might get stuck in his gullet. Everything has to be liquidised and even then he doesn't trust it, he has to check and recheck it. He's losing weight and I'm very concerned about him.' Straddley looked at Michael with desperation. The man was wonky himself, Michael had always thought, probably more fucked up than most of his patients. But so were a lot of psychiatrists.

He probably was too.

We're all barking. These poor sods come and see us, pay us a hundred pounds an hour because they think we have the answers. We stick a few pills down their throats and let them keep talking until they come up with the answers themselves. Or get bored.

Or, he thought, with a sudden sharp twist of guilt, *kill themselves*.

Michael began to sidestep around him. 'Can we talk about this later, Paul?'

Straddley did a clumsy shuffle so that he was blocking

Michael's path once more. 'Um, how much later exactly, Michael?'

'I don't know. I have a busy day and I'm late for my ward round.'

'Can you do lunch? The canteen?'

Michael nodded reluctantly, although he'd been hoping to pick up a sandwich and sit quietly by the river.

Straddley released him. Michael walked across the hall and up the grand balustraded staircase. The entrance hall was a huge space, filling most of the ground floor, with columns and a high, elaborately stuccoed ceiling; it had a grandiose air that seemed aloof to the imitation wood of the reception counter and the metal and plastic chairs arranged in the waiting area.

He took a quick walk round his in-patients, checking their charts and medications and asking how they were, then collected his list of appointments from Thelma.

At ten to nine his multi-disciplinary team of two nurses, a junior doctor, a psychologist and a social worker were crammed into his office for their twice-weekly review of his patients and departed shortly after nine ten.

His first patient hadn't arrived yet. Good.

Before he had even taken off his jacket, he sat down at his computer and logged on. Twenty-eight new e-mails, mostly from other psychiatrists and psychologists with whom he shared ideas and problems. Another confirmed details of timing for a paper he was to present at a conference in Venice in September. And there was one from his brother Bob, in Seattle, the usual chatty stuff about his wife (Lori) and kids (Bobby Junior and Brittany) and had he seen Mum and Dad recently?

There was no e-mail from Amanda Capstick.

But that was OK, it was early, he'd sent it to her office. No need to fret.

Yet.

There was no e-mail from Amanda at ten o'clock. Nor after lunch. Nor by five o'clock in the afternoon.

It had been stupid to send his.

Amanda was a tough, sensible young woman. She wasn't going to be won over by cheap, soppy sentiments, they would just be a turn-off.

His last patient of the day was due at five fifteen. Quarter of an hour's grace. He made a couple of notes in the file of the patient who had just left, then replaced it in the cabinet.

'Georgia On My Mind' was still playing over in his head. It wouldn't quit. '*Amanda* On My Mind'.

The sweet smell of freshly mown grass was in the air. He yawned, swivelled his chair around to face his desk, then slouched forward, rested his head on his arms and closed his eyes. He let his mind sink back to last night – or earlier this morning.

She had looked stunning. A long, shiny, leopard-print jacket, silky black T-shirt, short black skirt, loose gold bracelet on her wrist. Her face was even lovelier than he had remembered and he tried to picture it again now but, oddly, could not assemble an entire clear image in his mind.

He could see her blue eyes sparkling with laughter. Her teeth white, even, but large, which made her mouth seem sensual, predatory, and he longed to kiss it. Her slender arms, the tiny crow's feet around her eyes when she smiled, the flick of her head to toss back her hair, her scent. Calvin Klein. He'd seen the bottle in the bathroom.

How had her body language been?

She hadn't thrown herself at him, that was for sure. But neither had she done anything distancing. She'd been neutral; kept to her space. Yet she had watched him constantly, and that was a positive sign. Her smiles had been warm and her laughter genuine and open.

But he felt he had learned little about her, at least about her love life, which was where he had been trying to pry. There was some relationship that she was uncomfortable about. And it seemed to make her uneasy when he tried to get her to talk about it.

His intercom buzzed. His next appointment was in the waiting room. A new patient.

Hastily, Michael opened the new file he had prepared, and looked at the referral letter from the man's doctor, a GP Michael had never heard of. Dr Shyam Sundaralingham, who practised in Cheltenham, but that wasn't unusual: there were countless doctors he didn't know.

Dr Sundaralingham diagnosed that his patient was suffering from clinical depression and had specifically requested that Michael see him. That wasn't unusual: a lot of people heard him on the radio or read his articles, and asked for him specifically. He would give them an initial interview, but then, to keep his workload from spilling over, he kept only those patients who particularly interested him, and normally referred the others to psychotherapists for their long-term treatment.

This new patient was thirty-eight.

His name was Dr Terence Goel.

Chapter Twenty-four

'OK, Amanda, I think this would be helpful. I want you to describe Michael Tennent to me.'

Amanda was in the turquoise room of her therapist, and now in the airy quiet of this space, shaded by the Venetian blinds from the late-afternoon sunlight, she felt calm for the first time that day. She leaned back in the comfortable wicker armchair, closed her eyes, compiled her thoughts.

'He – I – uh – he reminds me – a sort of – composite. Let me think of an actor, sort of outdoors but intellectual, if you know what I mean. Kind of Harrison Ford in *Indiana Jones* or, maybe, Jeff Goldblum – he has that sort of quiet authority that Goldblum has.'

Maxine Bentham, in her usual position squatting on the floor against the sofa, nodded. 'He was in *The Fly*. And in the Jurassic Park movies.'

'Uh-huh.'

'OK, Amanda, let's think about these roles. In *The Fly* he plays a crazed scientist who evolves into a human fly. In *The Lost World* he plays a scientist who has to deal with the monsters. Do you see any significance in this?'

'A contradiction? Is that what you want me to say?'

'I only want you to say what you *feel*.'

Amanda tapped her teeth with a fingernail. She nibbled at it, aware that she was doing so, but unable to prevent herself. She had been appalled at what a mess her nails had looked recently. 'You think I'm seeing him partly as someone to be scared of? And partly as someone who can solve my problems? Who can slay my monster? Who can cure me of Brian?'

'Jeff Goldblum is a curious way for you to describe him, that's what I mean.'

'I don't think so, no. I'm just trying to give you a physical description. He's tall, dark-haired, good-looking, but in a – a kind of intellectual way. Maybe he has a little Jewish blood, just a hint.'

'Do you think he's a kind man?'

Amanda nodded vigorously. 'He's really warm. I . . .' She hesitated, searching for the right words. 'I feel safe with him, secure. I don't have to pretend anything with him. I'm *me* with him. *Me*.' She frowned. 'Am I making any sense?'

Maxine gave her a curious, rather wistful smile. 'Yes. Go on.'

'I don't know. Maybe it's because he's a shrink, so I feel he can see through me, so there's no point in trying to lie to him.'

'Lie to him about what?'

Amanda scratched the back of her neck. She was suddenly finding this difficult. 'He sent me an e-mail this morning. It was there when I got to the office. It was –' She fell silent.

The therapist prodded gently. 'It was what?'

'It was really nice!'

'What did it say?'

'It just said, "Four hours since I saw you. I'm missing you."'

'Did you reply?'

'No.'

'OK, why not?'

Amanda tugged at her nail again with her teeth. 'Because I –' She shrugged. 'I'm not sure how to reply.'

'Because you are not sure if this is Jeff Goldblum the Fly or Jeff Goldblum the Monster Slayer?'

'It's more complicated than that.'

Maxine waited for her to go on, but when she didn't, she said, 'You told me last time that you liked Michael Tennent, but you didn't know whether you were attracted to him. Has that changed?'

Amanda shifted her position in her chair. 'I haven't been entirely honest with him. I told him that we were making a documentary about psychiatrists, and that's only partly true. What we are actually doing is a pretty hard-hitting attack on the whole therapy culture we have in our society.'

Maxine Bentham looked surprised. 'Does this include me?'

Amanda shook her head. 'No, I wouldn't do that to you.' She crossed her legs, then uncrossed them, then crossed them again. 'Oh, God, this must sound terrible! It's not about *good* therapists, Maxine, it's about these people who do a three-month mail-order course, then set themselves up as hypnotherapists, or rebirthers or whatever. People go along to them and they make decisions that affect their entire lives based on what these instant therapists tell them.'

Now Maxine Bentham was starting to look distinctly uneasy. 'Surely Dr Tennent doesn't fit into that category? He's a highly qualified doctor, and very eminent.'

'Yes, he is. But therapy is a long process, right? In proper analysis you see a patient three to five times a week for years, right? But where it becomes a joke is something like when you have a radio show. Someone has a problem, they think they can just pick up the phone, call a radio show, and slam-dunk! Ten minutes of chat with Dr Michael Tennent and their life is back on track. He's bastardising his profession. He's lowering himself to the same status as the quacks. Here you have a brilliant man selling out to the instant-gratification culture.'

There was a long silence. 'Amanda, you're going to have to help me out, I'm getting a little confused here about where you're at.'

Amanda raised her arms. '*You're* confused? How do you reckon I feel? I think I'm falling in love with the guy!'

Chapter Twenty-five

Lawnmowers.

Michael could hear the drone of the mower's engine, the pitch of its blades, the rumble of metal vibrating, and every now and then the clacking of a ratchet.

Lawnmowers were one of the downsides of summer. The contraption outside, an old sit-on Atco cylinder cutter with a train of gang mowers clattering along behind it, had been getting steadily closer all day and now, finally, at twenty past five it was right below Michael's window.

Michael had a headache, which he blamed on his lack of sleep last night although his caffeine binge throughout today to stay awake was probably as much to blame.

Go home, gardener. It's nearly half past five. Don't you have a life outside cutting grass at the Sheen Park Hospital? Go home! Please.

He tried to concentrate on the form in front of him that was headed LIFE HISTORY QUESTIONNAIRE.

Title: ___ *Dr*   First name: ___ *Terence*
Surname: ___ *Goel*
Address: ___ *Flat 6, 97 Royal Court Walk, Cheltenham, Glos.*
Tel. (Day) ___ *01973-358066*   (Evening) ___ *same*
Marital status: ___ *widower*
Present occupation: ___ *Communications scientist*
Are you happy in your occupation? _____
If not, in what ways are you unhappy? _____
_____
Do you live in a bedsit flat or house etc? _____
Is it your own or is it rented from the council or a private landlord? _____

Who else lives at home? (please list the people)_____

_____

What is your current problem (s) that you want to
solve?_____

_____

What prompted you to seek help now?_____

_____

Michael turned over the pages. With the exception of the
first few lines, nothing else had been filled in. In his letter of
referral, Sundaralingham had already mentioned that Goel
was a scientist rather than a doctor of medicine.

'Prisms.'

He looked up with a start, wondering if he had misheard
his new patient. 'Prisms?'

'Do you have prisms in your glasses, Dr Tennent?'

Surprised by the question, he said, 'I do, yes,' then added,
quizzically, 'Why?'

Michael studied his patient carefully, checking for signs
that the man was agitated or guarded, suspicious or
distracted, but Terence Goel seemed none of these.

Making firm eye-contact with Michael, he was lounging
back on the sofa, legs apart, feet squarely on the floor, arms
spread out either side of him. A little *too* relaxed, perhaps,
Michael wondered, as if being here in this office was
boosting his confidence. That happened frequently, just
the same as someone going into a doctor's surgery and
immediately feeling better.

Goel had it all going for him in the looks department,
Michael thought. Handsome, impressively tall, great phy-
sique. With his gelled hair, collarless grey shirt, classy
charcoal linen suit and black suede Gucci loafers, he looked
almost self-consciously hip, like some technology guru
togged up for a media interview.

On first impressions, he seemed genial and far more self-
assured than most people who came in here. His voice had
a deep, assertive punch. Boston, Michael guessed, although
his knowledge of American accents was limited. The only

93

slight incongruity was the clipboard with an attached notepad, which Goel had brought in and now rested on the sofa beside him. He didn't seem like a man who would carry around a clipboard. Neither did he seem like an archetypal scientist – although there was a breed of gung-ho professors that the US specialised in producing and this was clearly one of them.

'Even without glasses, we look at a lot of things through prisms, Dr Tennent. We don't realise that, but we do. Do you ever look at the stars?'

Michael wasn't sure where this was going, but stayed with it. 'Yes, sometimes.'

'You understand why they twinkle?'

'I don't know the scientific explanation, no. I assume it's to do with their distance from us.'

'It has nothing to do with their distance from us. It has to do with moisture in the atmosphere. We can only ever look up at the stars through moisture. Each droplet distorts, makes a prism. We look at the stars in the night sky through billions and billions of prisms.'

There was a calmness in Terence Goel's voice, as he delivered his explanation, and that gave Michael his first insight into his patient. It was an emotionless calm, an artificial one, as if the man was exerting supreme control to present himself as something other than he was.

'Thank you,' Michael said. 'I wasn't aware of that.' Then he added, good-humouredly, 'I'll take a look up at the sky tonight with new eyes.'

'How often in life do we have the illusion that we are seeing things clearly, Dr Tennent, when in reality we are not.'

'Is this something you find is a big problem in your life?'

'It's a big problem for everybody.'

Michael glanced back down at the questionnaire, then looked up again, wanting to move the session forward. 'You don't seem to have filled in much of this question-naire.'

'You noticed that?'

94

There was such surprise in Goel's voice that Michael couldn't be sure whether it was genuine.

'Yes. Were you uncomfortable with the form?'

'No.' Goel gave him a warm, disarming smile.

Michael continued to watch him closely, but his body language was giving up no secrets. He decided to move on. 'Right. Terence. I'd like you to tell me a bit about why you want to see me.'

'Is that your Volvo outside? The silver grey one?'

Michael paused for a moment before responding, not wanting to waste time on non sequiturs. 'Yes,' he said dismissively. 'Can we get back to what it is you want to see me about?'

'They're strong cars, Volvos. I was told they're a good car to be in a crash in.'

Michael glanced fleetingly at the photograph of Katy. 'I think it's better not to be in a crash at all.' His eyes met Goel's, and suddenly, he felt himself flushing.

Did Goel know about the accident? Unlikely, although Michael *had* written some intensely personal pieces for several newspapers in the months following her death on bereavement. And it wasn't uncommon for a patient to try to play mind games with him, but rarely at a first consultation.

And Dr Terence Goel, sitting in the sofa, maintained his body in a perfectly relaxed stance, knowing that Michael Tennent was watching every twitch, every blink, looking for clues, trying to find those little dotted lines marked *open here* that would lead him into his psyche.

In your dreams, Dr Tennent.

Then, aloud, he said, 'I hate cocktail parties.'

'Why is that?' Michael replied.

Dr Goel blanked him. 'Why is what?'

'Why do you hate cocktail parties?'

'What makes you think I hate cocktail parties?' Dr Goel asked, with disarming innocence.

'You just said so.'

Dr Goel frowned at him. 'No, I didn't. I didn't say anything.'

On the top sheet of paper in the file folder, beneath where he had written today's date, 23 July, with his Parker fountain pen (a first wedding anniversary gift from Katy) Michael made a note. Some conditions made people speak aloud without realising they had done so.

Thomas Lamark had to work hard to suppress a smile. This was going to be much easier than he had feared. You might be smart, Dr Michael Tennent, but you have no idea how much smarter I am.

Tina Mackay had been his only slip-up so far. Not a big slip-up, but unnecessary. He had not done his research properly with her, hadn't known her father was so high profile, a big cheese in the civil service: the coverage they had given his daughter's disappearance was out of all proportion to her significance.

Every bloody day there was an article. Quotes from friends, quotes from her mother, quotes from the police. Everyone was getting more worried. And the police had no leads!

There had been six editors on the list who had turned the book down. Any one of them would have done fine. The coin had told him to take Tina Mackay.

He blamed the coin.

This office was a tip, it was disgusting, really it was. How could the psychiatrist work here? How could he find anything? Look at the wodges of paper, the loose floppy disks, the magazines, the files, just piled everywhere, haphazardly. Anyone would think he was in the middle of moving in but he had been here for seven years.

You are far, far filthier than a pig, Dr Tennent, and one day, very soon, you are going to squeal far, far louder than one.

And that's before I start to really hurt you.

Thomas had familiarised himself with the building before coming in. He'd strolled around the grounds, checked out the exits, the fire escapes, and then taken a good walk around the inside, carrying his clipboard. He reckoned it was a fair bet that if you carried a clipboard no one would challenge you.

Now he knew all the staircases, passages, doors.

He also knew he was Michael Tennent's last patient today. It would be easy to take him or kill him after the session. But that would be too easy, and he wasn't ready yet. He still had unfinished business.

'I'd like to know a bit about your parents, Terence. Are they still alive?'

Instantly, Michael saw the reaction in the man's face, as if he had touched a deep nerve.

Dr Goel did not reply.

Michael saw the man struggle to keep his composure. His body language had changed from a man at ease to someone under threat. Dr Goel leaned forward, arms tightly crossed, then he leaned back.

Michael gave him a couple of minutes, and when he still did not say anything, Michael asked, 'Do you find it difficult to talk about your parents?'

'I don't find it difficult to talk about anything, Dr Tennent,' he replied, with haunted eyes.

There was clearly a big key in his childhood, but Michael could not find the way into it today. All further questions about his parents simply made Goel clam up and rock backwards and forwards in his chair.

Michael moved to a different subject, planning to come back at the parents from another angle, and asked Dr Goel about his work.

'I'm afraid it is classified information,' he replied.

Michael looked down at the man's incomplete form. 'You are a widower. Shall we talk about your late wife?'

'You are asking a lot of questions, Dr Tennent.'

'Do you resent that?'

'Why should I?'

Michael changed tack again. 'How do you wish me to help? What is the problem you want me to solve?'

'I'm right, aren't I?' Dr Goel said. 'You are asking a lot of questions.'

At six o'clock, Michael shook Dr Terence Goel's hand, and Terence Goel told him he looked forward to seeing him again the following week, at the same time.

Michael closed the door, sat down and glanced through his notes. He felt zonked – exhausted and confused by the man. It had been a long day. Dr Terence Goel, what do I make of you? What the hell is going on inside your head? If you want me to help you, you are going to have to open up to me. What have I learned about you today? Every time I asked you a question you replied with a question. You have one hell of a personality disorder. You are stubborn. You are a control freak. You are confused. Delusional. You very definitely have an obsessive streak.

Your parents are your Achilles' heel.

The lawnmower was still going strong outside. Jesus, how much grass was out there?

He returned to the referral letter from Goel's doctor. *Clinical depression.* He wasn't convinced depression was at the heart of all this.

To the bottom of the list of notes he had written down, he added a mental one: 'FUBAB'. It stood for Fucked Up Beyond All Belief.

Then he turned to his computer and, once more, for the hundredth time today, checked his e-mail. With a beat of excitement he saw, finally, that he had a reply from Amanda Capstick. He dragged the mouse across the pad, and double clicked on the e-mail to open it. Like the one he had sent her, it was short and simple. It said: 'I'm missing you too.'

Chapter Twenty-six

Detective Constable Glen Branson eyed the brand new Jaguar sports convertible that was driving in the opposite direction to him, along the seafront towards Brighton, with its roof down, its wipers jerking across the dry windscreen and its hazard lights flashing.

In particular he looked at the driver, a greaseball youth who shot him a nervous glance. Although Glen was in plain clothes in an unmarked car, if the youth was a local villain he would be aware of the tell-tale signs: the make of car, dark colour, type of radio aerial. Glen noted he wasn't wearing a seat belt.

In the short time he had been with the force, Glen had earned respect and he was well liked; although a rookie detective, he was a mature human being, having joined the force relatively late, at twenty-nine. He had completed two years as a police constable, first on foot patrol then in cars, and had then successfully applied for the CID. He'd served the standard two years probation period then, just two months ago, had completed a further year as a temporary detective constable, following which he had taken and passed the CID course with honours.

In his former life, Glen had worked for ten years as a nightclub bouncer. He was black, six foot three inches tall, weighed a tad under two hundred pounds and was as bald as a meteorite. Not many people had given him trouble, and the job had paid so well he'd been scared to give it up. It wasn't until his son, Sammy, was born that he had plucked up the courage to change. He wanted his son to be proud of him. He didn't ever want his son to have to tell someone that his daddy was a bouncer.

Normally Glen brimmed with confidence but in these few weeks since passing his exams and becoming a fully fledged detective he had been nervous. There was a huge amount to remember and he wanted to get it right. He'd seen how easily the police could lose a case by a simple error in procedure. In the movie *Storm-10*, Kirk Douglas, quoting Einstein, had said, 'Heaven is in the details.' Good policing was in the *details*, too.

Glen was ambitious and he had some catching up to do in his new career. He had calculated he could make inspector or even chief inspector by his mid-forties. And that would be something he wanted to hear Sammy telling people. 'My dad's a chief inspector!'

I will be, Sammy, I promise you.

This Jaguar was definitely wrong.

So far he'd had a good day. He'd been congratulated on a piece of detection work by the DCI at the station. A suspected antique-jewellery thief had denied being in Brighton on the day of the raid on a shop in the town and had a strong alibi – a sworn statement from a witness that he had been in London the whole of that day. Glen had discovered a mobile phone registered in one of the suspect's alias names. From analysis of the bill provided by Vodaphone, he could see that two calls had been made on the phone at different cells along the London–Brighton line, travelling north, two hours after the raid.

A stolen car would add another small feather to his cap. He had one job to do this afternoon, which was to take a statement at a flat that had been burgled last night. It shouldn't take more than an hour, and then, he hoped, he could get off shift promptly at four in time to catch the four forty-five showing at the Duke of York cinema of a 1950s movie he had never seen on a big screen, *On the Waterfront*. Outside police work and his family, Glen ate, drank and breathed old movies.

He swung round the car in a U-turn, accelerated hard, overtook two vehicles and pulled in directly behind the Jag. The driver seemed to be struggling with the controls. Glen pressed the transmit button on the car's radio, and said, 'This is Charlie Hotel One-Four-Four.'

He heard a female voice at Central Control acknowledge him. 'Charlie Hotel One-Four-Four.'

The Jag driver continued, unaware of him, still apparently struggling, wipers arcing away.

'I am following a Jaguar sports car which I view with suspicion, navy blue, registration Romeo five-two-one Yankee November Victor, westbound on Hove Kingsway. Have a uniform patrol check it.'

'Jaguar sports, navy blue, registration Romeo five-two-one Yankee November Victor. Thank you, Charlie Hotel One-Four-Four.'

Then he heard his local control on the personal radio clipped to his belt, a cheery male voice, Ray Dunkley – Glen had met him a couple of times. He was putting out a call to a uniform police constable.

'Charlie Hotel One-Six-Two, we have a grade three for you, a resident at three Adelaide Crescent is reporting concern about an elderly neighbour who hasn't been sighted for three days. The name of the person she's concerned about is Cora Burstridge.'

Glen's ears pricked up. He fumbled for his radio, unclipped it and raised it to his mouth. 'Sorry to butt in, Control, this is Charlie Hotel One-Four-Four. Is that Cora Burstridge the actress? *The* Cora Burstridge?'

'I believe so, yes.'

'I knew she lived somewhere around there! I'm on my way to take a statement at fifteen Adelaide Crescent, I can check it out.'

'Do you want to be bothered? Uniform can get over there some time this afternoon.'

'It's no bother!'

'Thanks, Charlie Hotel One-Four-Four, if you don't mind? Be helpful – we're a car short today.'

Glen felt a surge of excitement. 'Cora Burstridge! Wow! She's something else. Did you see her in *Rivers of Chance* with Robert Donat and Cary Grant? Nineteen fifty-two?'

'Before my time. Afraid I'm not as old as you, Glen.'

'Ya, very witty.'

'The neighbour will let you in. Mrs Winston. Flat seven.'

As he released his mike switch, the car's radio fizzed again, and he heard the female controller putting out the details of the Jaguar. Moments later, he made a left turn into Adelaide Crescent, and watched the Jaguar continue on towards the congested traffic of central Brighton. Either the kiddie was innocent, or was planning to leg it on foot into the crowds rather than try to out-drive the police.

Glen parked his car almost directly outside number 3, Adelaide Crescent, a proud classical Regency terrace: columned porticoes, tall sash windows, white paintwork fading and flaking under the relentless corrosion of the salty air. Its air of faded grandeur made it just the right kind of building for a star like Cora Burstridge, Glen thought. It had real *style*.

He felt a guilty thrill of excitement just staring up at it, thinking about the actress who lived there. It ought not to matter to him who it was, his actions should be just the same for everyone, but of course this mattered to him.

Cora Burstridge!

He could reel off the names of every single one of her forty-seven movies by heart. *Safe Arrival. Monaco Suite. Forgetting Mr Didcote. Desert Tune.* Comedies. Musicals. Thrillers. Romances. She was so versatile, so beautiful, so graceful, and so very sharp-witted. Glen had seen her only recently in a television adaptation of a Robert Goddard novel, and she still looked marvellous and gave a powerful performance. And, of course, only on Monday night she'd been on television at the BAFTA awards, where she had delivered a slightly disappointing acceptance speech, he thought. But he could forgive her that: the poor woman had clearly been overwhelmed by the adulation.

Must be about sixty-five now, he calculated. Amazing how good she looked. He glanced up at the windows of the building and felt a lump in his throat. He hoped fervently that she was all right.

He rang the bell for flat seven. Mrs Winston met him on

the third floor. She was a pleasant woman well into her seventies, her grey hair elegantly coiffed.

Two bouquets were propped against the wall outside Cora Burstridge's door. The hall was musty and smelt of cats, and it was dark and much less impressive than the exterior of the building: everything was browned with age and it felt as sad as a railway-station waiting room.

'These arrived today,' Mrs Winston explained. 'Another eight or nine came yesterday – I've put them in my spare bathroom to keep them watered. And I took in her milk yesterday and this morning.'

'You've tried her doorbell, I presume?' he asked.

'Yes, again just now. And I've knocked.'

Glen knelt and peered through Cora Burstridge's brass letterbox. He could see a large amount of post scattered on the floor. Surreptitiously, not wanting to distress Mrs Winston, he sniffed the air. There were faint traces of a smell that had become as familiar as it was unwelcome to him; it made his stomach heave and gave him an instant, terrible feeling of dread. That cloying, putrid-fish smell.

He could hear flies.

He stood up, pulled out his notebook, and asked Mrs Winston a few standard questions. When had she last seen Cora Burstridge? Had she heard any noises? Did the actress have many visitors? A housekeeper?

To the last question, Mrs Winston surprised him by saying that Cora Burstridge was short of money. She had a cleaning lady who came once a week, on Fridays, for a couple of hours, that was all.

'I'd have thought she must be a very rich lady,' Glen said.

'I'm afraid not. She hadn't worked much in the past ten years. I think she'd made a few bad investments and her last husband was a gambler.'

Glen asked the woman if there was any other way into the flat and she directed him to the fire escape at the back. Then he persuaded her to go back inside her own flat: he didn't want her to see what he feared he was about to see himself.

He radioed the duty uniform-section sergeant, gave him

the facts and received authorisation to force an entry. Then he checked out the fire escape, a precarious metal super-structure which led up to a solid, rusted-up door, but gave no access to any windows.

He went back to the front door of Cora Burstridge's flat, rang the bell several times, knocked, and then, to be quite sure, called loudly through the letterbox. Nothing.

The door was secured with a fairly recent Banham dead-lock and there was no point, he knew, in even considering trying to pick it. Brute force was his best option. He tried gently with his shoulder, then much less gently with his right foot. The door yielded a fraction but the lock did not give. He debated whether to radio for a unit with a portable battering ram on board, but did not want to risk missing out on this himself. Instead, he continued to hammer away with his foot.

After some moments, he became aware of other doors opening and of voices murmuring. A young man in a T-shirt and shorts came to the top of the stairs, then stopped with a look of shock when he saw Glen, perspiring, in his grey suit.

'Police!' Glen called, to reassure him.

With a look of horror, the youth fled down the stairs. Glen made a mental note about that – he probably had drugs in his flat. Then he turned his full concentration back on the door, and kicked hard again.

Finally the lock tore away from the door frame, but the door swung open only a few inches then stopped tight against the safety chain. It had been installed well and it took several more very hard kicks before it yielded. He pushed the door shut as best he could behind him, to keep out prying eyes, then stood struggling against the smell and the nausea rising inside him. Then he pulled on the thin rubber gloves he carried in his pocket.

He was in a small hallway. Two exquisite abstract paint-ings of Parisian street scenes hung on one wall, and on the opposite wall were two framed playbills. Cora Burstridge and Laurence Olivier in *Time and the Conways* at the Phoenix Theatre, Charing Cross Road, and Cora Burstridge,

Anna Massey and Trevor Howard in *Lady Windermere's Fan* at the Theatre Royal, Brighton.

In spite of his anxiety, he could not help feeling awed at being inside the home of this great actress – one of *the* great actresses. Something about it that he couldn't pinpoint made it feel different from anywhere he had ever been before. It had an air of magic, of being in some other world, part of an exclusive club which you had to be a rich, famous celebrity to join. He was looking forward to telling his wife, Grace, tonight. She'd never believe he had been inside Cora Burstridge's home!

Then his anxiety returned with a vengeance. Stepping carefully over the mail he walked into a large drawing room, with the curtains partially drawn. Two bluebottles were batting themselves against the window. It was furnished almost entirely in art deco. It was utterly stunning, but gave Glen the eerie sense of being in a time warp, heightened by more old playbills and film posters, as well as framed photographs. In pride of place above the mantelpiece was a letter from the Princess Royal thanking the actress for the time and effort she had put into hosting a fund-raising evening for Save the Children.

This place was a treasure trove! So much to look at.

In one corner of the room was a writing desk on which an answering-machine winked furiously. As he went over to it, he saw a note, weighted down by a Lalique deco mermaid, written in blue ink, in a shaky hand. It said: 'I can no longer look at myself in the mirror.' There was no signature.

Glen read the words several times, and now, suddenly, it wasn't nausea he was struggling against: it was tears. The crackle of his radio brought him back into the real world.

'Charlie Hotel One-Four-Four?'

He pressed his microphone switch. 'Charlie Hotel One-Four-Four.'

It was his own section sergeant. 'Glen, could you attend a container that's been tampered with at Aldrington Wharf at the harbour?'

'I'm at Cora Burstridge's flat. I think I could be here a while.'

'She going to show you some of her movies?' his sergeant bantered.

'I don't think so,' Glen replied, grimly.

He went back into the hallway and walked along a narrow passage. The stench was getting stronger and the sound of flies more intense. The smell seemed to alter the density of the air itself, to weigh it down. *Don't breathe in, you are breathing death itself.*

He slowed his pace as he approached a door that was ajar at the end.

He stopped outside it. The room was in darkness, but he knew she must be in there. Sliding his hand past the door frame, he found the light switch, pressed it and pushed the door wide open.

The room filled with light from a large art-deco chandelier and matching wall sconces. Flock wallpaper. Fluffy slippers on the white carpeted floor. A solitary figure was lying in the massive bed, face turned away from him, something shiny covering her hair that he thought might be a shower cap. Flies hovered above the bed, and there were more on the curtains. Her arms lay outstretched in front of her, above the bedclothes, her hands sticking out of the sleeves of her pink satin dressing gown. Even from over here, by the door, he could see the tips of her fingers had turned mauve.

Taking a breath, despite the appalling stench, he walked past the dressing table, with a mirror completely bordered in light bulbs, around to the other side of the bed to see her face.

And that was when he lost it.

It wasn't a shower cap over her hair, it was a Waitrose grocery bag over her entire head, clamped tightly around her neck by her dressing gown sash tied, clumsily, in a bow.

With his gloved hands he undid it and pulled up the bag to expose her face. As he did so, a cloud of bluebottles exploded around him. He stared down in numbed shock. Her mouth was open, as if in a frozen scream of agony. Most of her face was bluish black. Maggots crawled over what remained of her lips and in what was left of her eyes.

He turned away in shock, gagging. *No, Cora, no, no, no. Why did you do this? Oh, sweet Jesus, why did you have to do this?*

Chapter Twenty-seven

Later she would tell her friend, Sandy, that she had been wrong about him all these weeks, this man who always came to her checkout counter and stared at her so strangely. He wasn't Liam Neeson at all!

Well, it wasn't totally improbable that he *might* have been. She'd had Patsy Kensit in only a fortnight ago. And Liz Hurley a few months back. And she wasn't sure but she *thought* it had been Billy Connolly just before Easter. Loads of stars came in here, to Safeways in the King's Road, but for some reason they always seemed to go to other checkouts, not to hers.

But now she looked up and there he was, this man she was convinced was Liam Neeson (but he always paid cash so she couldn't get his name from his credit card) was smiling at her. He was wearing a yellow polo shirt buttoned to the neck, and a brown Armani jacket.

'Hello, Tracey!' he said, as usual.

And, as usual, she blushed. People did sometimes say her name, it was easy enough to read it off her lapel badge, but this man's voice was something else, it was a dreamy English voice and he said *Tracey* in a very special way. And suddenly she couldn't remember whether Liam Neeson was English or American.

'I'm making Bahian crab soup,' he said, and gestured to the *incredibly* neat line of foodstuffs that waited on the far side of the NEXT CUSTOMER PLEASE! sign. It looked like he had laid everything out using a ruler or something. 'I'm making it for my girlfriend.'

He liked the way she nodded at him in acknowledgement that he had a girlfriend, that he wasn't a sad loner trying to chat her up. It felt good saying that he had a girlfriend. Suddenly he felt like a normal human being.

'Have you ever had Bahian crab soup?' he asked.

She wrinkled her face in distaste, hitting the button to start the conveyor moving. 'Don't like crab very much – don't like the way they look.'

'My mother didn't like crab either,' he said. 'She hated crab. She would never allow a crab in the house. Not even *tinned* crab.'

'I don't mind crab paste,' Tracey said. 'In sandwiches.'

A large bottle of freshly squeezed orange juice arrived first at the till. She slid it past the bar-code reader, reached down and gave Thomas Lamark a fistful of plastic bags. Then she slid four avocados through, followed by a pack of English tomatoes.

'English are the best,' he said. 'Some of the imported tomatoes get irradiated to kill the bacteria. Did you know that?'

Tracey shook her head.

'You have to be careful with radiation, Tracey. It can mess up your genes. Are you concerned about radiation?'

She glanced upwards warily as if checking she wasn't being irradiated by some unseen machine. 'I like English tomatoes too,' she said.

Then the crabs arrived, but they were in a white plastic bag and she couldn't see the creatures inside it. All the same, she still shuddered as she held the wet fish department's coded label up to the bar-code scanner.

Thomas watched the checkout girl. He felt sorry for her. And she reminded him, in her looks and perky demeanour, of his girlfriend at medical school, a nursing student. Liz. And he remembered how he had squirmed when he had brought Liz home to meet his mother, and his mother had made him realise all the things that were wrong with her.

There was so much wrong with this poor girl. She was such a thin little thing with fluffy blonde hair and a face that was pretty but vacant, and her teeth weren't that great, crooked and not well kept. Last week he'd noticed she'd had a ladder in her tights. The week before, the collar of her blouse had been badly frayed. 'Did you read that Cora Burstridge died?' he asked her.

'Cora who?'

'The actress. Cora Burstridge. It was in the papers this morning.'

She shook her head blankly, and passed a carton of free-range eggs through the scanner, then she tilted her head and opened her mouth. 'She the one who won an award, Monday?'

'The BAFTA award.'

'Oh, right, her. She died? Poor thing.' She gave a little nervous laugh. 'Not fair is it, to get an award and then die?'

Four mangoes trundled along to the end of the conveyor.

'Did you like Gloria Lamark's films?'

'Who?'

'Gloria Lamark,' he said quietly.

'Never heard of her,' she said.

She continued logging the groceries in silence, then helped him to bag them. Then, to her surprise, he handed her a credit card to pay for the groceries. On it was the name Dr Terence Goel.

While she was waiting for the slip to print out, Thomas took his coin out of his pocket and tossed it.

'Heads or tails?' he asked her.

She looked at him in surprise, then shrugged and said, 'Tails.'

He palmed the coin, then checked it. It was tails. He put the coin back into his pocket. 'You are lucky, Tracey. This is your lucky day!'

He pulled a slim white envelope from his pocket and handed it to her. 'I want you to have this. Put it away, open it later.'

Surprised and embarrassed, she took it clumsily and thrust it onto the shelf beneath the cash register. 'Wh-what is it?'

'Open it later!'

He signed the credit-card slip, loaded his groceries back into his trolley and wheeled it along to the exit doors.

She watched him go. No one else appeared at her

110

checkout, so she was able to continue watching him. *Terence Goel*. Not Liam Neeson. What was in the envelope? He stood on the kerb with his plastic bags and hailed a taxi.

Liam Neeson would probably have had a chauffeur, she thought.

She glanced over her shoulder. No one was approaching or paying her any attention. As the taxi drove off, she looked at the envelope. Her name, *Tracey*, was handwritten on the outside.

She opened the envelope. Inside she was shocked to find four £50 banknotes; they were folded inside an unsigned handwritten note on plain paper, which said:

> Thank you for always smiling at me so nicely, it is a great act of kindness. This is for you to buy some new things for yourself. There is not enough kindness in the world.

Chapter Twenty-eight

From the street, number 14 Provost Avenue was nothing special – a modest detached 1930s house, with a suburban mock-Tudor façade, looking much like all the others in the quiet, suburban backwater of Barnes in south-west London, just a few hundred yards from the Thames, and only a couple of miles from Michael's consulting room at the Sheen Park Hospital. But the conventional interior had been ripped away, and replaced with split-level flooring dividing the living area into three spaces. One, where Amanda sat now, while Michael was busy in the kitchen, had chairs arranged for talking, another had a sprawling semi-circular sofa for watching television, and the third, a steel Philippe Starck dining suite. The divide between the spaces was dominated by a mutant Swiss cheese plant that looked like it ate triffids for breakfast.

A wonderful smell was coming from the kitchen.

Prominently displayed on shelves was a wide range of three-dimensional puzzles. The clinically white walls were hung with modern paintings on small canvases. Intricately painted, complex abstracts, some with a nightmarish quality about them, others in brilliant blues, one in particular that reminded her of the calm beauty of a Hockney swimming-pool painting. She wondered which of the objects in this house reflected Michael's taste and which that of his late wife.

The puzzles were his, he had told her, but whose were the paintings? In a way, she quite liked them, they were intriguing, a mixture of contrasts, like Michael himself.

Part of her was desperately curious to know more about Katy, yet another part sensed it was a subject best left alone.

In any event, on their previous dates he had seemed reluctant to talk about her. There was some terrible sadness or guilt there, with which he still did not seem to have come to terms. A photograph of her, on the mantelpiece above a beautiful, modern open fireplace, dominated the room.

She stood up, carried her glass of Californian Mondavi Fumé over towards it, and stared at it, a colour photograph in a silver frame, showing an attractive woman, with shoulder-length blonde hair, Ray-ban sunglasses pushed up on her forehead, sitting astride a powerful-looking red motorcycle.

Amanda peered closely at her face. She was beautiful, but there was a coldness in that beauty, self-consciousness – almost, she thought, hardness.

She wondered, suddenly, whether people who were doomed to die young knew it.

Michael had had a shower only an hour ago, but already he was hot and sticky again. The kitchen, which had been spotless this morning, was now in chaos.

HEAVEN IN A SHELL!

The caption rose up at him from the recipe page. Beneath was printed: SKEWERED SCALLOPS WITH WARM BASIL DRESSING. The photograph of what the finished dish was supposed to look like was marred by a large stain from the balsamic vinegar Michael had spilled on the page. He had torn the sheet from the Saturday *Times* a few weeks back, and now it was spread in front of him on the kitchen table. Alongside, he had the ingredients. He read through them again, one final check before he committed the dish to the oven.

He was in a minor state of panic.

Four large fresh scallops. Olive oil. Basil leaves. Four slices of prosciutto. One garlic clove. One small tomato. Balsamic vinegar. An assortment of mixed leaves and fresh herbs. White and pink rose petals. Two wooden skewers.

The photograph that had looked so tempting was going to be impossible to re-create. It wasn't food, it was the Chelsea Flower Show on a plate. Not even his wooden skewers looked as good as the ones in the photograph.

And, as ever, the most important bit from the recipe was absent. Did you cook the scallops already wrapped in the prosciutto, or did you add the prosciutto afterwards?

He gave his mother, who was a brilliant cook, a quick, surreptitious call, keeping his voice low so Amanda couldn't hear. She didn't know the recipe, but suggested grilling the scallops first, then changed her mind, then changed her mind again. He wished he hadn't decided to experiment tonight. Delia Smith's old stalwart, grilled peppers with anchovies, would have been wiser, or gazpacho with prawns.

Since his medical-student days, Michael had been tearing out recipes, buying the ingredients and experimenting. In the past three years he had done little cooking for himself; he had lost his enthusiasm; there had been no one else to cook for. On Saturday nights with Katy, when they hadn't been going out, he had taken charge of the evening meal. The love of food had been something they had shared together.

Since her death, he'd survived on canteen lunches at work, and microwaved supermarket meals at home.

Tonight, though, he had someone to cook for again, and he had been thinking about his menu since Wednesday. He wanted this meal to be perfect. It would have been far easier to have taken Amanda to a restaurant, but he wanted to show her this side of him; he was proud of his culinary skills.

He had been unprepared for his attack of nerves.

He had read recently an excerpt from a paper published in the *British Journal of Psychiatry* on esteem. Women had a higher esteem of men who cooked, and it heightened desire in them. The old hunter-killer thing; the man as

114

provider. Civilisation pulled skimpy camouflage netting over our primal roots.

He grinned, wondering how Amanda would have reacted if he had greeted her at the door in a loincloth, wielding a wooden club. Then he tugged on his oven gloves and checked the Rosemary Lamb with Redcurrant Sauce. The potato and parsnip cakes, snow peas and spiced carrot purée were already in the warmer.

Then he dived through into the living room to check on his guest.

Amanda, standing at the fireplace, was still holding the photograph of Katy in her hand, and did not hear Michael approach. Suddenly she felt a vice-like grip on her arm, and the photograph was torn from her hand.

'Don't touch her things!'

His voice was an icy command.

She turned, startled.

His face was like thunder and, for a moment, she was frightened of him. His grip was hurting her.

Then he released her, and carefully set down the picture. She watched him in alarm. He turned to face her, as if shielding the photograph from her view, and gave an anguished smile, his flash of anger subsiding as fast as it had risen.

'I'm sorry,' he said, awkwardly. 'I –'

'It's OK.' She swallowed, watching him uncertainly. But he was calm now, back to normal.

He lowered his head. 'Forgive me, I'm sorry, I just have this thing about . . .'

'It's OK, really,' she said.

He stared helplessly at her, and suddenly she felt sorry for him. He looked so incredibly different out of the suits in which she had always seen him before, standing now in his white PVC apron with musical notes all over it, open red shirt and blue chinos. She liked him like this, he seemed much more vulnerable.

'I need to move on,' he said. 'But it's so damned hard.' He

stared at the walls. 'Sometimes I feel I'm living in a bloody mausoleum.'

She watched his eyes dart from painting to painting. 'I like your paintings.'

'Katy's. She painted them.'

'All of these?'

'All the ones in this room, yes. She called this lot in here her Brainstate collection. Maybe these were how she saw me.'

'She was very talented,' Amanda said, feeling inadequate by comparison.

Michael was still embarrassed by his outburst. 'Yes,' he said flatly. 'But she didn't believe it. She kept insisting it was just a hobby.'

Wanting to change the subject, Amanda said, 'You sure there's nothing I can do to help in the kitchen?'

'Nope. All set, I'll be with you in a tick.' He went over to the open French windows and peered out anxiously. 'You're really happy to eat outside? Won't be too cold?'

'I'd *love* to eat outside.'

'How's your drink?'

Amanda held up her glass, which was half full. 'Fine, thanks.'

'You know the difference between an optimist and a pessimist?' he asked.

'No?'

'An optimist says his glass is half full. A pessimist says it's half empty.'

'My glass is brimming,' she said.

The *Figaro* overture was playing on the CD. Michael listened to it and a surge of emotion lifted him. Why the hell couldn't he have just let her look at the damned photograph? He hoped to hell he hadn't blown it. He should have moved away from here, that was the problem. And he should have taken Amanda to a restaurant. Here, there was too much of Katy all around.

But he hadn't wanted to sell the house. It would have been the final break with Katy and he hadn't been ready to let go. Not until now. Not until this moment, with Amanda sitting on the sofa and the overture of *The Marriage of Figaro* roaring in his ears. And in his heart.

Amanda's hair looked freshly washed: it had a deep, silky sheen, prettier than he had ever seen it. Her face was even prettier too and he loved the clothes she was wearing: a white satin jacket over a black halter top, shiny black trousers, and high-heeled shoes that on someone less classy would have looked tarty, but on Amanda were just plain sexy.

He loved the way she smelt.

He grinned. Amanda lounging back on the massive navy blue sofa; the *Figaro* overture; the balmy summer air. This was a perfect moment. He raised his arms, closed his eyes for a second, and dreamily twirled his hands as if he was conducting the music.

When he opened his eyes again, she was staring straight into them. 'I'd like to die listening to Mozart,' he said.

Amanda considered her reply carefully. 'Do you think about death a lot?'

'All the time. You do, too.'

'I do?'

'Everyone does. Not consciously, but we do. It's a fundamental part of the human psyche. Dag Hammerskjöld, who was Secretary General of the United Nations, once said, "There is no thought that we have, no action we take that is uninfluenced by how our mind views its destiny and our body its death. In the final analysis, our view on death shapes the answers to all the questions life puts to us."'

'Do you believe that?'

'Totally. We are driven by survival instincts. Think of the decisions you have to make every minute when you're driving, or walking down a street and wanting to cross the road. When you go to a restaurant and you look at the menu, you don't just select the food that's going to do the best job of filling your stomach. Your choice is going to be influenced by all kinds of thoughts in your head about diet, nutrition – about what is healthy to eat. About what food is

117

going to help you to live the longest.' He looked at her quizzically.

'I never thought about it.'

'You don't need to. Most of the time your brain does it for you.' He tapped the side of his head. 'Your little grey friend.' Then he paused and said, 'Forgive me for being angry. I didn't mean it.'

She smiled at him. 'I was silly.'

'No, you were curious, which you have every right to be.'

He went back into the kitchen. Grill the scallops first, he decided, then roll the prosciutto around them. Live dangerously – what the hell?

Amanda sat down. Her arm hurt from where he had gripped it; it felt bruised. She had heard before starting research on her programme that psychiatrists were a strange breed. Several she had interviewed seemed desperately in need of treatment themselves.

Did Michael have a dark side? Or was this simply what the death of a loved one did to you?

Thomas Lamark was thinking about death, too. Earlier he had been thinking about white vans. Now he was thinking about Dr Michael Tennent's death.

He had been thinking that vans were good in the daytime because no one noticed them. You were a plumber or a butcher or a printer or anything you wanted to be: you stuck your name on the side and no one looked at you twice. The same way that you didn't look twice at the faces of bus drivers or men digging the road or sweeping the entrance to the tube station.

At night it was different. At night villains drove vans. You hung around in a quiet residential street at ten p.m. on a summer's night and sooner or later some Neighbourhood Watch dingbat was going to phone the police.

This was why he had borrowed Dr Goel's dark blue Ford Mondeo for tonight.

The Mondeo was now parked in Provost Avenue. He had a clear view of Dr Michael Tennent's house. He also had a clear view of Amanda Capstick's Alfa Romeo. She had left the roof down. He presumed that meant she was not intending to stay the night.

Chapter Twenty-nine

A finger clicked in front of his face. Glen Branson didn't see it.

'Hallo? Anyone home?'

Glen did not hear the voice.

His eyes were watching Cora Burstridge on the television. But his brain was elsewhere. In a darkened room. A plastic Waitrose grocery bag. A note. '*I can no longer look at myself in the mirror.*'

The words had become hardwired into his brain. He saw them in his dreams last night, and the night before. He saw Cora Burstridge's partially eaten face. He would never forget those words. Ever.

'Your tea. It's on the table. It's getting cold.'

He turned to Ari, blew her a kiss, he loved her to death, she had the patience of ten saints. 'Two minutes, angel, OK?'

Sammy looked up from the floor, where he was constructing a Playmobil circus with all the concentration of a heart surgeon. 'Is Mummy really an angel?'

'To me she is.'

Glen was amazed at the speed with which television had begun cobbling together Cora Burstridge tributes. He was watching one now, a string of clips. Dirk Bogarde had just been on, talking about what a true star she had been. And now here was a clip of the two of them, him dressed as an intern in a hospital ward with the young Cora Burstridge, her face a mass of scars.

'Cheer up, old girl, have you right as rain in a few days,' Dirk Bogarde said breezily.

She looked up at him. 'I can no longer look at myself in the mirror,' she replied.

Ari stepped between Glen and the screen. 'Want me put it back in the oven? I think I'm starting to get jealous of your new girlfriend.'

Glen did not hear her. He was transfixed.

'Daddy, if Mummy is an angel, does that mean Jesus loves her?'

He did not hear his son either. He just heard Cora Burstridge's words, on the screen, in the film *Mirror To the Wall*, made in 1966. It was about a model disfigured in a car crash. She becomes suicidal and is pulled back from the brink by a psychiatrist, played by James Mason, who gives her back her sense of worth and self-esteem, and in the end, marries her.

I can no longer look at myself in the mirror.

The coincidence was freaky.

The video was running; he had started to record the tribute the moment he saw it. He stopped the tape and wound it back.

'I cooked you steak, Glen! It's going to spoil.'

'I'm coming.'

He wound the tape back over the segment and played it again. As he listened to her speak the words, he closed his eyes, went back two days, to Thursday, to Cora Burstridge's flat with its art-deco furniture and the note on the dressing table.

I can no longer look at myself in the mirror.

He concentrated, fired up the synapses, tried to haul back a complete picture of Cora Burstridge's bedroom on the third floor of Adelaide Crescent on the Hove esplanade, overlooking the English Channel.

Slow Time.

That was the name the CID gave it when they sealed off a crime scene. They put the house, or the hotel room, or the flat, or the patch in the woods, or the stretch of pavement, or the area surrounding the car into *slow time*. Like freeze-frame. One frame at a time. The minutiae; hair follicles; flakes of skin; clothing fibres.

Slow Time.

This was suicide. It was not a crime scene. She'd chained the safety lock from the inside, written her note, downed her pills, and then –

The thought of what Cora Burstridge had done next gave him the shallows.

Before his grandfather had retired and come to live with Glen's parents in England, he had been first mate on a tramp steamer that plied for trade around the Windward Isles, delivering boxes of engine spares to one, collecting sugar beet from the next and taking coffins to another. Glen loved to listen to the adventures he'd had, but especially he liked to listen to the old man talk about *the shallows*.

Boats almost never sank in deep water, he told Glen. It was the shallows that got them. You got the biggest waves where the water was the most shallow; the most dangerous rocks were not the ones you could see, but the ones you could not see, the reefs a few feet below the surface. The shallows.

The shallows spooked Glen, yet he was drawn, each time, to ask his granddad to talk about them. They gave him a thrill, they gave him his own private demon to fight – and it was a demon that he never, ever, quite slayed.

Dark, raging turbulence. Froth, foam, razor-edged coral that could rip open the belly of a boat like a sardine can. The shallows instilled in Glen a fear that used to wake him some nights in his childhood, thrashing in his bed and screaming warnings to the skipper. When the fear subsided it left him high and dry, washed up from his sleep into a dark, only partly defined pool of dread.

Suicide. The word rolled around inside his head like the slop of dark water.

Suicide.

He tried to picture those last few minutes of her life. Writing the note. Taking off her slippers. Getting into bed. Pulling the bag over her head, tying the bow with her dressing-gown sash. The horribly claustrophobic sweatiness of the bag in front of her eyes.

What kind of thoughts did Cora Burstridge have during those last minutes of consciousness? What had driven her to it?

He'd spoken to her daughter, who lived in Los Angeles, and a couple of her friends had given statements – and spoken to the press. Cora Burstridge had been depressed since her most recent face-lift. She'd been finding it hard to cope with ageing, and the BAFTA award on Monday night had only exacerbated her sense of isolation.

She had not been made a dame, or given any other honour because, as she herself admitted, Buckingham Palace had frowned on her series of public affairs with three prominent politicians, then frowned harder on her anti-monarchist views.

'Better give the old bat some kind of recognition before she croaks,' was how she'd privately described Monday night to one friend.

Alone, money running low, her looks gone, dumped a decade back by her third and last husband, suffering from depression, she was a classic case for a suicide.

So why, Glen Branson asked himself as he hauled himself up from his armchair to confront his cold steak and now frosty wife, *why do I have a problem with this?*

Chapter Thirty

'This is Dr Tennent speaking. Gloria, would you please give me a call as soon as you get this message? I'm rather afraid I upset you this morning. It might be helpful if we had a quick chat on the phone.'

Click.

Thomas pressed REWIND on the car's tape deck. Then he pressed PLAY and listened again to the recording of Dr Michael Tennent's voice that he had copied onto a cassette from the answering-machine.

Click.

He swallowed. Gripped the steering wheel with his fists. He wanted to rip it out of the dashboard and stab Dr Michael Tennent to death with the column.

He played the tape again.

Saturday night. Ten o'clock. Big moon. Stars sparkling, a lot of prisms up there tonight. He was sitting in Dr Goel's midnight blue Ford Mondeo. Dr Goel was cool about him using it. The car was clean, immaculate, there had not been a speck of dirt on the paintwork when he'd begun his journey here. It had a Phillips tape player and CD deck, beige leather seats, electric windows, plenty of gadgets. There were buttons and switches everywhere you looked, with strange symbols on them. Tiny hieroglyphics drawn for midgets with magnifying glasses. What the fuck did they mean?

The only thing written in plain English was on the boss of the steering wheel in front of him. AIRBAG.

It was getting hard to see the dog turd on the pavement in the pool of shadows between two street-lamps. Thomas had been eyeing it for an hour. A fly was crawling up the inside of the windscreen. Flies ate dog turds. Flies ate dead birds. If it wasn't for flies there'd be dead birds everywhere. He didn't mind flies, they were OK, he had reason to be grateful to them. He hated dead birds. Dead birds were unlucky.

There had been a dead bird in the garden the day his mother died. There had been a dead bird beside Versace when he'd died. They could be messages from the Higher Authority – how could you know they weren't?

It was too dark for anyone to see his face inside the car now. He'd brought *The Times*, ready to shield his face if anyone walked past. He did not think anyone in this neighbourhood would bother to look twice at a man, sitting in a respectable car, reading *The Times*. So far, no one had walked past except the old man with the Labrador that had crapped on the pavement.

There was a piece about the missing editor, Tina Mackay, appeals from the police and her mother, another quote from her distraught boyfriend. No leads, no clues, no sightings of her E-registered navy Volkswagen Golf with a dented rear bumper. There weren't going to be. He had dismantled it in his garage at home, taken it, one bit at a time in his white van, to different junk yards. All in all, he cleared almost two hundred pounds for it. He spent the money on flowers for his mother's grave.

There was a far, far, bigger piece on Cora Burstridge. A eulogy of 2,324 words. It was written by the former film critic turned theatre critic, Peregrine Vernon.

Peregrine Vernon had once savaged his mother's performance in a play. It was in 1986, her attempt at a comeback; in Somerset Maugham's *Our Betters*, in which she played a dictatorial aristocratic lady of leisure. Peregrine Vernon suggested the director should have cast a wild pig instead of her. 'It would have looked more attractive and made less of a hash of the lines,' he had written.

Thomas could clearly recall the critic's face in the photograph above his by-line. The bow-tie, the silver hair, the bloated, broken-veined, lunched-out face. And his mother's tears when she had read those words.

At the play's first-night party, his mother had looked so beautiful, he had been so proud of her, the performance she had given in the play had been sensational – and the performance afterwards at the party, the grand lady making her comeback, welcomed by everyone, that had been fantastic! A triumph! They were all there. The Lloyd Webbers. Harold Pinter. Paul Scofield. Peter Hall. Cameron Mackintosh. Eddie Kulukundis and Susan Hampshire. Robert Fox. Vanessa Redgrave. Maggie Smith. Joan Plowright. Sir Michael Hordern. Albert Finlay. Judi Dench. Bill Kenright. *Everyone!*

There were tears of happiness in his mother's eyes that night. Then the terrible silence in the back of the car as they were driven home, the first reviews already read and the papers discarded. And in the morning, with the arrival of the *Mail* and those terrible words, she was broken.

Jack Tinker, the regular critic, had been on holiday. Peregrine Vernon had taken his place. Through her tears she kept repeating over and over that Jack Tinker would have liked it, Jack Tinker would never have said such terrible things.

And now Peregrine Vernon had written 2,324 words on Cora Burstridge.

A scandal that Cora Burstridge was never formally honoured by the country for the incalculable range of her services to it. From selfless volunteer in the Blitz, to giant of the screen and the theatre . . . we have lost one of the greatest actresses our country has ever produced and she will never be replaced . . .

Thomas's anger increased. Peregrine Vernon was wrong. There was a scandal, but it was quite different from the one he wrote about here. He needed to be told. The record should be set straight.

You stupid ass of a man, why did you have to write this article? I'd forgotten about you, really, I had!

Amanda Capstick's Alfa Romeo was still outside Dr Michael Tennent's house. The roof was still down. Two hours ago the national lottery draw had taken place live on television. His mother had despised the lottery, had sneered at the people who bought tickets. He wondered if Dr Michael Tennent bought lottery tickets. He played the tape-recording from the answering-machine again.

'. . . I'm rather afraid I upset you this morning. It might be helpful if we had a quick chat on the phone.'

Click.

Rewind.

Click.

He played it again.

He hated the lottery. Hated the little coloured balls that jigged around in the glass bowl. The lottery gave people hope, when in reality there was no hope. If you lost, you were miserable. If you won, your life became hell. It was never going to get you out of your loop of misery. It was like Dr Tennent's voice on the tape. Promising something it could never deliver.

There was another cassette lying on the passenger seat beside him. He would play that soon.

The flies had quit for the night. Even the one crawling up inside the windscreen seemed to have given up trying to escape, for the time being. He took a coin from his pocket, tossed it, palmed it, but did not yet look down at it.

Dr Michael Tennent, will you still be there in the morning?

127

Chapter Thirty-one

The flames of the two candles burned upright in the breezeless night, on the wooden table in the wrought-iron gazebo, beneath a canopy of vine leaves. Amanda ate the last mouthful of her lamb. It was seared on the outside, pink in the middle, seductively sweet from the redcurrant sauce. Michael had judged it to perfection. 'You are an amazing cook,' she said, wanting to see him smile. He was a completely different person when he smiled: he turned from a serious, remote character, wrapped up in his own thoughts, into an animated and gregarious personality.

She was having a good time with him, the earlier incident, if not forgotten, set aside, and she was enjoying the sense of being let into secrets as he told her about some of his more bizarre case histories. And he looked strikingly handsome tonight, with his strong, lean face, his dark hair, his small tortoiseshell glasses, his powerful frame clearly visible through his red Ralph Lauren shirt. She liked the smell of his cologne. The way he spoke.

She watched him cutting a piece of lamb on his plate. His shirtsleeves were rolled back midway to his elbows; his arms and hands were hairy. Strong, masculine hands with long fingers, *surgeon's hands*, her mother would have called them.

He was the kind of man she would have liked to have had as her father, she thought. Maxine Bentham had repeatedly told her that her attraction to Brian was her need of a father figure. Maybe that was true, and maybe that was the reason she was sitting here in this garden with Michael Tennent, feeling the same kind of snowstorm excitement in her stomach that she'd had on her very first date when she was seventeen.

Michael glanced away awkwardly: compliments always made him shy. Then he looked back at her, intently, and raised his glass of red wine. 'I think you're lovely,' he said quietly.

The angst he had been feeling about entertaining another woman in Katy's home was forgotten now – maybe the wine was helping, maybe the passage of time, but mostly it was Amanda. There was some kind of magic going on out here between them. Something so good that it scared him: it was too good to last. Nothing this wonderful could last.

The song that had kept coming into his head over the past few days, was back again now, 'Georgia On My Mind', and suddenly he realised why: a neighbour – or maybe a car out on the street – was playing it on a stereo.

Their eyes met. A midge hovered into view then fell back into the night. There was an intensity in her eyes that drew his own to them: they were shimmering with life, spangles of light like a burst of fireflies glittered in the dark of the pupils. They continued to stare at each other, locked in a slow, easy moment that stretched effortlessly longer and longer, dancing with their eyes to their own private, silent rhythm.

Tiny muscles quivered in Amanda's face. Her expression narrowed a fraction, then widened again, bearing the hint of a smile that was warmth, not mockery. Such incredible eyes. Michael longed to reach across the table and take her hand. He wanted to touch her, but this wasn't the moment, not yet.

The night was warm on his face. It carried her perfume to him. Here, in his garden, surrounded by exotic plants, they were alone in a dark, secret world, and he felt a growing tightness of excitement inside him, a sense of adventure, the start of some extraordinary, magical journey.

She blinked, and still she was staring at him. A slight frown now, as if there was something she was seeing that was denied to him, then she swung away her eyes and picked up her glass.

But instead of raising it towards him she pulled it into her chest and cradled it in her hands. Strands of her hair lay in a soft arc over her forehead. The thin gold chain around her neck glinted in the candlelight. She gave him an uneasy smile then raised a hand and, in a nervous gesture, flicked a few stray strands of hair back into place.

Then she curled her fingers around her glass and he saw her bitten nails. *Amanda, what is worrying you, you beautiful creature?*

Amanda was grateful to the darkness for hiding the deep flush in her cheeks, the guilt that she had carried here with her tonight and now wanted to exorcise. There wasn't going to be a good moment to do it and she wanted to get it over with.

'Listen,' she said. 'I –'

An aircraft thundered low overhead on a flight path down into Heathrow. She waited for the roar to subside.

Michael felt a flash of fear at the change in her tone. Was she going to break the news that she was in love with someone else? Or tell him she had been turned off by his anger with her for looking at Katy's photograph? Was the whole evening about to go south?

'I haven't been honest with you, Michael.' She continued to clutch the glass to her chest, like a child's comforter.

He didn't like the way she said *Michael*.

'I –' She smiled awkwardly, held the glass out a few inches in front of her with both hands. 'I have to tell you that . . .' She hesitated then ploughed on. 'That my original reason for coming to see you was –' She bit her lip, then found the confidence to go on. 'To trash you.'

Michael's face showed his surprise.

'You can throw me out now, if you want,' she said.

He looked hurt and puzzled. 'Why did you want to trash me?'

'Because that's the angle we're going for with the show. We're doing an attack on the whole therapy culture of our

130

society. I didn't tell you this when I first came to see you.' She looked down at the table, evasively.

'Why not?'

She peeped guiltily up at him from beneath her flopped hair, put her elbows on the table and rested her chin on her hands. 'Because you wouldn't have agreed to take part in the programme. I was going to make a meal of your radio show – showing the absurdity of ten-minute-per-punter sound-bite therapy.' Looking at him imploringly, she said, 'Please don't be angry.' She reached down under her chair and pulled up her handbag. 'Do you mind if I have a cigarette?'

'I didn't know you smoked.'

'I don't, I quit six months ago.' She opened the bag with trembling hands and took out a pack of Silk Cut. 'These are for emergencies. This is an emergency.' She lit a cigarette with a smart gold lighter.

As the smoke wafted across his face, Michael breathed in deeply. He had given up five years ago and had managed to stay off them even in the aftermath of Katy's death, but he still loved the smell. 'Use the shrubbery as an ashtray,' he said.

'Thanks.' She drew nervously on the cigarette, then exhaled as she spoke. 'I'm telling you this because in the short time I've spent with you, at the theatre, then at dinner on Tuesday and now tonight, I realise I was wrong about you. You are a sincerely caring man.' She stared intently at him. 'You're a really good man. If you want me to leave, tell me and I'll go.'

'Do you want to go?'

'No.'

There was a long silence. She drew again on the cigarette, then tilted her head and blew the smoke up at the sky. 'The only redeeming thing I can say is that if I hadn't come to trash you, I wouldn't have met you, and then I would have really missed something. I think you're incredible,' she said. 'I really mean that. You're a very special human being.'

Their eyes locked, but after a few seconds Michael looked away, embarrassed by the depth of feeling in her words.

'I'm not special,' he said. 'I just believe that all of us – all human beings who are lucky enough to be sane and healthy – should do something useful with our lives. We should try to make a difference in the world. We should try to leave it, in some small way, a better place when we die than when we arrived. That's all I try to do.' He added, 'I don't have the time to see everyone, and I do my best for my radio phone-in patients. I think you're wrong, we do give comfort to some of them.'

Amanda drew on her cigarette again. 'Yes, I'm sure you do.' She crushed out her butt into the soil beneath a bush. There was another silence between them, then she said, 'I'm not putting you in the programme. That's a promise.'

He smiled, wistfully. She was too lovely, it was impossible to be angry with her.

'Are you going to forgive me for deceiving you, Michael?'

For an answer, he took her hands. They slipped easily into his own. He had been expecting them to be delicate but the palms were coarse, as if she had worked a lot with them. It excited him, as if there was the promise of some other coarseness about Amanda that he had not yet discovered.

Moments later they were standing. His hands had slipped inside her jacket and were on her waist, and she was holding his shoulders, looking into his eyes.

He was intoxicated by her perfume, by the smell of her hair, by other faint, wonderful scents that were rising up from her. He squeezed her a little harder, brought her even closer, caressing the skin of her waist through the soft folds of her halter top. Their lips barely touched. Just a fleeting caress like the touch of silk in a breeze.

Then a second kiss, just as fleeting. Michael slipped his hands up from her waist and cupped her face. He felt he was holding the most precious thing on earth. Her eyes were on him, total trust in them. Then a smile. She put her hands around the back of his neck and pushed her fingers through his hair.

Then Michael was pulling her head back, running his tongue down her chin, down her throat, and she was fumbling with his shirt, pulling open buttons, sliding her hands inside against his bare skin.

His whole body quivered with pleasure. Their mouths locked, he felt her tongue slip up and around his teeth, while her fingers had found his nipples and were teasing them, tickling with a sensuousness so intense it was almost unbearable.

He fumbled with her top, then slipped his hands below it and, for the first time, touched her bare skin. She squirmed into him with a sigh. He found her bra strap, undid it and now he had her breasts in his hands, cool, large, heavy.

She was crazing him with the teasing of his nipples. He lowered his face, took her right nipple in his mouth.

Then, quite suddenly, she eased him away, took a step back, and looked up at the sky. 'Something I have to do,' she said. 'Take two minutes!' She hurried into the house.

Puzzled, he followed her but before he could ask her anything, she had reached the front door.

Noël Coward! The fag playwright. Thomas Lamark had been trying to think of his name for an hour, and finally it had come. It was Noël Coward who had written the line, 'the potency of cheap music.'

Gloria Lamark had liked opera. Grand opera. Thomas understood the potency of great music, of opera, choirs, chants. He reckoned Wagner was more potent than Ray Charles. And so were Berlioz, Verdi, Pergolesi, Strauss, Gounod, Mahler, Tchaikovsky.

The tape of 'Georgia On My Mind' was still sticking out of the cassette on the dashboard of Dr Goel's Ford Mondeo. He ejected it, put it on the seat beside him and pushed the tape of Dr Michael Tennent's voice on his mother's answering-machine back into the slot.

You like cheap music, Dr Michael Tennent. Does cheap music give you an erection? Can it send you into someone's arms? Does cheap music short out your brain, Dr Tennent? I'll play you cheap music. You can have all the cheap music in the world. But you won't have Georgia on your mind. You'll have me.

Dr Tennent's front door was opening. Thomas froze into a sculpture of himself. The woman – Dr Tennent's bit of fluff – was coming out, she looked dishevelled, she was in a hurry. Thomas wondered what had been going on.

He watched her reach her car, deactivate the alarm, climb in. She left the door open and he could see her, clearly illuminated by the interior light. She was fumbling to push her key into the ignition. Now she was reaching for another button. The roof raised. Even through the closed windows of the Mondeo he could hear the whine of the electric motors at work. Then the thud. He saw her raise her hand inside the car and close the manual catch. Then, to his surprise, she got out of the car and locked it.

Dr Tennent appeared in the doorway: his shirt was untucked, most of the buttons undone. She walked back towards him, he took her in his arms, and they kissed, right there, with the front door wide open.

Thomas felt something wrench inside him. A lump rose in his throat. He swallowed, crushing his eyes shut against the tears that were welling.

Why are you doing this in front of me, Dr Michael Tennent? Why are you tormenting me like this? Do you have any idea how this makes me feel?

Do you have any bloody idea at all?

Chapter Thirty-two

Amanda suddenly broke off, nuzzled up to Michael's ear and whispered, 'Someone's looking at us – across the road.'

Michael shot a glance: he saw lights on in some of the neighbours' houses, but no face at any window. He barely knew any of his neighbours and he wasn't bothered who was looking at them. Right at this moment he couldn't have cared if an entire flotilla of alien starship battlecruisers was hovering overhead with binoculars. He was zeroed on this woman, he wanted her, he was burning up inside for her. Nothing else in the entire universe mattered.

He steered her indoors; somehow they made it over the front step, still entwined, and he kicked the door shut. 'Need to be the man with X-ray eyes to see us now,' he said.

She tugged undone the last two buttons of his shirt, amazed at how hairy his chest was. Brian's body was so smooth and hairy men had always been a turn-off in the past, but this was different. She pulled him to her, kissed him savagely – this was how he was making her feel, savage, wild. A furnace was roaring in her belly. His lips were soft yet he was kissing her with an extraordinary feral strength.

She was being swept away by him. He was sending currents of electricity through her soul.

'Make love to me, Michael,' she whispered.

A maelstrom of thoughts swirled in Michael's head. It was so long since he had made love to a woman. He craved Amanda so desperately, but he was scared of failing, of messing this up. He looked into her eyes and he saw trust, an incredible, beautiful look of trust.

With trembling fingers he fumbled for her bra, forgetting he had already freed it earlier; it snagged on his fingers, then fell away. He cupped her breasts in his hands and she let out a tiny gasp. He wanted to get her clothes off, to feel her naked in his arms, he was raging with desire. She was pressing up against him, lunging against his erection, he could enter her now, here, right where they were standing, but he held back. He wanted to really make *love* to this woman. He wanted this first time to be sensational, he wanted to wake up with her in his arms, in bed.

They stared at each other. Time stood still. Her eyes were filled with bald, wanton desire.

He was anxious now how long he could hold back. *Slow it down. Just slow it down.*

There was an incredible silence as if the two of them were alone in a vacuum, in some other world, where nothing else existed, just each other and the magic of the feelings that were driving them. The softness of her mouth, the warmth of her flesh, the scents of her soap, perfume, shampoo, skin, the sounds of her breathing, the shimmering disks of blue that were her eyes, the haze of blonde hairs. There was a lump in his throat as he kissed her again. Nothing, nothing had ever been this beautiful, this perfect, this natural.

He lowered his hands down her body, slipped them inside her knickers and, kneeling down, levered them gently over her buttocks, over her knees and let then fall around her ankles.

The blonde fuzz of her pubic hair was right in front of him. He pressed his face into it, gently at first and then more firmly, and the prickle against his skin was soft as a caress. He buried his face in deeper, probing his tongue between the soft flesh of her thighs, becoming intoxicated on the raw musky tang. He found the moist folds of the entrance, and slowly, gently worked his tongue inside them.

Amanda threw back her head with a gasp.

Michael burrowed harder, the exquisite private taste of her in his mouth, the smell in his nostrils, these flavours, they were beyond the end of the Universe, they came from some other place, some other galaxy in some other universe in some other dimension, there was nothing, nothing on earth that was this good. He was trembling. He was gorging on her, praying for time to stop, to freeze over and for this moment never, ever to end.

Gently she lifted his face up and kissed him on the lips, tasting herself on his mouth. She unbuckled his belt and slipped her hands down inside his underpants and she felt the curls of his pubic hair. She loved the way he breathed as she played her tongue around his nipple.

And then she felt the rock.

It startled her; she recoiled as if it had given her an electric shock, then returned to it, unable to believe how hard it was, and its size! It was daunting, and wonderful, unreal. It was his. It was Michael. She held it and she was holding Michael. She wanted him desperately and yet she, she wasn't – wasn't, just no way wasn't – going to fit this inside her!

She felt a blowtorch heat of excitement.

Still holding him, she sank down. She kissed his navel, traced the contours of his belly button with her tongue. His hands were pushing in long deep strokes through her hair. She went on down and the smell was incredible, warmth, animal perspiration, hot skin, she pulled down his underpants, white boxer shorts, then slowly, treasuring it, savouring it, brought his vast, incredible rock up to her lips. The top was moist, she licked it, then again, pushing her tongue deep into the crevasse, the fluid was sweet, with a hint of saltiness, she ran her tongue backwards and forwards, she could feel from the sounds he was making, the grip of his hands on her shoulders, the bursts of breath, that she was tantalising him, and she loved the feeling as much as she loved the taste. She had him in her power, in her control, she was pleasing him, torturing him.

Adoring every second of him.

She took him, as far as she could, in her mouth.

Oh Jesus Michael you are huge.

She cupped his balls in her hands, squeezed them gently, felt him respond. His balls felt wonderful, the cold, sensuous skin, the soft hairs, she was entering a new space here, travelling through an uncharted trench deep inside her, or maybe she was travelling outside her body, outside all time to some distant point that was the centre of the universe, the centre of all time, all existence.

Then she was floating through air. She was being carried, swept, in Michael's arms, and now she was lying on a bed, a huge bed, she could feel a shoe being pulled from her foot, then another incredible explosion inside her.

She opened her eyes. He was naked on the bed, naked and covered in hair and holding her toes in his mouth, pulling softly on them with his lips, pulling deep shivers of pleasure like folds of silk down her body.

Now his tongue was tracing up her calf. Then he was exploring the space behind her knee, then on, up along the base of her thigh, and then, in one space-time continuum, his tongue was entering her again, deep inside her.

She clutched his head with her hands, some distant howl erupting around her, maybe it had come from within her, she didn't know, she didn't care, this was all existence, there was nothing beyond this moment, no past, no future, nothing else mattered, nothing else had ever mattered or ever would. She was in the clutches of some wild, primal force, this creature, half-human, half-beast, had her help-lessly in his control. She opened her eyes for a moment, saw flashes of a wall with a painting of apples, of a dressing table, a painting of a naked man and naked woman touching each other, she saw a drawn curtain, a single bedside lamp that was on, then Michael's face blurred through the fuzz of her pubic hair.

Then her eyes were rammed shut as a wave of pleasure welled in the pit of her stomach, pushing outward, grow-ing, swelling inside her, rippling her skin, her body, her brain . . .

Now his face was right over hers and the pleasure that could not get any stronger was getting stronger.

He was entering her. She was gathering him into her, clawing his back.

Michael was trying desperately to hold back, he was trying to think, to concentrate, to remember all the things you were supposed to remember – not that he'd ever been that great, or that experienced, a lover – things like taking his weight on his elbows, entering slowly, trying to think of something to distract him, something boring or horrible, anything to turn him off, to try to contain himself for just a while longer, for a few minutes, to please her. He wanted desperately to please her, he didn't care about himself, not at this moment, he just wanted to hold it, to make it special for her.

I didn't even think about a condom.

She didn't say anything.

Their eyes met. He thrust himself in even further. She was smiling, that look of trust, and this trust gave him confidence, there had never been anything like this in his life, he could hold himself, he could hold back, he really could!

She was taking him into her. This *thing* of his. This huge, incredible thing-beast-serpent was pushing up inside, pushing away ripples in its path, pushing ripples that spread out into vast shock waves of pleasure way beyond her physical body, and deep into her soul. She was dreaming, nothing could feel this good, she had to be dreaming, this was –

OhMichaelohMichaelohmyGodMichael!

He was coming in deeper still. This thing, this thing that she couldn't – couldn't take in further – this was the nucleus of her body now, everything else clung to it.

And now she and this man-beast-Michael were locked together, travelling together, racing on some rock that had broken free from Earth, free from gravity, soaring through a firmament of darkness and stars, with a fuse burning inside each of them, burning harder, faster. Pumping, pumping her insides, pumping these waves that were engulfing her.

Then the bomb imploded inside her, and seconds later, inside him too. She was drawn, screaming with pleasure into some dark hole, some black hole, wormhole, incredible black vortex of pleasure that felt like it would never, ever, end.

Afterwards she lay there in shock. She couldn't believe how good it had been, and he was still on top of her, still inside her, still hard as rock. It was a full minute, maybe two, maybe even longer than that, before either of them was capable of speaking.

Chapter Thirty-three

Oriental massage – call Viki!

Strict discipline! Call Miss Whiplash!

For a really sensuous massage, phone Carla.

Fantasy woman. Let delicious Divina pander to your whims!

Twenty minutes after he had left Michael Tennent's house, Thomas Lamark dialled the number on the card. He was hesitant; he had never done this before. A woman answered. Her voice was common but maybe he could get her to change that.

'I saw your ad. Divina?'

She sounded wary. 'Where did you get my number?'

'In this call box. At the bottom of the Earl's Court Road.'

'You'd like an appointment?'

'Are you free now?'

'I have an hour, if you come round right away.'

'What colour is your hair?'

'Red.'

'Do you – do you have a blonde wig? Long blonde hair? Wavy?'

'Want me to put that on for you?'

'Thank you.'

Ten minutes later, Thomas pressed the buzzer of the narrow door sandwiched between a betting shop and a café. He identified himself through the speaker-phone, entered and climbed a narrow, dimly lit staircase.

When he reached the landing at the top, a door opened. A woman stood there, much younger than he had imagined from her voice, mid-twenties at the most, and plumper than he had visualised. She had a friendly, soft-featured face that he found neither attractive nor ugly, long platinum blonde tresses and was wearing a cream satin dressing gown loosely fastened.

'Thomas?'

He stared at her cleavage. 'Yes.'

She eyed him carefully, then beckoned him in, closing the door behind him.

He entered a small room lit with a red bulb inside a paper globe lampshade. There were large mirrors on the wall and on the ceiling. The narrow double bed had a candlewick coverlet, and there was a mangy red carpet on the floor. Ventilation was from an open window behind Venetian blinds, and an electric fan on the dressing table.

'Would you like a drink, Thomas?'

'No thank you.'

'Not a Coke or anything?'

'Nothing.' He was feeling awkward. There was a sickly sweet smell of perfume that he did not like. This was not what he had imagined.

'Let's get the financials out of the way before we start, shall we, Thomas? It's one hundred pounds for the hour, unless you want anything a little kinky, then it would be extra.'

Startled by her directness, he fished two fifty-pound notes from his wallet and handed them to her. In return she gave him a condom in a foil wrapper.

Then she untied the sash of her dressing gown, let the front fall open, and leaned back provocatively. 'What would you like me to do to you, Thomas? A little massage first?'

Her breasts were nothing like his mother's. These were bigger, rounder, upright, they looked unreal. The nipples were horrible, tiny dark things, like studs.

And she had a thick, unruly bush of black pubic hair.

His eyes went up to her wig, then down to her pubic hair.

His mother's had been blonde, tinged with grey recently, but still blonde.

This black was horrible.

'Something wrong, Thomas?'

'You have black pubic hair.'

She grinned. 'Sorry, I haven't got a pubic wig, darling!'

He did not like the way she made fun of him. He was making a mistake in being here, he realised. This wasn't how he had imagined it; this wasn't what he wanted. From what he had seen in films, he had imagined he would be in some vast gilded chamber, with a sunken bath, crystal chandeliers, champagne on ice.

And a woman who looked like his mother.

In her cheap wig, this woman was insulting his mother's memory.

'Can you speak differently?' he asked.

'Speak differently?'

'Do you know the actress Gloria Lamark?'

She shook her head.

Anger rose inside him.

'Did she speak lah-di-dah, Thomas? Do you want me to speak lah-di-dah?' She feigned an upper-class accent. 'Do yew meeeen speaaakke laike theas?'

'Tell me that you want to touch my choo-choo,' he said with an edge of desperation.

Reverting to her normal voice, she said, 'Your *what*?'

Reddening. 'My choo-choo. Tell me that you want to touch my choo-choo.'

'Choo-choo? What's your choo-choo, darling?'

He pointed at his flies. 'My thing. Penis.'

'You call it *choo-choo*?' She looked at him in astonishment, then burst into a cackle of laughter. 'Choo-choo!'

He stared lividly back at this ghastly creature, with her sickly sweet smell and her studs for nipples and her fat flesh and ghastly black tangle of hair, then dug his hand into his pocket and pulled out his coin.

He tossed it in the air palmed it.

She caught the glint of gold and asked, 'What's that?'

'Tails,' he said. 'Tails, Divina. You're very lucky.' He

143

turned and walked out of the room, ran down the stairs, and out into the street, then hurried around the corner to where he had parked Dr Goel's Ford Mondeo.

Chapter Thirty-four

What's wrong with me?

The Gregorian chant filled the car with a sound that alternated between high and low pitch. The choral voices crashed out of the speakers, unearthly, like voices of the dead. They shrilled in Thomas's ears, boomed in his heart.

He drove in a mist of rage, a man possessed, with demons in his soul. He wanted to kill someone tonight, anyone, it didn't matter who – a guy, a girl, a junkie, a wino, anyone.

It would be Dr Michael Tennent's fault.

You will have blood on your hands, Dr Tennent.

With the sickly sweet smell of the prostitute's perfume still in his nostrils, he headed towards the West End, anxiety nagging him: maybe the psychiatrist had caught sight of his face. What if the bitch had made a note of his licence plate?

No. They'd just glanced at him, that was all. They hadn't seen his face, hadn't written down his number. They weren't interested in him. They were just interested in each other. Even so, he had been careless. Stupid.

Why couldn't he and Divina have been interested in each other?

Why did you laugh at me, Divina?

What on earth is the matter with me?

The traffic was heavy up the King's Road. He was forced to slow down, drift along with it, part of a long line, like jigging along in a cut-out car in some theme park ride.

The ride was called *Virtual London*.

Weirdos swirled past in the current; some were hovering in groups as if they were caught in eddies, some were massed outside the entrance to clubs like scum slopping

145

against a river bank. Everywhere he looked the street was full of floaty weirdos. *Come on, step off the pavement in front of me, make my day.*

He cruised Sloane Square, then traversed Belgravia to Hyde Park Corner and on down Piccadilly. He was driving fast now, except the traffic was gumming up ahead as he closed on Eros. He was doing better, he had found a rhythm, found the trick of bullying past slower vehicles. It was easy, all you had to have was nerve! Force open a gap! And ignore the angry flashing of lights!

He crossed the junction on a dubious amber, then accelerated hard up Shaftesbury Avenue, pavements flooding over with kids, freaks, spilling off the kerb. He wanted to feel the thud of a body on the front of the car, he wanted to see some freak come barrelling over the bonnet and explode against the windscreen. He swerved in towards the kerb but nothing happened. He was driving right through people as if nothing was there!

He wondered if his memory was tricking him, the way it did trick him sometimes. Maybe he wasn't in Terence Goel's navy blue Ford Mondeo 16 valve, maybe he was at home, sitting at his computer, playing a game, driving through Virtual London.

This was just a game!

I'm indestructible!

He overtook a stalled taxi, caught another light on the final flicker of amber, made a left into Tottenham Court Road. Then his rear-view mirrors threw a dazzling glare at him. Some jerk behind driving on full beam. He heard a siren, just a short burst of two-tone, the lights flashed again, full-beam then low-beam and when they dropped back to low beam, his mirrors were a riot of strobing blue light.

He felt a flash of anger at himself, then flipped his indicator and pulled over into the kerb. Headlights swung in behind him.

Concentrate!

Had he been mistaken about how much Dr Tennent or

146

the girl had seen? Had a neighbour reported the number-plate of the car?

He lowered the window and in his mirror watched a policeman climb from the car behind, pull on his cap and approach him, a flashlight in his hand.

The beam momentarily struck Thomas in the face, dazzling him, then was switched off. He blinked, annoyed, but kept calm. The policeman was in his mid-twenties and looked younger. Thomas observed that he pressed his face right up close to his own, presumably to try to detect alcohol on his breath.

'Your house on fire, is it, sir?'

He looked at the officer blankly. In his surprise at the question, he almost forgot to adopt the Bostonian accent of his friend Dr Goel whose car he was driving. 'My house?'

There was a faint reaction to his accent. The policeman seemed to soften, but only a fraction. 'You seem to be in a bit of a hurry, sir.'

Thomas applied maximum charm. 'Oh, I'm sorry, I guess I get lost in London. I'm trying to find my way back home, down to Cheltenham and I'm going round in circles.' He accompanied his explanation with a suitably beguiling smile.

'You'll be going round in an ambulance if you carry on driving like that, or else some innocent person will. Have you been drinking this evening?'

Still utterly charming. 'No, I do not believe in drinking and driving.'

'You mean you can drive as badly as any drunk when you're sober? Is this your vehicle, sir?'

'It is.'

'And who is the registered owner?'

'I am.'

'And your name is?'

'Dr Goel. Dr Terence Goel.' Thomas spelled it out for him.

'Right, Dr Goel, the manner of your driving leads me to believe you may be driving while under the influence of

147

alcohol, and I'm going to ask you to take a breath test. Step out of your car, please.'

Thomas climbed out; the officer shielded him from the passing traffic and ushered him onto the pavement. He noticed a woman police officer sitting in the car that had pulled up behind him. She was talking on the radio. Probably checking his licence plate. Thomas had no worries there.

'Are you a resident of this country, Dr Goel?'

'Yes.' People were looking at him and he didn't like this.

'Do you have an English driving licence?'

'Yes, I do.' A whole group of people had stopped and were gawping. They were irritating him. The clammy air was irritating him. This policeman was irritating him. He had the square, bony face of a flyweight boxer.

Now the policeman was shining a torch in through the passenger window of the Ford Mondeo. 'Where have you been tonight, Dr Goel?'

Thomas figured it was best to stick as close to the truth as possible. 'Visiting friends in Barnes.'

'This is a bit of a detour if you're heading for Chelten-ham, isn't it?'

Thomas silently cursed his error. 'Uh, you know, I'm like – I get real confused in London.'

The officer opened the passenger door, reached in and picked up the two tape cassettes off the passenger seat. He held the first one to the interior light, then turned to Thomas. 'A Ray Charles fan?'

'Uh-huh.'

' "Georgia On My Mind" – great song.' The officer gave him a brief, stiff smile. Thomas was not sure whether to read anything into it. Had someone reported him playing it outside Dr Michael Tennent's house?

'And this other tape, sir? What does it contain?'

'Work.'

'What do you do?'

'I'm a scientist – I work for your government. The information on that tape is classified. I have to insist you put it down immediately.'

A fraction chastened, the officer put the cassettes back on the seat. Thomas enjoyed the moment. He dug a hand into his pocket and closed his fingers around his coin. Then as he followed the policeman towards the car, and waited as he reached in and removed the breathalysing equipment, Thomas flipped the coin and trapped it on the back of his hand.

Tails.

'It's your lucky night, Officer,' he said.

The breath test was negative. The policeman asked Thomas to blow a second time and it was still negative. He gave Thomas a brief lecture on road safety then released him with a caution and detailed instructions to the M4.

The cemetery was only a small deviation from the route.

It was half past midnight. Thomas borrowed the torch Dr Goel kept in his glove-box. The gates were locked and he had to clamber over them; then he dropped down onto the drive. It was light here, close enough to pick up some of the glow of the street lighting, but ahead the centre of the vast cemetery lay as black as a lake, beneath the stars.

He switched on his torch, and swiftly made his way through the car park, past the chapel, and along one of the well-tended paths.

The newer graves were towards the rear. He didn't need to look at the dates on the headstones: he could tell from the glints of Cellophane that wrapped recent bouquets, from the scents of flowers and recently turned earth.

It took him a full five minutes of walking fast to reach the ragged strip where his mother lay. Then he stood still, his anger rising as he scoured the grass with the beam of the torch.

Bitch.

She was here, under this soil, stiff and silent, the way she had been when he had last held her in his arms, the way all the rest of the people in here were. Dead. Gone. No longer a person, reduced to the state of *cadaver*.

He stared down at the ground, then suddenly shouted,

'You stupid bitch, why did you have to die? Why?' His voice rose to a scream. *'Why? Why? Why?'*

Then he sank to his knees. The moon was riding high in the sky, it was nearly full, but there was one bit missing; it looked like a bent coin.

He pressed his face right down into the grass and breathed deeply, trying to catch just a small trace of Chanel No. Five. But all he could smell was earth and grass. He got to his feet, kicked the strip of grass sending a divot skimming into the shadows.

Lie there, you bitch, what do I care?

Then, aloud, he said, 'Lie there all fucking night!'

Chapter Thirty-five

A dying drumbeat of fear rolled through the fading dream.

The darkness was loud, deafening, pressing in on him. Michael burst out through it, from deep sleep to instant thrumming consciousness.

Someone was walking across his bedroom floor. A shadowy figure appeared by the window.

Oh, Christ.

In his confusion he remembered a car. There had been a car outside and Amanda had been freaked out by it –

Amanda?

It was coming back fast now.

Amanda was here, they were sleeping –

Where was she? He put out an arm and felt empty sheets. Fear roiled through him. *Phone the police. Find a weapon.*

A clank. Brass curtain rails rattling on the rod. A strip of streetlighting exploded into the room and the figure shone like a ghost.

A naked woman. Amanda, peering out of the window.

In his relief, the whole room seemed to lighten up. Michael held his breath, watching her in silence, drenched in her musky smells and his own perspiration.

The curtains rustled back together, not quite as tightly as before, leaving an orange chink.

'No one there,' Amanda said, turning towards him as if knowing he was awake.

She slipped back into bed and he felt the hard goose-bumps on her flesh as they worked their arms around each other and kissed and held each other close, lying on their sides, their faces up close, resting on the same pillow. Her breath was minty, she must have just brushed her teeth, he thought, hoping his own mouth didn't taste too bad. He loved the feel of her nakedness in his arms, pressed against his own body.

'You're still worried about that car?' he asked.

'It's OK. I – I just wanted to make sure that it . . .'

'Wasn't your ex?'

'I couldn't see clearly but I didn't think it looked like Brian. I wouldn't put it past him to have me followed though.'

'I have some binoculars. If the car does come back we can take a closer look.'

She raised her eyebrows with a grin. 'Are you the neighbourhood Peeping Tom? Is that what you have binoculars for?'

'Horses, actually.'

'Horses? You like racing? Flat or jumps?'

'The jumps. Katy liked –' He stopped abruptly, not wanting to get drawn, and instantly regretted mentioning her.

There was a brief, uneasy silence, and sensing it, Amanda gently pushed some hairs back off his forehead, then changed the subject. 'Tell me more about yourself. Do you have any brothers or sisters?'

'I have a brother, three years older than me.'

'What does he do?'

'He's a metallurgist. Works for Boeing in Seattle.'

'Are you close?' she asked.

'No, not really. We get on when we meet up, but we don't know each other that well – three years is a big age gap when you're a kid.'

She kissed each of his eyes gently. He tightened his hold on her, and she moved closer still against his body as if silently comforting him, slipped one hand down his stomach, let her fingers drift through his groin and then began, with incredible tenderness, to stroke him. 'Are your parents alive?'

'Yes.' He breathed in sharply from pleasure.

'What do they do?'

This woman is incredible, Michael thought. Their lovemaking had been beyond anything he had ever experienced. And now he felt an extraordinary sense of ease and peace with her. He realised he had never, ever felt so comfortable with any other human being. Nor so horny.

I could fall in love with you, Amanda Capstick. I could fall seriously, utterly and hopelessly in love with you.

'My father's retired – he was a doctor – a GP in Lymington – down on the edge of the New Forest. My mother was his secretary.' He was growing further in her hand, and she continued the light, tantalising strokes.

'Beautiful part of the world. Is that where you grew up?'

Clenched teeth. 'Yes.'

'Does he still practice?'

An even sharper intake of air. *You are driving me crazy!* 'No, he's eighty-four. He married quite late. Just potters around with his little boat. My mother gardens, plays bridge and worries about me.'

'My mother worries about me, too' she said. 'We always remain little children to our parents.'

'Yup. That only changes at the very end when they turn into the helpless children we once were.' He caressed her hair. 'Tell me about your parents?'

'My father was an artist – a painter. He left my mother when I was seven because he wanted to go and sit on a mountain in India in search of enlightenment. He was in a motorcycle accident out there and died of septicaemia in a hospital in Delhi.'

'I'm sorry.'

'I barely knew him, he was hardly ever around when they were together. And my mother – she's nuts.' Amanda smiled, her face all blurry. 'Nicely nuts, she's lovely, but she's always been eccentric – rather bohemian. She lives in Brighton and she's fifty-four and she still hasn't decided what she wants to do in life.'

'Did she remarry?'

'No, she's had a succession of lovers, mostly unsuccessful artists, or actors or writers. She was a graphic artist by training, but has always dabbled in other things. She's into

153

Feng Shui at the moment. Large companies pay her a fortune to rearrange the furniture in their offices.'

'Is there good Feng Shui here?'

'I think she'd approve of your living spaces.'

'That's a relief.'

'You'd like her. Everyone does.' She paused, then added. 'I think she'd really like you.'

There was another silence, but now it was an easy, secure space they had made for each other. Michael lay still, scarcely able to believe this was real, that Amanda Capstick was here, naked in his arms, pressed up against his erection, her warm, minty breath on his face.

'Are you worried about Brian?' he asked. 'Is he violent?' As he spoke, he ran his hand lightly over the flat of her stomach, then with his fingers began to tease her pubes.

'He has a vile temper. But I don't think he's going to be turning up here at three in the morning with a pickaxe – that wouldn't be his style.'

'I'm OK with axes,' Michael said. 'I got attacked by a mental patient with one.'

'Why? What happened?'

He wanted to make love to her again. 'Later.'

'Tell me *now*!' She squeezed him hard and he exhaled a blast of air, laughing, then kissed her forehead.

'OK! I was an expert witness in a child-custody case. I told the court the mother wasn't fit to look after her children. A year later, she was waiting for me in the hospital car park with a logging axe.'

'Did she hit you?'

'She tried to hack my leg off, but luckily she hit my briefcase. Then I managed to disarm her.'

'I didn't realise psychiatry was a contact sport.' she said.

Michael grinned. 'I hadn't either, when I went into it.'

She was quiet for a moment and then she said, 'Why did you become a psychiatrist? Did you always want to be one?'

It was a question he was asked often.

'I was always interested in biological things as a kid – I suppose partly from my father being a doctor. I did a degree in psychology, then realised that psychiatry is much more biological. I've always been interested in people, in what makes us tick. Psychiatry is the natural combination of the two. I just wish the public image of psychiatry was better.' He gave her a quizzical look.

'I think the public image is good,' she said. 'In fact I'm getting more impressed with psychiatrists every moment.'

'Actually, we're pretty much at the bottom of the food chain in medicine. We're the last resort for GPs, when all else fails. We're just one rung above snake-oil salesmen.'

'Are you angry with me, for what I told you I was doing with my documentary?'

'Did you ever hear the saying that, when you have their balls in your hands, their hearts and minds will follow?' he murmured.

Their eyes met again, explored each other and, as if in reply, she slid her head beneath the sheets, took his balls in her mouth and closed her lips around them.

Then she began to hum.

Chapter Thirty-six

'Open your present!'

She couldn't sit still either! Spangles of April sunlight darted like fish in the deeps of her emerald eyes. 'Go on, yes, open it, Tom-Tom, open it now! Happy birthday!'

She was even more excited than he was!

The folds of her silk dressing gown rustled as she sat, a Peter Stuyvesant cigarette burning in the ashtray, her blonde tresses shimmying; she was leaning across the table towards him.

The present was for him, but he knew how much it meant to her that he liked it. *She was imploring him to like it!* And he knew how angry she would be if he did not.

Thomas always wore his best suit on his birthday, with a tie, a plain shirt and black shoes. He was sitting in these clothes now at the large table in the breakfast room, which overlooked the garden, secluded from neighbours by tall trees and dense, immaculately tended bushes and shrubs.

He liked to go out there, but it was only rarely that his mother gave him permission. She had explained many times the dangers. Bad people could be hiding in the shrubbery waiting to snatch him and take him away for ever. Sunlight corroded human skin. London air was unhealthy to breathe. There were insects that could bite or sting, animal faeces that could make him blind. Horrendous stuff came out of aeroplanes when they flushed their lavatories and just hung in the air, slowly dropping down on people.

There was a gym and a sauna downstairs in the basement where the two of them worked out every day. There was no need to go outside except for specific visits, like today, when they were going to the Science Museum. Only the underprivileged and people who were doing bad things went outside when they didn't need to. And only children who did bad things, or whose mummy and daddy didn't love them, were sent to school, where they had to learn in classrooms with lots of other kids, instead of having their own private teacher, like Mr Goodwin, come to their house every day.

Under his mother's guidance, Thomas prayed every night to God, to thank him for making him normal, and for giving him a mother who loved him. And he prayed for God to help him find new things to love about his mother each day.

There were three cards on the breakfast table. One was from Grandma Lamark and showed an elephant holding a balloon in its trunk; a ten-pound banknote was clipped to the inside. The second was from his Aunt Stella, who had sent him a five-pound book token. On the front of her card was the number '6' in large letters and the word 'TODAY!' beneath it.

He didn't know that some children got toys on their birthdays. No one had ever told him that, and he had no way of finding out; the kind of books to which he was given access were not the kind that mentioned toys on birthdays.

He didn't know either that the staff employed by his mother – the cook (Mrs Janner), housemaid (Elvira), personal maid (Irma), butler (Dunning), secretary (Enid Deterding), chauffeur (Lennie), gardener (Lambourne), and his tutor, Mr Goodwin, were expressly forbidden to give him cards and gifts. The same rule applied at Christmas.

There was a click of the door and Thomas turned round. Dunning, an elderly, courtly man in tails, with hair as smooth as sealskin, stood attentively. At a signal, he addressed Thomas.

'Good morning, Master Thomas. Happy birthday to you.'

'Thank you, Dunning,' he replied.

Then the butler turned back to his mother. 'When you are ready, Madam?'

'Your special birthday breakfast, Tom-Tom, are you excited?' his mother asked.

He nodded. He was! Porridge, bacon, egg, tomato, sausage, baked beans, fried bread, toast, marmalade! The *treat* breakfast he got when he had been especially good and didn't have to eat the boring muesli that came in a box from Switzerland and had a picture of an elderly man in spectacles on the front.

'Are you more excited about your present or your breakfast?'

Thomas hesitated. If he gave the wrong answer, there was the danger of losing both. 'My present.' His voice travelled in hope.

Such joy in her face! He beamed. This was going to be a good day today!

'Can you guess? Can you, Tom-Tom? Can you guess what it is?'

It was about two feet square, little more than two inches thick and wrapped in cream paper with a blue ribbon. Heavy. He turned it around in his hands. Hard and heavy.

No, he couldn't guess. Really he couldn't!

His brain was searching for possibilities. He wondered what could be in a flat box. For Christmas she had given him a Meccano set which had come in a flat box and weighed a lot. In the booklet that had come with the set were instructions on how to make a swing bridge. He'd built a cage with it. He captured spiders and put them in the cage to see how long they could live without food or water. Sometimes they lived a long time.

Maybe it was more Meccano.

Eagerly hoping so, he untied the ribbon and let it fall free.

'Don't tear the paper, Tom-Tom, we don't want to waste it.'

'No, Mummy.' He worked loose the wrapping paper, being careful not even to add further creases, then finally he pushed it open to reveal the gift.

It was a photograph in a silver frame. His mother, in a long dress and black gloves, was talking to another woman, who was also wearing a long dress and gloves.

'That's Princess Margaret! Isn't that a wonderful present, Tom-Tom?'

He said nothing.

'I thought it could go on the wall in front of your bed so you can see it when you wake up. Would you like it there best?'

Thomas looked down at the table, not wanting to let her see his disappointment.

'That's the film première I told you about, the one before you were born we did to raise money for Oxfam, to help children less fortunate than you. Princess Margaret told me she adored my films! Would you like to meet a princess?'

Thomas wasn't sure what a princess was. 'Yes.'

'You'll have to be good for a long time. Princesses don't visit anyone who is bad. You're not looking at your picture. Are you sure you like it?'

Thomas looked at it and nodded.

'The princess was upset with me when I gave up my career to have you, Tom-Tom, because it meant she wasn't going to see me in any more films. She asked me if you appreciated the sacrifice I had made, and I told her you were a wonderful son and you did appreciate it. I was right to tell her that, Tom-Tom, wasn't I?'

He nodded.

'You do appreciate that, don't you, Tom-Tom?'

Barely a whisper. 'Yes'.

His mother took the photograph, turned it round and peered closely at it. 'This was seven years ago. Am I still as beautiful now?' Her voice sounded forlorn.

The sight of her looking sad made him forget his own disappointment. He couldn't bear it when his mother was sad. 'You look even more beautiful now,' he said.

She reached out a hand that smelt of pine soap. He took it in his own tiny hand and kissed it.

'I'm glad you like your present,' she said. Then she smiled.

He smiled back and squeezed her hand. Happy now.

Chapter Thirty-seven

Much calmer now. Dust on the photograph. Thomas wiped it with a cloth, then stood back. His mother talking to Princess Margaret. An old photograph. One of the dozens of photographs of his mother in his den. He hadn't looked at this one in a long while.

How long?

Where was it taken? What was the occasion?

His memory was letting him down again, as if someone was following him around, tearing pages out of his brain at random. Useless junk never got torn out: he could remember with photographic clarity the circuit boards of every computer he had ever owned, every chip, switch, wire, nut, bolt, solder. Completely fucking useless. Yet stuff that did matter just went. Stuff like the reporter, Justin Flowering, who was his house guest, who needed his hospitality, his care, his attention: he'd forgotten all about him yesterday, hadn't taken him any water, any nourishment.

One wall of his den was lined floor to ceiling with bookshelves containing science, medical and technological books, the other walls were filled with photographs of his mother.

There was a powerful microscope on his desk and a stack of glass slides containing preserved animal and human cells. He liked to study the intricacies of life; one day maybe he would take up biological research. He wasn't happy with Darwin. He preferred his namesake, Karl Lamarck. One day he would get around to it. He liked the methodology of research. The hours, days, months, years of observation, experiments, patience.

Order.

Downstairs in the kitchen the microwave pinged.

He prowled over to the window, tall and proud, the master of this house now, and peered out through the curtains that he kept permanently closed to stop the molecules of shit and urine that came out of aeroplanes from getting into his room. Dawn was leaching away the darkness. He heard a taxi rattle past, saw tail-lights through the railings.

Sunday.

Are you chilling out today, Dr Tennent? Taking it easy? Enjoying fucking your bit of fluff?

Another picture of his mother caught his eye, one of his favourites. She was lying on a divan in a négligée, the tops of her breasts clearly showing. She was drinking a glass of champagne, smoking a cigarette from a long holder, and laughing.

He tried to remember the last time they had laughed together, but that page had been ripped out.

Dry lips. He needed a drink of water or something. He wondered if it was dry in the grave.

Down in the kitchen he removed the Pizza San Marco with wood-smoked ham and mushrooms from the microwave. He eyed some shrivelled red bits embedded in the melted cheese surface with suspicion. They looked like dried tomato skins he had seen in vomit.

He brought it to his nose and the odours were fine. It had been a while since he'd eaten or drunk anything. He'd had nothing for twelve hours before he began his surveillance of Dr Michael Tennent's house, not wanting to have to break off to evacuate bodily fluids or substances.

NIL BY MOUTH. The signs that were hung on the ends of patients' beds in the wards sometimes, when he was a medical student. He'd once managed to leave the sign on a grumpy man's bed for five days and no one had questioned it.

There was an electric clock on the kitchen wall that made a faint click at one-second intervals. The fridge and freezers hummed. The noise in the room sounded like a wasp's nest inside his head. A neon strip in one of the units had blown and needed replacing. The dishwasher needed emptying – he couldn't remember when he had filled it, but the cycle-finished light was on. Dirty dishes were stacked in the sink and on the drainers. He couldn't remember putting that stuff there – another page that had been ripped out.

He cut the pizza into four segments, put one on a plastic tray, with a jug of water, and went down the cellar steps into the gym, switched on the lights and walked across to the sauna.

As he opened the door, a blast of heat and the stench of excrement greeted him. Justin Flowering, still in the suit and hideous tie he had worn at his mother's funeral, now blotched with dried blood, lay in the same position, pinned down by the bonds around his arms, midriff, thighs and ankles.

His eyes were shut, his face was gaunt, his skin waxy, his hair matted; he had lost a lot of weight.

'I've brought you some pizza with wood-smoked ham, Justin, and some water.'

There was no response.

Thomas put down the tray, briefly studied the blackened, cauterised stump at the end of the reporter's right arm, then compared it with the stump at the end of his left arm. Both were healing nicely and he was glad about that. No sign of gangrene.

'Healing well, Justin!' he said.

Then he checked the young man's pulse. Weak. The skin felt clammy. He stood back, wondering whether to put the young man on a saline drip and nurture him back to strength. Perhaps with what he had learned down here he would now be a better reporter.

But he was a distraction. Thomas had to remind himself of that. Justin Flowering was a distraction. He could not afford to let his heart rule his actions.

I really would like to make you better, Justin, but I can't, there are too many complications. I'm going to have to let you go. I'm sorry about this.

He climbed the stairs up to his den, took a hypodermic syringe from a drawer, then went back down to the kitchen and removed a vial of curare from the fridge. Obtaining medical supplies was easy for him. He printed out fake prescription forms copied from one of his own doctor's, on his computer, then filled them in by hand. No problem.

Back in the cellar, he injected sufficient curare into a vein in the reporter's wrist, then sat beside him, on a slatted pine seat in the sauna and waited.

After a few moments Justin's eyes opened in shock. He was shaking. Struggling to breathe. His lips, cracked and blistered, parted a fraction, still connected by a thin strand of saliva.

Thomas looked him in the eye, feeling a confusion of emotions. 'Back with us again now, Justin!' he said, trying to sound encouraging, hoping to give this creature at least a few moments of kindness while he died.

The reporter made a wheezing sound. His face was starting to darken, the flesh tones turning blue. His whole body was juddering.

'I'm here for you, Justin,' Thomas said, taking his wrist and holding it. 'I'm here for you.'

Justin Flowering juddered for a full two minutes, eyes bulging, making tiny sounds somewhere in the depths of his throat. Then he fell silent. Thomas continued to hold his wrist until a further sixty seconds had elapsed with no tremor from the pulse.

Now he needed to take the reporter down to his final resting place, alongside Tina Mackay. This was the messy part. This he really did not relish doing, but he should do it now, he knew, now, before he forgot, before any bad smells started to come from the man.

But first he took the tray with the slice of pizza back up to the kitchen. No need to waste it. His mother had taught him never to waste food.

Three hours later, exhausted, but elated by the power of what he had just done, Thomas carried a tray with four slices of pizza on it up to his mother's bedroom, went in (no need to knock! he thought, joyously) sat down on her bed, then lounged back on it, deliberately keeping his shoes on, and balanced the plate on his lap.

He watched his reflection in the mirror in the top of the canopy. And on the wall opposite. And on the side walls. His mother's smells rose up off the pillows and mingled with the pizza. He lifted a quarter segment and melted cheese rolled off the side like a lava flow. Crumbs fell onto the sheets. He smiled a defiant smile at his reflection. Then he closed his eyes and tried to conjure up his mother's face. Instead, he saw the cheap wig and stark black bush of pubic hair of the woman, Divina.

Hope you're watching, Mummy!

Hope you can see me, lying on your bed, getting pizza crumbs everywhere, thinking about other women!

Hope this is making you mad as hell.

There was a rubbery smell on his hands and an unpleasant odour of disinfectant on his clothes and in his hair. Jeyes fluid. He'd put on protective clothing, but the reek had got through it. And the embalming fluid. He wasn't used to housework, but it had to be done, when you had guests staying.

Need a new light bulb for the kitchen unit.

His mother used to dictate a list each week. Dunning or some other member of staff would go out for the shopping. But in the last few years, when it had been just the two of them together, he had done it.

He liked shopping. It gave him pleasure to see that the things he saw in advertisements on television were real. You could buy them! It still gave him a guilty thrill to take something off a shelf that he had seen on television only hours earlier.

He tried to remember the weekly list of duties. The page was still there, but it wasn't as clear as the circuit boards of the computers.

Cut the grass.

Hoover carpets.

Washing up.

Laundry.

Feed the fish.

He had remembered that he needed to feed the fish, but had run out of food. It didn't make any sense to him that they had pet fish in the pond in the garden. His mother never went out there, so she never saw them. Why did she have them?

Must buy fish food.

Going to be a lot of changes around here, as soon as – His thoughts hit a stop light. He waited for it to change to green, then went on. *Soon as* – He stopped again. He had lost the thread. He was trying to remember the wattage of the neon strip bulb he needed for the kitchen.

He was trying to concentrate on the list. The list was important. He had to get the house clean, tidy, ready. He had a new guest coming soon.

Only the coin knew exactly when.

But he had a feeling it would be tonight.

Chapter Thirty-eight

'Forty-five,' Amanda said.

The boom and echo of the Tannoy system drowned Michael's reply.

'Didn't hear you!' she shouted.

The sun beat down hard. A mist of dust hung over them, stinging their eyes. Then the exhausts of fifteen large, tatty, beefcake-engined saloon cars shook their eardrums like an earthquake. The crowd, which had opened up like a sponge, now contracted again, squeezing in on them from all sides. Michael craned his neck but all he could see so far was empty track. The stadium stank of spent racing fuel and fried onions.

'So Brian is sixteen years older than you,' he said.

She cupped her hands over his ear and said, 'Maybe I have a thing about older men!'

He glanced at her and smiled. She was joking but it was probably true. After her father had left home, her mother had had a string of boyfriends, all unsuccessful artists of one kind or another. She only had a sister, there had been no strong male throughout her childhood to whom she could look up. In her ex-boyfriend, Brian, she had clearly found a father figure. Maybe now with him too.

The male commentator boomed, through the Tannoy, 'Just waiting for car twelve.' Then in a more chatty tone, he added, 'Good to see Dave Spall out there, in car four-three-two, having his first drive for five years. Car twelve is now ready. The course car is out! The start of the Len Wardle Memorial Trophy is under way!'

Michael saw a flash of metal. A gleaming red saloon pace

car glinted past, followed by fifteen stock cars in a tight but haphazard formation, like a shoal of fish.

Amanda's face was alight with excitement. 'Come on, Dave Spall!' she shouted. 'Come on, number four-three-two!'

Michael, anxious now, craned his neck over the crowds, peering through the wire mesh fencing, trying to get a fix on Dave Spall's yellow Toyota. There were four yellow cars in the race and it was difficult to make out his patient's.

He had been treating Dave for four years. The one-time national champion stock-car driver, whose day job was machine-tool engineering, had suffered depression after a freak accident five years ago in a demolition derby, when another competitor's seat-belt mountings had sheared and he had been flung through the driver's window onto the track, under the wheels of Dave Spall's car, which had killed him; a novice of seventeen.

When he'd first been referred to Michael, Dave Spall had been unable even to cope with driving on public roads. Slowly Michael had coaxed him back to normality and now, today, Dave was taking to the track again, and had asked Michael if there was any chance he could come along. He'd told Michael it would be a big boost to his confidence if he knew he was out there in the audience watching him.

Michael liked the man and had been touched by the request. Amanda had leaped at the suggestion of joining him, and the meeting, at Eastbourne, was only half an hour's drive from her sister, where she was going later that afternoon to her niece Leonora's fourth birthday party.

The pace car reached the start line and swung off into the exit lane, then all hell broke out behind it. Two cars collided on the first bend; one spun, a third car hit it broadside and was badly rear-ended by a fourth. Dave Spall swerved past the mess and was lying in fifth place at the end of the first lap.

Amanda squeezed his hand excitedly; Michael squeezed back, it was an incredible feeling, just this tiny communion with her, amid the roar and shouts, under the blazing sun.

She looked beautiful in her simple outfit of jeans and white T-shirt, and he was proudly savouring the admiring glances she was getting from other men.

Dave Spall held fifth place throughout the second and third laps. He was doing fine. Michael saw his head twitch and wondered if he was trying to spot him in the blur of faces. *Just concentrate, Dave, get round that track, don't try to win, just finish!*

In the fourth lap a car tried to pass Spall on a curve, slid outwards into him, locked sides with him and pushed him over towards the barrier. Michael felt Amanda's fingers biting into his flesh; she'd gone with him to the paddock and shaken Dave Spall's hand, and then proceeded to ask him a raft of technical questions about his car that had amazed Michael, who had been left behind totally.

The two cars stayed locked together right down the length of the track then, to Michael's relief, Spall eased off and let the other car go ahead. The grip of Amanda's fingers eased also.

Michael glanced at her and she shot a smile of encouragement back at him that said, 'Relax, he's going to make it!'

He did make it. He finished sixth, intact. They hurried through the crowds back to the paddock, and Spall called Michael a great big four-eyed hairy bastard, threw his arms around him and planted a kiss on each cheek. Then he kissed Amanda and asked Michael why psychiatrists always pulled the best-looking birds, and told Amanda she could come and work as his mechanic any time, and spent the next ten minutes discussing the merits of superchargers versus turbochargers with her.

They left the paddock before the start of the last race. Amanda wanted to avoid the traffic – she was already running late for the party. As they walked towards the car park, arm in arm, Michael said, 'I'm impressed! Where did you get your mechanical knowledge from?'

She gave a funny little shrug that Michael found endearing. He'd noticed she always did that when he paid her a compliment, as if she wasn't very good at accepting them.

'Brian was car-mad. I was forever going with him to race meetings, and getting stuck at dinner parties next to men who ignored me because all they wanted to talk about was engines. I decided I wanted to stand my own ground with these people, so I learned everything I could on the subject.'

Michael shook his head, grinning. 'You're amazing! You really are!'

She gave another little shrug. 'Actually, engines are really interesting when you get to know about them.'

She was full of surprises. It seemed that every few minutes he found something new to like about her. They stopped and slipped their arms around each other's waist. The whole sky was dancing in her eyes. Michael's heart was aching: he wondered whether it was possible for a human being to feel any happier than he felt at this moment.

He wanted to say it to her right now. *Amanda Capstick, I love you.*

It was a fight to hold the words back. But it was too soon. Even after their incredible night of lovemaking – four times! – it was too soon; he didn't want to frighten her off.

He was scared at how happy he felt.

And as he watched Amanda driving off in her little red Alfa, clouds of dust kicking up under her tyres, her hand waving, so cheery, so fragile, he felt scared that something bad was going to happen and rip the happiness away from him once more, just as it had been with Katy's death.

As if mirroring his sombre change of mood, a cloud rolled across the sun like a tarpaulin.

170

Chapter Thirty-nine

sunday, 27 july 1997.
Amanda Capstick used to have a dog called Ollie.

Sweet.

There is a colour photograph of Ollie on her website. A brown cocker spaniel, sitting on a pebble beach with its tongue hanging out.

Probably crapped on the beach, and some eight-year-old kid put his finger in it and then stuck it in his eye and got a Toxocara parasite in there which infests the retina, causing inflamation, granulation and permanent damage.

But Amanda Capstick won't be concerned about that. A woman low enough to want to be penetrated by Dr Michael Tennent isn't the sort of person to worry about children being blinded.

Some words of wisdom for you Dr Tennent. From a poet who does not use capital letters, e.e. cummings.

> *be a little more careful of love*
> *than of anything else.*

I expect you might wonder why I should be concerned about your welfare, Dr Tennent. You might wonder why I am nervous of your relationship with a woman who puts photographs of her dead dog out on the Internet.

Si vis pacem, para bellum. If you want peace, be ready for war.

You are a doctor, you should be able to speak Latin. These are the words of Julius Caesar. Are you ready for war, Dr Michael Tennent?

Julius Caesar murdered two million Gauls during his conquest of France. He is revered today as a great leader. Does that tell you

171

something about mankind, Dr Tennent? Does that help your understanding of the human condition? Do you draw upon a reservoir of such knowledge when you see your patients? Did you when you saw my mother? When you rang her afterwards and left your message on her answering-machine?

I'm rather afraid I upset you this morning. It might be helpful if we had a quick chat on the phone.

I'm rather afraid I'm going to upset you now, Dr Michael Tennent. One of the things that will assist me in this is a thumbtack.

I wrote some days ago that I would explain about the thumbtack. It's really very simple. As a medical man you will be aware of curare. Curarine is the type alkaloid of Guianese curare. Native South Americans extract it from a plant found in the rainforest; when rubbed on the tips of arrows, it induces almost instantaneous paralysis in victims. When their respiratory muscles become slack we see first cyanosis, in which the victims start to turn blue from oxygen starvation. They are able to breathe out, but not breathe in. Fatal asphyxia follows.

I have learned that there is an elegance to the natural world. The equations of mathematics; the balance of nature. Gödel's theorem is especially elegant. So is Pythagoras's. In good science there are elegant experiments, elegant solutions. I have made a special thumbtack: the needle of a hypodermic syringe carefully cut off a quarter of an inch below the tip and fitted with a tiny rubber bulb. I attach the thumbtack to the palm of my hand with a mild adhesive, then I fill the bulb with curare.

What could be more elegant than to shake hands with one's victim?

If the dosage is measured with care and delivered subcutaneously, the respiratory muscles will be among the last affected. But just in case, as I have done before, I will take a portable heart-lung resuscitator along with me in the white van. This relieves me of the hassle of losing valuable time in performing manual cardiopulmonary support.

I must take the greatest care. After all, a human life is at stake here.

It would be a real tragedy for death to come too quickly.

Chapter Forty

A long, single-storey building with grey pebbledash walls, and a covered drive-in one side, deep enough to take an ambulance or a small truck. Two pillars with open wrought iron gates, and a Tarmac car park, distance the building from a traffic gyratory system that includes in its congested circuit a grimy Victorian viaduct and a J. Sainsbury's superstore. The subdued sign beside the brick pillars carries the cheerless words: BRIGHTON & HOVE MORTUARY.

The rain adds further gloom, but even on the brightest summer day this place looks horrible.

Glen Branson had never been afraid of ghosts; it was the living he considered dangerous, not the dead. Normally the detective constable didn't have a problem with human corpses, but this was not a normal corpse that was lying on the steel table, under the glare of four massive fluorescent lights.

Cora Burstridge might once have craved the spotlights, but these lights today, hanging on heavy chains from the high ceiling, were doing her no favours. This cold room, with its drain gullies, its grey-tiled walls with bright purple covers on the plug sockets, stainless-steel sinks, and stainless-steel work surface on which lay an assortment of surgical instruments and an electric rotary saw, was an indignity too far.

On another surface lay the paperwork, several forms, including the standard G5 form Glen had filled out in Cora Burstridge's flat.

Glen was having a hard time keeping a grip on himself. His stomach felt like it was churning wet cement as he swallowed hard, trying to cope with the smell that was worse than a venting sewer. He looked everywhere but at the corpse. The mortician, a cheery matronly woman in her mid-forties, in a white apron and white boots, had just finished packing Cora Burstridge's skull cavity with shredded paper and was now fitting the back of her head back into place.

Wincing he turned towards the coroner's assistant, Eleanor Willow, a pleasant-looking woman in her mid-thirties with neat black hair, an elegant grey suit and pearl earrings, and she gave him the flicker of a smile. He glanced at the other two stainless-steel tables in the room, which were empty.

On the far wall was a blackboard divided into sections: *Brain. Lungs. Heart. Liver. Kidney. Spleen.* A set of butcher's scales with a digital read-out sat in front of it. The pathologist, Nigel Church, stood facing away from them all, dictating into a machine he held in his rubber-gloved hand.

'Petechial haemorrhaging in the whites of the eyes,' he was saying. 'This looks normal, consistent with suffocation.'

Glen always considered him an incongruously handsome man for the grimness of his profession, and today, with his youthful face, his flourish of ginger hair, his blue scrub suit tucked raffishly into white boots, he looked quite the swashbuckler. In other circumstances, he might have been chosen for this part as the perfect foil to Cora Burstridge.

Except, Glen thought grimly, this was neither a theatre nor a film set. And although he respected Dr Church well enough, he was disappointed that the coroner hadn't considered it necessary to call in a Home Office pathologist to conduct a more rigorous post-mortem.

He shivered in his wet clothes. It was tipping down outside and he had got drenched just sprinting to the building from his car. A damp chill tunnelled into his bones. He tried to cheer himself with images from Cora Burstridge's films. He saw her hurl an ashtray at Stanley Baker, who was two-timing her in *She Always Wore*

Scarlet. He saw her driving an open Mercedes sports on an LA freeway, swerving in and out of the traffic and laughing while kissing Peter Sellers passionately in *California Belle*.

Now he saw her lying on the shiny steel table. She had an incision from her neck down to her pelvis; the skin was clamped open, and her yellowy intestines bulged out of her midriff. A large triangle comprising her sternum and front rib, the flesh still attached, had been placed, in an act of grim modesty, over her pubic hair. Her breasts, once so famously flaunted in *The Temple of Pleasure*, hung at a skewed angle, resting squashed on the table top on each side, and a creamy brown lump, that was her brain, sat on her chest.

Her fabled legs stretched out straight, marbled with veins. A brown tag hung limply from the big toe of her right foot; it was marked 'Brighton and Hove Mortuary' and gave her name. Her lower arms seemed pathetically bony, the tops fleshy and wrinkled.

He could barely bring himself to look at her face. The hideously blackened and ravaged features framed, almost in mockery, by her shock of gleaming platinum hair. He was relieved that one of the worst bits, the cutting off of the back of her skull and the actual removal of her brain, had been done by the mortician before everyone had arrived.

Finally he pulled himself together and forced himself to look at her properly. He felt in some way that he owed this to her. She had given him such pleasure through her films; now, in whatever way he could, he wanted to repay this debt.

He had been brooding all of yesterday, and had lain awake during much of the night, trying to work out what was wrong with her death, why he was unable to accept that it had been suicide.

It didn't feel right, that was the simple truth. Maybe his judgement was being clouded because of who she was, and the horror of what had happened to her face. Maybe it was naïveté and when he was older and more experienced he would learn to accept that things like this happened, that people really did do these things to themselves.

I'm here for you Cora. I'm here to make sure we're getting the truth about your death. And I'm staying with it until I'm satisfied. I promise you that.

He watched dutifully as the pathologist carved his idol's brain into thin slices, inspecting each one closely in turn, then scooped them onto the scales.

Swallowing bile, he forced himself to keep watching as the pathologist pushed his arm up to his elbow inside her chest cavity and cut out her lungs. When he put them down on the work surface, they oozed blood the colour of engine oil.

The pathologist placed each lung in the scales, dictated the record of their weight into his machine, then dumped them alongside the sliced brain inside a white plastic bag. Next he removed her bladder held it up and, as if addressing Glen, said, 'The bladder contains a moderate amount of urine. We're retaining some for analysis.' Then he cut it open and poured some of the urine into a glass tube.

Glen had been to enough post-mortems to know the procedure by heart. When Dr Church had finished eviscerating her, all her internal organs would be in that plastic bag. The top would be secured and it would be placed back inside her. Then her chest would be crudely stitched shut.

But he wasn't able to hack this any longer. He left the room, fighting back tears.

He walked through into the tiny pink lounge area, made himself a cup of sweet tea, then phoned into the office to check his messages. Nothing urgent, a quiet Monday so far.

When he had drunk his tea, he went back into the room. Dr Church was working on the intestines now, taking fluid samples for analysis. He stayed on until the pathologist had finished, but held back his private thoughts from Dr Church and the coroner's assistant. Wild speculation wasn't going to help anyone at this stage – all it would do was make him look unprofessional.

While the pathologist and the coroner's officer conferred on formalities over by the work table, and the mortician had left the room to take a phone call, Glen walked across to Cora Burstridge and stared silently down at her. He wasn't sure what he expected to see that the pathologist might have missed. Her eyes were shut.

'One small anomaly,' the pathologist said, walking across to Glen. 'The blowflies. Your report says that when you found her the plastic bag was secured tightly around her head. If that was the case, how did the blowflies get in?'

Glen turned to him in surprise. It was a good question and he wondered why he hadn't thought of it himself.

He looked down again at the dead actress. Cast his mind back to the moment that he discovered her. How tightly was it secured around her neck? Were there any gaps? 'I – I hadn't considered that,' he said.

'Blowflies can smell a human cadaver two miles away,' another mortician, a shrewd looking man with Dickensian mutton-chop sideburns who had just entered the room, said with an air of almost macabre relish.

'OK, but how did they get inside the bag?' Dr Church asked.

For a moment, Glen's hopes rose. Then they were dashed by the mortician.

'They find ways. Her skin would have shrunk after she died, probably created a gap.'

'The windows were shut,' Glen said. 'How would they have got in?'

He gave him a good-humoured but withering look. 'They don't need a very big space to get in. Not like you or I. They don't have to have the front door opened for them.'

'Thanks,' Glen said. 'I get the picture.'

He asked the coroner's officer to send him a copy of the pathologist's notes, then left. It was a relief to get back outside into the torrential summer rain, to be back in his car, to head back to his office, to the incessant warbling phones and the putter of keyboards and the smell of stewed coffee and the banter and bad jokes of his colleagues.

To the living.

To normality.

Chapter Forty-one

On Mondays, Michael had his clinic at the Princess Royal Hospital Medical School. When he'd been a student, he had determined to stay away from Harley Street, not wanting what he perceived as the 'fat cat' image of medical practitioners in that exclusive manor. He had always intended to be a psychiatrist of the people, not just of the wealthy, and at the Princess Royal he was able to do this.

All the people he saw here were National Health research patients, often deeply underprivileged and more prone to depression than the wealthy sector of the community. His pay for this work was modest, but he was happy with the balance of his work. Sheen Park, his radio programme and his article for the *Daily Mail* gave him his living. He had no ambitions to become rich, but he enjoyed the comfort of not having money worries.

This morning he had a different kind of worry.

The Doppler wail of an emergency vehicle went past two floors below. Rain ticked the window. This office was larger than he liked: he preferred the intimacy of his room at the Sheen Park Hospital. It had once been a drawing room in a grand house: high-ceilinged with moulded cornices; a massive fireplace with an absurdly small, unlit gas fire; formal antique furniture with a regal chaise-longue and two Victorian armchairs facing his desk that were more elegant than comfortable.

In front of him sat Lucinda Ryan, a former top model, who was now so obsessed with her figure and skin tone that she cut herself constantly to let out what she imagined to be surplus blood.

Michael was fond of her, but today the session was

dragging. He glanced surreptitiously at the tiny silver clock on his desk. It had been a Christmas present from Katy – or maybe a birthday present, he was no longer sure. Details of their life together were slowly slipping below the surface of the water. Saturday night had been the clearest sign yet that he was starting to let go.

It was hard to concentrate this morning. While Lucinda was studying her face in her tiny mirror, he brought his hand up to his nose, like a besotted schoolboy, and quietly sniffed his fingers. He had only washed his hands lightly and traces of Amanda were still on them.

'I've been doing it again,' Lucinda said. 'But it's working, isn't it? I'm less red in the face. I've got two blood donor cards now.' She smiled proudly. 'Managed to wangle the second – they made a clerical error with my old address. So long as I go to different clinics, they don't find out.'

Michael wrote a note in her file. He was concerned about the way she looked. 'Right, we'll have to end it there for today. Please would you see my secretary on your way out, Lucinda? I'd like you to have a few tests.' He registered the alarm in her face. 'I think you're looking too pale. I just want to make sure that all this blood you're losing from your system isn't causing anything else in your body to overcompensate.'

'Will the tests involve them taking blood from me?'

'Yes.'

She looked happier.

As soon as she had left his room, Michael turned to his computer and logged on to the Net. A dozen or so fresh e-mails had arrived in the two hours since he had last checked, shortly before nine. To his disappointment, there was nothing from Amanda.

He was aching for her. He wanted to see her name on his screen, wanted to read a cheery message from her, wanted to hear her voice.

She had said she would call him when she got home from her sister's last night, just to say hi, and to let him know she was back safely. She hadn't rung. Michael was worried that she might have had an accident. More likely, because it had been such a fine day, the traffic to London from the coast had been terrible and she'd got back later than she'd intended.

But she could have phoned him on her mobile.

He'd lain awake until well past one, thinking about her, the bed full of her smell, analysing in minute detail how she had been towards him on Sunday. She couldn't have gone off him, surely?

Had she lied to him about going to her sister and seen Brian instead?

No. All she had said about Brian had come from her heart. And although he knew his understanding of women was limited, in spite of all his years of psychiatry, he found it hard to believe that after the incredible night of love-making between them Amanda could have gone on to sleep with her ex.

Unless she'd become riddled with guilt. But he really didn't think so.

He'd been tempted to phone her at half past one in the morning, on the pretext of making sure she was OK, but he hadn't wanted to risk irking her. Instead he'd sent her an e-mail. Just a simple message. 'Hi. Hope you got back safely. I'm missing you.'

He'd hoped when he woke this morning to find a reply awaiting him. He'd checked again just before he left for the office and then again when he arrived.

A great dark swell rolled inside him. How long could he leave it before he phoned her? He didn't want to show her he was anxious. Nor did he want to play games. There were all kinds of complex rituals that followed the simple human spark of male-meets-female. But he didn't want to be bothered with them. He just wanted to hear her voice again.

He picked up the phone and dialled her office number.

A plummy-voiced young woman answered, and told him Amanda had an early meeting and wasn't expected in until noon. He hesitated when she asked if he'd like to leave his name, then thanked her and said no, he would call back.

He felt a modicum of relief. *An early meeting*. She'd

probably got back too late to phone him, and this morning had dashed off in a rush without checking her e-mail.

Michael's next patient was waiting. He reminded his secretary to put Amanda Capstick through to him if she phoned, then walked across to the door to greet his patient.

He would give it until lunch-time. Surely she would call by then?

She didn't.

Chapter Forty-two

You could be blindfolded and still know you were in a police station, thought Glen Branson. They had the same linoleum floors, the same long, beat-up corridors, the same noticeboards with the same junk on them you'd find in any hospital, or school, or in any other hard-used institutional building.

But they didn't smell like hospitals; they didn't have the constant background shouting of schools. They had a quiet energy all of their own. Constantly ringing phones, gentle banter, graveyard humour, steady concentration, a sense of being part of a community. Glen liked that.

Monday was football day. All everyone talked about was the weekend's games. Gary Richardson, at the desk behind him, was a former professional goalkeeper, disabled out after a knee injury, who had joined the force and was now a detective constable like himself. He ran the local forces team. Tall, gelled hair, hip. Glen could hear him talking now.

'What happened Saturday, for Chrissake? I mean, this guy's a striker. It was a fucking disaster! They're the worst team in the league right now!'

The bacon roll sat untouched on Glen's desk. Grease was sweating through to the outside of the paper napkin in which it was folded. It was midday. He had been back in his office for an hour and it felt good to be in the warmth of this room, to listen to the chatter, to be with the living. He liked football, but he didn't have football on his mind right now.

He was still feeling queasy from the mortuary. He needed to eat, needed some energy, he'd been at the mortuary since eight thirty this morning and had had no breakfast, but wasn't ready yet to swallow anything solid. Instead he was sipping his way gingerly through a mug of treacly sweet tea.

The detective constables' office was on the first floor of Hove police station. It was a narrow room, packed tightly with six desks down each side, paired up so that their occupants faced each other. At the far end, partitioned off by a bank of filing cabinets, was a large oval conference table used by the ProActive section.

Just inside the entrance was a work area housing the room's one computer terminal, an ancient electric typewriter and a television set. Half-way down the room was a ceiling-mounted ForceLink closed-circuit TV screen, which played a loop, updated throughout the day, of descriptions of wanted criminals, with warnings if they were either violent or armed, licence plates of cars to be stopped, and anything else that Sussex Police should be on the look-out for, plus crime statistics and targets.

On the screen at the moment in bright colours, it announced: OVERALL CRIME DETECTION RATE. JUNE 1997. 26.2%.

'So this is what happens, I get called out at three thirty on Saturday morning,' Glen heard another colleague's excitable voice. 'Two gays, right? They lit a candle Saturday night to create the *right atmosphere*. They fell asleep after the *right atmosphere* had done its stuff. Burned their flat down and the flats on the next three floors above them. You know who the only casualty was? A cat! The guy in flat six threw his cat out the window and it died.'

Glen's feet were sodden from treading in a deep puddle and his suit was damp. Chilly air blasted him from the air-conditioning and an equally hostile draught came at him though the windows.

He glanced outside. It wasn't much of a view, the asphalt roof of the floor below, the car park, some garages; leafy branches swinging around in the wind. A patrol car was heading out, wipers clouting the rain, and some poor sod was cycling, plastic cape flying behind him.

Petechial haemorrhaging in the whites of the eyes. This looks normal – consistent with suffocation.

Everything the pathologist had found was consistent with suffocation. No abnormal marks on Cora Burstridge's body. Her doctor had told the coroner's officer that the actress had been on antidepressants for five years. There was an inevitability about the findings. He already knew what the bright young coroner, Veronica Hamilton-Deeley, would say in her summing up at the inquest. Cora Burstridge was a sad, lonely actress who could not face the deterioration of her looks, her reduced income, the absence of hope. *Suicide while the balance of her mind was disturbed.*

Glen sipped some tea and looked at the pile of files and forms on his desktop and in his in-tray. Paperwork was the only thing he didn't like about this job. *File Content Checklist. Defendant Details. Case Decision Information Form. Summary of Evidence. Remand Application Form. Witness List. Exhibit List. Cautions.* Endless forms. Hours and hours of pen-pushing, never able to catch his tail. Everyone in here was overworked. That was good and bad.

They were divided into three sections, each of four detectives, with a detective sergeant in another office. Three male and one female detective per section. The female detective in his section, Sandra Denham, was out taking a statement from a rape victim in preparation for a court hearing. One of his other partners, Mike Harris, sat opposite him, and Will Guppy, the team's resident comedian, was across the narrow aisle.

Guppy, beanpole tall, with crew-cut blond hair, a mournful crag of a face that masked a sense of humour even more grotesque than his taste in ties, sat in his shirtsleeves, hunched over his desk. He liked to give the impression that he was a man of culture. On the wall beside him was a drawing of two large squares, underneath which was printed the words: PICASSO'S TESTICLES.

The room was half full. Colleagues were slowly drifting in and it would be packed by two o'clock for the Monday briefing, when the previous week's activities would be reviewed. Everyone liked to report results, and Glen had two good results: a petty burglar he'd been responsible for catching had been sent down for two years on Friday, and the arrest of a serious antique-jewellery thief.

His mind drifted back to Cora Burstridge's flat. The blowflies. The terrible sight of her face inside the plastic bag. What a way to end up. To have been loved by the whole world, and to end up alone, being eaten by flies.

He shuddered.

Then he thought again about the pathologist querying how the blowflies had got there.

Two actresses of similar ages had killed themselves in the past three weeks. First Gloria Lamark, then Cora Burstridge. He'd spotted the news of Gloria Lamark's death by chance, when he was waiting in a private house to take a statement and the only thing to read had been a copy of *The Times*. Poor old Gloria Lamark, he thought. Whatever happened to her? She'd made quite a few pictures, some very good, but then her career had petered out way back in the mid-sixties, whereas Cora Burstridge's had taken off. They had been famous rivals at one time, he remembered, Halliwell or Kim Newman had talked about it in one of their books on the movies of that era.

He could remember how beautiful Gloria Lamark had been. She'd been called England's Marilyn Monroe and there were indeed similarities. She'd had that same quality of innocence and charm as Marilyn. He remembered in *Double Zero* with Michael Redgrave and Herbert Lom, the way she had smiled so innocently while lifting Michael Redgrave's wallet as they embraced on the dance floor and –

'Glen, it was you last week put out an alert on a suspect Jag on the seafront, wasn't it?' Will Guppy said, without turning his head.

'Last week?' His mind was a blank for a second.

'You prat! I was out with a uniform crew and we stopped it.'

It came back now. The Jaguar he had spotted on his way to Cora Burstridge's flat. 'Right! Got it!'

'You are a fucking tosser. Know who was driving it?'

'Who?'

'Only Glen Drury. Only Glen fucking Drury, who just got a seven-million-pound transfer fee to Newcastle United and is probably going to be the next England striker, and you go and report him as having nicked his own brand new set of wheels. Good one!'

'I hope he plays football better than he drives,' Glen replied, unfazed. He was about to take another sip of his tea when his phone rang. He picked up the receiver and heard the voice of the female switchboard operator.

'Glen, I've got a DC Roebuck from the Met, wants some help from someone in Hove. Can I put him through to you?'

'Sure.'

The London Metropolitan Police considered themselves the cream, and could be arrogant when dealing with provincials. This one wasn't. He had a polite, good-natured voice.

'Hi,' he said. 'I wonder if you could do me a favour. I need some help on a missing person. Her name is Tina Mackay. Thirty-three years old, editorial director with a London publishing house. Has not been seen since early evening, Wednesday July the ninth, when she failed to turn up for a date with her boyfriend.'

Glen had his notepad open in front of him and was jotting details down as he listened. 'I'm familiar with her name. We've had pictures of her sent down. There's been a fair bit of press coverage, right?'

'Yes. She's quite prominent in the publishing world. She was last seen by a colleague just before seven that day, leaving the office. Collected her car from the multi-storey nearby where she had a contract parking arrangement. The attendant was distracted by two car alarms that had gone off simultaneously. He noticed her car leaving, but only from a distance and can't identify who was driving. No one has heard from her since.'

'Is this a murder inquiry?'

A brief silence. 'We don't have a body but we're stepping up our inquiries a little. That's all at this stage.'

'How can we help you?'

'I've been going through her expenses. She put in a standard claim form for the week ending July the fourth. There was a petrol receipt for a PDH garage in Old Shoreham Road, Hove dated June the twenty-ninth.'

Glen flicked through his diary. 'That was a sunday?'

'Yes. All she put down on the form was "Lunch, Robert Mason". That name is not known to anyone in her company or to her family. She doesn't appear to have mentioned him to anyone.'

'If she put expenses in that means it's to do with her work,' Glen said.

Then he detected a wry note in the reply. 'Assuming she was honest with her expenses.'

'Aren't we all?' said Glen.

DC Roebuck laughed. 'Of course. Wouldn't dream of trying to stick a day at the seaside on *my* expenses.'

'I wouldn't need to,' Glen said. 'Life's one long beach here.'

'Lucky sod. You ever need any help with topless sunbathers, let me know, I'll be straight down.'

'I'll bear it in mind. But you'll be at the back of the queue.'

'Thanks, pal. OK, business. Could you check out this Robert Mason for me, so we can eliminate him?'

'You have any other details on him?'

'Sorry, that's it.'

'No problem. What's your first name?'

'Simon. Simon Roebuck. You?'

'Glen Branson.'

'Any relation to Richard?'

'I wish!'

Roebuck said he would fax down full details about the inquiry, gave his direct line and his mobile number, thanked Glen and hung up.

Glen entered the name Robert Mason into the Sussex Police computer files but nothing showed up. Then he opened the phone directory and saw, to his dismay, about a hundred and fifty Masons listed.

Bastard! he thought, realising that Roebuck had off-loaded a pile of thankless donkeywork on him. He ran a finger down the names. Fifteen had an 'R' among the initials. At least that narrowed it down.

While he waited for Roebuck's fax to come through, his thoughts turned back to Cora Burstridge.

It would take a couple of days for the blood and fluid samples the pathologist had taken from the body to be analysed by the lab. By the time he got the pathologist's report through from the coroner, it would be early next week. If Dr Church found nothing suspicious, her body would be released by then and her funeral arrangements made.

He had a week to satisfy himself that she really had committed suicide.

And he didn't yet have any idea where or how to start looking.

Chapter Forty-three

The same woman as earlier answered the phone.

'Oh, hallo,' Michael said. 'Could I speak to Amanda Capstick?'

Irritation. 'She hasn't come in yet. May I take a message?'

'I'll call back, thanks.'

He hung up.

It was one o'clock. His next patient was due at two fifteen. He felt ragged from lack of sleep. She would call, of course she would call. She was busy, her work was hectic, she'd already told him that. Her early meeting had gone on later than she'd expected, that was all.

He looked out of the window but it was still raining hard. Even so he decided to brave it, he was hungry and he needed fresh air. If he went out for half an hour, he'd arrive back to find a message from her.

He checked his e-mail again. Another dozen had come in but he barely noted who they were from: he was looking for one name only, and it wasn't there.

He took the main section of *The Times*, the blue and yellow golfing umbrella that someone had left in his waiting room a year back and had never claimed, slipped his mobile phone into his raincoat pocket, told his secretary at the Princess Royal Hospital, Angela Witley, whom he shared with two other psychiatrists, that he was popping out, and asked her to give Amanda Capstick his mobile number if she rang.

He walked down to Tottenham Court Road, crossed over, then cut through into Cleveland Street and joined the short queue at the counter of his favourite sandwich bar. He wasn't hungry but he needed energy; the slice of toast and bowl of cereal he'd forced down at breakfast had gone and he was aware that his gloomy mood was being exaggerated by his low blood-sugar level.

'Don't worry, it no gonna happen!'

Michael looked up with a start to discover it was his turn. The irrepressibly cheery Greek owner beamed up at him like a man with six numbers up on his lottery ticket. He smiled back drily. 'Your people were all right. You had Byron to solve your problems.'

Still beaming like a lottery winner. 'And you have Mr Blair.' He made the name sound like a deity.

'Blair's not a poet.'

'But he's good Prime Minister, yes?'

'He doesn't have much to beat,' Michael replied.

He ordered a tuna-salad sandwich on sourdough, a banana, and a can of Coke, which he normally only drank as a hangover remedy. The rain was easing and he took the dainty brown carrier bag across into Regent's Park and strode briskly towards the lake.

Every time he saw a flash of blonde hair his hopes rose, and he looked carefully, just in case it might be Amanda. It was the kind of coincidence that *could* happen, he reasoned against logic.

There was a bench close to the water, sheltered under the overhang of a massive chestnut tree. He folded his Burberry and sat down on it – remembering the day Katy had dragged him off to Simpson's in his lunch hour to buy it, because she could no longer stand the battered mackintosh he'd worn for years. Dirty old man's raincoat! she called it.

He checked that his phone was switched on and there was a reception signal. All five black dashes were lit. The signal could not be stronger. If someone tried to call, it would ring loud and clear.

He unwrapped his sandwich, took a bite and, chewing slowly, started to scan his newspaper. He was finding it hard to get into any of the stories until one headline caught his eye.

THE HIDDEN TRAGEDY OF MISSING PERSONS.

249,762 persons went missing in Great Britain last year, according to figures published this week by the National Missing Persons' Helpline. Astonishingly, 34% will never appear again if the trend of the past decade holds true.

Wheelchair-bound mother of three, Paulette Flowering, is one of the latest parents to experience the nightmare of a missing child.

Her son, 19-year-old trainee journalist Justin, disappeared twelve days ago, after leaving the offices of the *Mill Hill Messenger* newspaper, where he had been working for the previous six months.

'Justin was finding the job very stressful,' she said. 'And he was unhappy about the attitude of some staff members towards him. He ran away from school twice, but on both those occasions phoned me within a couple of days to let me know he was all right. I'm very worried about him.'

Michael took another bite of his sandwich and read on. The highest percentage of missing persons was among teenage children, but there were plenty of adults too, in all walks of life. A senior editor at a London publishing house had been missing for nearly three weeks – Michael recalled there had been heavy press coverage of that, and pictures of the attractive, dark-haired woman had been on national television news.

A fair number of seemingly successful professional people disappeared each year: in the past twelve months there had been bank managers, lawyers, estate agents, an airline pilot and – a *psychiatrist*.

'We can assume a small percentage of these people have engineered their own disappearances for convenience,' said retired Chief Superintendent Dick Jarvis of the National Missing Persons' Helpline. 'Insurance deceptions and bigamous marriages are two of the most common reasons; you may remember the famous case of the postmaster general, John Stonehouse, who left all his clothes on a beach in Miami in 1974, to imply he had drowned. In fact, he was alive and well and living under a different identity in Australia.'

Michael ate the last mouthful of his sandwich. Then he checked his mobile phone. All five black dashes sat there in the window, smugly reassuring him of perfect reception in this area.

She's probably stopped for lunch with whomever it was she was meeting. You're not likely to hear from her until after two, so stop fretting.

But he couldn't.

He got back to his office on the dot of two. By a quarter past she still had not rung. His next patient was in the waiting room. A twenty-eight-year-old hot-shot commodities broker, who worked eighteen hours a day to earn one and a half million a year and wondered why he was suffering panic attacks.

Michael told his secretary to send him in. At least his mind would be occupied for the next forty-five minutes. By then it would be three o'clock.

Amanda would have to be back in her office by then.

Surely?

Chapter Forty-four

Michael's four-thirty appointment was late. He had two more patients this afternoon, a short staff meeting, and he had to visit, briefly, two in-patients. Then he was finished – at least, here in the office. This evening, at home, he had to write his weekly piece for the Thursday *Daily Mail* and fax it through in the morning. Tuesday, ten a.m., was his copy deadline. Any slippage on that, and his editor would get twitchy. He didn't like to be late, it was unprofessional.

He didn't imagine Amanda would be unprofessional either. Which was why the news he was now hearing from the yahoo-voiced young woman on the other end of the phone disturbed him.

'I'm sorry,' she said. 'She still hasn't arrived. You've rung earlier, I recognise your voice.'

'Yes, I'm Dr Tennent. Amanda's doing a segment with me in your documentary series on therapy.'

The young woman's tone warmed considerably. 'Dr Tennent! Yah, of course. I'm Lulu, her assistant.'

'Right. Lulu, do you have her mobile number? Maybe I could try that.'

'Yah, I'll give it to you, but I think it's switched off. I've been trying and I just get the answering-service.'

Although they had slept together, Amanda was still a stranger to Michael, and her private world – home and business – was unfamiliar territory to him. He was aware that he had no right to pry into her life but he just could not believe she deliberately wouldn't call him.

'Look,' he said, 'Lulu, is she OK?'

The assistant hesitated. 'Actually, we're getting worried.'

The words sent a deadweight of fear plunging in free-fall through him.

Lulu went on, 'She had an important nine-thirty meeting at the BBC this morning, and I've just heard that she never showed up – or rang. And we were expecting her in the office for a meeting here at twelve and haven't heard a word from her. She's normally very good about keeping in touch. I hope she hasn't had an accident over the weekend or something.'

It was too soon to start panicking, but Michael couldn't get the feeling out of his system that something was very wrong. He had no idea how close or otherwise Amanda's relationship was with Lulu, but knew he should not be divulging details of her private life to her office staff, so he kept it as professional-sounding as he could. 'Amanda and I – we . . .' He hesitated. 'We met on Sunday afternoon. I had a patient driving in a stock-car race at Arlington, near Eastbourne. Amanda thought it might add a bit of production value to the piece if –'

Lulu saved him from having to go on. 'Yes, she told me she was seeing you. She was looking forward to it.'

Michael could have sworn he detected a hint of humour in her voice, as if Amanda had told her a *lot* more than she was letting on. 'She left the race meeting about half three to drive to her sister, somewhere near Heathfield.'

'Chiddingly,' Lulu said. 'If she hasn't come in by the end of the day I'm going to go round to her flat and make sure she's not lying unconscious or anything.' There was a brief pause, and then she added, unconvincingly, 'There's probably a perfectly good explanation. Maybe she's double-booked herself and completely forgotten about the Beeb meeting. And she's just got a new mobile – she's been complaining about the reception. I'm certain there's a perfectly good reason.'

She didn't sound at all certain.

Michael felt agonisingly impotent. He wasn't sure what else he could do or say at this point. Yet he wanted, desperately, to do *something*.

He clutched at one final straw. 'Lulu, tell me something.'

He was glad he had her name: using it made him feel he was now at least some part of Amanda's inner circle. 'Is it like her to forget a meeting?'

'No,' Lulu said. 'It isn't. It isn't like her at all.'

196

Chapter Forty-five

A woman answered the phone. Polite.

He needed to be tactful. For all he knew, Tina Mackay could have been having an illicit affair with someone down here. 'This is Detective Constable Branson from Hove Police making a routine inquiry. Does a Mr Robert Mason live at this address?'

'*Robert* Mason? No, no Robert Mason. You don't mean *Dave* Mason?'

'We're looking for Robert Mason.'

'I'm sorry. My husband's name is Dave.'

'You don't by any chance know a *Robert* Mason?'

Brief pause for thought, then, 'No, no, I don't.' Not over-bright, but she sounded straightforward enough.

Glen thanked her, hung up, and put a line through the photocopied phone-book entry. Nine down. Six so far were negative. One hadn't answered, and two were answering-machines, neither of which gave a name. He cursed DC Simon Roebuck of the Met yet again for lumbering him with this search.

It was a quarter to five, and he'd only just got back to the office after going off with his partners to arrest a suspect drugs dealer, who was a former kick-boxing champion. They'd gone in a team because they thought he might be violent. He turned out to be a pathetic, ageing wreck, in a drugged stupor, and gave them no trouble.

Glen tried the tenth number on the list. Eliminated that. And the following six. At ten past five, he tried one of the numbers he had rung earlier. This time instead of the answering-machine, he got a breezy male voice with a mid-Atlantic twang.

'Hi, Robert Mason!'

Glen introduced himself, then asked him if the name Tina Mackay meant anything to him.

'Tina?' All the energy seemed to drop from his voice. 'Sure. Jesus, we had lunch just a few weeks back. This is terrible about her disappearing, I've been reading about it. Did you find her yet?'

'I'm afraid not. Would it be convenient if I were to come up and ask a few questions? I won't take much of your time.'

'Sure. You want to come now? I have to go out at seven.'

Glen needed to be home by six thirty to baby-sit Sammy. Monday nights Grace went to her English-literature evening class, but he didn't say that. He said, 'No problem.'

His instincts told him that Robert Mason had not abducted Tina Mackay, and when he met the guy twenty minutes later he was convinced he was right. Mason was a thirtysomething record producer and lived in a palatial, ostentatiously decorated flat overlooking the sea, only a short distance from Cora Burstridge's. He had met Tina at a book launch, and had invited her down to one of his regular lavish Sunday-lunch parties, at which 'I throw people in the arts together'. Simple as that. Innocent.

Dead end.

Glen drove slowly past Cora Burstridge's building as he headed home. The rain had stopped and the evening sun was breaking through the clouds over the Channel. The tide was out. A row of gulls sat on a weed-draped breakwater. An old man swung a metal detector backwards and forwards on the shiny wet sand beyond the end of the pebble beach. This had been Cora Burstridge's view.

He stared up at the actress's third-floor bay window and wondered if anyone was up there now. Her daughter, Ellen? The one he'd phoned in Los Angeles and to whom he'd broken the news? She'd sounded deeply upset, the kind of grief that has a whole load of guilt attached, the worst kind, when you realise it's too late to do all the things you should have done.

I'm still with you, Cora. I'm still fighting your corner. I'm out here in my car and I'm thinking about you day and night. It wasn't your looks I loved, it was your brilliance as an actress. You've given me so much in my life, I'll do whatever I can to give you something back.

That's my promise.

He built a Lego tower with Sammy, then put him to bed and read him a Roald Dahl story. Sammy liked to go to sleep after laughing at a story, and Glen liked to watch him close his eyes with a smile on his face.

Grace had left his dinner in the microwave, and all he had to do was switch on the timer. But when she came back from her class, at half past ten, her head full of Graham Greene and *Brighton Rock*, and of strange characters called Pinkie, Spicer, Dallow, Cubitt, Ida, she found a mess of Lego bricks on the floor, and Glen sitting on the sofa, his face buried in a thick tome titled *Postmortem Examination*, by Dr Nigel Kirkham, MRCPath.

And she found his chicken casserole with mushrooms, tomatoes, runner beans and duchesse potatoes, still sitting, mortuary cold, in the microwave.

Holding on to her temper, she gave him a wan smile, and perched down beside him, nuzzling his cheek. 'Good book?'

For an answer, he turned and looked at her with big round eyes that were fogged with exhaustion.

Chapter Forty-six

Michael sat in his den at home in front of his Mac Power-Book, typing his notes for his *Daily Mail* article:

Symptoms of mental disorder include: Altered perceptions – frequently visual and taste. For instance, flowers smell like burning flesh. Sweet food tastes bitter.

Illusions. Hallucinations. Elementary: Hearing bangs and whistles. *Complex*: Hearing voices, seeing faces, whole scenes. (Need to elaborate.)

Disorders of thinking: Delusions, obsessions, disorder of stream of thought, formal thought disorder, abnormal beliefs. Talking past the point. There is a German word for this, *Vorbeireden*. The patient is always about to get near to the matter in hand, but never quite reaches it.

He folded his arms. The inspiration wasn't coming, the article was going to be crap. The Grolsch he had poured lay untouched. He looked at the clock on his screen. It was seven thirty. Amanda's assistant, Lulu, hadn't rung him. She promised she would after she had been to Amanda's flat. So why hadn't she?

He dialled Amanda's home number again. Listened to her voice on the answering-machine. It sent a pang of yearning through him.

'Hi, sorry I can't come to the phone right now. Leave a message and I'll call you back!'

He tried her mobile instead. As before, the answering-service cut in before it had even rung. 'You've reached Amanda Capstick. Leave a message and I'll get right back to you!'

He hung up. *Why haven't you rung me, Lulu?*

He looked back at what he had written on the screen. There was no flow. It was a mess. Normally when he sat down, some miracle happened, the muse came, the words poured out.

Maybe I should go over to Amanda's flat.

But Lulu was already doing that.

He picked up the phone, dialled Directory Enquiries and asked for the number of the Sussex Police headquarters.

When the switchboard answered, he asked if anyone could give him information about road-traffic accidents in their area during the past twenty-four hours. He was put through to the traffic control room. A helpful male voice. 'Amanda Capstick? One moment, sir.' There was a pause, then he came back on the line. 'No one of that name has been reported in any accident in the Sussex area, sir. I've checked the past forty-eight hours for you.'

'Thanks. You don't by any chance have a list of hospitals in that area with Accident and Emergency departments? She might not have had a car accident, she might just have been taken ill.'

The operator suggested a few hospitals he might try. Michael phoned the first two and was about to call the third when Lulu rang. Music was blasting in the background and he could barely hear her, even though she was shouting.

'Michael Tennent? Hi, sorry about the noise, I'm in a pub – the only phone I could find, my mobile's battery's dead. Look, I've been round to Amanda's. No answer from her doorbell. One of her neighbours has a key and we went in. No sign of anything wrong. Her car's not outside – I've taken a good look around all the side-streets, so I'm pretty sure she's not there.' A brief pause, then, 'Also I rang her sister before I went there. Amanda left her house to drive back to London at nine last night. She said she seemed very happy.'

The words were like a torment to Michael. *Very happy.* He saw her drive off from the race-track, waving, so cheery, so vulnerable.

Very happy.

He remembered a film he had seen, *The Vanishing*, where a guy's girlfriend – or was it his wife? – disappeared from a motorway service station forecourt and was never seen again.

These things happened.

But not to Amanda, no, please not. This couldn't have happened to her, there was some other explanation, something simple that both he and Lulu had overlooked.

What?

'I've tried Sussex Police,' Michael said. 'And I've started phoning hospitals. I'm going to work out the route she would have taken back to London from her sister and check with all the police stations and hospitals on it.' He hesitated. 'There is one other thought I have. Um – her previous boyfriend?'

'Brian?'

'Yes.'

'I already rang him, this afternoon. He said he hasn't heard from her.'

'It's just that she struck me as being a bit nervous about him. There was a car parked outside my house for a while when she was over and she got quite twitchy.'

'I don't think she's with him.'

'No?' He felt embarrassed now. 'OK.'

'I'm heading home,' she said. 'I have the numbers of some of her friends – I'll do a ring round. Will you call me if you get any news? You have my home number?'

'Yup, you gave it to me. Likewise, you'll call me if you hear anything?'

She promised she would.

Two hours later, Michael phoned Lulu. He'd drawn a blank with the police and the hospitals. Lulu had drawn a blank with Amanda's friends, her sister, whom she'd tried again, and with her mother, and with Brian once more.

He went out for a walk around the block to try to clear his head. There were no messages on his machine when he got back.

202

He microwaved a seafood lasagne and ate it, dutifully but with no enthusiasm, in front of *News At Ten*. Then he went back to his computer and knocked his article into shape. It still felt ragged and stilted, but it would have to do. Shortly after midnight, he faxed it to his editor at the *Daily Mail*.

He tried Amanda's home and mobile numbers and again got nothing but her recorded voice. On the off-chance, he tried her office number, and there he got Lulu's recorded voice.

He took two paracetamol and went to bed.

At three in the morning he stuck a melatonin tablet under his tongue.

But it didn't bring him sleep.

Chapter Forty-seven

Thomas Lamark observed the dials on the dash of Dr Goel's navy blue Ford Mondeo. He checked each one in a sequence that had become routine to him.

The odometer showed he had driven one hundred and nine miles since leaving Holland Park at seven o'clock this morning. Exactly half a tank of petrol remained. Oil pressure was fine. Temperature was fine. Speed was zero. RPM was a steady five hundred.

No warning lights showed on the panel.

Good.

The strip-light bulb from the kitchen that required replacing sat on the passenger seat beside him. The tape of Dr Michael Tennent's voice on the answering-machine was in the slot of the cassette-player. He would listen to it again, soon. Once every half-hour was good.

Just to remind him.

He checked the gauges on the dash again. Everything was fine. He looked in the mirrors and the rear view was fine, too. He looked inside his head and retraced his steps out of his house. He had checked the window locks. Checked the door locks. Set the alarm. Brought in the milk. Locked the front door. This was the way to combat his memory lapses. Step-by-step checks.

Later, he would look for a shop that sold strip-light bulbs. But this was not the reason he was sitting in Dr Goel's car at traffic lights on the outskirts of the handsome spa town of Cheltenham at half past eight on a Tuesday morning. He had not driven one hundred and nine miles in order to buy a strip-light bulb.

Green now. Just to make sure, he looked at the traffic

lights again. The car behind hooted. Thomas glanced in his mirror and did not like the face of the man in it. He looked at the lights a third time. Definitely green. Satisfied, he drove on.

Today he was a commuter going to his office. Just an ordinary man in an ordinary motor car. He stopped at another set of lights and looked out of his window at the car on his right. Another ordinary man in a suit: this one had ginger hair and a sad face. Thomas watched him, enviously. Just a normal man going to work. With a normal life. Friends. Probably a wife. Children. He gave the man a nod. *I'm like you*, he wanted to say. *I'm just an ordinary man going to work. I'm normal, I'm not wrong in the head. I'm the same as you. I'm normal.*

The man did not see him, did not nod back. The lights changed and the man drove out of his life. Thomas ran through his checks, then he drove off too. He'd only been to Cheltenham once before, but the map of the town was printed in his mind and he knew exactly where he had to go.

There were plenty of parking spaces outside the elegant but slightly dilapidated Georgian terraced crescent, whose Cotswold stone façade glowed a soft gold in the morning sun, the pavement stippled by shadows of leaves. He could feel the warmth of the sun on his back. It was going to be a fine day.

His watch read 8.40, the car clock 8.42. He remembered a quotation: 'A man who wears one watch always knows the exact time. A man who wears two watches never does.'

He played the tape of Michael Tennent's voice on the answering-machine, and listened to it intently. When it had finished, he said, 'How many watches do you wear, Dr Michael Tennent?'

At nine o'clock he got out of the car and walked a short way along the terrace to number 20. The steps up to the front door were spattered with birdshit. The door had been painted green a long time ago, and needed redecorating. Beside it was a metal entryphone panel in much better condition than the building. There were several names against the buzzers and he selected the one that said, CHELT. BUSINESS COMMS. CENTRE LTD.

A pukka man's voice crackled a brisk, 'Hallo?'

Terence Goel identified himself.

There was a sharp buzz. He pushed open the door and went into a large hallway with tired cream paint and a tired red carpet. The place was dingily lit and smelt of failure.

There was a staircase in front of him and a dubious-looking lift to his right. A wooden panel on the wall listed the companies in this building. The Cheltenham Business Communications Centre was on the second floor. Beneath the panel was a shelf on which lay an assortment of post. He glanced down. Mostly mailshots, addressed to a foreign-sounding company.

In an office somewhere above him a phone was ringing, unanswered.

He decided to take the stairs.

Why didn't anyone answer the phone?

There was a mirror at the foot of the stairs, screwed to the wall, a fine, gilded mirror, but the glass needed dusting. He checked himself in his reflection, touched his hair with his fingers. Today he was wearing Terence Goel clothes. Dr Goel was an American working in England. The differences between an American working in England and an English-man working in England were subtle. Nuances. From his studies of Americans on television, more American men than Englishmen wore wedding bands.

Dr Goel wore a plain gold wedding band.

He wore a cream Daks linen suit, properly crumpled, a button-down midnight-blue shirt with a yellow tie, matt leather shoes with thick crêpe soles. Americans, he had noticed, went in for practical shoes rather than stylish ones.

He looked OK, he decided. He looked fine, he looked the way Terence Goel always looked.

Then suddenly he leaned closer to the mirror. Closer still. Shock. How come he hadn't noticed this before?

He took off his jacket and looked at the left shoulder. A tiny strip of the fabric, only a few threads wide and less than half an inch long, was missing. It must have snagged on something. Getting out of the car?

Luckily it hardly showed: the lining was the same colour and you'd have to look pretty closely to see anything. Anyhow, Dr Goel was a scientist, an academic. Academics the world over tended to be slovenly. If Terence Goel had a rip in his jacket that was no big deal.

He shook his head and his reflection echoed his confirmation of this. 'No big deal. Uh-huh.'

Second door on the right along the corridor. A smart brass panel fixed to it bore its name. The panel added a touch of style, Thomas thought. Like a lawyer's plaque. The style began and ended with this plaque.

The door opened onto one small room, with a telephone switchboard, a clapped-out-looking computer, and about twenty telephone-answering machines. One wall was lined floor to ceiling with wooden pigeon-holes of the kind found behind a hotel front desk. Coffee simmered in a glass jug, surrounded by a handful of squalid-looking mugs. Blue curls of cigar smoke hovered below the ceiling, and slowly leaked out through the slats in the Venetian blinds that were lowered against the sunlight.

A solitary golf-club was propped against a wall. Beside it, a cheap suitcase lay with its lid sprung open and a mass of folders spilling out. There were several dusty certificates on the wall, one of which proclaimed, MEMBER OF THE CHELTENHAM CHAMBER OF COMMERCE.

The bulky proprietor of the Cheltenham Business Communications Centre looked like he had been lowered into the chair behind his ludicrously small and cluttered desk, and then the rest of the furniture had been dumped all around him. Amid the clutter, Thomas saw a national lottery ticket with two numbers circled.

The man's full title, according to the wooden sign on the desk, was Nicholas R. Lubbings, BA Com, MBA. Next to the sign, a soggy cigar burned in a round metal ashtray with Martini emblazoned on it. From where he sat, Lubbings could operate the switchboard, the computer, and reach a bank of filing-cabinet drawers without moving.

He was a massively overweight man in his mid-forties, whom Thomas decided could do with a bath and some fresh air. He had a large square head with sagging jowls, topped with short, neat, Brylcreemed black hair cut in an old-fashioned style. His beer gut sagged out of his blue blazer, straining his shirt buttons.

Lubbings studied him warily, then his eyes gleamed in recognition. Thomas had once seen a documentary on television in which an elephant was hoisted out of the cargo hold of a ship. The manner in which Lubbings now rose to his feet reminded him of this.

'Good morning, Dr Goel! Good to see you again!' He seized Thomas's hand as if he had found a long-lost billionaire uncle, pumped it hard and beamed furiously, exhaling brandy vapours, despite the early hour.

'Good morning, Mr Lubbings,' Thomas replied stiffly.

'And how is the world treating you on this fine morning?' Another blast of brandy breath. Lubbings released his hand, plodded out from behind his desk and swivelled round a beat-up leather chair for Thomas to sit down.

Thomas did not reply. Instead, he said, 'You have the package for me?'

The telephone rang. Lubbings lunged back towards his desk and tapped two keys. Instantly, words were displayed on the computer screen. Reading them, Lubbings lifted the receiver and said, 'Southern and Western Import-Export Limited, good morning.'

Thomas watched him.

'No, I'm afraid he's not in the office. May I take a message?' Crooking the phone under his ear, he typed out a message on the computer, his fingers working the keyboard with a dexterity that surprised Thomas.

As he hung up, the phone rang again. He raised an apologetic finger, again tapped the keyboard, and read off the screen as he answered it. 'Cheltenham Sporting Saloons, good morning.'

Thomas cast his eyes at the huge rack of pigeon-holes. Many contained letters and larger packages. Now he noticed on the floor beside the desk a grey Royal Mail sack, with a mass of post inside it spilling out onto the carpet. Ranked alongside it were several small piles. Lubbings was presumably sorting them out for the different companies for whom he provided an accommodation address and related services.

'A Ford Granada Scorpio, not more than fifty thousand miles?' Lubbings said. 'I'm afraid none of our sales staff are available at the moment. If I could take your number, I'll have someone call you back in a few minutes.' Lubbings again typed furiously, thanked the caller unctuously and returned his attention to Thomas. 'Not usually so busy this early! Now, your package – ah, yes, yes indeed. It came yesterday. You rang, didn't you, Dr Goel? Can I get you some tea? Coffee?'

'Just the package.'

'I have a new brochure, since your last visit. More services, might be of interest to you, won't take a moment to run through them.'

He thrust a drab leaflet at Thomas, then went over to the pigeon-holes, stared up at them blankly. 'Ah, yes!'

He ducked down beneath his desk and retrieved a large square box, marked FRAGILE. It was addressed to Dr Terence Goel, PO Box 2876, Cheltenham, Gloucestershire GL7 8RS.

'We now have an e-mail facility, Dr Goel. And voice-mail. I don't think we offered voice-mail before, did we?'

'I don't think you did,' Thomas said, 'but I must go now. I'm keeping someone waiting.'

'Of course! Good to see you, Dr Goel. If you ever need conference facilities, we can offer those too. I could show you the conference room, if you like?'

'Another time.'

'Of course. Absolutely. Any time, pop in – you're always welcome. This is your office, after all!' He gave a silly little laugh.

Thomas returned to his car. The box was heavier than he had expected. He was anxious to check the contents. But not here.

He put the box in the boot and checked carefully that the

lid was shut. He got back into his car, then out again, and once more checked that the boot was shut.

He checked one more time before he finally drove off.

Chapter Forty-eight

'You are troubled this morning, Dr Tennent,' the old man said. 'You are finding it hard to concentrate.'

Michael, seated in his comfortable chair in his office at the Sheen Park Clinic, stared at the former concentration-camp officer, who was sitting ramrod upright on the sofa but looking even frailer than he had a fortnight ago.

He didn't need Herman Dortmund to tell him this. He didn't need Herman Dortmund to be sitting in his office at all right now. He didn't want to see anyone. Least of all this loathsome creep.

He wanted the session to finish and Dortmund to go. He glanced at his watch. Nine thirty. Fifteen minutes and he would have a gap. He would phone Amanda's office and see if there was any news, and if there wasn't, he'd already decided on his next course of action. His eyes were gritty from tiredness, but he was running full-throttle on adrenaline.

'Let's talk about you,' Michael said, not wanting to be deflected.

Dortmund was dressed as always like an English country gentleman. He wore a Harris tweed suit that looked far too warm for this fine summer morning, a checked Viyella shirt, a National Trust tie, held in place with a discreet gold pin, and brown suede brogues.

Dortmund's fingers were steepled in front of him, his small, cold eyes staring over the them. In his arrogant voice, with its guttural accent, he said, 'Last time I was here I explained this ability I have to foreshadow tragedy. I told you I had known that you were going to lose a woman whom you love.' There were beads of spittle in the corners of his serpentine lips. And there was smugness in his tone. Satisfaction, even. 'It is this person you are worrying about now, Dr Tennent.'

Michael studied him. As before, he did not want to legitimise this man's warped fantasies by asking for details, yet he couldn't ignore what he had just said. 'All right,' he said. 'Can you add to that?'

Without moving, without averting his stare, Dortmund said, 'No.'

Michael had the feeling he was playing games. 'Tell me why you think I am worrying about someone.'

'I understood that I was paying you to help *me*, Dr Tennent.'

'Yes, I am, but you told me originally that you had come to me in search of redemption for your time working in Belsen. And you are the one who mentioned it. So?'

'It is not important to me. An observation, that's all.'

Michael broke off the stare by glancing into the man's file: he was giving Dortmund time to speak again.

The silence continued. Michael glanced at his watch. Ten minutes left.

'I read in *The Times* that Gloria Lamark had died,' Dortmund said, finally. 'The actress. She used to be one of your patients – I sat with her in your waiting room one time. I remember her in the film *Double Zero*, with Michael Redgrave.'

Michael looked up at him sharply. There seemed to be reproach in the old man's eyes – or was he imagining it? He was not going to be drawn into talking about Gloria Lamark.

'I told her that I liked her in this film,' Dortmund continued. 'She was pleased. Actresses are easily pleased. You just have to stroke their egos, that is all. I am sure that is something I do not need to tell you, Dr Tennent.'

'Did you see *Schindler's List*?' Michael asked.

Dortmund looked away. It was a cheap point to score, Michael knew, and a dangerous one on a man whose sanity was fragile enough from guilt over atrocities he had committed during the war. But he didn't care. If this ageing creep was going to read his body language and try his hand at mind-fucking him, he too was willing to cut up rough today.

Dortmund did not speak again until the session had ended. Then he gripped the polished mahogany handle of his walking stick, levered himself up off the sofa, wished Michael a terse, 'Good morning,' and left, like a man stepping through his own shadow.

Michael snapped his file shut and angrily replaced it in the cabinet. He would sack Dortmund, he decided. He had only kept the man on as a patient because he interested him but he was still trying to fathom out what had really gone on in Dortmund's mind all those years back, in the Second World War.

Did you have to be born evil to commit evil? Or did you have to be born with the *capacity* for evil? Or did something happen to you when you were a child? Or an adult?

What was evil anyway? What was it that made it acceptable for Christians in the Crusades to have murdered Muslims in their attempt at world domination of their beliefs, yet unacceptable for Nazis to have murdered Jews, blacks and the disabled?

Did you have to be sane in order to be truly evil? Sane and weak or sane and strong?

He picked up the phone and dialled Amanda's office. Lulu answered. She had just tried Amanda's home number and her mobile, her sister, her mother and Brian once more, without success.

His heart was screaming, but his voice was calm. 'Lulu,' he said, 'I'm going to phone the police.'

Chapter Forty-nine

Brighton police station rises at a level angle off the apex of a steep hill. Architecturally, it could not be anything other than an institutional building of the kind found in any modernised town centre. Concrete and glass, stained by urban grime and corroded by salt from the Channel, it is neither visually appealing, nor is it an eyesore. But it is very large. It is the second busiest police station in England.

The engraved coat-of-arms over the front entrance gives it authority. There's a wide mixture of people in this part of town. Some of them are uncomfortable walking down the street past that long wall of glass they can't quite see into. Many avoid this street altogether.

An office of the Brighton and Hove Coroner is located on the ground floor, and has a view of the staff car park and the gymnasium.

Glen Branson stood in the open-plan room in which the coroner's assistants divided their time between here and their office behind the mortuary, in front of the desk of Eleanor Willow, who had been present at Cora Burstridge's post-mortem.

'Why exactly do you want the key?' she asked.

'Cora Burstridge's daughter is coming over from Los Angeles. I thought I'd have a tidy-up, make sure there's nothing left that might upset her,' he lied.

She frowned. 'Yes, OK, if you think that's necessary.'

'You're not intending having SOCO go in there, are you?'

'No,' she said. 'You don't have to worry about prints. The pathologist is pretty happy. We're just waiting on the stomach fluids, blood and urine analysis.'

She rose from her desk, opened a file drawer, rummaged inside it and produced a brown envelope on which was hand-written, 'Cora Burstridge. Flat 7, 93 Adelaide Crescent. Hove.'

'You'll bring these straight back to me?'

'Absolutely.'

The door Glen had kicked in on Thursday had been repaired and there were barely any scars from the damage he'd caused. The lock sprang easily on the twist of the key, and he slipped inside, closing the door behind him, glad no one had seen him.

He did not want any interruptions, he wanted to think clearly, he wanted time, *slow time*.

He had already ascertained as best he could what had happened on Cora's last day from her neighbour, Mrs Winston, who seemed to have kept a close eye on her. Cora had done an interview with the local newspaper, the *Evening Argus*, in the morning. A photographer had turned up while the reporter was still there. Afterwards she had gone shopping – she had told Mrs Winston she wanted to buy a little present for her new grandchild in America, something light that she could post, and Mrs Winston had suggested a small item of clothing. Cora was going to visit her daughter and see her grandchild for the first time at Christmas and she was looking forward to it. The grandchild was all she talked about. A little girl, just three months old. Her name was Brittany.

Cora Burstridge had left her flat shortly before one, and Mrs Winston, who had gone to visit her daughter for the afternoon, never saw her again.

Glen stood still. The bad smell was almost gone, just a trace lingered, but maybe that was in his mind.

He tried to imagine he was Cora Burstridge. *Walking in the shoes*, the psychological profilers called it. He snapped shut the safety chain, which had also been fixed. Then he walked in Cora Burstridge's shoes across the hallway, slowly. He was tired, elated from winning a BAFTA award,

215

but tired from the late night in London, and beyond that, he had an underlying tiredness of life.

He hated being old, he hated being short of money, he was lonely and the future stretched ahead of him like a rusted railway track into a dark tunnel.

A much younger version of himself, standing shoulder to shoulder with a young Laurence Olivier, looked down at him from the *Time and the Conways* playbill on the wall.

The past. Those days were gone and they weren't coming back. You got your BAFTA Lifetime Achievement Award, you said your piece, and then you were supposed to get out of everyone's face and go home to die in quiet obscurity. If you were lucky, and didn't leave it too long – until no one was left who remembered you – you might get a memorial service in a smart London church.

So now he had his BAFTA award. He went home. Money was running out, not even enough to pay for a decent nursing home. He had the option to go to California, live with his daughter, growing decrepit in a city where he might have been loved once, but now was just another has-been.

Not many friends left.

The only jewel in his life now was the grandchild, Brittany, he hadn't yet seen, seven thousand miles away. His best way to celebrate his award was to buy a present for Brittany.

So where was it?

He walked through to the drawing room. Bright sunlight filled the place. It glinted at him off the deco frame of a mirror. It dazzled him from a silver cigarette box on the coffee table. A red light was flashing. The answering-machine on the bureau in the recess near the window. He walked across to it. Eleven messages on the counter. He hit PLAY and listened to them.

The messages were in addition to the ones he had heard on Thursday but left on the tape. Requests for interviews and more congratulations from friends, all of these during Thursday night before the news had hit the press. There was one message timed at earlier this morning, a sales call from Brian Willoughby of Everest Double-glazing wondering if she would like to take advantage of their low midsummer offer.

It was hot. Double-glazed windows. She already had double-glazed windows. A lorry accelerated along the seafront. The double-glazing muted the sound but did not keep it out. It kept the blowflies in. A solitary fly was batting against a pane. Several more lay dead on the sill. Jesus, he was glad he had come: he could at least spare Cora's daughter those.

And the blowflies still bothered him.

He stared out, across the wide, busy road, across the promenade, the pebble beach, at the wet sand. Breaking waves. Low tide. Shallow water. He remembered his grandfather. *The shallows.*

The roughest water is in the shallows. The dangerous rocks are the ones in the shallows, just below the surface, not the ones you can see but the ones you cannot see.

What was in here that he could not see?

He put himself back into Cora Burstridge's mind.

Had it been this hot in here last Tuesday afternoon? Would I have opened a window? He tried but the glazing unit was bolted shut with a window lock. Where do I keep the key?

She was security-conscious. Some elderly people felt the cold badly and didn't mind heat like this. He would check the windows, but first, *Did I buy a present? Where did I put it? Did I mail it before I killed myself?*

Then he saw the carrier bag. A large, elegant, dark blue plastic bag, clipped shut at the top. Hannington's was printed on the side.

Glen opened the bag. Inside was a pink Babygro. He lifted it out, unfolded it, held it up. Tiny arms, tiny legs. The word CHAMP! embroidered across it in bold lettering.

He put it back in the bag. Hannington's was the best department store in Brighton. Of course, nothing but the best for Brittany. Grandma's prerogative to spoil Baby! He'd

217

had plenty of experience of that. Ari's mother was nuts about Sammy.

He walked back over to the window and now his brain was motoring. I'm Cora Burstridge, I'm depressed, and I'm going to kill myself. Last night I win a BAFTA award, I buy a Babygro to celebrate and I'm going to mail it to my granddaughter, Brittany, in their nice house on Palm, north of Wilshire, in Beverly Hills. I imagine Brittany in it, I try to think what she looks like.

I come home. Why do I kill myself before mailing it?

This does not make sense.

He glanced behind him, looked at the dark passage down to her bedroom and shivered suddenly, as his brain presented him with a snapshot of what he had seen down there last Thursday.

Then the whole atmosphere of this flat got to him. The silence. The sense that Cora Burstridge had vacated this place – and yet had somehow not gone. Not yet. Spirits hung around, people said. They hung around until the funeral. Then they went over to the Other Side.

Shadows everywhere. Was one of them Cora's?

Was she angry with him for being here?

I'm intruding into someone else's life, someone else's death and I'm only doing this because I'm nosy, because I want the chance to snoop around the great actress Cora Burstridge's home.

Not true!

I'm doing this to help you, Cora.

He looked into the Hannington's bag again. There was a receipt at the bottom and he lifted that out. Brittany's little outfit had cost fifty-seven pounds.

That was a staggering amount!

I spent fifty-seven pounds I could not afford on an outfit for my little grandchild. I wanted to see her rolling around in it. I wanted to hear her gurgling in it. I was going to mail it to her, and then a few weeks later I was going to get sent a whole roll of Kodak prints of Brittany in her new outfit, and I was going to put them on the mantelpiece and in the kitchen, and keep some in my handbag.

Glen put the receipt back in the bag. Then he tugged

from his pocket his rubber gloves, and pulled them on.
Cora Burstridge had not committed suicide.

No way in hell.

Chapter Fifty

A gap in her memory. Darkness inside her head. Darkness outside.

Darkness in her ears, in her eyes, in her mouth, in her lungs. She breathed in darkness and breathed it out. Smelt darkness.

Her eyes hunting, the pull of their muscles giving her their bearings, finding nothing, not in any direction, not up, down, right, left.

She was lying on her back, she knew that much. Nothing else.

Exhaustion. Her bones felt as if they had been filled with lead. Too sapped to fight against the pull of gravity, she lay motionless, left high and dry on a dark beach of consciousness by the retreating tide of sleep.

Breathing.

In some kind of waking state. Hypnogogic, hypnopompic, Amanda's mind rambled. Waking states. Hypnogogic was the confused dream-state you were in when you were drifting off, hypnopompic was the confused dream-state you were in when you were waking. Or maybe it was the other way around.

She tried to remember where she was. What place did she know that had darkness this dark?

She was cold but she was perspiring. Water was beading off her skin, down through her clothes, through her hair. She shivered. Cold, hot, cold, hot.

Feverish.

The darkness smelt of concrete and of something else, like disinfectant, but not disinfectant. She knew this smell, it was familiar, an old smell that was triggering recognition but not memory.

Am I dead?

Let's take this one step at a time.

Amanda closed her eyes, the lashes crunching softly against each other in the silence, then opened them again. There was no difference. Darkness. Her throat was sore. Darkness. She blinked. Darkness.

Too hot.

I *know* this smell.

She wondered, panic starting to unravel her calm, whether she had gone blind during the night. It happened. People went to sleep and woke up blind. Strokes. Detached retinas. Panic unspooling inside her now, she groped with a hand for the light switch. Her bedside table was on the right. On it were a glass of water, a handkerchief, a wristwatch, clock radio and lamp.

Nothing. Her hand found cold, coarse, hard . . . Now her brain was whipping up a blizzard of confused thoughts.

Stone? Concrete?

She blinked again, squeezed her eyelids shut and, in the silence, listened to her heartbeat. She could feel the muscles flexing away inside her chest, catching sometimes, vibrating, speeding and slowing. Blood hissing in her ears as if she had conch shells pressed over them.

Oh, Christ, please, dear God, don't let me be blind.

She tried to concentrate her hearing, to listen for the sound of sleeping. For Michael? For Brian? She moved a hand through the darkness, searching for contact, but her fingers found only more cold, coarse stone.

Tell me where I am, someone. Tell me what has happened. Tell me what this smell is that is like a hospital but not like a hospital.

Am I in hospital?

Please tell me I'm not blind.

Her body told her she was on a mattress. Her hand told her the mattress was on a stone floor. The smell was her clue. She clung to it, a cloying, astringent reek that stung her eyes, her throat.

There must be a light switch. A bell. There are always bells in hospital. Above the bed. She reached up her hand, but it found nothing, no wall, no switch, no bell. Just empty darkness.

Her ears were hurting, popping, panic filling them with pressure, like going up in an aircraft, or down with a scuba tank. She found her nose, pinched it, blew. Her ears cleared but the panic threw other switches inside her. She was gulping air, her legs banging together. Starting to freak out.

Calm down. Listen. Work this out.

It was as quiet as a tomb all around her.

Try to remember, she told herself. *Work backwards.* But from when? Now? She was in bed with Michael, they were making love, they –

A car had been parked outside. A man in it had been watching them.

Brian?

She shivered. Her hand found her mouth. She sucked the edge of a finger and the flesh was warm. It was good to feel contact, a relief to feel something living in this darkness, even if it was only part of herself.

I need to pee.

I don't know where the lavatory is.

Oh, sweet Jesus, I can't be blind.

She pushed her bladder thought away. Got to figure this out, got to remember where I am. Then I will remember where the light switch is and I can find the lavatory. Not blind, it's dark, that's all.

NOT BLIND.

Can work this out from the clothes I'm wearing. She touched her left wrist, and the Rolex that Brian had bought her years back was still there. She cursed that the dial wasn't luminous. Now she felt down her body. She was wearing a T-shirt. Her Versace jeans, she could feel the metal Versace bobble. Her favourite belt that she had bought in a shop in Menorca two years ago. No tights. Flat black shoes.

Wearing these clothes – yesterday? With Michael, at the stock-car racing. It was all coming back now. Then she had

222

gone on to Lara's. Georgia's fourth birthday party. The conjuror had produced a white rabbit from inside a glass jam jar.

And then?

Drove back to –

Blank.

Her hand found stone and air. Her need to urinate was worsening. Got to get up, stand up, find my bearings, this is ridiculous.

Maybe I'm dreaming.

Yes. Dreaming. Good. This is just a lucid dream, I will wake up in a minute.

She rolled over onto her side, off the mattress, onto her knees on the stone floor, then stood up. Disoriented by the darkness she swayed, stumbled, then fell, hit the ground hard and cried out, her hand stinging from a graze.

Jesus.

Her head was spinning. She got back onto her knees. Then upright again, more slowly this time. Upright now. Steady. Stand still and hold it there. Good girl.

My throat is sore.

I drove back to London after Georgia's fourth birthday party. I arrived at home, I parked the car, I took my handbag, locked the car, unlocked the front door of the building, went into the hallway, checked for any mail even though it was Sunday.

And then?

Blank again.

Fogged film.

Dark, murky liquid slopped around inside her mind. A sheet of bromide paper clacked from side to side in a tray, an image forming. The image was a man coming down the stairs that led up to her flat, a tall, good-looking man, his hand outstretched in a greeting. Big easy smile on his face, the smile of an old friend, yet she couldn't place him, couldn't remember ever having seen him before.

'Amanda! Great to see you! What on earth are you doing here?'

He shook her hand. She felt a light prick in her palm, as if

223

perhaps a ring he was wearing had dug into her skin. She still couldn't place him.

'I live here!' she remembered saying.

Then blank.

Chapter Fifty-one

North London. Heavy lunch-time traffic, people on the move, the whole city caught by the sudden weather shift, jackets off, ties loosened, sodden armpits. Like his own. All traces of yesterday's rain had gone and the wide avenue with its grimy Victorian houses felt as arid as it looked. Already the leaves on the trees looked dusty.

Michael's shirt clung to his chest and there was just one cool area in the small of his back where his sweat lay pooled. He crawled up Rosslyn Hill in the Volvo, behind a smoky lorry, his A–Z open on his lap, regretting now that he hadn't gone for the air-conditioning option when he'd bought the car. He had the windows down, the roof open, the fan going full blast in his face. Pages of the map riffled in the draught, and every few seconds the brochure that lay beside his mobile phone on the passenger seat flapped open and shut.

It had been biked over to him by Amanda's assistant, Lulu. It advertised the services of 20–20 Vision, and contained two pictures of Amanda. One, two inches high, had a brief career resumé beneath it, the other was an action long-shot and Amanda's face was scarcely bigger than a microdot.

Amanda, where on earth are you? What has happened?

She could be lying in her upturned car in a ditch. Brian might have kidnapped and killed her in a fit of rage. Jealousy turned people's minds. She could have drowned, or lost her memory and be wandering around. People flipped, sometimes they lost their grip on reality.

Or –

He pushed the thought away that some stranger might

have abducted her. Fred and Rosemary West had been caught, but there were still other monsters out there every bit as bad.

Oh God, Amanda, please be all right.

It was ten to one. Thelma, his secretary at the Sheen Park Hospital, had come up trumps: she'd managed to reschedule his last patient of the morning and the first two of the afternoon, which gave him a three-and-a-half-hour window before Terence Goel, whom she had been unable to contact, arrived at three forty-five. Michael had calculated that he should be comfortably back by then. He would have to be. He would never let a patient down.

As he drove up the hill he saw the police station immediately ahead of him across the road, a rather grand-looking red-brick building sporting a massive flagpole with nothing hanging from it. Hampstead was the most local police station to Amanda's flat, and the detective he had spoken to required him to come in and make a statement. He wasn't prepared to take it over the phone.

Michael parked in a side-street, pocketed his mobile phone, hoping that at any second it was going to ring, hoping desperately to hear Lulu's voice saying that Amanda had turned up and everything was fine.

He buttoned his collar, straightened his tie, then climbed out and pulled on his lightweight navy suit jacket. Then he scooped up the brochure, entered the station and went up to the side of the counter marked 'Detailed Inquiries'. There was a bell with a sign saying 'RING FOR ATTENTION.' On the wall was a crime-prevention poster warning GRASSED UP, BANGED UP, AS A MUGGER YOU ARE NEVER SAFE. Beside it was another poster, with a colour photograph of a small boy and across the top, the words MISSING – HAVE YOU SEEN THIS CHILD?

He could see several desks and phones on the far side of the counter, all unmanned. The only other person in here was a grubby-looking girl, late teens or early twenties, sitting sullenly on a chair in the waiting area, holding an equally sullen-looking dog, a boxer-collie cross, he guessed, on a short chain.

He pressed the button, which vibrated hard with a sharp ring. After a few moments a door opened and a WPC came up to the counter. 'Are you being seen to?'

'I have an appointment to see Detective Constable Gilpin.'

'And your name please?'

'Dr Tennent.'

'Right, I'll see if I can find him for you. I have a feeling I saw him go out.' She looked at a chart of numbers, lifted a phone and dialled. After a moment she said, 'Hi, it's Sue at the front desk – is Roger there? No, I thought so. There's a Dr Tennent who has an appointment with him.' She nodded, then turned to Michael. 'I'm afraid he's been called out on an emergency. Did you especially need to see DC Gilpin, or could someone else help you?'

'I want to report a missing person,' Michael said, swallowing the rise of anger he felt. *This* was an emergency. Amanda could be in extreme danger. Equally, he'd had several patients over the years whose children had gone missing, and he was only too uncomfortably aware of how little the police could do to find missing people, unless there was clear evidence of a crime.

A couple of minutes later the door opened again, and a gentle-looking bear of a man came through it, in an open-necked yellow shirt. He was in his early thirties, with a hefty rugby-player's frame, but overweight and uncomfortable in this heat, Michael judged from the sweat streaming down his cheeks and his sodden shirt front. He had fair hair cropped to a fuzz and a big, slightly rubbery, baby face.

He looked quizzically at Michael. 'Dr Tennent?'

'Yes.'

'I'm sorry, DC Gilpin has been called out, can I help you?' He had soft, kind eyes, and a quiet voice, but looked nonetheless like a man well able to take care of himself in a fight.

'Yes, I want to report someone missing – it's serious. There is something very definitely wrong.'

The officer frowned. 'Dr Tennent? You wouldn't by any chance be the Dr Tennent that's on the radio?'

'Yes.' Michael was pleased at the recognition: this might help him to be taken more seriously.

The officer smiled. 'My fiancée's a great fan of your programme! Never misses it.'

'Thank you,' Michael said.

'She really rates you. She'll be well chuffed when I tell her I met you! Come through to an interview room. Would you like a tea or a coffee?'

'I'd love some coffee,' Michael said. Then, although he never normally took sugar, he added, 'White with sugar.'

They sat in a small, claustrophobically hot room, with one tiny frosted-glass window high up that didn't open. It reeked of stale cigarette smoke. There was a fan, which the officer switched on, then he seated himself opposite Michael at the battered metal table, opened a notepad and took out a biro. The room reminded Michael of the radio studio; it even had the same brown colours. The fan pushed the air around, without cooling it much.

After he had taken down Amanda's basic details, the officer asked, 'Was Miss Capstick depressed at all? Or suffering from any mental disorder?'

'Not in my opinion, no.'

Watching Michael's face carefully. 'Was there any disagreement between you?'

'Absolutely not. We . . .' Michael checked himself then decided the officer should know the truth. 'I don't think either of us could have been in a happier frame of mind when we last saw each other.'

'All right. Can you tell me what happened the last time you saw her?'

Michael gave the officer all the details he could; it was a laborious affair, waiting for him to write everything down. When he had finished, Michael handed him the brochure, showing Amanda's photographs inside it.

The officer looked at them. 'Very attractive young lady.' He handed back the brochure.

'Don't you want to keep it?' Michael asked, surprised.

'Not at this stage, sir.'

Michael looked at him angrily. 'What do you mean, *not at this stage*?'

'Sir, with respect, it has been less than forty-eight hours. Obviously we want to help all we can, but this isn't a long time for someone to be absent. Miss Capstick is not suffering from any mental illness. For all we know she might have decided she needs a little space on her own.'

'Forty-eight hours is plenty long enough for her to have bled to death if she's in a wrecked car somewhere, or to have been murdered.'

The officer put down his pen and leaned forward, studying Michael's face intently. 'What do you think might have happened, sir?'

The man's scrutiny made him feel uncomfortable. He knew the police would be bound to have some suspicions about him, as one of the last people to see her, and for reporting her missing.

Michael told him about Amanda's relationship with Brian, and her concern about the car that had been sitting outside his house, and the officer made notes about this.

'She had no enemies, so far as you were aware, sir?'

'Not that she mentioned.'

'Did she appear in any of the documentaries she made? As an interviewer or narrator?'

'I'm not sure. Why?'

The officer shrugged. 'Celebrities often get targeted by stalkers. It's only a thought at this stage. I wouldn't get alarmed.'

'It's very hard not to be alarmed. Amanda is not some flake, she's a very bright, very together, sensible person. Even if she never wanted to see me again in her life, there is no way she would fail to turn up to business meetings and not make contact with her office.'

'I'm afraid it happens more frequently than you think, sir. People disappear, then turn up days later with perfectly acceptable explanations. I'm sure as a psychiatrist you must have encountered people who have done this.'

Michael had, but he was reluctant to acknowledge this. He stared back at the man, not wanting to give him any leeway. He wanted the police to get out there and start searching for Amanda. Right now.

'So what are you going to do? Anything?' he asked, testily.

'At this stage, sir, we'll circulate details to other police forces in Sussex and London that Miss Capstick has been reported as a missing person.' He smiled to try to give Michael some reassurance. 'Dr Tennent, I'll keep a special eye on this for you and make sure that everyone knows about it, but beyond that there isn't much more we can do at this stage.'

'When can you do more about it?' Michael asked, frustration fuelling his anger now. 'When you find her body?'

The officer had the grace to blush a little. 'Two hundred and fifty thousand people are reported missing every year, sir. Most of them turn up again. I'm sure she will and that she's fine, sir.' He fished in his top pocket and pulled out a card. 'Any time you need to contact me, day or night, it has my direct line and my mobile.' Then he turned it over and wrote on the back. 'I've added my home number, sir, as it's you. Please call me if you hear anything – or if you just want to talk more about it.'

Michael took the card and looked at it.

The name printed on it was Detective Constable Simon Roebuck.

Chapter Fifty-two

Dresses. Shoes. Hat boxes. Wigs. Silk scarves. Jewellery boxes. Two entire rooms in Cora Burstridge's flat were full of nothing else. Glen found it hard to believe how many clothes the star had had.

He found a diamond-studded antique Cartier watch in one box that was just sitting on top of a chest of drawers, and more fine jewellery lying around in cupboards and drawers.

Everything was generally tidy – or as tidy as this massive jumble of stuff could ever be. There were certainly no tell-tale signs that an intruder had been rummaging around. Not until he opened the door to the broom closet in the kitchen.

There was disarray in here. A bucket and pail had been knocked over; the handle of a carpet sweeper lay awkwardly on a crate of sherry bottles; several cloths had come off their hooks and fallen onto objects below them; a dustpan and brush had been dislodged and lay on the floor along-side a tin of Brasso, which had leaked out its contents.

A gleam of light shone above his head. It was coming through a loft hatch that was very slightly ajar.

Was someone up there now?

He froze.

The hatch cover was only a foot above his head. He could reach up and touch it easily with his gloved hands. Listening, he stood still, held his breath. His radio crackled and he switched it off, tuned his ears into the loft. Nothing. Music playing faintly under him, a piano tinkling – maybe the flat below?

Reaching up, he placed his palms against the cover. He

was over six foot tall, Cora would have needed a step-ladder. Where was it? When did you last go up here, Cora?

He pushed the cover further open. In the stark light he could see up into the rafters. They looked in OK condition, a few flaps of roofing felt hanging down, that was all. Moving the wooden cover carefully aside, he gripped the edges of the hatch and hauled himself up.

As his head rose up into the loft, he saw the figure towering above him, looking down icily.

A rash of goosebumps erupted on his skin. He let go involuntarily, and crashed down. *Oh, fuck, oh, fuck, oh, sweet Jesus!*

He was backing out of the closet, his heart berserk inside his chest. All he could see was the figure, the cold smile, the glossed lips, the long blonde hair, the full-length black silk dress.

Get a fucking grip, man!

Just an almighty bloody scary-looking mannequin.

Remembering now. Of course. *The Lady Is Out.* One of Cora Burstridge's best films, a real shocker, in which she played the demented victim of a stalker, Anthony Perkins in a reprise of his *Psycho* role. In the climax scene, she had set a trap for him by having this mannequin dressed up to look like her, and standing it in a room behind a net curtain while she waited behind the door with an axe and butchered him when he came in.

He went back into the closet, but slowly, hauled himself up and looked again. The sight of the mannequin was almost as bad the second time. Watching it carefully now, taking his time, just to make sure – that it didn't move, that it wasn't a ghost.

The face had been made up with exquisite care in every detail; it looked horribly, terrifyingly real. 'Nice sense of humour, Cora,' he whispered, wishing he could share this little joke with her, but not quite able to.

He heaved his whole body up into the loft, his feet kicking out at the walls for a grip. This was how the cloths had come to be on the floor, he thought, and probably the dustpan and brush and the Brasso tin.

On his knees, he looked around. A solitary lightbulb hung from a flex a short distance in front of him. A large water cistern. Suitcases and trunks piled all around. Stacks of pictures or paintings wrapped in brown paper and tied with string, coated in years of dust. The mannequin, too, was dusty, and a large cobweb had been spun on the wig.

This was a treasure trove of Cora Burstridge memorabilia, and Glen would have loved to have had the time to explore it. Instead, he hefted himself upright and concentrated on his task.

Maybe Cora had come up here and left the light on. OK, I'm Cora, what am I looking for? I've come home from buying my grandchild Brittany a Babygro. I have people sending me flowers, phoning me to congratulate me on my BAFTA award. So I put down the bag with Brittany's present, I get out the steps, I climb up into the loft. What am I looking for?

Something for Brittany? Something that winning this award has reminded me to look for?

Glen pulled out a small torch he had brought with him, switched it on and ran the beam over each of the trunks, suitcases, brown-wrapped parcels. Dust, cobwebs, mouse droppings. None of these cases had been opened for months – years, maybe.

Careful to step only on the joists, and keeping his head ducked against the low rafters, he made his way across the loft into the darkness beyond the throw of the lightbulb. Then he stopped and turned to look at the mannequin. It spooked the hell out of him again. And his bald head touched a large spider's web. He jumped, then brushed it away in revulsion. As he did so he felt the feet of the spider running around his neck, and he snatched at it with his hand, shuddering. 'Yuk! Get away!'

He scrunched his shoulders and shook himself. As he did so, the beam of his torch caught what he thought at first was a moth hanging asleep on a wooden upright.

Free of the spider now, he walked over and looked closer. It was a tiny strip of cloth hanging from a nail. Shoulder-high to him.

233

He looked at it closer still. Cream threads. Had Cora snagged herself up here? But Cora was only five foot four. This would have been head-high to her.

He left it as it was, without touching it, and walked on, over towards a rectangle of light he could see at the far end of the loft. As he got closer, playing the beam of his torch on it, he could see it was an ancient fire-escape door. Rusted, probably disused for years.

It was secured by a padlocked hatch. Except the hatch had come away from the door and was hanging, twisted, four rusted screws still in place in it, four gaping holes in the door where they had been.

Someone had kicked this door open. Recently.

Chapter Fifty-three

In 1966 the BBC banned from transmission a documentary made for them by director Peter Watkins, about a fictional H-bomb attack on Britain. It was called *The War Game*. It included footage of shadows on walls in Hiroshima that were the vaporised remains of tens of thousands of people caught in the atomic blast. It showed footage of others, even less fortunate, whose entire body skin was sloughing off them as they ran in blind, screaming agony.

In the notoriety following its banning, *The War Game* became compulsive viewing in art-house cinemas and at private screenings. Gloria Lamark saw it at a special invitation-only preview at the National Film Theatre. Afterwards, like a lot of other people who had been terrified by it, she commissioned the construction of a nuclear shelter beneath her home. It would be dug out beneath the house's existing cellar and its walls were to be of three-yards-thick concrete.

In common with others who had built such shelters, Gloria Lamark kept it quiet. In the event of a nuclear attack, anyone who knew about your shelter would kill you to get in there first. She went to elaborate detail to disguise the shelter's existence. If you took the staircase down at the back of the hallway, you would find yourself in a small gymnasium containing an exercise bicycle, some weights, a rowing-machine and a jogging-machine. A wooden door led into a small sauna. The entrance lay through a door below this sauna, of the kind used on bank vaults.

Beyond the door was a chamber, monitored by a closed-circuit television camera. A second vault door, with a similar lock, opened onto a spiral staircase down to the shelter itself, which was accessed by yet a third door.

The shelter was a small network of rooms, each hermetically sealed by steel doors, like the watertight compartments of a ship. If one room developed a leak, the others would still be free of contamination. There was ventilation ducting, and provision for a generator-run air-purification plant and a water-purification system. Gloria Lamark had intended that she and Tom-Tom could remain down here for months if necessary, living off tinned food and bottled water.

However, the costs of constructing the shelter had been astronomic, even by her own extravagant standards. The shell had been completed in 1965, but by then her fears had subsided a little. She never completed plumbing it, nor did she put in the air purifier or the food stocks. Instead she had locks put on the outside of the doors and sometimes imprisoned Thomas there during his early childhood when he was bad. She stopped this after he reached his teens, and never entered the shelter after 1975. In fact, she had virtually forgotten all about it.

But Thomas hadn't.

And now, in a sealed chamber deep inside the shelter, thirty feet beneath the ground-floor rooms of the house, Amanda Capstick lay in darkness, deafened by her own heartbeat.

She had fallen again. Tripped over the mattress. She lay still, ear to the cold stone floor, listening. But the darkness was so loud. It sucked each rasp of her breath then echoed it back, the volume turned up as far as it would go. Her ears pulsed with fear. She was a mass of pulses, that was all, pulses, driven by one beat. Pulses, thoughts, pain – those were all that separated her from the void around her. The need to urinate, that separated her, too.

She got back on her feet again, feeling more alert with every moment that passed, trying frantically to figure out where she was.

One step at a time.

Starting with this giddying darkness; scouring it, smelling it, still trying to work out what that acrid reek was. She was finding it hard to stay upright. Every few moments she would become disoriented and stumble against a wall, or trip on the mattress and fall.

Surely, however dark a place is, there must be some light – under a door, around a window, through a crack in the ceiling? But not here. Nothing. No relief from the desperate blackness of the void.

She touched her own body, checking it out, finding reassurance that she was still solid, still flesh. She pushed her fingers through her hair. Not dead. Definitely not dead.

She had filmed once in a ward full of stroke victims. Some people could be trapped, deaf, dumb and blind, inside their bodies, with their consciousness still functioning normally.

Me?

If I could find my handbag. Cigarette lighter in there.

The need to urinate was starting to dominate her thoughts. She could fight it off, but every few minutes it came back, worse than before. Now another rush came and this time the pain of fighting it was so bad that a tear rolled down her cheek. She stood, hunched against a wall, legs crossed, shaking, perspiring, her insides twisting as if someone was winding a tourniquet in there.

Then, finally, the wave passed. She was OK again, for a few minutes.

If I was in a hospital, paralysed, blind, I would have a catheter.

She called out again for help. But the mere effort of shouting brought another rush from her bladder, and now, again, she put all other thoughts out of her head.

Loo. Jesus. There must be a loo.

Find a loo and then – and then think straight.

Her left hand was hurting like hell from the last time she had fallen over. With her right hand, she began to feel the walls. Methodical. *Must be methodical.* One inch at a time, top to bottom. She reached down to the floor, then up, as far as she could stretch. Cold smooth stone.

I got in here somehow, so there must be a way out.

Wild thoughts flashing in her head now. Did Michael

Tennent have something to do with this? Brian? Who was the man who had come down the stairs and shaken her hand?

She stumbled, lost the wall, tried to find it. Her arms flailed, she let out a frightened yelp as she fell again, crashing hard on the stone floor, her face finding the mattress, the dank, musty, old-smelling mattress. She swept the floor with her arms, every inch of the floor, looking for her handbag. It wasn't there.

'Oh, God, please someone help me!'

On her knees again. Upright. Calming. Deep breath. Steady, balancing now, taking it easy, one step at a time, over to the wall. Start again.

Her hands moving again across smooth stone. She tried to tell herself that this was one of those really bad dreams of being trapped, running on the spot while the train bears down on you, or the murderer is coming towards you and your legs won't work.

But the pressure of her bladder told her she wasn't dreaming. She was awake. She was pressing against the wall again, legs crossed, swearing now, anger leaching out through her gritted teeth.

I am not going to wet my knickers. I am not going to piss on this floor.

Sweet Jesus, I am not.

Chapter Fifty-four

'Do you know about the bower-bird, Dr Tennent? Are you interested in ornithology?'

The lawnmower was at it again outside in the garden of the clinic. The heavy traffic, all the way back from Hampstead, had done nothing for Michael's frayed nerves, and now Dr Terence Goel, sitting relaxed on his sofa, in a cream linen suit and moccasin loafers, was doing nothing for his nerves either.

Each time Michael asked him a question he answered with a question. Michael had removed his jacket, but sweat was still running off him. The air in this office was oppressively hot; it had been mitigated a little by the scent of cut grass, but now it was heavy with the pungent cologne that Dr Goel was wearing.

'The bower-bird? I don't, no. Is ornithology one of your interests?'

The drone of the mower was getting louder still. Michael sipped some water, glanced down at the American's file.

'How do you define an *interest*, Dr Tennent? At what point does *knowledge* become *interest*?'

'When do you think it does?' Michael asked.

Goel placed his palms flat on the cushion either side of him, leaned back and stared with a worried look at the ceiling. '*Ptilonorhynchus violaceous*.' He looked at Michael and, in response to the psychiatrist's blank expression, added, 'The satin bower-bird. Have you heard of the *satin* bower-bird?'

'I'm afraid not.'

'It mixes pigment from berries and charcoal. It builds a bower like a thatched house, nine feet high, with rooms. It manicures the lawn beneath each day and decorates it with insect skeletons and fresh flowers. Then it constructs an avenue of sticks leading up to its home, fabricates a paintbrush out of fibrous plant material, then decorates this avenue with the pigments it has mixed. It is the only animal in the world other than humans that makes tools and decorates its home. You have to admire that, don't you, Dr Tennent?'

'Yes,' Michael said, guardedly, as before with Goel, not knowing where this was leading. He waited for his patient to continue.

Dr Goel stared back at the ceiling. Michael glanced at his notes from their previous session. Goel had talked to him then about prisms, he had explained why stars twinkled. He appeared to like imparting seemingly irrelevant facts. Michael was having to make a supreme effort to keep up his concentration. Amanda, he kept thinking. Amanda, my love, where are you? *Where are you?*

'Are you knowledgeable about ornithology, Dr Tennent?'

'You just asked me that. No, I'm afraid not.'

'I don't think I asked you,' he said.

Michael made a note in the file. Terence Goel seemed to forget things. A defence mechanism.

Thomas Lamark watched Dr Tennent. *You are not having a good day today, are you, Dr Michael Tennent? You think I'm a screwed-up psychotic who forgets things he has just said. You can't wait for this session to end. You are worried sick about your bit of fluff, Amanda Capstick. You have good reason to be worried about her. You should be desperately worried. You should be even more worried than you are.*

And you will be.

'Did you know that many bird species mate for life?' Dr Goel said.

Michael paused before responding, hoping to encourage Goel to continue speaking. But Goel was waiting for him.

'No, I didn't.'

'If they lose their mate they just pine and die.' Now he fixed his eyes firmly on Michael.

Breaking contact and looking discreetly down at his

notes, Michael remembered now that, at the last consultation, Goel had brought up the subject of car crashes. He recalled wondering then whether the man knew about Katy. Now he wondered again. No, he concluded, probably not; almost certainly not. He was just making this connection himself.

'Do you think, Dr Tennent, there would be a difference in the way the male bower-bird would mourn its mate depending on how the mate died?'

Remembering Goel's Achilles heel, his parents, Michael replied, 'I don't think I'm qualified to make that judgement. Let's talk a little bit about you. You're coming to see me because you're suffering from depression. We didn't get very far last time. I'd like to know a little more about you. Perhaps you could give me a brief life history.'

'I'd like to ask you something first, Dr Tennent. Something that is bothering me.'

'Go ahead.'

'I read an article which said that too many people of the video generation are convinced they have what it takes to kill in cold blood. I'm a child of this video generation, but it seems to me that civilisation is a thin veneer over basic human nature, and basic human nature has no problem with killing at all. Would you agree with that?'

Michael was determined to make his patient talk more. He turned the question back to him. 'Do you?'

Goel closed his eyes. 'I'd like to consider the bower-bird a little further. There are all kinds of hazards that face a bird. Imagine a bower-bird is flying free, and she does not see power lines stretched across her path. She flies into these power lines and is killed by the impact. She falls to the ground.'

He opened his eyes, stared at the psychiatrist, then continued, 'Now imagine this bower-bird is flying free, and she lands in a trap that is set by a hunter who is collecting birds to sell to zoos. He has a specific commission to capture a bower-bird. Her mate, the male bower-bird, is out elsewhere, gathering food. Which would be the most traumatic, do you think, Dr Tennent? To see the corpse of his mate? Or for his mate simply not to return home?'

Michael squirmed in his chair. The man's eyes were fixed on him. Jesus, if only this man knew how close to the knuckle he was. He wasn't in any kind of a state to answer this question right now, that was the truth. It felt like his patient had tipped over a barrow inside his head.

Amanda. Amanda darling. Call! Call me, tell me you are OK, oh God, Amanda, call me.

Under the guise of looking at the man's file, Michael glanced at his watch. Twenty minutes still to go. He wanted to call Amanda's secretary, Lulu, just to hear her voice, to feel some kind of proximity to Amanda.

And Thomas Lamark was finding it hard to keep his face straight. This was perfection! He had liked as a child to capture insects – flies were good, big ones, bluebottles were best – and then to stick a pin through one wing and press the point into a table top, and to watch the fly struggling, to feel the insect's confusion as it went through all the motions of flying, but could not.

'Let's . . .' Michael said, but he had lost the thread. He tried to regain his equilibrium. 'Which – ah – which do *you* think would be the most traumatic?'

Terence Goel slipped his hand into his jacket pocket, then pulled out a coin. He tossed it, then trapped it on the back of his hand. 'Call,' he said. 'Heads or tails?'

Michael was not sure whether to go along with this. Then curiosity got the better of him. 'OK,' he said. 'Heads.'

Terence Goel lifted his other hand. 'Good call.'

'And tails would have been a bad call?'

Goel smiled. 'No, that would have been a good call too. One's good for you and one's good for me.'

'Is that a gold coin?' Michael asked.

'An heirloom.' Goel slipped it back into his pocket.

'Do you use it to make decisions?'

'How do you make decisions, Dr Tennent?'

The session was fast heading out of control. Before they had begun, Michael had studied his notes from the previous week. At the last session Goel had produced an endless string of *non sequiturs*, and they'd achieved nothing. He was doing the same again now. Evading the real issue. Blocking it out. Talking about anything but.

Maybe this was his problem? Goel clearly had an obsession with death, and another with loss. And he definitely had a slanted handle on reality. Where did the roots of all this lie? Had he lost someone he loved?

Almost certainly.

'I'd like to know something about your childhood, Terence,' he said, deliberately switching to his first name. 'Let's talk about your family life when you were a child.'

The effect was like turning a switch off. Goel seemed to shrink in on himself. He sat motionless on the sofa, frozen like a wax tableau in an art gallery labelled MAN ON COUCH.

Nothing that Michael said could snap him out of it, or elicit a response. Not until he said, finally, 'Our time is up now.'

Then Goel rose and, without speaking to him, without looking at him, walked towards the door.

'If you see my secretary on the way out, she'll arrange your next appointment,' Michael said, secretly hoping that Dr Goel wouldn't bother.

Thomas Lamark wrote the next appointment down in his black leather diary. He was pleased, it had been a good session.

Perfect.

He played it back in his head as he drove Dr Goel's blue Ford Mondeo back towards Holland Park, looking forward to getting back to his bower. He drove gently, not wanting to shake around the box he had collected from Cheltenham that was still in the boot.

Looking forward to opening it.

Michael continued to think about Dr Goel during the rest of the morning. Something did not add up about the man. His doctor had referred him because he had diagnosed that he might be suffering clinical depression. Yet Goel did not act as if he was depressed.

With depression, people's self-esteem sank. They failed to take care of their appearance. They lost their social skills.

Dr Goel seemed to have a very high self-esteem. His body language was that of a confident man. He took immaculate care with his appearance. No way was this man depressed.

There was something very wrong with him for sure. A deep darkness. Psychotic, perhaps. A sociopath?

Not depression.

Chapter Fifty-five

The need to urinate was now a critical mass of pain inside Amanda. She was not going to be able to hold out much longer.

Then her hands found an opening in the wall. A door!
How the hell did I miss this before?

It was impossible that she could have missed it: she was certain she had been all the way around, many times.

Who had opened it?

Jesus. Was someone else in here with her?

Knees knocking hard together, thighs gripping, pain shooting up through her kidneys, spiking right into her chest, she stepped into the gap. The open doorway. Stepped forward in small, agonising steps.

The smell was even more horrendous as she entered this new area of darkness. It was stinging her eyes, stripping her throat, hurting her lungs. But she could sense something in here.

A human presence.

She called out, in a voice so distant and choked that she barely recognised it as her own, 'Hallo?'

Loud black silence greeted her.

She kept inching forward, beyond the doorway now, feeling her way along another smooth wall. Then, suddenly, in spite of her cautious pace, her feet struck something solid that caught them out, her hands lost contact with the wall, she stumbled, windmilling her arms in the darkness, then fell forward, crashing down on a hard, lumpy object.

'Sorry,' Amanda said. 'Sorry. I'm –'

No movement from this rocky unyielding mass beneath

her. Her hand was touching something soft. Soft, yet coarse at the same time.

The reek of this chemical was unbearable.

Hair! She shivered. She had fallen on some dead animal. As she jerked her hand back it touched something cold and rubbery. And this was unmistakable.

This was a human face.

Whimpering, she snatched away her hand, backed off, tried, desperately, to find the doorway into the other chamber, understanding now, remembering the smell, from the biology lab at school. The chemical that frogs and other animals were preserved in.

Formalin.

Then she fell over the second body.

She screamed her lungs out into the darkness.

But the darkness had no sounds to offer back, beyond those of her own terror.

Then the warm trickle of water between her legs. But she was beyond caring about that now.

Chapter Fifty-six

Glen Branson's immediate boss was Detective Sergeant Bill Digby, who occupied a small office of his own across the corridor from the detectives' room at Hove police station.

Mid-afternoon on Tuesday found him in a sour mood.

Digby was a quiet, deep man. Burly, with a narrow, military moustache and crinkly black hair, he looked old-fashioned in contrast with some of the sharp young turks of the detectives' room. He acted in an old-fashioned manner too, always steady, methodical, rarely panicked, seldom rushing except on the dozen or so occasions a year when he was called to a murder scene; then he was out of the door at an altogether different speed. Digby, like most police officers, was as fascinated by murder as the general public; hardened, yes, but always hooked.

Some people thought that because he was slow Bill Digby was probably a bit thick; but those people didn't know him well. His hobby was playing Scrabble, and he had won his share of regional tournaments. In his work he applied the same laborious, tortuous methodology with which he played that game. He never liked to make a move until he had considered the maximum possible value that could be gained from it.

The detective sergeant had clocked twenty-five years in the force. He'd been shot at, knifed, hauled over the coals for blowing the prosecution of a burglar by a breach of procedure, and he'd once had a brick with a dead cat attached to it thrown through his living-room window by the family of an armed building-society robber he'd just seen sent down for twelve years.

He was a survivor. A big part of policing was making

decisions that were tough, and not always fair. Every newly reported incident in the county requiring police action appeared on his computer screen; on an average day a new one appeared every sixty seconds. Almost five hundred thousand incidents had been logged last year.

Most were minor. With only limited resources, senior officers had to make decisions all the time about what should be investigated and what should be ignored. The police were judged on results. Statistics. Villains in court. *Convictions. Winning a better quality of life for the community.* Winning the war against crime. Stopping icebergs. Walking on water. Take your choice, Digby thought sometimes, when he became exasperated, they were equally impossible.

Most of the work of detectives was relatively small-scale: burglaries, robberies, assaults, fraud, but occasionally something big came along. And when it did, if you handled it right you could get yourself noticed for promotion – and on some substantial cases, you could end up making a significant contribution to the community.

Operation Skeet had had such potential. Detective Chief Inspector Gaylor, his direct boss at this station, had given him free rein with it, and believing in his abilities, Gaylor hadn't even put a detective inspector over him.

Using a network of informers run by Glen's fellow detective, Mike Harris, Bill Digby had spent three years building a case file on a local ring of drug traffickers who were importing cocaine through Shoreham, the local commercial seaport. At night the drugs, in weighted packages and tagged with low-frequency lost-golf-ball transmitters, were dropped overboard, then collected, also in darkness, by divers.

The mastermind was a known paedophile Welshman, Tam Hywell, a creep whose cunning Digby respected but whom he put on the bottom rung of the social food chain, somewhere between a tapeworm and slime mould. With less charm than either.

Four weeks ago Operation Skeet, on a textbook-perfect dawn raid, had netted the entire ring. Digby had enough on Tam Hywell to be confident of making him sing his heart out in court. Either Hywell came clean on his drugs operation, turned prosecution witness and gave them all they wanted to know, or he would be prosecuted on a charge of procuring small boys. Hywell knew that no one in their right mind would want to enter a British prison convicted of a sexual offence involving children.

Against all Digby's entreaties, a smart-arse solicitor had convinced a dithering stipendiary magistrate to grant Hywell bail. And on this past Sunday morning, one of Hywell's neighbours had reported an intolerable smell coming from the penthouse where Hywell lived alone. When the police broke in they found the bloody remains of the man. He had been hacked to death with a machete, his tongue had been cut out of his mouth and replaced with his genitals.

The detective sergeant was looking at the scene-of-crime photographs now, and trying to work out just how much damage Hywell's death would have done to his chances of securing convictions on the others.

He looked up, his thoughts interrupted by a rap on the door. Before he could say anything, it opened, and DC Glen Branson peered in. 'Got a moment, Sarge?'

Digby gestured for him to come in, and Glen sat down in the cramped space in front of his modest desk, then leaned forward, nosily looking at the photographs. 'Tammy Hywell?'

'Yeah.' Digby smiled drily because, with all his pent-up anger, he couldn't resist the line that had suddenly come into his head, and added, 'Looks a real dickhead, doesn't he?'

Glen resisted the temptation to reply with a further wisecrack. He sat back. 'Cora Burstridge,' he said. 'Last week?'

His sergeant nodded, with instant recall.

'I'm not happy. I'm not at all convinced it's suicide. I've done a little investigating –'

Digby interrupted him. 'On whose authorisation?'

'I did it in my own time, Sarge – I'm off today, I visited her flat this morning.'

Digby raised his eyebrows. Glen was a good man, ambitious, he liked him, but sometimes the inexperienced DC got too enthusiastic. 'OK, go on.'

Glen told him his thoughts about the Babygro Cora had bought for her grandchild, and about the fire-escape door in the loft that had been forced open, and about the pathologist's concern about the blowflies. Then he added, 'I did a check on the flats in the block behind, which overlooks that fire escape. One lady I spoke to says she saw a man with a clipboard going down that fire escape one afternoon early last week, Tuesday or Wednesday.'

'When did Cora Burstridge die?'

'The pathologist can't tell exactly. But he thinks, because it was first-stage maggots and blowflies, that she'd probably been there two days, which would be Tuesday. She was last seen going out shopping on Tuesday morning.'

'Not a very precise tally with this lady witness,' Digby said.

'No, Sarge, but I talked to the managing agents of Cora Burstridge's building to ask whether they had had any surveyor or workman in there last week, and they were categorical that no one had been there.'

'Did the building have a fire certificate?'

'Yes, current, issued November the nineteenth last year.'

'So why was this exit padlocked?'

'It's a disused route. There's a newer one, approached from the common parts of the building.'

Digby skewed his mouth to one side and briefly checked out the inside of his cheek with his tongue. 'The safety chain was applied from the inside, wasn't it?'

'That's my point!' Glen said. 'The safety chain was on. The windows were all locked from the inside. If there was an intruder, then he had to have climbed up into the loft after killing her and escaped that way. In his panic he didn't shut the hatch properly, he left the loft light on, and he had to break his way out.'

Digby scooped Tam Hywell's photographs together and

tapped them on the desk-top to line them up, before slipping them into an envelope. 'We searched her flat last Thursday. Why didn't we find the loft hatch open then?'

Glen shrugged. 'I've been asking myself that. I can only think we must have missed it.'

'Cora Burstridge was a very famous lady, Glen. Her death has made big news in all the national press. Don't you think some piece of scum might have taken the opportunity to break into her flat knowing it was empty?'

'I don't think anything's been taken, Sarge. There's jewellery, fine watches, beautiful art-deco ornaments all over the place. No burglar has been rummaging through there. It's tidy.'

'Unless you disturbed him when you went in?'

'It's a possibility.'

'You're assuming he came in through the front door of the flat and then left via the loft and fire exit. Are you sure he didn't come in that way, Glen?'

'There are no marks on the outside of that door – but I'd need someone from SOCO to take a look to confirm that. I'd like to have a SOCO examination of the entire flat and loft, Sarge. I found some clothing fibres on a nail in the loft, which again indicates someone in a hurry. There might be a lot else for them.'

Bill Digby sat in silence, considering Glen's request. 'You're aware of the costs of a forensic operation, aren't you, Glen?'

Glen was. Two hundred pounds per item of clothing or clothing fibre. Fifteen hundred pounds to process fingerprints. Putting the scene-of-crime team to do a thorough sweep of Cora Burstridge's flat would cost a minimum of ten thousand pounds.

'Yes, Sarge, I am. But I think the evidence justifies it.'

'You were at the post-mortem. Did the pathologist find any marks on the body?'

'No, Sarge.'

'You haven't seen the results of any tests on fluids yet?'

'No.'

Digby shook his head. 'We have a mountain of work on

251

Skeet now with Hywell dead. I just can't justify this, Glen. We have a doctor's report saying the deceased was depressed, a suicide note, the door locked from the inside, nothing appears to have been stolen. I hear everything you're saying, Glen, but it's not enough to convince me. She wasn't an invalid – if someone had tried to kill her, she would have fought back. There would be some signs of a struggle, some marks on her body.'

'She was elderly,' Glen said.

'But capable of going out shopping on her own. The time to raise these points, if you think it appropriate, will be at the inquest, but you don't have enough there to convince me we should be regarding this as a suspicious death. OK?'

Glen shrugged, disappointed, but he knew better than to press his argument any further right now. In his own mind, though, he had decided he wasn't just going to let it stop here.

'Tomorrow, early – you got anything fixed?'

'No, Sarge.'

'Good. I want you to accompany Mike Harris to Luton to bring down an informer on the Hywell case – he's doing time in Luton jail, so we're getting him out on an overnight release to come and talk to us. You'll pick him up at nine and you should be back down here by eleven.'

Glen liked Mike Harris, and he enjoyed the more experienced DC's company. And, he thought, he would be able to pick his brains on the way. Cora Burstridge's daughter was arriving Thursday to identify the body. She was intending to stay in her mother's flat.

If SOCO were to have any chance of finding anything, tomorow would be their last chance.

Chapter Fifty-seven

'Have you washed your choo-choo?'

Tom-Tom in the oval pink bathtub, head sticking out of the foam. A special treat – he loved it when his mother tipped the bubble bath stuff in, and it was like snow, only even frothier, even lighter; he could scoop great armfuls of it up.

'Yes, Mummy.'

Standing over him, her white satin dressing gown open at the front. He could see her breasts poking through, with their big red nipples. He could see the line down the centre of her stomach where she had been cut open *to let him be born*. And the thick straw bush of hair below it.

'Let me see, Tom-Tom darling. Let me make sure you've washed him really thoroughly.'

Nervous now. Scold or treat today?

She leaned over him. One breast touched his cheek and rested cool against it. Her hands slipped below the froth, gripping a bar of Camay. He felt the hard slippery soap against the inside of his legs and it gave him a strange kind of excitement.

'Good boy, darling, Tom-Tom, what a beautiful clean choo-choo. Mummy will clean it a little more now.'

Treat today.

Relief inside him. And the excitement building.

Now he felt her soapy hands working on his penis, massaging it, teasing the foreskin back, then forward again, covering the tip. She soaped her hands some more and teased his foreskin back then forward again, and he was hardening now, growing in her fingers.

'Such a big choo-choo. Going to have such a big,

beautiful choo-choo when you grow up, aren't you, Tom-Tom?'

He giggled excitedly. He loved it when she smiled, when she approved. He wanted, desperately, for her to smile at him all the time.

Slipping off the white satin gown now, she let it drop in a heap, like a pool of white liquid on the pink carpet. Naked in front of him, her huge breasts, the thick, straggly triangle of blonde hair; the flesh around her stomach a little loose. That was where he had been, in there, curled up inside her, behind that wall of flesh.

Hard as a rock now. He showed her proudly, knowing this made her pleased, and she rewarded him with a kiss on the forehead. 'Good boy, Tom-Tom, I love you.'

He looked at her, wanting her to say it again. She didn't, but she was smiling, and that was good.

She stepped into the bath, sat down facing him, knees sticking up through the froth. 'How is your choo-choo now, darling?'

He wanted her to touch it again, wanted desperately that tight sensation that drilled through him when she held it. She reached forward, soaped her hands and held it again now, and it was harder than ever and he loved that feeling of the soapy hands playing up and down it.

Now she handed him the Camay. He gripped the pink bar in his small hand. 'Mummy needs washing now, darling,' she said.

He leaned forward, rubbed the bar in slow circles around her navel, really slow, following it in equally slow, circular motions with the flat of his hand, up and over her breasts, working around her nipples, then back down over the soft flesh of her stomach.

She arched back, raising herself a little, and her blonde bush of hair, darkened almost to brunette from being wet, rose up through the froth. He pressed the soap into it, slowly down through it, and under the front, touching her velvety Secret Place now. The Secret Place that only he knew about.

And had sworn he would never tell anyone about. Ever.

254

Chapter Fifty-eight

'You look terrible, Mike.'

'I'm fine.'

'No, I mean it, you look *terrible*. Are you ill?'

You're in my office, when I don't want you to be in my office, you're making me feel ill. Piss off, leave me alone, get out of my face.

That was what Michael thought when his colleague, Paul Straddley, walked into his office just as he was dialling Lulu, but he didn't say that. He replaced the receiver and said, 'I'm tired, that's all.'

Straddley peered at him more closely. 'Are you sure?'

'I'm a fucking doctor!' Michael snapped.

His diminutive, boffiny colleague, in an even more depressing suit than usual, was startled by the outburst but held his ground. 'I'm a doctor too, Michael.' His voice had more authority than his appearance.

There was a brief moment of stand-off. Paul looked at him reproachfully, then he said, 'Michael, you were going to get back to me on Thursday. I need to talk to you about this patient of mine with his fear of vomiting.' When he saw Michael's blank expression, he reminded him, 'I told you about him – he's scared of food, can't eat anything that hasn't been liquidised, scared he's going to get tiny lumps stuck in his gullet. This is your field.'

'Right,' Michael said, remembering vaguely.

'Can you do lunch tomorrow?'

'Let me check my diary.'

Michael sat down at his computer and called up his Claris Office Manager diary. He hadn't looked at it for some days. His radio show tomorrow evening – Christ, he wasn't in any mood for that, although he was hoping to persuade the station to put out an announcement about Amanda – and on Saturday he was reminded, with shock, that he was taking part in a charity pro-am golf tournament, for the mental health charity, SANE.

He'd been talked into this months back by his best friend, Nick Sandford, with whom he had roomed at medical college for four years. They had originally been at prep school together, back in the late sixties, where they had hated each other, and at the age of twelve, in the school boxing finals, Michael had knocked him out, much to the horror of the teachers and parents.

But when they had met by chance in their first term at King's, there was an instant bond between them. The years of maturing at their separate public schools had changed them both. Neither could remember clearly why they had so disliked the other. Michael thought it was probably because Nick had been a bully. Nick thought it was because Michael had irritated him by being the best sportsman in the school. From out of the hazy mists of the past, a brilliantly strong friendship now burned.

After qualifying as a doctor, Nick had worked for a brief spell as a medical information officer for the pharmaceutical giant Bendix Schere and had then started his own generic-drug manufacturing company. He was now a squillionaire. Both still shared a love of fast motorbikes – or had, until Michael had lost all interest in driving after Katy's death. But they still played golf together.

Nick and his wife, Sarah, whom Michael liked, had been a great strength to him in the past three years since Katy's death.

Lunch tomorrow was clear. Except that he was reluctant to commit any time at the moment: he had intended to cancel all his appointments for tomorrow to concentrate on Amanda.

Straddley was studying his face with a distinctly worried look. 'What is it, Michael?'

'Lunch tomorrow. One o'clock – meet you down in the restaurant?' Michael said, buoyantly.

256

'Fine.'

It was the fastest way Michael could think of to get the man out of his office. And he could always blow out the lunch date in the morning. He desperately wanted to call Lulu before his four-fifteen patient arrived.

As Straddley closed the door behind him, Michael picked up the phone again and dialled Lulu. She was sounding weary and increasingly edgy – all the confident Sloany punch had gone from her voice. Michael had already recounted to her his frustrating meeting with DC Roebuck on his mobile phone while driving back from Hampstead an hour earlier.

'Nothing – you?' she said. These were almost always her first words now when she heard his voice.

They hadn't met, but Michael had an image in his mind of how she looked. Neat, he thought, but large and horsy, judging from her voice, rather conservative, velvet head-band, navy two-piece, twinset and pearls. 'No. Look, could you do something? Could you fax me or e-mail me a list of Amanda's immediate family, names, addresses and phone numbers, and all her friends, including Brian Trussler?'

She said she would do it right away.

The name Brian Trussler was lodged darkly in his mind. He couldn't forget Amanda's look of fear when she had seen the car in the darkness across the street.

Brian Trussler.

Is she with you, Brian Trussler? If you've harmed her, Brian Trussler, I swear to God I'll rip your head off.

Then he hung up, and stared thoughtfully at his computer screen. Thelma still hadn't buzzed to say his patient was here. He logged onto the web, opened Alta Vista and typed the search request, 'missing persons'.

It was a long shot, but that didn't matter, he was determined to try everything.

A few seconds later a message appeared on the screen announcing there were 257,891 matches to his request. The first ten were for missing individuals in the United States.

257

He cancelled the request and made it more specific: 'missing persons – United Kingdom'.

His door opened again. Paul Straddley came into his office once more. 'Michael, you're in some kind of trouble – you must be, looking the way you do. I can't believe you can concentrate properly on your work. Do you want to talk about it? What is it? I am your colleague, you can talk to me.'

Michael sighed. Why not tell him? 'Someone – a friend – has gone missing, Paul. I'm worried about her, that's why I'm a bit chewed up. That's all.'

Paul nodded, looked a little less concerned, but not much. 'National Missing Persons Helpline – they're the people. Tried them?'

'I've never heard of them.'

'Worth a shot.'

Straddley retreated once more as Thelma buzzed to tell Michael his patient had arrived.

Michael asked her to cancel his entire list for tomorrow.

Chapter Fifty-nine

Shivering, Amanda lay curled up on the mattress, which she had dragged as far away in the darkness as she could get from the –

Things.

Dead things. Not dead people, not corpses, not cadavers, no, please not.

Who were they?

She had not prayed since the second year at Brighton and Hove High. She'd had problems believing in a God who never answered her prayers. Wednesday, 24 November 1979, the date she had got the results of her maths test and learned she had failed.

It was no big deal of a test; God could easily have given her good marks. Instead he had chosen to ignore her prayer the week before. So she had never prayed again. Until now.

Pressing the sides of her hands together, she sank her face into the palms, closed her eyes, even in this absolute darkness, and whispered, 'Please, God, tell me this is just a bad dream. Give me something, please, just something to help me.'

Parched throat. Her heart aching to understand where she was, and why she was here.

She could smell her urine through the reek of formalin. Felt the raw, stinging dryness in her throat from the chemical. Her thirst was terrible, so bad she almost wanted to press her tongue to the floor. *People drink their own urine. You can survive on it for days. I was stupid, I wasted it.*

She thought of Michael, his strong arms holding her, his strong brain, his strong, manly smells, how good and safe she had felt with him.

Now I've found you, Michael, don't tell me I've lost you already. Please don't tell me I'm going to die down here without ever seeing you again.

Brian Trussler's company had made a documentary series about survivors. They had interviewed people who had survived the Zeebrugge ferry disaster, two girls who had escaped from a plane that went down in the Indian Ocean, and others. Always it was the same characteristics. Mental strength. Determination. The will to live. *Staying calm and thinking things through.*

Wherever I am, however I came to be in here, if there is an entrance there must be an exit.

The thought had crossed her mind that she had been in an accident, mistaken for dead, and had been locked in some storage room at a mortuary. But the mattress on the floor kept contradicting that idea.

All the immediate possibilities had been exhausted and now she was searching for new ones, trying to keep her grip on reality, trying to focus, to make a list, to hold it.

And trying to ignore a scratching sound she had heard a few minutes ago that might have been a mouse or, worse, a rat.

She had searched the walls in both chambers for exit routes. She had found ridges in the wall in the chamber with the bodies, which indicated there was a door, but she could find no way of opening it.

There must be ventilation in here, she realised. Air must come in from somewhere.

Where?

She stood, folded the mattress double, her left wrist hurting like hell from where she had fallen on it earlier, jammed the mattress up against the wall, *getting good in the dark now*, and climbed onto it. This gave her a couple of feet extra height. Balanced precariously, stretching her arms as far up as she was able, she checked every inch of the wall that she could reach, then stepped down, moved the mattress exactly two lengths of her own feet, then repeated the process.

Thinking for a moment when she stepped down again,

she pulled off her T-shirt and dropped it to the ground as a marker, so she would know when she had completed a full circuit of the room.

It was as she reached the end of the first wall and turned the corner, that her right hand struck something of a completely different texture from the concrete of the wall.

A metal grille.

Holding her breath, see placed the palm of her hand flat against it. A cold draught. An air vent!

Clenching her fist, she made a measuring prong of her forefinger and thumb that she estimated was about two inches wide, and walked them along the base of the grille. Twenty-four inches. Less deep on the vertical, about twenty inches.

Wide enough to fit through?

How was the grille fixed to the wall? She worked her fingers around the edge. Found a small raised lump, a quarter of an inch across, no more. A screw.

Now she moved her hands along, counting. Ten screws.

Without warning, the mattress sagged. She clawed at the wall, trying desperately to get a purchase. Then, with a yelp, she was plunging through the blackness, torn by the savage forces of gravity, down, headfirst onto the unseen floor, her forehead shattering the concrete silence with a crack as sharp as twisted glass.

Chapter Sixty

'I'm afraid he's in a script conference and can't be disturbed.'

'It's really very urgent,' Michael said. 'I just need a quick word with him.'

Brian Trussler's secretary had a cutting voice. 'Can you tell me what it is about? Perhaps I can help you?'

Yes, Michael thought, sourly, maybe you can tell me if your boss has kidnapped Amanda Capstick. 'It's a private matter. I'd like you to interrupt him and tell him I'm on the line. My name is Dr Tennent.'

Michael hoped perhaps his name might mean something to her, but from her response, it didn't. She clearly wasn't a *Daily Mail* reader or a Talk Radio listener.

'Perhaps I could get him to call you back after the meeting, but it's likely to go on for another two hours.'

Michael looked at his watch. It was five o'clock. 'Surely to God you could slip a note in to him.'

'I'm sorry, he absolutely cannot be disturbed.'

Was she covering up for him?

'OK, I'll be in my office for another hour or so. Then I'll be on my mobile. I'll give you my office, mobile and home numbers.' Then using his warmest bedside-manner voice, he tried appealing to her better nature. 'Please ask him to contact me tonight. I'm a psychiatrist and someone's life is in danger. He may have some vital information.'

She hesitated and for a moment he thought she was going to relent, but then she said, 'Can you be more specific?'

Michael thought. Amanda had been having an affair with Trussler; even in his frantically worried state, this did not give him the excuse to start being indiscreet. 'I'm sorry, no, I would be in breach of a confidentiality.'

Softening, but only a fraction, she said, 'Give me your numbers, Dr Tennent. I'll see what I can do.'

Michael spent the next hour on the phone to Amanda's mother, then her sister, then her three closest girlfriends, whose names and numbers Lulu had given him. He arranged to meet up with all of them in turn tomorrow morning, starting with her mother in Brighton at nine o'clock. It was no good over the phone: if any of them was sheltering Amanda they would be able to mask it in their voice, but not so easily in their face.

Brian Trussler had not rung back. Michael decided, from the attitude of his secretary and from the way Amanda had talked about him, that he was a man who only returned phone calls that were about making money or getting laid.

He decided to visit him. Now.

It was shortly before seven by the time Michael had battled through the traffic and found the Bedford Street, Covent Garden, premises of Trussler's company, Mezzanine Productions. There was a parking space almost directly opposite, in front of a smart-looking bookshop called Crime In Store; tight, but just enough room. Michael braked sharply without checking his mirror, and a cyclist swerved past him with an angry shout.

He reversed into the space and switched off the engine, but kept the fan blower going, grateful for the gale on his face, though it was just as warm as the heavy air outside.

He had a straight-line view, through the gap between two parked cars, of the front door of Mezzanine Productions. The downstairs looked suitably media cool: smoked-glass windows, angled slats of limed grey wood. He dialled the number, which he had already programmed into his mobile. It rang several times before Ms Super-Defensive answered.

'I'm sorry, he's still in conference. I have given him your message,' she said, in a tone that gave Michael no grounds for confidence that the call would be returned tonight, if ever.

'Would you tell him that I'm now on the mobile number I gave you and I'll be on it for some while.' As an inducement he added, 'I'll keep the line clear for him. You have conveyed how urgent this is, haven't you?'

'Yes, Dr Tennent, I have.' Her tone sounded now as if she was repelling a double-glazing salesman.

Michael killed the call. At least Brian Trussler was still in the building. He felt shattered, but his brain was whirring. He dialled Amanda's office number, hoping Lulu was still there. She was.

'Lulu, do you by any chance know what car Brian Trussler drives?'

A man in denims and Walkman headphones strode past with a fierce expression as if he was heading into battle.

'Oh, God, he has a Porsche, a Bentley – um – a Range Rover and a Harley Davidson motorcycle, but he's off the road at the moment,' she said. 'He got banned for drink-driving about two months ago. Second offence, he's off for three years – and he only just scraped out of a prison sentence.' Then, as if imparting a great secret, she said, 'I don't think that's public knowledge.'

He thanked her, hung up and dropped the phone next to his briefcase on the passenger seat beside him.

It was a fine evening, and sunlight still daubed the pavement on the other side of the road. The café a short distance down had put tables and chairs outside, all occupied. Further along, a crowd of people stood drinking outside a pub.

Then he saw movement behind the front door of Mezzanine, and stiffened, watching carefully. Two men came out, both in their twenties, one in T-shirt and jeans, carrying a large film can under his arm, the other in a loud shirt and Lycra shorts, who made sure the door was shut. They stood chatting for some moments, before walking off in different directions, the one in shorts stopping at a lamp-post a few yards up and unchaining a mountain bike.

Michael hoped this was the only entrance to the offices.

At least, since Trussler didn't drive, he wouldn't have a car secreted somewhere around the back.

Seeing the people drinking at the café and the pub reminded him of his own thirst – and hunger. He'd had a glass of water and a cup of tea in the office, and eaten one of the two shortbread biscuits that Thelma had put on the saucer. Other than that, and the cup of coffee at Hampstead police station, he'd had nothing since this morning. But he was reluctant to leave the car now to get something in case he missed Trussler.

Keeping one eye on the front door, he hauled his Mac PowerBook out of his briefcase, and booted it up. Then he attached a cable from the modem serial port into his mobile phone, logged onto the Internet, and called up the Mezzanine Production web page, which he had book-marked earlier.

The download was interminably slow and he wondered if the machine had hung or the line had dropped. Then, finally, the image began to fill out the screen. He clicked on the icon, which was marked DIRECTOR'S BIOGS. After another interminable delay, Brian Trussler's colour photo-graph appeared, above a long list of his television credits.

Although he had already memorised the man's face, he studied it hard again now. Trussler seemed fairly distinctive-looking, and ought to be easy enough to spot. Short-cropped, thinning hair with a few pathetic vanity strands across his dome; collarless black shirt fastened at the neck with a jewelled stud. He looked like a flash, smug, middle-aged criminal. *Amanda, what did you see in him?*

And he knew she would never be able to answer that question, because the truth was that humans seldom understood the forces of attraction that ensnared them. You could make informed guesses, sure, in her case an element of father-figure, but that was only one part of a massive composite.

The door was opening. A woman strode out, brown hair cut in a chic but dated style, silk scarf draped around her shoulders, clothes that were smart but sensible. The kind of woman who might run Brian Trussler's life and secretly yearn for him, who'd be adept at fielding unwanted phone calls from psychiatrists, but less so at finding love.

She checked that the door was locked. Then she adjusted her scarf, glanced at her reflection in the glass, and walked away in fast, neat, sensibly spaced steps.

He jerked the modem cable out of his mobile phone, switched it off then back on again to clear it, and dialled Trussler's direct-line number again. This time there was no intervention by the secretary. Instead, after six rings, the voice-mail kicked in. The secretary's voice.

'You have reached Brian Trussler's phone. Please leave your name and number and we'll call you back.'

Michael pressed END. So, almost certainly, that woman had been the secretary. Did that mean the meeting had now ended, or was she simply leaving the office for the day?

He was trying to decide whether to go over to the door and try to bluff his way in, or whether to continue waiting here, when the door opened: three men and a woman came out. One man had a pony-tail, one a shaven head, one had gelled black hair. The woman, thirtyish, raggedly attractive, held the door and a fourth man came out, dressed in a cream suit. Short, thinning hair with a few strands straddling his almost bald dome, he was talking and gesturing with his hands. He had a commanding air about him; this was his call, this was his meeting, these were his minions.

This was Brian Trussler.

Chapter Sixty-one

In the privacy of his den, Thomas opened the box that had been mailed by UPS carriers to Dr Terence Goel's PO Box in Cheltenham. Inside, it was beautifully packed, each component nestling in its own polystyrene compartment. Two lenses stared up at him through the shredded paper wadding, like some fat, creepy bug.

'Beautiful,' he whispered.

He laid his face against the wadding. *Beautiful*. It felt like straw. Today felt like Christmas. *Beautiful*. The cold plastic rims of the lenses touched his cheek like two kisses.

This is for you, Mummy, I'm doing this for you. Is this making you happy? I hope so.

A copy of Dr Goel's Midland Gold MasterCard credit slip, in an envelope, was attached to the invoice. A payment for one thousand, nine hundred and forty pounds to the CyberSurveillance Mail Order Company Ltd.

Thomas tucked this proof of purchase into his black crocodile-skin wallet, sliding it down behind the lining, just in case the apparatus had a fault and he needed to send it back. Then, in the grate of the disused fireplace, Thomas carefully lit the label addressed to Dr Terence Goel that had been on the outside of the package and burned it. The Ford Mondeo parked in the garage alongside Amanda Capstick's Alfa Romeo was unavoidable but, other than that, he tried to ensure that nothing in this house could connect him with Dr Terence Goel of Cheltenham. The white van was secure on a long-term contract in a multi-storey car park.

Fetching the vacuum cleaner from downstairs he hoovered all the ashes out of the grate. No dirty fireplace in this room, thank you. He wanted it clean, spotless, sterile, like a hospital operating theatre. That was the way he liked it. Carpet, desk, computer, chair, armchair, books, pictures of his mother. No bugs. No bacteria. Behind closed curtains, double-glazed windows were sealed against the shitty London air. Better to be hot than poisoned. No dirt, none, no thank you.

Now this room wasn't clean any more, there was shredded paper all over the floor around the box and this angered him. *Bitch Amanda Capstick.* This was her fault. If she hadn't allowed herself to be penetrated by Dr Michael Tennent he wouldn't have had to order this piece of kit, and if he hadn't ordered it, then he wouldn't have this shredded paper as messy as straw over his grey carpet.

He could vacuum it up soon, but not yet, not until he was finished.

He had to read the instruction book. He removed it from its Cellophane wrapper. On the outside was printed AN/PVS NIGHT VISION GOGGLES MODEL F5001.

This was the model he had ordered. Good.

He read carefully, memorising the diagrams. Then he lifted the goggles out of the box and held them up. They were beautiful to look at, beautiful to hold, he pulled them to his eyes, smelt the rubber cushioning. So comfortable, such a snug fit. He could see nothing through them yet, of course: the lithium battery wasn't installed.

He checked out all the features. The IR-on switch. The low-battery indicator. The IR illuminator. The F/1.2 objective lens. The momentary IR-on indicator.

Beautiful!

He couldn't wait to use them. This was going to be something else altogether!

He lifted out the head mount, a complex arrangement of straps. Now the excitement was really growing. He attached it to the goggles and, from the diagram he had memorised, put it on. One strap went around the rim of his skull, like a headband, clamping the goggles to his forehead. Another bracing strap went beneath his chin; a third went around his neck, and a fourth went from the headband in front of his ears to the neck strap.

Wonderful! He stood up, unable to see yet, but entranced. This strapping device was comfortable, so snug, he could wear these goggles for ever!

I wish you could see me now, Mummy!

He raised his hands to remove them and winced as his right arm twinged. Anger at Amanda flared up inside him again. *You hurt my arm, you bitch.*

She was so heavy! Why was someone so small and so thin so damned heavy when they were unconscious? Getting her out of the hallway of her building and into her Alfa Romeo while trying to make it look like they were two lovers entwined hadn't been easy! He'd wrenched his arm getting her into that damned car.

But the pleasure that lay ahead helped him forget the pain. Oh, yes. This was going to be good. He removed the goggles, knelt down on the floor, took out the lithium battery and the charger, inserted the battery in the small compartment at the base of the goggles, then plugged in the charger. He pressed the switch and the indicator light came on. He smiled.

Thunderbirds are go!

Amanda heard the click of a door.

Movement.

Someone was sharing this darkness with her. Stifling her first instinct to call out for help, she lay still, held her breath. A muscle plucked at the base of her throat. She tracked the darkness with her ears.

Beyond the drumroll of her heartbeat, silence.

Then a sudden movement, like one single footstep. A thud close by. Then the unmistakable sound of sloshing water. The squeak of a rubber-soled shoe.

Thomas nearly kicked over the bucket. He cursed his clumsiness. He had almost tripped, dammit. Jesus! You stupid bitch woman, do you realise all the trouble you're putting me to?

She was so close he could reach out and touch her, but he didn't want to do that. He didn't want to touch anything

269

that Dr Michael Tennent had had sex with, not yet, not until he was ready. And she stank of body odour and urine; she'd only been down here two days and she was turning this place into a pigsty. He could smell her even over the reek of formalin. And why was the stupid bitch lying on the floor and not on the mattress?

Should have brought her the food and water yesterday, he knew, and something for her to do her latrine stuff into. Somehow it had slipped his mind.

He looked at her in the green night-vision light. The tiny red glow of the battery indicator showed he had ten minutes left. The batteries had needed a twenty-four-hour charge but that was an impossible length of time. They'd had to make do with four hours, and that had been a hard enough wait.

But now, the main thing was, the goggles worked! Clear enough to see the fear on her face.

No, not *her* face, he corrected himself. *Its* face.

This was the mistake he had made with the editor, Tina Mackay, and the reporter, Justin Flowering. He had thought of them as people and in the end he had been distressed by what he had done to them. Keep this one at a distance. *It's an animal. Just an animal.*

And, just like an animal in its lair hearing a sound, it lifted its head, staring around in the darkness, eyes open so wide in terror he could see the whites all the way round.

Not taking care of itself; there was a bad bruise on its forehead. Its hair was a mess, all tangled up, it needed combing or brushing, or both, he was tempted to tell it to make itself more presentable but it was better just to watch it in silence. It even had its T-shirt on back to front.

He thought how slovenly this animal looked compared to his mother. His mother liked to sit in front of the mirror, with him standing beside her, combing and brushing and caressing those long blonde tresses. Sometimes she would sit naked and he would stand beside her, also naked, combing and brushing, and she would reward him afterwards by doing something good with his choo-choo.

He made another noise now as he put down the second

bucket, this time scraping his foot deliberately. It was looking straight at him now, and for a moment he wondered if it could make out his shape in the darkness, but, of course, that was impossible. These goggles gave off nothing. Military specification. They were fabulous! He was invisible.

Could it hear him breathing? Was that what it was focusing on now? He stepped silently in his Nike Air trainers several paces to his right. It was still staring ahead, staring at where he had been.

In the land of the blind . . .

'Hallo?' it called. 'Hallo, who's there?'

Pitiful, croaky little voice.

'Hallo, please, hallo? Who's there? Please help me.'

He retreated silently back through the darkness, into the outer chamber, past the bodies of Tina Mackay and the reporter, Justin Flowering. Then he stopped again and looked back.

The dirty thing on the floor stiffened, turned its head in short, jerky, startled movements.

It called out again, 'Hallo?'

A door clanged shut. The echo rumbled around the chamber until it was blotted up by the darkness.

Then, suddenly, an explosion of light.

Amanda threw her hands against her eyes in pain and let out a gasp of shock, her eye muscles straining inside their sockets. A clear red glow now through her hands.

Slowly, fearfully, she removed them, blinking, still dazzled, her headache making it hard to think clearly, but as she began to adjust to the light, she looked around. She was in a square, windowless room, about twenty feet by twenty feet, and about ten feet high. Four downlighters flush with the ceiling lit the room. Otherwise it was solid concrete, with no hatch. She looked at the duct vent, directly above where the mattress lay against the wall. Other than the door that was the only possibility. It was big enough to get into – if she could find a way to unscrew the grille cover.

She pressed her hands to her head to try to squeeze away the pain, but as she touched her forehead, it was so bad she nearly cried out. Over to her right was the open door through into the room where she had found the bodies, which was in darkness. Then her eyes swung down to the two plastic buckets and the tray on the floor just short of the doorway.

One bucket looked empty. The other contained a soapy froth and had a flannel draped over the edge. A beige towel was folded neatly beside it, and a brand new roll of lavatory paper. On the tray was a large plastic jug of water, a plastic beaker, a paper plate on which were several chunks of wholemeal bread, and another on which were thick slices of cheese. A handful of cherry tomatoes and an apple lay loose on the tray. No knife. Nothing that she could try to use as a screwdriver.

She fell on the water jug, grasped it in both hands and began to gulp it down gratefully, greedily, so fast it spilled out of her mouth, running over the sides of her lips and down her chin.

When she did stop, she'd already drunk three-quarters of the contents and was desperate for more, she could drain it right now and it still wouldn't be enough. But she did not know how long would be before she was given any more. She needed to ration herself, needed to –

The time.

I can read my watch now.

Time and date.

7.55. Tue. Jul 28.

One more swig of water, just a small one. She kept it in her mouth, swilling the delicious moist substance around, savouring it, treasuring every drop. Two days.

Oh, sweet Jesus. *Two days.*

A swirl of panic tore through her. Two days. *Two days.* Seven fifty-five in the morning or the evening?

Why isn't anyone looking for me? Why hasn't anyone found me? She stared at the food, grabbed a piece of cheese and some bread and crammed them in her mouth, chewing savagely, tears rolling down her cheeks.

Michael, do you even know I'm not at home or at work? Lulu, are you wondering where I am?

Oh, Christ, who the hell is going to miss me?

She drank another precious mouthful of water, then ate more bread and cheese and a tomato, a ripe, delicious, incredibly sweet, beautiful tomato. Even this little bit of food going down was making her feel stronger. *Think.*

It's Tuesday. Maybe Tuesday morning or Tuesday bloody night. Two days. Forty-eight hours. Lulu, you must be wondering where the hell I am. What are you doing about it? What have you told Michael? Do you think I'm just lying at home with a bloody migraine or something?

What the hell are you all doing?

Anything? Are you doing anything at all?

The light went out.

For a moment she stared into the darkness in anger, not fear.

Chapter Sixty-two

Michael watched Brian Trussler shake hands with the other three men on the pavement outside the offices of Mezzanine Productions. Positive body language: they'd had a good meeting.

The one with the pony-tail clamped his mobile phone to his ear, and stepped away. Brian Trussler pulled his phone out also, dialled and strutted a few yards down the street, looking pleased as hell with himself. In his cream linen suit, purple collarless shirt and white loafers, he had an even flashier air than the mental image Michael had already formed of him, and he was filled with a sudden intense loathing for and mistrust of this man.

Michael opened his door and was half-way out of his car, when Trussler broke into a sprint, one arm raised in a frantic signal, flagging down a cab at the intersection a short distance down the road.

He debated whether to run after him, then decided instead it might be more useful to see where he was going. He slammed the door and started the engine. To his relief he could see that the cab, in a distinctive bottle-green, was stopped at traffic lights at the T-junction with the Strand. He swung the Volvo out, deliberately cutting up a van, forcing it to brake hard, accelerated down to the end of the road and pulled up hard on the tail of Trussler's cab, which had its right-turn signal on.

Grabbing his phone off the driver's seat, he dialled Lulu's home number. The lights changed as it was ringing, and he steered one-handed, trailing the cab into the heavy evening traffic of the Strand.

Lulu's answering-machine kicked in after four rings. The

cab crossed a traffic light on orange and Michael, a split second later, on red. They stopped again at the next lights, in front of Charing Cross station. He dialled Lulu's mobile. Three rings, and then to his relief he heard her, against a hubbub of voices, a clattering of cutlery or glasses, and background music that was numbingly loud.

The lights were changing. The cab was entering Trafalgar Square and a chauffeured Mercedes was trying to cut into the gap between them. Driving recklessly close to the cab's bumper, ready to change direction whenever it did, Michael froze out the Mercedes. 'Hi, Lulu, it's Michael.'

She couldn't hear him.

Under Admiralty Arch and into the Mall. The cab was accelerating and Michael eased back a short distance in case the driver was observant. Raising his voice he said, 'It's Michael! I need Brian Trussler's home address.'

'Umm, it's – oh, God, number four, West Crescent, NW1,' she shouted back. 'Regent's Park – do you know Albany Street?'

'Uh-huh.'

'It's somewhere off that, I think.'

'Thanks. No news?'

'Nothing – you?'

She was too breezy tonight. No one had a right to be happy, not until Amanda had been safely found.

'No,' he said.

They were stopping at the lights by St James's Palace. Buckingham Palace dead ahead. No flag, the Queen was out – having a nice time somewhere? Everyone else in the whole bloody city was having a nice time tonight.

A convertible BMW pulled up on his right, a blonde driving, hair all tangled from the wind, and he looked at her with a sharp pang, reminded of Amanda. There was another attractive girl in the passenger seat and one in the back, all laughing, sharing a joke, having a good time. Now a guy and a girl in a grey Jaguar pulled up on his left, impossibly beautiful, as if they had stepped out of a chocolate commercial. The girl was nuzzled up against the guy's face, kissing him. Michael wanted to scream at them

275

all to stop having fun, fun was on hold, everyone had to concentrate.

Help me find Amanda.

Brian Trussler was not heading home.

At the top of Constitution Hill, entering Hyde Park Corner, the green cab should have looped round to Park Lane, but instead it turned off left down Grosvenor Crescent behind the Lanesborough towards Belgrave Square, and Michael, before he could follow, had his exit route cut off by a bus.

'Bastard, damn you, get out of the sodding way,' he mouthed angrily, swerving over into the extreme right-hand lane without looking, without caring what the hell might be there, his only option now to do a complete circuit of Hyde Park Corner, and pray.

He ran the red light, slewing round the first corner, tyres yowling, then wove through a gap, forcing a despatch motorcyclist to swerve, through another, blasted his own horn hard now as both he and a black cab made for the same gap. At the last moment the cab gave way and he was heading round the outside lane, playing chicken with a bus thundering up from Victoria. He braked sharply, swept across right behind it and made a left turn.

Now he was out of the murderous traffic and accelerating hard down past the Lanesborough, into Belgrave Square, hunting with his eyes for a bottle-green movement, checking the first exit, the second, and then he glimpsed it, fleetingly, on the far side of a junction, before it disappeared down Chesham Place heading towards Sloane Street.

He threw the Volvo up to the white halt line of the junction. Traffic was streaming down Belgrave Place, and he couldn't wait. *Give way, you bastards, let me out!* He started nosing the Volvo out, bullying his way into the centre of the road until a car braked with an angry blast of its horn.

Michael floored the accelerator, the front tyres scrabbled for grip for a second, the nose of the Volvo lifted and yawed, the steering wheel kicked hard in his hands, then he was thundering down Chesham Place, rev counter flying, scanning the road for stray pedestrians or cyclists, and he caught another sight of Trussler's cab, crossing the lights at Sloane Street into Pont Street.

The lights stayed green long enough for him. He overtook a line of cars, and now, pulse hammering, he was right up close behind the cab again, and braked hard, killing his crazed speed. He could see Trussler's head through the rear window, moving animatedly as he talked on the phone.

The cab threaded a route along Chelsea back-streets towards Fulham, and following it was easier now. They emerged into the Fulham Road, crossed the Beaufort Street lights by the ABC cinema, then suddenly the cab braked and made a sharp left. Almost immediately it went left again into a smart, expensive-looking residential mews. Michael stayed back, watching it go down the cobbles, then stop outside a house.

He drove into the mews and pulled up far enough behind a parked Saab to keep a clear view. Trussler climbed out, paid the driver, then rummaged in his pocket. To Michael's surprise, he pulled out what looked like a set of keys, walked up to the front door and put one in the lock.

Did the bastard have a secret lair? Was this where he was keeping Aman –

His speculations were interrupted by the door opening. A striking-looking woman with long brown hair erupted out of it, threw her arms around Trussler's neck and embraced him passionately.

Michael watched in amazement as Trussler kissed her with almost savage abandon, right there on the doorstep. They were mauling each other and she, wearing what looked like a dressing gown, was almost ripping off his clothes right there. After some moments their lips broke free, and their faces pressed together, they mouthed something to one another. They both grinned, then they kissed again unashamedly, like a couple of courting kids, before going inside and closing the door.

Michael stared dumbly, trying to take all this in. Was this a new girlfriend since Amanda? Or had Trussler been two-timing Amanda as well as his wife? He had a key to this place, so did he own it? Was this his secret knock shop? Or had this woman given him a key? If she had, the relationship must have been going on for some while. How long? Since Amanda had dumped him, or before that?

Whatever, his theory that Trussler might have kidnapped Amanda out of jealousy was fast heading south. He didn't look like a man capable of caring enough for anyone to want to bother hurting them.

Michael gave them twenty minutes, hoping to catch them off-guard. Opening his Mac, he tried to get his head around a lecture on obsessive compulsive disorder he was due to give at a conference in a fortnight but he was too distracted to concentrate.

A sleek Burmese cat gave him a cursory inspection, then disdainfully entered a flap in a garage door. A woman with punk hair and designer jeans strutted past with a clutch of Yorkshire terriers yapping on leads. A dusty Porsche 911 arrived home, its driver, a tired-looking man in his early thirties, in pinstriped trousers and red braces, hauled himself out, then ducked back into the car to retrieve his briefcase.

Michael waited until he had entered his house, then walked along the mews, up to Trussler's door and rang the bell.

There was no response. He gave it a reasonable length of time, then rang it again, this time for longer, then repeated the ring again twice more in rapid succession.

After a few moments he heard footsteps. The door opened and the woman he had seen earlier stared out at him, displeased. 'Yes?'

A slight accent – Italian, he thought. She was good-looking, not as beautiful close up as she'd looked from a distance, but there was an overt sexuality about her, even more so with her makeup smudged, her hair awry and her breasts loose inside the towelling dressing gown she was holding closed with one hand.

'I need to have a word with Brian Trussler,' he said, and caught the flash of panic in her eyes.

Tightening her gown around her, then folding her arms, she replied, 'Who?'

'Brian Trussler.'

She shook her head and said, 'I'm sorry, you have the wrong house.' She reached back to close the door.

She was so convincing that Michael found himself considering the possibility that he had followed the wrong person, except that that flash of panic he had seen had given the game away. 'I don't think so,' he said firmly. 'Look, it's very important. I just need a couple of minutes of his time.'

'I'm sorry, you have the wrong house.' She tried to close the door in his face, but Michael lurched forward, placed his foot over the sill and against the jamb.

She flared in anger, 'Get out!'

Michael forced the door back a few inches. She was stronger than she looked and resisted hard. But he held steady, easing himself in.

'Get out!'

Fear as well as anger in her face now. She smelt strongly of a classy perfume he did not recognise. Glaring at him, face to face, confrontational but nervous, unsure of her ground, she let him pass.

There was a staircase immediately in front of him and as he climbed it, her tone changed. 'Brian!' she warned. 'Brian!'

He reached the landing and pushed open the door on his right, but that went into an empty kitchen and dining area. Down the short corridor he heard music, Luther Vandross singing, it was coming through an open door ahead of him. He walked in.

Dimmed lights. A candle burning on a bedside table; double bed with black satin sheets and lying on it, naked, cosseting an erection in his hands like some sad little Plasticine tower he had just made, was Brian Trussler.

As Michael entered the room, he dived for a sheet, pulling it over his midriff with a mixture of surprise and alarm. 'Who the fuck are you?'

'Brian, I don't – I couldn't stop this man!' the woman called behind him.

Michael marched over to the bed. 'You didn't have the courtesy to return my phone calls.' He glanced over his shoulder at the woman then back at Trussler. 'I think you'd rather hear what I have to say in private.'

'You want to get the fuck out of here before I call the police?' Trussler said.

'Amanda Capstick,' Michael said, and gave him enough time to absorb this. 'You and I are going to have a chat about her – you want to ask your friend to leave the room? I don't mind if she hears about her.'

Trussler's eyes widened. He stared back at Michael warily, then he said, 'Gina, five minutes, OK?'

She gave Michael a scalding look, glanced back at Trussler for reassurance, then went out.

'Close the door,' Trussler said.

Michael shut it.

Trussler heaved himself up in the bed. There was a half-empty tumbler containing what looked like whisky on the rocks on the table beside him, as well as an open packet of white powder and a clear Perspex biro casing with no innards. 'What's all this about?'

Michael glanced away, checking out the room. Erotic paintings, a massive mirror on the wall beside the bed. Maybe she was a hooker. Unlikely: hookers didn't greet their clients the way she had him. He turned back to Trussler and studied his face carefully as he said, 'My name's Michael Tennent. Amanda and I have started going out. I last saw her on Sunday afternoon, when she went off to her sister for tea.'

'Lara?' he said, sharply.

'Yes.'

'You know that she's missing.'

'Her secretary told me. Yup.'

'You don't seem very concerned. Is she just one of a whole string of mistresses that you run?'

'You have sixty seconds to get out of this house, Mr Tenby. OK?'

Michael scooped up the packet of white powder. Trussler sat up vigorously and made a grab for it, but Michael stepped back out of reach. 'I'm a doctor, you little shit, OK? You want me to flush this down the toilet or take it to the police?'

Trussler rolled out of the bed and lunged at him. Michael parried his arm, the jolt sending the cocaine flying, and brought his foot hard up between Trussler's legs. The film producer doubled up, making a metallic gurgling sound like water in a drain, pressed his hands to his crutch and rocked backwards and forwards, gasping.

Michael marched over to the phone, lifted the receiver. 'Here, call the police – want me to do it for you?'

Trussler sat on the bed, naked, clutching his groin. His head lolled forward and he retched, but didn't throw up. 'What do you want?' It came out as a hoarse gasp.

'I want to know where Amanda is.' Michael replaced the receiver.

Trussler closed his eyes. 'Jesus, man,' he lolled forward again, 'she dumped me. I haven't seen her for – I don't know – two, three weeks.'

'Why aren't you more concerned?'

He opened his eyes again. 'She's a very independent lady. Needs a lot of space. That's her way of coping with pressure.'

'Has she disappeared before?'

'I really think you're overreacting, Mr Tenby. If you've been after her this obsessively, I'm not surprised she's disappeared. She's probably terrified of you.'

Michael looked at him with loathing. 'It's you she's frightened of, shall we get that clear?'

Trussler pointed at the door. 'Out. Now. You think she's missing, go to the police, that's what they're for. Just what the hell do you think gives you the right to barge in here and start interrogating me?'

Michael grabbed the man's thinning strands of hair and jerked him to his feet, pulling his face right up close to his own. 'I'm in love with her,' he said, through clenched teeth. 'That gives me the right to barge in anywhere. I'll go to the ends of the earth to find her and, my Christ, if I find that you've done anything to her, or there's anything you know that you're not telling me, I'm feeding your balls to your neighbour's Burmese cat. Understand?'

Michael had to shake him twice before he nodded, and not until then did he release his grip on the man.

'I love her, too,' Trussler said.

'Sure, I can see how concerned you are for her,' Michael replied. 'It was more important for you to come round here for a shag than return my call. My God, you're *really concerned*, aren't you?'

He turned and marched out of the room.

Chapter Sixty-three

The car was falling apart. It smelt horrible. The M1 was horrible too, rain-lashed, roadworks, contraflow, red and white cones as far as the eye could see. An endless convoy of lorries kicking up spray that was denser than fog.

The wipers squeaked. Every few minutes the glove compartment lid would spring open and crack down on Glen's knees. A load of wiring dangled loose beneath the dash and he was careful to avoid getting his feet tangled in it. It took the CID about two years to trash a pool car, and this Vauxhall was on the wrong side of its third birthday. Someone had smoked two million cigarettes in here. More recently, last night probably, someone had thrown up in the back. At eight o'clock in the morning, Glen didn't know which was worse: the smell of the vomit or of the Dettol that had been splashed around to mask it.

Mike Harris drove. They were heading north, and the Watford Gap service station was coming up in a few minutes. They were stopping there for breakfast. Glen was tired and hungry; he'd been up most of the night, scanning through two more books on post-mortems and thinking. When he finally lapsed into sleep, he dreamed of a woman with a plastic bag over her head, struggling for air.

Mike Harris had a strong, kind face. He was wise, solid, he knew the ropes, understood people, had long ago sussed how the world worked. He always reminded Glen of the saying, 'a good man in a tight corner'.

In cramped moulded chairs, they faced each other across an absurdly narrow Formica table. Fried eggs, bacon, sausage, beans, black pudding, fried bread, the works. While they ate, they talked. In half an hour they would arrive at Luton and they'd be accompanied back to Hove by the prisoner turned informer, who was hopefully going to help them with their drugs case, Operation Skeet. Right now Glen had his far more experienced colleague to himself, and he'd made use of the journey by giving him all the background to his concerns about Cora Burstridge.

Mike Harris scooped beans onto a slice of bacon and forked the heap into his mouth. While he was chewing he asked, 'Did you go to Hannington's where she bought the Babygro?'

'No, I didn't think of that,' Glen replied.

'Whoever served her, they'd remember whether she was with someone or on her own.'

'Good point. I'll check that.' Glen drank some tea, and then said, 'Mike, what do you really think? That I should accept what Digby said and drop it?'

'No. If you really feel this strongly, do a G30 report and give it to the governor.'

'DCI Gaylor?'

'Yes, he's a very accommodating guy. Put on the form all the inquiries you've done and the reasons why you believe this is suspicious – put down exactly what you told me. Tell him that if he can't afford to spare you the time, you'll work your two rest days this week, if you can just work solely on Cora Burstridge on those days. He might agree to that, so long as you don't want to start spending money.'

'On forensics?'

'Absolutely.' The detective constable looked at his watch. 'Eat up, we're running late.'

Glen chewed a large slice of sausage. 'I need Forensics to take some prints, and to look at a broken lock for me – I think that's crucial,' he said, a little despondently. 'I need to have them there today, somehow, her daughter arrives tomorrow.'

They finished their breakfast in silence. Then, as they were walking past the slot machine arcade, Mike Harris said, 'Look, I've been a copper for thirty years. When we get back, go and speak to Ron Sutton in SOCO in Brighton.

284

Mention my name and ask him if he'll do you a favour. He owes me.'

Glen thanked him. 'I know him,' he added. 'Good bloke.'

They ran across the car park, through the torrenting rain, back to their car. As they drove down the slip-road, Mike Harris said, 'Thursday night – you doing anything, or are you on lates?'

Glen looked out through the rear window at the traffic. 'No. I start lates next Monday.'

The detective accelerated hard, pulling out into a gap. 'I'm going to a leaving do in London, chap I've known for years, did the initial CID course with him in 'seventy-nine. He's been seconded to the National Criminal Intelligence Service. Should be a good evening, doing all the sights of London booze-wise and finishing up in Soho with a Chinese. Fancy joining me? Might be some good contacts – there'll be some brass there. Never know who you might meet who could help your career one day.'

'Yeah, I'd like to come, thanks, thanks a lot.'

'Get a pink ticket from your wife.'

'No problem,' Glen said, with bravado, although it *was* a problem. Ari wasn't jealous, but she had a thing about men and stag nights.

As if reading his mind, Mike Harris said, 'Tell her it's work.'

'We never lie to each other.'

'You don't have to lie.'

'I'm not scared of her, or anything like that.'

Harris grinned and said nothing.

Soon Glen couldn't stick the grin any longer. 'I'm not,' he insisted. 'Really I'm not!'

'There's a train from Hove station at five twenty. We'll take that, OK?'

'What do I wear?'

'Anything that won't show beer stains or lipstick.'

Chapter Sixty-four

wednesday, 30 july 1997. 8.35 a.m.
The Botvinnik queen's rook defence! This is an incredibly old move! Deeper Blue used a variation of this in game three against Kasparov in 1997. And just now my friend Jurgen Jurgens, in Clearwater Springs, Florida, has used this same move.

It is important to keep up my chess games on the Internet. Chess exercises the brain and I am worried about these gaps in my thinking that seem to be happening with more frequency. It's quite scary that chunks of time can go by of which one has no recollection. I really cannot account for much of Monday. I forgot the woman – the thing – it! No water, no food, nothing.

I'm not that bothered. Any bitch prepared to be penetrated by Dr Michael Tennent deserves whatever she gets.

So maybe it wasn't that I forgot the bitch, after all. Perhaps it was my subconscious taking over and punishing it by ignoring it. We should all let our inner voices take control from time to time. Let them have their say. We let them take control when we're driving down the motorway sometimes, and they don't do a bad job. Maybe we all need to have a little more faith in ourselves.

Terence Goel must ask his psychiatrist about these memory lapses next time he sees him.

The weather is bad this morning. Heavy rain. The thing doesn't realise how lucky it is to be in a warm, dry place.

I must ring my stockbroker today, haven't spoken to him in a while. Lots of movements in the markets. And I need some groceries. I must buy some more of the solvent that removes grease from hands. Dismantling the bitch's Alfa Romeo is hard work.

So far it's had it pretty cushy. I really haven't been unpleasant to it at all, and I've given it no cause for alarm. It has a mattress, food, drink, soapy water, a towel, nice-quality lavatory paper, life could be a lot worse for it.

I wonder how Dr Michael Tennent will react tonight when he hears it scream?

Chapter Sixty-five

The fat boy was telling a joke. He liked to use this time, before the teacher arrived, to tell unfunny jokes to the assembled class. His name was Martin Webber. Ginger hair, freckles, small ratty mouth, cheeks like hamster pouches. He told his jokes loudly in a squeaky, self-important voice.

The one he was telling now he had told before. Thomas Lamark remembered that, even if the rest of his class were too stupid to.

'There was this Irishman called Paddy, who tried to commit suicide by jumping out of a basement!'

Thomas watched as everyone roared with laughter. He still failed to see what was funny. A man wanted to commit suicide. That was tragic, not funny. The man did not have enough intelligence to understand that to kill himself he needed to jump from a considerable height. The fact that the man was Irish seemed to add resonance. *Irish* was some kind of shorthand for inferiority or stupidity, but Thomas did not understand why it should be so.

'Thomas doesn't get it!' said another boy, Justin Watts-Weston.

'God, you're such a thick bastard, Thomas!' said Tony Dickinson, leaning right over his desk and sticking his face right in front of Thomas's. 'Thicko! Thicko! Thicko! Dwooorrrr! Dwoooorrrr! Dwoooorrrr!'

Dickinson had spiky fair hair, a snub nose and nasty little bulging eyes, like a frog. Thomas had been wondering for some weeks what would happen if he slit one of those eyes open with a razor. He had a razor blade inside his desk now, his Stanley knife for modelling. It would be so easy –

'Hey, precious boy, if your mummy's such a famous

actress, how come she hasn't been in a new film this year?' Dickinson taunted further. 'My dad says your mum's a has-been.'

Thomas was about to lunge at Dickinson, when the boy retreated to his own desk, and the class fell silent. Mr Landymore, the history teacher, entered.

Thomas, seething, glared at Dickinson. Mr Landymore began writing on the blackboard, but Thomas had nothing to learn from this ignorant man: he already had a far better knowledge of history than his teacher.

He raised the lid of his desk and stared down at the bluebottle, which was still alive, rocking from side to side. Suddenly it spun around in a circle, several times. Without its wings, it made no sound.

He had captured it earlier. Using a magnifying glass, tweezers and a modelling knife, he had removed its wings and legs. He lowered the desk lid and wrote down in his notebook, 'Spiders spin webs. Flies just spin.' Now that *was* funny.

Then he closed the book to stop anyone else reading it.

Martin Webber told jokes that were not funny and knew nothing about Max Planck's quantum theory. He had tested his classmate out on this. Martin Webber had no idea that quantum mechanics was a mathematical system for computing the statistical behaviour of subatomic particles.

He doubted also that his classmate had ever read *Gray's Anatomy*. Thomas had found it in Kensington library and had read it from cover to cover, memorising every diagram. It would be a simple job to excise one of Webber's kidneys. It would be possible to capture him, anaesthetise him, excise the kidney, suture him and send him home. Then afterwards he could post the kidney to Webber's parents. He had worked this out, every detail, and he liked this idea a lot.

Almost as much as he liked the idea of slitting Tony Dickinson's froggy eye with a razor.

He wondered if Martin Webber would spin round in circles if he cut his arms and legs off.

*

'The ball, you wanker! The ball! Kick the ball, you wanker!'

Dickinson again. Now the playground, during morning break, was the place of torment.

Thomas's mother had said to him recently, 'You do understand don't you Tom-Tom? About not being quite right in the head? You do understand that, don't you?'

Yes, he understood. Something was wired up wrong inside him, but no one knew that, just himself and his mother, it was their secret. They shared it with Dr Brockman in Harley Street, who gave him medication and saw him less frequently now than he used to, and they all knew that Dr Brockman would never tell anyone else either.

His mummy had sent him to school as punishment for not loving her enough. She had warned him not to tell other boys their secret; that if anyone else knew their secret, they would come and take him away, and lock him up in an institution and he would never be able to see his mummy again, *ever*.

They were pointing fingers at him in the school playground now. Something that he'd done wrong but he didn't know what it was. They didn't like having him here, they didn't want him here. They were always telling him here that he wasn't quite right in the head and he got scared sometimes, that his mummy was leaking this information out to them to punish him for when he was bad.

A football rolling towards him, that he was ignoring. This was why they were bawling at him? A silly football?

Someone shouted, 'Hey, Thomas, creep, kick the ball!'

Richard Grantham ran up, panting, trapped the ball with his foot, dribbled around him twice in a tight circle. 'Hey, you know something, Thomas, you're weird. You know that?'

Today they were getting at him because he was supposed to have laughed at something, and he hadn't. Yesterday they were getting at him because he *had* laughed. This place, this school, everyone in it, they all operated on some level of consciousness he wasn't tuned in to at all. He didn't want to kick balls. In this place, if you didn't want to kick balls you were a freak.

The rush of footsteps behind him now. Then, before he could turn, he felt the shock of the hard toecap in his backside and he stumbled forward, crashing into the wire-mesh netting that surrounded the playground.

Winded, his face stinging, he turned and saw Tony Dickinson standing, arms folded, smirking. Several other boys were standing still, too. He turned, walked away, trying not to let them see that he was limping from the pain, went inside to his classroom, opened the lid of his desk and took out his modelling knife.

He tested the steel razor blade, to make sure it was really sharp, by making a tiny incision in his own finger and watching the thin line of blood appear.

Perfect!

Now, concealing the knife inside his hand, he sat down at Tony Dickinson's desk and monitored the clock on the wall, waiting for the end of break. He listened to the shouting outside, Then, finally, the sound of footsteps, chatter coming closer, chairs scraping, classmates drifting back in. And now, Dickinson's voice.

'Hey, jerk, you're in my place.'

Thomas stayed where he was, looking at the blackboard on which Mr Landymore had written in large, clear writing, MAGNA CARTA 1215, listening to the footsteps closing behind him.

Then his head was yanked back hard, by his hair, and he was staring straight up into Tony Dickinson's bulging eyes.

'Out of my chair, creep!'

Thomas did not move.

Dickinson lowered his face. 'I said *out*, creep!'

He started to hoist Thomas out by his hair. As he did so, Thomas raised his right hand and brought the blade in one fast, firm, horizontal slash across the boy's eyeball, straight across the white, the greeny grey iris and the black pupil. It was like slicing a grape. He saw the clean parting following the line of the incision, and then, in that brief (exquisite!)

291

moment before Dickinson realised what had happened, clear fluid oozed out.

It looked just like grape juice.

Chapter Sixty-six

The smell hit Glen Branson as he walked down the corridor on the second floor of Brighton police station, hands in his mac pockets, tired from his early start for Luton this morning. Although it was now only just after one p.m. he already felt he'd done a full day. And now this smell to contend with.

A WPC he recognised, who was with the Child Protection Unit, also housed here in the Serious Crimes Unit, walked past him and wrinkled her nose.

'Cor!' she said.

Glen nodded. Death. For the second time in a week. This putrid, rancid smell, growing stronger as he walked down the corridor, was exactly like the smell that had been in Cora Burstridge's flat last Thursday, although, if it were possible, this was even stronger.

And it got stronger still as he reached the open doorway of the photographic studio. Brilliant white light inside. A bloodstained cotton jacket was lying on a sheet of white background paper in front of a camera mounted on a tripod. Standing beside it, in a white protective suit, rubber boots and rubber gloves, was Ron Sutton, a scene-of-crime officer Glen had befriended during his two years' uniform apprenticeship at this station. Ron, like Glen, had a passion for old movies.

Tall, fair-haired and bearded, with a quiet, methodical air, Ron Sutton never seemed fazed by even his most gruesome tasks. At this moment, he was pulling a blood-stained beige sock out of a black plastic sack.

Glen stuck his head through the doorway and felt the

heat of the lights in here. 'Jesus, man, that is one fucking awful smell.'

'Tammy Hywell's clothes.' Ron turned to him and raised his eyebrows.

Glen nodded. Tam Hywell, their key prosecution witness in Operation Skeet who'd been hacked to death with a machete in his flat.

'I was wondering if you were busy,' Glen said. 'Stupid question.'

Ron stood behind the camera, took a series of photographs of the jacket from the same angle, but with different apertures. Glen let him concentrate, watching him. Ron then lifted the jacket, dropped it into another bag and laid out the sock on the background paper. 'You? How you getting on over in Hove?'

'Up and down. I need a favour.' Glen hesitated, then gave him a hopeful grin. 'Mike Harris said to mention his name.'

'He did, did he?'

'Yup.'

Ron moved the tripod forward, adjusted the tilt of the camera, then squinted through the lens. 'What kind of favour?'

'Would you mind bringing your gear to look at a loft hatch, and doing a little dust around a flat for me?'

Ron took a sequence of shots, removed the sock, then rummaged in the bag and produced the second sock. He laid that out on the paper. 'Not sanctioned?'

'It's a suicide, but I'm uncomfortable with it – I'll show you why.'

'Can't you get your DS to sanction a dusting?'

'No, I've tried Bill Digby – he's convinced it's suicide. Mike advised me to put in a G30 to the governor, which I'm doing.'

'I can't get prints processed without a sanction.'

'That's fine. I'd just like you to hang on to them, so at least you have them if we ever need to take it further.'

Ron gave him a strange look. 'You want to put your neck on the block, and mine? Why?'

'I'll tell you who it is, Ron. *Cora Burstridge!*'

Sutton's demeanour changed a little. 'That makes it more interesting. I might have guessed you'd find an excuse to go sniffing around her place.'

'It's not quite like that. I was the bugger that found her, and something's wrong, I tell you. Tomorrow her daughter and family tip up and there'll be prints all over the place. You don't just owe Mike a favour, you owe me one, too.'

'I do?'

'Remember that videotape I got you – of *Clockwork Orange*? Stanley Kubrick insisted the film was never shown again. The tape I seized in a haul last year and you said you'd give your back teeth to see it. I could have lost my career for getting you that tape.' Glen stepped in front of the camera lens. 'It's that favour, Ron.' Then he waved at the camera. 'Hi, Mum!'

'You're a pain, Glen. You're a big, bald pain.'

'And I'm black.'

'That, too.'

Chapter Sixty-seven

She was beautiful, and he was finding it hard to look at her. Partly because of the pain in her face, and partly because she reminded him so much of Amanda – the sound of her voice, the way she articulated, the way she moved, certain expressions in her face. She was, perhaps, an inch or two taller than Amanda, but the difference wasn't significant. With her long straight auburn hair, her tight black T-shirt and equally tight jeans, Teresa Capstick had more the air of an overgrown teenager than a woman of fifty-two.

Michael smiled wistfully as he looked around the drawing room, thinking how accurately Amanda had described her mother and her home. True Bohemia; trapped in a time warp from the late sixties. Aztec scatter rugs; bean bags; lava lamps; paper globe lampshades; joss-stick holders; a glass pyramid; a shelf piled with chunks of rock crystal. Self-help and mysticism books everywhere, and a framed quotation from Jonathan Livingstone Seagull on the wall.

Yet there was plenty of modern taste and style in evidence too, in this handsome Regency terraced town house. Some curious abstract paintings on the walls, several equally curious sculptures, a riot of plants, and stunning cream and black striped curtains. Through French windows that looked out onto an attractive, well-tended garden, Michael could see that the rain had stopped, but from the colour of the sky, it could start again at any moment.

He sipped some of his chicory-scented black coffee, then leaned forward and gratefully ate one of the smoked-salmon sandwiches she had bought for him from Marks and Spencer. He still had no appetite, but it was almost two in the afternoon, and as yesterday, he'd eaten only a meagre, hurried breakfast.

There were several framed photographs of Amanda in the room, some on her own, some with her sister, Lara, whom he had visited this morning before coming on here.

Lara looked quite different from Amanda. Brown-haired and with a heavier build, she was pleasant but much less confident than her sister, and today with her three small children all at home, ill with bugs, and her sister missing, stress showed in her pale, drawn face.

Michael had learned nothing from Lara that he didn't already know. Amanda had been to her niece's birthday party, she'd mentioned to Lara that she had a new man in her life – himself – and she'd also told Lara that her work was going brilliantly. She'd left to drive back to London on Sunday evening in as buoyant a mood as Lara had ever known.

And now her mother, who had also been at the birthday party, was saying the same thing. Nothing that Amanda had said to either of them on Sunday had given them any indication that something was wrong.

Teresa handed him another photograph album. 'These are her early teens.'

Michael wiped his fingers and lifted up the heavy leather cover. Amanda, with some fifteen years seemingly air-brushed away, grinned up at him from a gondola in Venice. Another Amanda, harder to recognise here, looking decidedly drunk, was singing at him from a crowded table in what looked like a ski-resort inn, and precociously holding a cigarette. Then another photo, of her standing on skis against a mountain backdrop, with an absurdly cool look-at-me! pose.

It was painful to look at these pictures, and yet he didn't want to stop.

'You spoke to the police again this morning?' she asked.

'Detective Sergeant Roebuck, yes. He had no news.'

'And her assistant, Lulu? She's very efficient.'

'We speak every few hours. Nothing. How well did you know Brian Trussler?' he asked.

'I met him once in seven years – Amanda invited me to her flat to meet him over a drink. He was very charming, but it's a difficult position for a mother to be in. You want the best for your daughter. An affair with a married man is not ideal. Do you know him?'

'I met him last night. I wanted to try to assess whether he could have done something to Amanda, out of anger at being dumped.'

'And what was your opinion?'

Michael wanted to say that he thought Brian Trussler was a complete tosser, but he didn't. Instead, he said, 'I don't think he cared enough for Amanda to want to harm her. But I can't be sure. I've told the police they should talk to him.'

'What do *you* think?' Teresa asked him. 'You don't think it is Brian Trussler, so what do you think has happened to her?'

When he looked up at her he saw the intensity of her gaze. The woman was no fool, she had studied psychology, she understood body language and now she was watching his.

She's checking me out. She suspects me, he realised, although it did not surprise him. I'd suspect me too, if I was her, he thought. I'd suspect anyone at this stage.

'I think Amanda is too stable to have simply taken off on her own accord because of pressure of work – or because of . . .' He tailed off.

Teresa filled in the words. 'Because of her emotional life?'

'Yes. She wouldn't have missed key business appointments, certainly not without phoning to cancel. At the very least she'd have spoken to Lulu.' He glanced down at the album, avoiding eye-contact for a few seconds. 'I think the best-case scenario right now is that something's happened to cause her to have amnesia – a trauma, or a knock on the head, something like that, and she could just be wandering around somewhere.'

Her lips tightened, and Michael could see she was quivering from her distress. 'And the worst?'

Michael stared at her levelly. 'That she's had an accident and hasn't been found yet.'

It wasn't the worst and they both knew it. Teresa nodded slowly, stood up and walked over to the French windows. As she spoke, she was choking on her words. 'Amanda used to love playing in the garden, when she was little. I had a sandpit – she liked to build imaginary film sets out of sand and put in her dolls and little cars. She'd make up whole stories around them. I grow herbs in it now. Mint, thyme, chives, rosemary, sorrel, dill. Do you like dill, Dr Tennent?'

'Please call me Michael.'

'Amanda taught me to cook fish with dill. She's always been so interested in everything around her. She teaches everyone she meets things. Has she taught you anything?'

There was a long silence during which he, too, was struggling for control, then he said, quietly, 'Yes.'

Teresa turned around and watched him through red eyes.

'She taught me how to live again.'

Chapter Sixty-eight

Thomas lay naked in the fine white lace-trimmed sheets in the canopied two-poster in his mother's bedroom. Chanel perfume and the smell of her hair, her oils, her skin still rose around him.

He watched her moving in front of him, dressed in her finery, climbing into the passenger seat of a convertible Ferrari outside the casino in Monte Carlo, while Rock Hudson held the door for her.

'You look so beautiful, Mummy,' Thomas whispered, rapt.

Tears ran down his face.

Three weeks and two days. In a coffin, cold and lonely, underground, in the dark.

He reached out and pressed the freeze-frame on the remote. His mother jigged in close-up, starkly lit. He lifted the small Sony tape recorder off the side table and pressed PLAY.

Dr Michael Tennent said, 'The bower-bird? I don't, no. Is ornithology one of your interests?'

He stopped the tape, replayed it, listened again to Tennent's voice. 'The bower-bird? I don't, no. Is ornithology one of your interests?'

He stopped the tape, then picked up a second tape-recorder and into it he said, 'Hallo, Amanda. How are you?' He paused then said it again, a little happier with the second attempt.

He played back the psychiatrist's voice. Then he played back his own voice. Still not right. His mother's face jigged on the screen. He wiped his recording of his own voice and tried again. 'Hallo, Amanda, how are you?'

Better! Oh, yes, *much* better!

He slid open the drawer in the bedside table and removed his mother's cream plastic vibrator and rolled its smooth, rounded surface against his nose. Still traces of her smell. He inhaled deeply, watched her face jigging away on the screen.

'Hallo,' he said again. 'Hallo, Amanda, how are you?'

His mother's face jigged away on the screen. Smiling. Approval!

Chapter Sixty-nine

'*Safe Arrival* – did you ever see that?' Ron Sutton asked, looking up at the framed production still on the wall of the passage through to Cora Burstridge's bedroom.

'With Ernest Borgnine and Walter Pidgeon,' Glen said.

'Good film, I liked that.'

'I didn't like the ending.'

'You're right, it was crap.'

Sutton, carrying a large black bag, was togged up in white protective clothing and rubber gloves, and Glen, in his brown suit, felt under-dressed beside him. 'This is where I found her.'

Sutton stared at the bed. 'Where was the note?' he asked.

'In the living room.'

They went through and Glen showed him the writing desk, where the note, which was now with the coroner, had been weighed down by the Lalique mermaid.

'And what did it say?'

' "I can no longer look at myself in the mirror." '

Sutton frowned.

'It's a quote from her film, *Mirror to the Wall*.' With James Mason, and Laurence Harvey, nineteen sixty-six,' Glen added.

'I never saw it.'

'You didn't?'

'No, I always seem to miss it when it's on television.'

'It was on BBC 1 last month.'

'I know. My son recorded something over it.'

'I think it's her best. I can't believe you've never seen it, man', Glen said, chidingly.

But Sutton was barely listening. He was looking around, thoughtfully. 'Seems a little strange, to quote from one of your own films in a suicide note.'

'That's what I thought.'

'Barry Norman was talking about *Mirror to the Wall* last night on television – I caught it half-way through, some tribute to Cora.'

'I recorded it, haven't seen it yet – I went to bed early.'

'He was saying there was a lot of controversy about that picture.'

'What did he say?'

'Gloria Lamark was originally cast in the role. Then something happened and she got bumped.'

Glen nodded. 'That's right. There's some stuff about it in one of Cora Burstridge's biographies. They used to go around slagging each other off in public, and one time Gloria Lamark threw a glass of wine over her at some royal première – *The Ipcress File*, or something around that time – right in front of one of the royals.' He shook his head. 'I can't believe you never saw it. Shit – that was the film that *made* Cora Burstridge's career. That was the film she got an Oscar nomination for.'

Sutton walked through the hall to the front door. He opened it, examined it, closed it, then opened it again. 'This has been fixed since you broke in, presumably?'

'Yes.'

'So if someone had entered via here, you effectively destroyed that evidence when you kicked the door open.'

With mock-contrition on his face, Glen said, 'Sorry about that.'

Sutton looked happier when he saw the mess inside the kitchen broom closet. He removed a brush and a tin of powder from his bag, and proceeded to brush dust carefully on the walls directly beneath the hatch, and on the entrance to the hatch itself. Then he took an ultraviolet floodlight from his bag, switched it on and examined the area he had dusted.

'Footprint,' he said.

Glen could see it also, a clear impression, the front half of a shoeprint.

Sutton photographed it. 'Size thirteen. What size are you?'

'Me? Eleven.'

'Anyone else from the force been up here?'

'No.'

'Big man,' Sutton said. 'Tall.'

'How do you know it's a man?'

Sutton gave him an odd look. 'Ever met a woman with size thirteen feet, Glen?'

'Nope. But there's always a first time.'

'I go for smaller builds myself.' Sutton studied the hatch surround. 'That's clean. Give me a leg up.'

Glen bridged his hands, and hoisted Sutton up. Then he followed him, switching the light on and getting a smirk out of Sutton's start when he saw the mannequin towering above him.

'*The Lady is Out*,' Glen said.

'The one with the size thirteen feet?'

'No, prat, her film, with Tony Perkins.'

'That was a good film. Scary.' He eyed the mannequin with the same wariness Glen had on his previous visit. 'So which way's the fire exit?'

Glen pointed, then followed him across the joists. 'There's a strip of –'

He stopped in mid-sentence. The scene-of-crime officer had already spotted the cream cloth hanging from a nail in a rafter.

Sutton shone his torch on it. 'This hasn't been here long,' he said. 'No dust on it.'

Glen's spirits lifted. He hadn't wanted Sutton to think he'd wasted his time coming here. The footprint in the closet had been a good start, and his reaction to this cloth was encouraging. 'Can you tell what it's from?'

'Not without analysis. Looks like linen. Could be a jacket, trousers, skirt, anything.'

'It's five and a half feet off the ground, Ron, it could hardly be trousers or a skirt.'

304

'Could be your woman with her size thirteen feet,' he said drily, carefully unhitching the strip and dropping it into a small plastic bag, which he handed to Glen. 'Hang on to it, keep it safe.'

They progressed slowly across the loft, checking all the rafters in turn, and the gaps between the joists, then finally reached the fire exit door. Sutton dusted the inside and surround for prints, but found nothing. Then he opened the door and blinked against the brilliant mid-afternoon light that burst in. The sky was clearing and the sun was out. It was going to be a fine evening.

They went on to the fire escape. Glen looked around at the rear of the neighbouring buildings. Such beautiful old houses from the front, but the backs were all bleak and ugly, scarred with fire escapes like the one they were on.

'High summer,' Ron Sutton said. 'Someone came up into the loft and now they've come out through this door, and there are no fingerprints. Not many people wear gloves in summer unless they don't want to leave prints lying around.'

'Or get their hands dirty,' Glen added.

Sutton was examining the area around the broken hatch. 'This has been opened from the inside – much the same way that you got into the flat – with a good kick.'

'You're sure?' Glen asked, a little flatly. It would have been much better if Ron could have shown that someone had broken in from the outside.

'No marks on the outside. If you'd wanted to break in from the fire escape you'd have had to lever the door open, and any tool you used would have scored the jamb or the door itself.'

Glen nodded; he could see it plainly. 'So, we have a shoeprint and a strip of cloth. I'm sorry, Ron, I hope you don't feel I've wasted your time.'

'People have been hanged on less evidence, Glen.'

'I don't think it's enough to convince Digby. Not yet. Half a footprint and a strip of cloth that could be from a suit or a skirt.'

'You have a lead now, Glen. You have a woman with size thirteen feet doing handstands in a loft.'

Glen gave him a cautioning look.

'Sorry,' Ron Sutton said. 'It's been a long day.'

Chapter Seventy

The National Missing Persons Helpline is housed on two floors in an anonymous, squat low-rise above a Waitrose supermarket in a bustling high street in Mortlake, a few miles west along the Thames from the Sheen Park Hospital. Visitors are discouraged. Its business is more effectively carried out by phone. Michael discovered this when he stood outside the entrance, the damp pavement steaming in the strong afternoon sun, and listened to the woman's voice through the entryphone. She was pleasant but firm.

'If you are reporting a missing person, we would prefer you to phone us. We have no facilities for seeing visitors.'

Michael was tired and fractious, fresh from a row over his mobile phone with DC Roebuck at Hampstead Police. The detective had told him that so far he had made no inquiries. Perhaps Michael would care to call him again later in the week?

It was four o'clock on Wednesday afternoon. Amanda had been missing now for over two and a half days. In three hours he was due on air at Talk Radio, and – although he didn't intend telling his producer in advance – he was going to give out a description of Amanda on that. Why not? What did he have to lose?

On the drive up from Sussex, Michael had retraced the route that Lara reckoned Amanda would have taken back to London on Sunday evening from her house. Several times, during the first part of the journey, which had been along rural roads, he'd stopped on bends where there was dense foliage or undergrowth that could have concealed a crashed car, and taken a look.

His shoes were muddy and his hands and face scratched

from brambles; he was glad there was just an entryphone and no closed-circuit television camera looking at him. He stared into the metal grille of the entryphone, and played his strongest card, hoping it would appeal to them. 'Actually, there's something I want to discuss. My name's Dr Michael Tennent. I'm a psychiatrist and I have a radio show on Wednesday nights. I could give your organisation a mention.'

There was a pause, then her voice again, reluctant. 'Please come up to the second floor.'

Michael could see what she meant when he pushed open the door at the top of the stairs, and walked through into a long, open-plan office. Some forty desks, he guessed at a rough count, ranked down either side. On the left were windows looking out onto an urban landscape, and on the right a wall covered, floor to ceiling along its full length, with missing-persons posters printed in bold red, blue and black lettering.

Almost every desk was occupied. People on the phone, or tapping on computer keyboards. A quiet air of activity and a much deeper, underlying sense of urgency. It was a diverse group of people behind the desks, male and female, mostly middle-aged, mostly white.

A stern, fair-haired woman of about forty, smartly dressed in a blue suit, came up to him. She eyed the state of his clothes with distaste and gave him a doubtful look. 'Dr Tennent?'

'Yes, look, I'm sorry to bounce in on you.'

'I'm Caroline Nelson,' she said, frostily, 'duty co-ordinator. I have actually listened to your show.'

He couldn't tell from her expression whether she liked it or not. But it was a good sign at least that she knew who he was. He smiled. 'They're always chucking the ratings figures at me. Nice to know that at least one of the listeners is genuine!'

'I'm afraid I'm not a regular listener,' she cautioned. 'Just occasional.' She glanced down at his shoes, then peered more closely at his face. 'Are you all right? Have you had an accident?'

'I'm fine. You'll have to forgive my appearance, I've been looking for someone – and I fell into a ditch.' He could see from her expression that the explanation had not gone down well, and he made a bid to retrieve the situation. 'Look, I'm sure you are inundated with people, but I'm not a crank. Someone I know has gone missing and I don't seem to be able to get the police to take this seriously. I'm going on air in three hours time and I could maybe say something useful if I was given guidance – and perhaps say something about your Helpline. I'm sure you need all the publicity you can get.'

'Can I offer you some tea? Coffee? Squash?'

'Tea, thank you.'

Caroline Nelson led him through into a small staff rest room, brought him tea in a plastic beaker, and sat down. She remained cold and wary. 'We get two hundred and fifty thousand people reported missing each year, Dr Tennent. If we let people come and make reports in person we'd have a queue to the end of the high street and back ten times.'

'I understand.'

'I'm making an exception for you. Just promise me you won't put out our address on the radio, only the phone number.'

Michael smiled. 'I promise.'

'Good.' She thawed a fraction. 'Now, tell me what on earth has happened to you.'

Michael told her the full story. When he had finished, instead of looking at him with sympathy, she looked at him testily. 'You didn't have a fight with her, Dr Tennent?'

'No! Absolutely not.'

'You're sure about that?'

'Of course. We – we had –'

'You didn't threaten her?'

'Not in any way. We were having a warm, loving time.'

'With no disrespect, that's something a lot of men say.'

'I'm not a wife beater. I don't have a dark side.'

'Even though you've come in here looking as though you've been in a pub brawl?'

She was starting to irritate him, and he had to make an

309

effort to remain cool. 'I told you, I was retracing Amanda's steps and fell into a ditch.'

She watched his face and said nothing.

Uncomfortable under her scrutiny, he stared out of the window. Two starlings sat on a television aerial. Amanda was somewhere out there, beyond that window. Where? *Oh, my darling, where are you?*

'You have to appreciate that we get men contacting us all the time, telling us their girlfriends or wives have gone missing, and the reason usually turns out that they had a fight and the woman ran off, terrified, either to a hotel or to a safe-house with friends.'

'It was nothing like that. Absolutely nothing like that. We had a perfect, beautiful day, we were walking arm in arm. She went off to her niece's birthday party and we were going to talk later. It was magical. We were two people in love. And it's not just me she's vanished from – she hasn't turned up at work, she's missed important business meetings. This is absolutely not like her. Her staff are extremely worried.'

'You were in love. You are assuming she was.'

'If she was faking it, she was a great actress.'

She drank some tea. 'You barely know her. It's quite possible she has a secret life that she's keeping from you.'

Michael put down his cup and stood up, clenching his fists in anger and frustration. 'Jesus!' He looked at her. 'What's with this screwed-up world? I've told you, I've been through it all. Even if she does have a secret life that she's keeping from me, she wouldn't have kept it from her assistant. Lulu was her confidante. Amanda's in trouble, she's in really terrible trouble – God forbid, she may even be dead. Am I the only person in the whole sodding country who cares about her, and who's trying to help her?'

Caroline Nelson raised her hands. 'OK, please calm down! We'll help.'

Michael turned away and watched the starlings again. 'Thank you.'

'Do you have a photograph of her?'

'Several.'

'We'll make up a poster and circulate it, see if we can get some television stations to put out an announcement. All right?'

'Anything,' he said. '*Anything*. Thank you.'

'If it's any encouragement to you,' she said, 'the majority of missing persons turn up within thirty-two days.'

'I can't wait thirty-two days. I'll be in a white tunic in my own clinic.'

She smiled, fleetingly, then looked serious once more. 'I'm sure she'll turn up. Over seventy-five per cent turn up within the first thirty-two days.'

'And the other twenty-five per cent? What happens about them?'

She stared him back in the eye and said nothing.

Chapter Seventy-one

Outside in the sun, Lara's husband, Oliver, in a Homer Simpson apron, was prodding sausages on the barbecue. The rest of them were sitting at the wooden table in the shade of the giant willow; Alice aged two, Leonora, four, and Jake, almost six were all laughing at a joke. Lara was laughing too.

Happy. Cloudless sky, total stillness. Beyond the hedge an oceanic field of ripening wheat swayed away into the distance. Alice was still chortling after the others had stopped.

'I'm in love,' Amanda announced.

They all turned towards her, smiling warmly, urging her to go on, to tell them more.

'I'm incredibly in love. I've never felt this way before, ever, I've found a man who –'

Her voice sounded strangely disembodied, as if she were eavesdropping on herself. Then, like a sharp focus pull, something changed. The sunlight was fading away, blotted up by the darkness.

Amanda became aware of the hard, lumpy mattress beneath her, and with it the fear returned as she opened her eyes into the horizonless darkness that was now her world.

She lay still, wondering what the time was. Was it night? Day? Morning? Afternoon? There must be a way to calculate the time, she thought, but how?

She badly needed to urinate.

Last time she had woken, she had aligned the mattress in the direction of her latrine bucket, and, stiff from lying down, she crawled forward slowly, then halted as she heard a faint scratching sound.

Jesus. A rat?

Something touched her face, a mosquito or a midge, some insect, she slapped it hard, savagely, heard the slap echo around the chamber.

She reached the bucket, which stank of earlier urine. After relieving herself, she sponged her face and arms from the wash bucket. As she dried herself, standing up to stretch her legs, she felt a little more clear-headed.

And now she could feel, acutely, the silent presence of the two corpses in the next-door chamber. One was a woman; she hadn't had the courage to check the other. A woman editor had gone missing a few weeks back; she'd been in the papers, on television, a pleasant-looking woman, with short brown hair, of about thirty. Was it her?

Had they all been kidnapped by some monster like Fred West or the man who skinned people in *Silence of the Lambs*?

Then she stiffened as she thought she heard the scuff of a foot.

Her brain raced with a plan that had been forming earlier, that she would stand by the door next time he came in, and slip out in the darkness behind him.

Another option was to hit him when he came in, but what with? There was nothing here. A mattress, plastic buckets, paper plates, paper tray, plastic jug. Nothing heavy enough to bring a man down, not even a full plastic bucket would guarantee that.

Then, suddenly out of the darkness, came Michael's voice. 'Hallo, Amanda. How are you?'

She spun round in deep shock. 'Michael?'

Silence.

'Michael?' she said again, afraid she had imagined it.

'Hallo, Amanda, how are you?'

It was Michael. A cold, detached Michael; it was his voice, but it was as if some other personality was speaking it.

The room stank of urine. Messy thing, rolling around in its

own filth. This was disgraceful; it needed to be punished for the state of this room.

Thomas, brandishing a cattle prod, watched her through his goggles. Such clear green vision! He could see every reflex. She was standing with her back to the wall, staring in the wrong direction, staring at where he had been just a moment ago.

'Take your clothes off, Amanda,' he said, still mimicking Dr Michael Tennent's voice.

'Keep away from me.'

'Would you like my choo-choo inside you?'

Even more nervous now. 'Keep away from me.' She raised her voice. 'Michael, keep away!'

Silently, he took a step towards her, then another. 'Where would you like me to begin hurting you, Amanda?'

'I thought you loved me, Michael,' she said, in a choking voice, and took a step forward from the wall, thinking she was moving away from him. But silently, on his trainer shoes, he stepped sideways until he was in front of her once more. And she did not realise it but she was looking right into his eyes.

With immense satisfaction he jabbed the cattle prod as hard as he dared into her stomach and fired the electrical charge.

The sudden, ferocious stabbing, winding pain, followed by a juddering that ripped through her body, sent her tumbling backwards against the wall with a gasp of shock and agony.

There was another fierce pain, this time in her chest. Her whole insides were pinched tight then sprang free, then pinched tight again, then sprang free again, as if she were plugged into an electrical socket that was being switched on and off. The pain moved to her thigh, then to her face, each time the agonising constriction, then release. Screaming again, arms protectively over her head, she rolled across the floor, trying to escape, crashed into a wall, barrelled through the buckets, begging him to stop. 'Please!

Pleeeeaaaassssseeeee. I'll do anything. Tell me what you want. Ooowwwwwwwwwwwwwwwwww.'

Then silence.

An eternity of silence. She lay still, waiting for the next pain. But it did not come.

A floodtide of nausea burst through her. She vomited.

Chapter Seventy-two

Marj was on the line. She phoned in every week, without fail, hoping to get through to Michael, with yet another nugget she'd hauled out of the collective works of Jung or Freud to test out on him.

The small studio felt more cramped than ever tonight. He couldn't get far enough away from the microphone, the damned foam bulb was in his face, angled aggressively towards him like some bird of prey that was about to peck out his eyes.

Chris Beamish, the producer, sat in the control room on the other side of the wide rectangle of soundproofed glass, watching him. *Why?* He never normally watched him, just screened the callers and left him to get on with it.

And behind Beamish, the studio technician, also bearded, was farting around with some Dexion shelving, which Michael was finding irritatingly distracting. The previous occupant of this studio had stuck about a dozen yellow Post-it notes to the console top and these were disturbing him too. He tried to avoid them but his eyes kept being drawn down to them to escape Beamish's stare. 'Virtual Reality?' one said. 'Artificial Life? If it looks like a duck, walks like a duck and swims like a duck, then it probably is a duck.'

Michael pressed the microphone switch and, trying not to sound too weary, said, 'Good evening, Marj from Essex!'

'Good evening, Dr Tennent. I wonder if you could enlighten me on Jung's acausal connecting principle?'

'Certainly, Marj, what's bothering you about it?' he said, a trifle facetiously, but this was lost on her.

'Well, I'm not sure I understand it,' she said, in her

deadpan voice. 'I'm worried that events may be happening in my life for reasons I don't understand.'

Michael looked at the clock on the wall: seven ten. Eighteen minutes before the commercial break. Time for Marj and one more caller. He would make his own announcement after that. This was a big subject Marj had bounced on him, and he was trying to think of a succinct sound-bite to cut through it. 'Do you ever have coincidences, Marj?'

'All the time.'

'Jung believed in *meaningful coincidence*. I seem to remember he once said that coincidences were God's calling cards.'

'I like that!' she said.

'You're aware of Jung's *collective unconscious* theory, Marj?'

'I won't say I understand it but, yes, I am aware of it.'

'Jung had several personal paranormal experiences, Marj. These confronted him with events that seemed inexplicable in terms of normal physical or psychological causes. Therefore he felt that normal causality was insufficient to explain these events and he began to term them *acausal*. Is that clear?'

'Ermmm, no, not really. Didn't he fall out with Freud over the nature of coincidence?'

Michael tried to bring the focus back to Marj's own personal problems, but she held him pinned to the attitudes of Freud and Jung for the remainder of the session.

'Hope that's clarified it for you Marj,' he said finally, killing her call with relief, glad to have muddled through that one, although from his producer's bemused expression, he knew he hadn't done brilliantly.

On the small computer screen to the side of his console he could see there were six callers waiting. They were listed by their first name and the area where they lived. If they had called previously, 'Reg' appeared in brackets beside their name, so Michael could welcome them back.

Top of the list now was a peculiar name. Nadama from

317

North London. Next, below her was Raj from Ealing. Then Ingrid from Notting Hill Gate, and Gareth from Ickenham.

He pressed the switch and said cheerily, 'Hallo, Nadama from North London!'

Through his headphones, in a quavering, terrified voice, he heard Amanda. She said, 'Michael?'

In joy, he almost shouted, 'Amanda? Where are you? Are you OK?'

'Michael,' she replied, 'I'm scared. I don't like this game. Can we stop playing it, please?'

He saw the strange look on Beamish's face, but he didn't care. He had Amanda on the line. He gave Beamish a frantic signal to cut live transmission, to go to music, anything.

'What game? Game? I'm not playing any game, Amanda. God, are you all right? Thank God you've called, I've been going out of my mind. Where are you?'

'Keep away from me.'

The ON AIR light was still on. He gave Beamish another frantic CUT signal. An almost imperceptible nod of acknowledgement, then the light went off.

She sounded terrible, there was an unnatural edge to her voice.

As gently as he could he said, 'Amanda, please, I don't understand. What's happened? Why are you upset?'

'Keep away from me.' She raised her voice. 'Keep away!'

This was freaking him out.

'I thought you loved me, Michael. I thought you loved me,' she said.

Wild thoughts banged through his head. Had Brian got to her and said something venomous? 'Amanda, listen to me, tell me what's happened. What have I done? Has someone said something –'

The line went dead. She'd hung up. The name Nadama disappeared from the screen.

Nadama. Jesus. A crude anagram. He looked up. Beamish was gesturing at him in despair. Then his voice on the intercom. 'Mike, for God's sake, what are you playing at?'

Michael stared back at him numbly.

'One minute to the end of the news, then you're back on air.'

'Can you trace that call?' he replied.

'Forty seconds.'

'Trace that fucking call!' he yelled.

'I'll do what I can, OK? Twenty seconds.'

Michael hit the button, and Raj from Ealing was live on air.

Chapter Seventy-three

Michael.

She tried to get her head round it as she lay in the dark silence, surrounded by the smell of her own vomit – and could not. She was in so much pain it was hard to think clearly.

How could someone who had seemed so sweet and lovely be capable of doing this?

Michael was smart; he might be insane but he was smart. He would know that releasing her could never be an option.

She thought back to that night they had spent together, in some other universe, in some other time-frame, how safe she had felt in his arms, how she had wanted nothing else but to lie there making love with him for ever. And she was remembering now that chilling look on his face when she had been holding Katy's photograph. The grip of his hand on her arm.

Christ, I was a fool to ignore that.

She should have bailed out then and there. In those few brief moments, his dark side had been plain to see. But she had chosen to ignore it, deluded herself that it was a manifestation of grief, nothing more.

She felt a terrible, cold, falling sensation of dread inside her. How would anyone ever find her? She could imagine Lulu and Michael talking on the phone. Michael feigning concern, giving all sorts of advice, telling her how happy they had been together and acting distraught.

Everyone would believe him. Michael was above suspicion. No one was going to come and find her. Her only choice was, somehow, to get out by herself.

Where am I?

She tried to think back to those brief precious moments when the light had been on. Some kind of man-made chamber. Sterile. Modern. From the total absence of light, and complete silence, she guessed underground.

A bank vault? Possible. Some kind of disused command post, built during the Cold War, when every county in Britain had fallout shelters for key civil servants and emergency services? It wouldn't be hard for someone like Michael Tennent to know the whereabouts of such a place and even to have access.

She could be anywhere in Britain, she thought.

How long since he'd been gone? An hour? Two hours? *Got to find a way to measure time down here.*

The screws of the vent grille were about the diameter of her little finger-nail. Her thumb-nail fitted snugly into the groove. She needed a screwdriver.

Painfully, she got to her feet, found the wall, and fumbled her way around the chamber until she came to the open doorway into the second chamber. As she stared ahead, tiny flecks of light came out of the darkness at her. Shapes moving. Shadowy figures swirling. Her imagination running riot, she stepped back a pace, goosebumps covering her skin.

They're dead, they're not up and walking about. They're dead, Amanda.

Dead.

You'll be just like them if you don't do something. Remember *survivors*. Survivors stay calm, they put their fear into another compartment, they think logically, they are utterly determined to live.

Keeping contact with the wall, she made her way through into the second chamber, until her left foot suddenly struck something solid. Even though she'd been searching for it, actually touching one of the corpses froze her in her tracks.

It was some while before she had sufficient courage to kneel down. Close to the cadaver's skin, the acrid reek of formalin was almost unbearable. She put out her hands and

321

felt nylon. A stockinged ankle. Hard, like a piece of furniture, not human flesh. Thin ankle strap. Small flat shoe, a woman's shoe.

The heel was solid, it might come in useful, she logged it mentally, then moved her hands up the leg. Reached a skirt. Cotton and viscose mix. Then a blouse, cotton. No belt. Moving up the body was horrible, feeling the arms, the bare flesh like cold, hard rubber. Down the left arm to the wrist, and she came to a watch, a slim metal watch on a leather strap. But the dial wasn't luminous, it was of no use to her.

Now the worst bit. Up to the face. A light, tentative touch with her fingers then she waited, plucking up the courage to explore further, trying to feel the contours of this woman's face, to get some clue about her age, what she looked like. She explored higher, feeling her hair now. Short, layered cut.

Like the missing editor had. *Tina Mackay*. She remembered the name now: a name that for the past couple of weeks had been in the nation's consciousness.

Tina Mackay, have I found you?

She moved away, shaking uncontrollably, her eyes streaming from the formalin, her throat tight with fear.

Down on her knees now she groped with her hands for the second body and then had to fight hard to keep control of herself when she found it, when her hands touched fabric and the hard motionless shape inside it.

A jacket. Shirt. Tie.

She drew back, hesitated, then touched the body again. Felt the tie. Polyester. Then the shirt, that was polyester also. A belt. Trousers. A wide, robust belt with a hard metal buckle. Good, this was good.

She explored upwards to the neck, then the face, the soft stubble on the chin. Definitely a man although his face felt free of wrinkles, and there was only such soft stubble. Maybe he was young, early twenties?

Had any young man been in the papers, missing, in his early twenties?

She felt inside the jacket pockets for anything that could

be useful, but they were empty. He was wearing loafer shoes and they had good, hard heels also. Now she worked her way down his right arm, feeling for a watch. *Please have some kind of digital watch with a light source.*

There was no hand at the end of the arm. Just scabby, cauterised flesh.

She dropped it in shock.

Then she leaned across, found his other arm, traced down the length of that, and found the scabby stump at the end of that, too.

Michael, what did you do to him? What did you do to her? What are you going to do to me?

Fighting back more tears, she removed his belt and shoes, then hurriedly returned to her own chamber.

Kneeling in a corner, she examined the belt and buckle with her fingers, the smell of leather reminding of the outside world, of shops, of the interior of cars, finery, the handbag department at Harvey Nichols. She brought the belt up to her nose, pressed it to her nostrils and breathed in the luxurious smell.

I'm getting out of here. Somehow. I'm going shopping in Harvey Nicks. I'm going to walk by the ponds on Hampstead Heath. I'm going to drive my car under the blazing sun with the roof down. I'm going to hold my nephews and nieces in my arms. I'm going to drink cold wine and smoke a cigarette.

She craved a cigarette now.

Focusing again, she gripped the belt hard in her right hand, pulled back the buckle, leaving the spike out, gripped the buckle hard against the belt with the spike between her fingers. Then she rotated her hand to the right, and to the left. Easy. She had a good, firm grip.

Now, with her left hand she pushed the buckle hard down on the floor so that the spike lay flat and, with her right hand, gripped the front of the dead man's loafer, and brought the heel down hard, like a hammer.

On the first blow, she hit the floor wide of the mark. On the second she hit her knuckles and, with a stifled cry of pain, dropped the shoe and the belt. Then she wound the belt around her fingers as a makeshift guard, and tried again.

The metallic ping told her she'd struck the right spot. She brought the heel down again. THWACK. Missed, struck the floor. Then again. PINGGGGG. It found its mark. Then again. And again.

After several successful hits, she checked the spike. It was warm. That was good. She knew from all she had learned about engines that the warmer metal got the more pliable it became.

Thomas stood just a few feet away, watching her through his goggles. What on earth was it doing? Kneeling on the floor hitting a belt buckle with the heel of a loafer?

Whatever was going on inside its pea-brained mind was OK by him. He didn't care, it could do what the hell it liked.

He retreated as silently as he had come in.

The light came on, detonating an explosion of fear inside her.

Turning in shock, Amanda closed her eyes tightly against the searing glare, dropped the shoe, unravelled the belt and clamped her hands over her eyes.

Silence.

Fearfully, she removed her hands slowly and then, gradually, opened her eyelids, letting increasing amounts of the glaring light in.

Now they were wide open, darting around the chamber, her muscles tensed, ready to fight the bastard with anything she could. But not ready for what she saw.

On the floor, just four feet behind her, she saw a tray of food, with a fresh jug of water. There was an apple on the tray. A pizza. Her red plastic latrine bucket had been replaced with a yellow one, the orange plastic washing bucket with a green one. There was a fresh towel. The old tray had gone.

The light went out again.

Chapter Seventy-four

'Michael, I'm scared. I don't like this game. Can we stop playing it, please?'

Michael sat at his desk in his study at home, staring at the square black speakers either side of his Aiwa sound system.

'Keep away from me.'

It was ten twenty p.m. He'd been home for over an hour and a half, just sitting here in his den, drinking a mug of coffee, playing the tape over and over, trying to think things through.

Trying to come up with something that made sense.

Beamish at the radio station said the call was untraceable. It had been one of hundreds that had come into the switchboard this evening. There was no logging system. In fact, as his producer had wryly pointed out to him, total anonymity was one of the advertised gimmicks of the show. Anyone could phone in; their identification was never checked.

And Beamish was angry with him. He wasn't a man to express his feelings, but Michael could see the signs plainly enough in his face. And yes, Michael could scarcely blame him. A domestic row live on air. Great. Beamish, afterwards, had asked quietly if he had any idea quite how much damage to his credibility as a psychiatrist this little public row might have caused.

He didn't have any idea, nor did he care right now.

'I thought you loved me, Michael. I thought you loved me.'

What is this about, Amanda?

He rewound the tape. Paced around the study. Sat down on the edge of his Parker Knoll recliner armchair, sipped his tepid coffee.

'I thought you loved me, Michael. I thought you loved me.'

I do love you. God, I love you more than anything on earth. I love you more, even, than – He stared, guiltily, at Katy's photograph in the frame on his desk. She was lying down on a picnic rug in a field, in striped leggings and a loose black shirt, giving him a great big warm grin.

He hadn't rung Lulu. He'd promised to call her if he heard anything, but what the hell was he going to say to her? That Amanda was sounding scared of him, that that was why she'd disappeared?

He picked up the phone, began to dial Lulu's number, then hung up. If Amanda had phoned him, then quite probably she had phoned Lulu too. More than probably, he thought. *Certainly.*

Maybe she'd kept Lulu in the loop on this all along. Told her to pretend she didn't know where she was to keep him off her back.

Had Lulu been lying?

That seemed so improbable. And yet . . .

She had phoned him on the radio station, live on air.

Why?

Back to Saturday night here. Their meal. Amanda's concern about the car across the road. Their lovemaking. Amanda looking out of the window, worried again. Sunday morning, just an incredible, wonderful morning. Their visit to the stock-car race-track had been relaxed, happy.

So what had poisoned her?

He could think of nothing that he had said or done that could have given her any reason to behave like this towards him. He turned his thinking to her mental state. What she had said in the phone call bore the hallmarks of paranoia. Was she suffering from some paranoid psychosis triggered by the stress of a new relationship? Or was she on drugs? Cannabis, crack, ecstasy and amphetamines could all cause this kind of psychosis.

One behavioural pattern of paranoids was to read hidden meanings into innocent remarks, and to misinterpret things. Compliments in particular could be seen as veiled criticisms. If you told a paranoid woman she looked beautiful, she could take this as meaning that she had not previously looked beautiful. If you told her you loved her, she might take this as a ploy to get more out of her.

Paranoids tended to display labile moods, normally stubborn, sarcastic or openly hostile. But there had been no anger in her voice.

It was more like fear.

He thought about the physiological effects of a neurological condition. That was one possible cause of a sudden personality change. Was she suffering from temporal lobe epilepsy? Or a brain tumour?

He rang Lulu's home number. She answered almost immediately, sounding sleepy. He held back from saying he'd spoken to Amanda, instead he said, 'Lulu, sorry to call so late.'

'S'fine. Any news?'

'Listen, tell me something. Amanda doesn't have any history of epilepsy, does she?'

'God, no, not that I know of.'

'Would she have told you?'

'Yah. Anyhow, she had a thorough medical recently, one of those BUPA check-ups for a key-man insurance cover we took out. I filled in the forms with her. I'd have seen if she'd written down anything like that. Why?'

'She rang me tonight, when I was live on air on the radio. She doesn't sound right.'

'She rang you?' The surprise in her voice sounded genuine.

'Yes.'

'Thank God! I've been going out of my mind. She's all right? She's OK?'

'I – I'm not sure.'

'Where on earth is she?'

'She didn't say.'

'Tell me! What did she say?'

'I have it on tape.'

'But she's OK?'

He hesitated. 'I don't know.'

'What do you mean?'

'Listen, Lulu, you know her much better than I do, I'd like you to hear her. I –'

'Can you play it over the phone? No, look, where are you? I could jump in a taxi. Just give me time to get dressed.'

'I'll come to you. Whereabouts are you?'

'Clapham Common.'

'Give me your address. I'll be with you in twenty minutes.'

'I'll put some coffee on.'

'I'll need it.'

Chapter Seventy-five

The lawn needed mowing. He remembered now: in summer the grass needed cutting once a week. There was a man who came and cut it with a machine. The same man who did the flower-beds and fixed things that went wrong in the house and drove them around in the Bentley which, like the white van, Thomas had put into a multi-storey on contract parking. The garage was a bit full right now, with Terence Goel's Ford Mondeo (lucky Dr Goel didn't have a bigger car) and what was left of Amanda Capstick's Alfa Romeo convertible (lucky *she* didn't have a bigger car).

He was going to have to make some space for Dr Michael Tennent's grey Volvo, otherwise he could foresee it causing problems when it arrived. And these weren't the kind of problems he needed.

I'm not a fucking car-park attendant.

Someone had thrown tinfoil into the fish pond. The *lagoon*, his mother like to call it. Vandals must have been in the garden. This pissed him off. He shone the torch onto the water and the tinfoil glinted. Above it, the tiny Baroque folly that was the island in the middle stood like a silhouette.

Night. Dark now. Eleven o'clock. A woman's laughter on the other side of the garden wall. The long grass was wet, but it was a dry night. Stars up there shimmering through the prisms. Someone was barbecuing. He smelt burning olive oil and grilling meat. Lights on in his neighbour's house, in a second-floor window. The woman's laughter chipping away at the silence of the night. It was quite late to eat, he thought.

The neighbours in the house on the right were Swiss.

They lived mostly in Connecticut, and only used next door a few weeks a year. They kept a Filipino maid to look after the place. In the house on the left, a retired stockbroker. He travelled a lot too.

The tinfoil in the water wasn't tinfoil.

He remembered now that his mother had sacked the man who cut the grass, just before she'd –

Sometimes it was easier not to think that word. *Died.* That put a certainty on it that he did not like. It was still possible that she'd gone away for a little while and would be coming back. Sometimes, walking around the house or strolling around the garden like this, he really felt that she was still around. Not her ghost, nothing like that, just herself. Any moment she would call out his name.

What was the *thing* doing with the shoe and the belt buckle? This needed more investigation. He made a mental note to check this out. But not right now. Now there was the tinfoil that was not tinfoil on the surface of the *lagoon.*

And now he remembered that this man who came and cut the grass, and who fixed things in the house and who drove the Bentley, and who had been fired by his mother, this man had also fed the koi carp. He should have been feeding them but there wasn't any food, and he'd forgotten to get any.

Now they were dead and floating on the surface.

He stood right at the water's edge and pointed the beam of the torch down. Their eyes looked back at him. Their stench hung in the air – he could smell it now, here, away from the barbecue smells.

I should have remembered to feed you.

This was all Dr Michael Tennent's fault. He had been distracted. *You killed my mother, Dr Michael Tennent, and now you've killed her fish. Would you like to kill me now? Would that complete your trinity?*

He went back inside the house, closed the side door from the kitchen, locked and bolted it. Then he stood still and listened to see if he could hear any sound from the thing down in the shelter.

Of course he couldn't! Thirty feet underground, encased

in concrete. It could hit belt buckles with shoes all night. It could detonate a small nuclear device and it wouldn't make any difference. Nobody would hear it.

He could do anything he wanted to it. So much choice. He wondered what it would be like to try out his choo-choo on it. That thought made him redden. As if his mother was in the room with him now, scolding him, reminding him. *'You do understand, don't you, Tom-Tom? About not being quite right in the head? You do understand that, don't you?'*

It was easy to forget things. It was important not to complicate his life. Take one thing at a time. He had forgotten the fish and he had nearly forgotten why he had brought Dr Michael Tennent's bit of fluff here.

He had not brought it here for its body to give him pleasure, he had brought it here to punish Dr Michael Tennent. There would be no point in trying his choo-choo out on it until Dr Michael Tennent was watching.

'Your father left because you were not right in the head. He couldn't stay and look after you, he was too embarrassed, Tom-Tom. I sacrificed my career for you. Remember that, darling, remember that always.'

He sat down in the drawing room and stared at her photographs all around the walls. He reminded himself how big his debt to her was and that he must not squander this chance to repay it in frivolity.

He tried to think what tonight would have been like with her. They would have had dinner together, then watched a video, and maybe, if she was in a good mood, she would have let him watch one of her old films. They would have done this together, tonight, if it were not for Dr Michael Tennent.

He switched on the television, and saw, to his anger, that a Cora Burstridge film was showing. Punching the remote, he brought up the news on Teletext. There was an item on Tina Mackay. The police had no leads. They were widening their search, appealing for information.

They were showing Cora Burstridge's films because he had killed her. They were putting Tina Mackay on the news because he had taken her. The realisation began to dawn on

331

him that he was *making news happen*. He had caused television schedules to be changed to accommodate Cora Burstridge retrospectives. The power lifted him. No one had come to Gloria Lamark's funeral, but he would see to it that her death went on affecting the nation for a long time to come.

I matter.

He had taken Tina Mackay three weeks ago tonight. They could widen their search all they liked. They could appeal to everyone on the planet for information. Fine by him. This wouldn't have happened if he had released her. Suddenly he did not have a problem over what he had done to her.

He only had a problem with Jurgen Jurgens, of Clearwater, Florida, who had thrown at him a Karpov pawn attack that he had failed to spot. It had been so obvious. It had cost him a bishop to stay in the game, and that was a heavy price to pay.

He went to his den to deal with Jurgen Jurgens. As he sat down at his computer, he started thinking about his biography of his mother. There would be enormous interest in it, now that she was dead. He must send it off to another publisher. Perhaps to several publishers all at once, make a big splash this time, try to get an auction going. A bidding war!

Amanda Capstick was not on the news yet.

Which would hurt you the most, Dr Michael Tennent? To think that she did not love you any more, or to receive part of her body in the mail?

Chapter Seventy-six

Michael had formed a mental image of Lulu as a tall, power-dressed, horsy Sloane.

The creature curled up on the floor in front of the speaker, cradling a mug of coffee the size of a small chamber-pot, in ragged leggings, a baggy Oasis T-shirt and spangled flip-flops, was a tiny rotund ball of energy, with an impish face, huge saucer-like eyes and short, spiky black hair.

Her flat was cosy and cramped, the walls lined with posters of obscure plays and poetry readings, the floor piled high with videotapes, CDs and books and strewn with cushions. It felt like being in a nest.

Michael sat in lopsided armchair with wonky springs beneath a large sash window, open in the muggy heat of the night, that let in the roar of traffic from the busy thoroughfare of Clapham Common West. As they listened to the tape he watched her face, unable to stop himself cringing, as he always did, at the sound of his own voice.

'Amanda? Where are you? Are you OK?'

'Michael, I'm scared. I don't like this game. Can we stop playing it, please?'

'What game? Game? I'm not playing any game, Amanda. God, are you all right? Thank God you've called, I've been going out of my mind. Where are you?'

'Keep away from me.'

'Amanda, please, I don't understand. What's happened? Why are you upset?'

'Keep away from me. KEEP AWAY! I thought you loved me, Michael. I thought you loved me.'

Michael gave Lulu a signal and she hit STOP, those big

saucer eyes fixed on him. Baleful. She said nothing for some moments, then she said, 'Can we play it again?'

He picked up his own enormous mug, sipped the hot sweet coffee and nodded. On the wall directly in front of him was a poster that had just words on it, a quotation. Light green words on a dark green background. They said, 'If you ever thought you were too small to make a difference, you've never shared a bed with a mosquito.'

He looked back at Lulu. In other circumstances, he'd have been amused.

They played the tape through twice more, then Lulu stood up and paced the tiny floor space, wringing her hands. 'Her voice is wrong,' she said.

'You think so?'

'It's – oh, God – it's her, but there's something very wrong.'

'In what sense?'

'She's frightened, Michael.'

'I think that, too.'

'I can't put my finger on it. It's not sounding *natural*. Do you know what I mean?'

'Yes, I do.'

'Can we play it again?'

They listened once more.

'It's the way she's responding – like – like there's nobody home. It's as if she's on drugs or something, but she *can't* be.'

'What makes you so sure she isn't?'

'Because she took something once, about ten years ago when she was a student, and she freaked out. Had a really bad trip, I mean *seriously* bad, OK? She ended up going to see a shrink.'

'I didn't know.'

Lulu was animated when she talked, gesticulating with her arms, her face wildly expressive. 'Acid. LSD, I think, it wiped her, big-time. She's always told me how scared it had made her of drugs. Brian was into coke and other stuff and she told me he used to try to get her to take stuff with him

334

and she always refused. She's a very together, very determined lady. I know she'd never take anything again. Ever.'

'OK,' Michael said. 'We eliminate that she might be on drugs.'

'How about Brian?' she said.

He told Lulu of his visit to Trussler last night, and she didn't seem surprised to hear he had another woman. 'The guy's a shit. I never told Amanda, but he has a reputation, right?'

Michael detected an almost wistful look in those huge eyes, as if she regretted, almost felt slighted, that Trussler hadn't made a pass at her.

'So we can discard Brian Trussler?'

'For the moment,' she said. 'You're a psychiatrist. Tell me what other explanations you have for a mood change like this.'

'It is possible to get a sudden personality change from neurological causes. The most likely are either temporal lobe epilepsy, a brain tumour or a stroke.'

She looked aghast.

'All these conditions can bring on paranoia, but it tends to be aggressive paranoia.'

'Never fear?'

'It's possible to have persecution delusions – maybe Amanda believes I want to harm her in some way.'

'What do you think is the most likely cause in her case?'

'Of her paranoia?'

'Yes.' She knelt and picked up her mug.

'The altered brain chemistry results in the condition causing personality change. Things that we normally repress can be released. You see it particularly in someone who's been hiding a low self-esteem.'

'That doesn't sound like the Amanda I know.'

'No. But she's displaying a dramatic behavioural change consistent with a neurological disorder. One of the classic symptoms is to misconstrue friendly actions by other people as hostile. This could be what we're hearing here.'

'And this is what you really think? That she's had a total

personality change because of developing epilepsy, or a brain tumour or a stroke?'

'You're absolutely certain she has no history of depressive illness?'

'As certain as I can be. You'd have to be an idiot to lie on a medical insurance form, wouldn't you?'

'It would invalidate any claim.' He drank some more coffee. He was hungry, yet he didn't want to waste time eating. Life was on hold. Amanda was the only thing that mattered and his concerns were growing with every second.

It felt strange being here with Lulu. Almost as if he was close to Amanda,

'I'm not convinced there's anything neurologically wrong with her. There are always exceptions to all conditions, but normally a person suffering any of the above turns aggressive. If she had a depressive illness that would be different, but as we know she hasn't, it gives us a problem.'

She nodded. 'Why she's sounding afraid – right?'

'Uh-huh.' He rewound the tape and ejected it from the machine.

She held out her hand. 'Can I take a look?'

He passed it to her.

'This was made by the studio tonight?'

'Yes.'

'What about getting her voice analysed?'

He stifled a yawn, tiredness seeping through the adrenaline. The air in the room felt heavy and slow. 'I know the person to do it.'

He pulled out his mobile phone and called his producer at home.

A sleepy voice grunted into the receiver. When Chris Beamish heard it was Michael on the other end, he became hostile. 'Ten to twelve. Jesus, I'm trying to have an early night. Michael, you've already given me one headache tonight. Call me in the morning.'

Michael yelled at him not to hang up. The line stayed

open. 'Listen,' Michael said. 'This is a real emergency, I need your help.'

He listened for a response, but all he heard was the faint hiss of static.

'Chris, you used to work for the police analysing audio-tapes, right?'

'Yes. I still do,' he said sourly. 'And insurance companies and detective agencies. What of it?'

'You love your wife and children. Three children, right?'

'What the hell is this, Michael? You're phoning me at midnight to throw a questionnaire about my life at me? I think, maybe, after your performance earlier tonight, you ought to go and see a shrink. Sorry I can't recommend one – I used to know a really good one.'

The line went dead. He'd hung up.

Michael stared at the phone in frustration then called back. It was picked up on the second ring and Beamish, in a more resigned and less hostile tone, said, 'Yes, Michael?'

'This is not a questionnaire, Chris. The woman who rang, who I told you was missing, I think she could be in terrible trouble. I need your help. She means to me what your wife and kids mean to you. I haven't lost my marbles – I wouldn't be phoning you at this hour if I didn't think that every minute mattered right now. Help me, Chris. I've never asked you for help before and I won't ask you again, but for God's sake help me this time.'

A brief silence. 'Do you want to bring it over now?'

'*Now?*' Michael responded with excitement and relief.

'I'm awake. Sue's awake. The kids are awake. The dog's awake. The damned budgerigar's awake and the goldfish and the hamster. Let's do it.'

'I'm sorry.'

'No, you're not sorry, Michael. Just bring the tape over.'

Chapter Seventy-seven

This had to work. She had no idea how much time she had left. Michael might have night-vision glasses. He might have seen her working on the belt buckle when he'd brought in the tray – but if he had, why had he let her carry on?

Pushing these questions to the back of her mind, she concentrated on her task. She doubled the mattress against the wall, on the spot she had marked with the spare shoe from the dead man then, holding the belt, with the end of the buckle spike beaten flat like a screwdriver blade, she climbed onto the mattress, careful to keep her balance. She raised her arms and groped for the ventilation grille.

To her relief, the fit was perfect: the blade nestled firmly in the groove of the first screw. Holding it firmly, she twisted it. Nothing happened. She twisted harder. Still nothing. Harder still. The point of the spike was holding in the groove.

A loud snap and a sudden painful jarring in her right hand; something stabbed her, tearing the skin of the palm. The buckle had broken under the strain.

Fighting tears of disappointment, she climbed back onto the floor, straightened out the mattress and pulled it away from the wall, not wanting to give any pointers if Michael came back.

Then she squatted down and carefully examined the buckle with her fingers. One of the cross bars felt as if it had snapped. And two of the studs that fixed the buckle into the leather had sheared. The spike was fine and the rest of the surround was fine also. It needed strengthening. But what the hell with?

Something was sticking into her, some lump in the mattress. She put her hand down onto the mattress, pushed hard, testing. Then she released the pressure and the indent in the mattress sprang back into shape.

Obvious!

She felt a sudden lift of elation.

Then she heard a sound, like the squeak of a rubber sole, only a short distance from her. Her mouth went dry. He was back in the room with her.

'Michael?' a shaky voice called out. Her voice, but she barely recognised it. Shivering with fear, she said, 'Michael, is that you?'

She could feel his presence.

'Michael?'

Silence.

'Michael, please, can we talk? Please let's talk about this.'

A sudden explosion of light erupted from the darkness, scalding her eyes, like acid. She threw her hands over them, but the light had already gone again. And in that brief fleeting moment she had heard a familiar sound. A click followed by a brief whir.

He had taken a photograph.

Chapter Seventy-eight

Michael drove the Volvo down a well-lit suburban London street of small, uninspiring, modern-box houses. Lulu was curled up on the passenger seat, cradling the cassette in her lap like a piece of priceless porcelain, navigating from an A–Z.

'Michael,' she said suddenly, 'you were asking whether Amanda had any history of depression.'

'Yes.'

'I don't know why I didn't think to mention this earlier. She has a therapist she goes to once a week.'

He braked and stared at her. 'A *therapist*? What kind of a therapist?'

'A sort of *relationship* counsellor.'

'Who is it?'

'Her name's Maxine Bentham. It's to try to see her through her crisis over ditching Brian Trussler.'

'I've never heard of her but that doesn't mean anything. Why the hell didn't you tell me before?'

'I don't know – I – sort of didn't – remember.' She looked uncomfortable. 'It was only thinking about what you were saying about depression. Amanda's not depressive.'

'You don't go to see a therapist because you're feeling happy.'

'No. But it's not like that with her. She's been seeing this therapist for a while, and she was making good progress.'

'You have this woman's number?'

'It's in Amanda's file in the office. OK, we just passed the first turn, we want the second – coming up, turn right here.'

Michael made the turn. 'I'll call her in the morning.'

They were in another identical street of modern-box houses.

'Number thirty-seven,' she said. 'That's it.'

In the front garden, a gnome with a pointy hat and a fishing rod sat on a rock in a round ornamental pond, illuminated by green floodlights.

Maybe the gnome was his idea of a joke, Michael thought, or maybe he really liked it. Behind the seclusion of his heavy beard, Beamish was always unreadable.

The radio producer opened the front door, in a Talk Radio sweat-shirt and tracksuit bottoms, and ushered them inside. He led them through an internal door into what Michael presumed had been the garage but was now a soundproofed room filled with electronic apparatus.

He introduced Lulu to Beamish, who relieved her of the tape, slotted it into a deck beneath a monitor, and went off to fetch a tray of coffee. There was only one chair in the room, in front of a computer keyboard. Michael and Lulu both stood, worn out, and gazed at the elaborate rig: panels of switches, dials, strobing lights, monitors, consoles.

'Eat your heart out, NASA,' Lulu said.

Michael smiled thinly.

Beamish came back in and set the tray down on a flat console between two reel-to-reel tapes.

'Quite a set-up,' Michael said.

Beamish gave a curt nod of acknowledgement, then pressed a sequence of buttons on the cassette deck. The tape began to play and spikes jumped on the monitor. He sat on the chair and turned to face Michael. 'What are you looking for?'

'Its provenance,' Michael said.

'We don't think her voice sounds right,' Lulu explained.

Beamish raised his eyebrows. 'We're not travelling in the same bus, Michael.'

341

Michael explained Lulu's relationship with Amanda. 'She knows this woman really well, Chris.'

'Yes, fine, but I'm still not sure what it is you want from me.'

'This may sound daft, Chris,' Lulu said. 'We're not sure what we want either. I – I – Isn't there some way you can analyse her voice to see if there *is* something wrong?'

'With her or with the tape?'

'Anything.'

Without any hint of humour, he said, 'I might be able to tell you if there's something wrong with the tape. I think Michael would be more qualified to say if there's something wrong with her.' He blinked two slow, heavy-lidded blinks. 'How does she sound normally? Do you have a tape of her voice to compare against it?'

Michael and Lulu looked at each other. Lulu said, 'I could dig around the office and find something – one of her dictation tapes, something like that?'

He turned back to his keyboard and tapped out a command. 'Let's work with what we have.'

A green 3-D bar graph appeared on the monitor. Beamish replayed the tape and they all sat in silence watching the spikes jumping as Amanda spoke.

When the replay ended, Beamish stopped the tape and rewound it again. He tapped out another command, and the shape of the spikes rotated, becoming more complex, then rearranged into a geometrical pattern that made no sense to Michael.

'OK, that was her voice,' Beamish said. 'Consistent throughout. The pattern indicates it's the same person.' He glanced at Michael then Lulu for verification. 'Now we're going to take a look at the silences.'

The tape played through once more. Again, he tapped the keyboard. More spikes appeared. This time there was an even more elaborate pattern made from a row of peaks and troughs. Beamish turned to them both, then pointed at the screen.

'This is a spectrum analysis. It gives a high-resolution frequency analysis, like a fingerprint. I'm not picking up anything significant from her voice, but I'm getting something interesting from the silence.'

He ran his finger along the spikes on the screen. 'Either of you know anything about ambient sound?'

Michael shook his head.

'No,' Lulu said.

'Right,' Beamish said, looking more animated than normal. 'Let's give you an example. If you looked at one small section of an ocean on a calm day, for several minutes, you aren't going to see anything change. It all looks the same. Yes?'

Michael nodded.

'Right, it looks the same, but it isn't. No two waves are quite alike. There's a current running, there's a very complex pattern in the water, all the way through. You couldn't see it with your naked eye, but imagine you froze a slice of that ocean and lifted it out. The segments either side wouldn't match up, not *exactly*. If you looked closely enough you would be able to see a break in the pattern.'

'Right,' Michael said, unsure where this was heading. Then, when Beamish went on, he began to understand exactly.

'This spectrum analyser does exactly the same thing with silence. You remove a slice of a silence – doesn't matter what silence, *any* silence – and the other two halves won't match up. That's what we have here.'

'So what does that mean, exactly?' Lulu asked.

Michael was already there. 'It means that what Amanda is saying has been *edited*, right?'

'Now we're all riding in the same elevator car,' Beamish said, with a triumphant smile.

The colour drained from Lulu's face. 'Oh, Jesus,' she said. 'That wasn't Amanda speaking to you in person?'

'No,' Michael said, quietly, watching Beamish's face for acknowledgement. 'It was an edited recording of her voice. Right, Chris?'

'On the button.'

'Why – why would – she – do that?' Lulu asked.

'I think,' Michael said quietly, 'we ought to work on the possibility that it wasn't Amanda who did it.'

Chapter Seventy-nine

After only four hours' sleep, Michael rose shortly after six, his brain wide awake, his stomach aching from hunger.

He showered, shaved and doused himself in the Boss cologne Katy had always bought for him, hoping it might help him stay fresh for the long day ahead. The *Today* programme warned of a heatwave, London in the nineties. He made himself a breakfast of cereal and scrambled eggs, then dressed in a white lawn cotton shirt, his Jasper Conran beige linen suit, which was the lightest weight suit he had, and brown loafers. For decorum, but with reluctance, he added a tie, with a sober geometric pattern.

At seven o'clock he dialled the home phone number that DC Simon Roebuck had written for him on the back of his card.

Now barely an hour later, in Hampstead police station, Michael sat leadenly on the hard plastic chair in the small interview room that stank of stale cigarette smoke. On the tired Formica table in front of him sat the tape cassette, a brown envelope containing a printout of Beamish's tests, and a buff folder belonging to DC Roebuck, who had gone to fetch some coffee.

The first beads of perspiration were already popping on the detective's forehead as he lumbered back into the room gripping the tops of two Styrofoam coffee cups in one hand. He put them on the table, and showered down beside them an assortment of plastic spoons, sugar packs and creamer tubs. Then he closed the door and lowered his hefty frame into the chair opposite Michael.

'Going to be a warm one,' he said, standing up again, briefly, to switch on the fan. He pulled out a handkerchief, mopped his brow, then ran his massive hands through his light fuzz of close-cropped fair hair.

Michael watched him warily, mindful of the blazing row they'd had on the phone yesterday afternoon, when the detective constable had told him that so far he'd done nothing to follow up Michael's missing-person report. Today, the policeman seemed surprisingly receptive to him.

'I hear you had a bit of an incident on your radio show last night?'

'Yes.'

Roebuck peeled away a foil lid, and poured creamer into his coffee. Then he tore open a sugar pack and tipped that in. His eyes rested on the tape cassette, and the envelope containing the printout from Beamish, which Michael had laid on the table.

'My fiancé was listening to it, Dr Tennent. She heard your conversation before it was cut off.'

'What did she think?'

'She's a police officer, she works for the CPU – the Child Protection Unit,' he added, when he saw Michael's blank look. 'She listens to a lot of phone calls of people in distress. She said in her opinion that this young lady, Miss Capstick, sounded in deep distress. Would you agree with that, sir?'

The detective's eyes, in contrast to his almost clumsy-looking frame, were hard, quick-moving and intelligent. Michael could see this man turning mean in any circumstance that required it. And he was aware now that he was being scrutinised carefully.

He removed the spectrum analysis printout from the envelope, and talked the detective through it.

Roebuck opened his folder and jotted down some notes on a pad. Then he looked back at Michael. 'Are you able to account for your whereabouts on Sunday afternoon and night, sir?'

Michael stared back at him. It was a fair question, sensible police procedure, yet in this context, and probably because his patience was frayed with tiredness, it angered him. 'Probably not, no,' he said, testily.

346

There was a lengthy silence, disturbed only by the hum from the fan, and the riffling of the edges of the report in its draught.

He stared Roebuck back in the eye. 'Want to lock me up as a suspect?'

'I don't think so, sir.' Roebuck smiled, his tone conciliatory.

'But it's crossed your mind?' Michael said.

After a moment of hesitation, the detective said, 'I'd be failing in my duties if I didn't consider all possibilities.'

'So that means you are at last concerned that something might have happened to Amanda Capstick? Good, I'm delighted. It's only taken four days.'

Roebuck gave him a wry smile of acknowledgement that he'd walked into the trap. 'I'd like to listen to the tape.'

Michael removed it from the box. The detective put it into one of the twin decks, and ran it.

When it reached the end, Roebuck nodded in thoughtful silence, then he said. 'The spectrum analysis shows the tape has been edited, through mismatches in the silences, you said?'

'Yes.'

'Mr Beamish has worked for us in the past. He's good.' He stirred his coffee, then drank some. 'Did you bring a photograph of Miss Capstick?'

'Yes.' Michael was encouraged by his attitude this morning. From the same envelope as the spectrum analysis, he produced a handful of photographs Amanda's mother had given him, and pushed them across the table.

Roebuck sifted through them. 'She's a very attractive young lady.'

'She is.'

'I'd like to get posters put up in all the areas where she was last seen. Presumably her family have no objection to publicity?'

'None.'

'We'll try to get her picture up on the missing-person slots on television covering this area.'

'If she's been abducted she could have been taken out of this area.'

'We'll go as wide as we can, sir.'

'What else are you going to do?'

'I'd like the names, addresses and phone numbers of all her family, friends and acquaintances.'

Michael produced the printout Lulu had already prepared from the envelope and handed it to him. 'What else will you do?'

'I'm going to take a look at our own missing-persons records and see if there are any similarities that could link them.'

'Link them to what? To the pattern of a possible killer?'

There was another silence, broken only by the hum of the fan and the riffling of paper.

'You're not going to give me some crap about it being too soon to start jumping to conclusions, are you, DC Roebuck?'

The policeman ejected the tape from the machine and slipped it back into the box. 'Do you have a back-up copy of this?'

'Yes.'

'We'll make another.' He tapped the edge of his cup. 'You want to talk straight, Doctor, so let's be open with each other. This tape changes everything, all right?'

Michael nodded grimly.

'And there's something else, which I'd like you to keep to yourself. I'm not telling this to the press because it wouldn't be in our interests at the moment. I don't want to distress you more than you already are, but since you want me to be open . . .' He picked up a plastic spoon then put it down again. 'There are some parallels here with another missing-person inquiry. A young woman editor at a publishing house, who went missing three weeks ago.'

'Tina Mackay? The one who's been in the news?'

'Yes. She's a similar age to Miss Capstick. Also a professional woman, attractive, similar build. She disappeared without trace, with her car.'

'None of that publicity's helped you?'

'Not in Tina Mackay's case so far, no.'

'Are you treating it as a murder inquiry?'

'We've set up an incident room, and we're giving it the same attention we would give a murder inquiry, if that answers your question.'

'And are you going to set up an incident room for Amanda?'

Their eyes locked. Roebuck said, grimly, 'I'm going to show this tape to my governor this morning. I'll do everything I can.'

'You'll keep me informed?'

'Yes.'

They stood up and Roebuck escorted him through to the main entrance. Then he took Michael's hand and shook it firmly, looking into his eyes once more, this time with deep concern. 'Call me any time, Dr Tennent. Day or night. All right?'

Michael thanked him, and left.

Chapter Eighty

Beneath the lurid glare of the mid-morning sun, the slack sea water in the harbour was the colour of tinned peas.

Glen Branson watched the steady stream of bubbles a hundred yards out from the dock wall where he was standing, breathing salt air richly tanged with rotting seaweed, rusting oil-cans and freshly sawn timber, thinking about Cora Burstridge.

The tide on the far wall was down to the low-water mark. A gull swooped low then rose again; several more sat in the water, rich pickings from this busy port. A crane winched a container from the hold of a freighter lying low on its Plimsoll line, flying a Norwegian flag. A tiny harbour patrol boat chugged past, dwarfed by the freighter's bulk. Ripples of wake bobbed the red buoys that marked where the two police frogmen were diving.

Sandwiched between a bunkering station and a lumber depot, behind the green screens they had erected an hour ago, were parked two police cars, a white crime scene investigators' van, the diving team's grey van, and a dark blue van belonging to a local firm of undertakers.

Danny Leon, the informer whom Glen and Mike Harris had brought down from Luton prison yesterday, had given them the unwelcome news that the reason they couldn't find a second key witness for Operation Skeet, Jason Hewlett, was because he was at the bottom of the harbour, without an aqualung. He had drawn a diagram showing the exact spot. Any minute now and they would find out whether he had told them the truth.

Hanging around, waiting with him, were a police photographer, two crime-scene investigators, two undertakers who looked as out of place as extras hanging around a film set, Glen thought, and Glen's immediate boss, Detective Sergeant Bill Digby.

Digby, in a brown suit and golf-club tie, feet apart, hands behind him, like a soldier at ease, crinkly black hair gleaming in the sunlight, shrugged and said, 'So far, Glen, all you can produce is one small strip of cloth retrieved from a loft, and an unreliable, elderly witness, who may or may not have seen a man on a fire escape.' He turned to the detective constable and gave a twitch of his trim moustache.

'Don't forget the Babygro, sir, the one she had bought that afternoon for her baby granddaughter. I think that's very important.'

'There's been nothing from the post-mortem?'

'No, Sarge.'

Digby pulled a pack of cigarettes from his pocket and lit one. 'Glen, do yourself a favour and forget about Cora Burstridge.'

'Her funeral's tomorrow. I –'

The detective sergeant gave him an interrogative look.

Glen hesitated, then said, 'I know it would cause distress to the family, but I'd really like to have the funeral delayed.'

'What's that going to achieve?'

'It could save an enormous amount of hassle if . . .' he was going to say, 'if there were any further developments', but decided not to. Digby wasn't in a good frame of mind, and he was going to be in an even worse one if the informer was right about Jason Hewlett.

And, he thought, dispirited, perhaps the sergeant was right. He stared at the bubbles and wondered if maybe he was obsessed with this because it was Cora Burstridge. Was her fame clouding his judgement, making him unable to accept that she really had taken her own life?

Digby was sending him clear signals that he disapproved of his giving all this time to the actress's death, and even the governor hadn't responded with any great enthusiasm to the form Glen had put on his desk.

Cora, you are being cremated tomorrow and I'm fast running out of road. I've done my best for you, and I don't know how much more I can do.

A sudden eruption of bubbles. The surface of the water between the diving buoys turned to a roiling, milky foam. A frogman's hooded, masked head, broke the surface, then the other's. The first raised a hand in the air and signalled a thumbs-up to the shore.

Then a third head broke the surface between them. Except that this head wasn't wearing any mask, or any skin, or any hair. It was a bare white skull.

Glen edged closer to the wall and peered down now, watching the divers in a mixture of horror and near disbelief. The skull was still, bizarrely, attached to its clothed body.

There was a flurry of activity around him as the undertakers rapidly pulled on white protective suits, as did the two crime-scene investigators. Then all four ran down the steps to a ledge in the harbour wall and helped the divers wrestle the corpse onto dry land.

The smell hit all of them simultaneously. Glen turned away, close to retching, and saw Digby react in the same way.

'Fuck me!' Digby said, pinching his nose shut.

Glen pinched his nose shut, too. That putrid-fish stench of death again, but unbearably strong. Looking down at the ledge, he could see why.

The body was in leather motorcycling gear, which had bloated right out. The hands were covered in leather gloves, the feet in boots. Wound several times around the midriff, pinioning the arms and legs was a length of anchor chain, which was also wound and secured around a small concrete breeze block.

The skull, protruding from the collar, and completely bare looked ludicrously small for the body, as if it had been stuck on as some appalling sick joke.

'Been there three weeks,' Digby said, grimly. 'Crabs have picked his head clean.'

'You reckon that's Jason Hewett?' Glen asked.

'Want to go and check the body for some ID?'

Glen swallowed. 'I'll get some overalls and gloves.'

Digby said, quietly, 'Take a good look at him, lad. Remember him, next time life throws you a curve. OK?'

The detective constable stared back at his sergeant, uncertainly. 'Remember him, Sarge?'

Digby nodded. 'Just remember him. You're all chewed up because you think I'm not being fair to you over Cora Burstridge. Next time you think life's a bitch, just remember how lucky you are that you're not that sad bastard lying down there.'

I don't think Cora Burstridge was very lucky either, sir, Glen wanted to say, but didn't.

Instead he went, silently, to the crime-scene investigators' van in search of the protective clothing and face mask they had laid out for him.

Chapter Eighty-one

After his ward round, Michael looked at his list of patient appointments for today, then frowned at his secretary, who was pecking at her keyboard. 'Terence Goel again? It's Thursday – he only came on Tuesday. Why the hell's he coming twice in one week, Thelma?'

In her nervy, defensive manner, she said, 'Well, you do have several patients who you see twice a week.'

'I can do without this one today.'

She looked at him with quiet sympathy. 'I'm sure he needs you, Dr Tennent. All your patients need you very much.'

He felt so drained that he was close to tears. He turned away so she couldn't see his face.

'Mrs Teresa Capstick – Miss Capstick's mother – phoned you about ten minutes ago, wondering if there was any news.'

Crushing a tear with his eyelids, he said, 'I'll call her.' Then he stepped out of her office and into the corridor.

'Dr Tennent?' Her tone softened.

He stopped. 'Yes?'

'I'm sure that Miss Capstick will turn up safe and well.'

'I hope.'

'Shall I send Mrs Gordon in?'

His first patient of the day, Anne Gordon, suffered from desperately low self-esteem. It was nine thirty, and he was fifteen minutes late for her after his drive across London from Detective Constable Roebuck, and a problem in one of his wards. She would be thinking she did not matter to him, and this was why he was keeping her waiting.

'Apologise to her. Give me two minutes to call Amanda's

354

mother. Also, could you call Lulu, I haven't been able to get hold of her yet, and ask her for Maxine Bentham's phone number? Got that?'

'Maxine Bentham, yes, Dr Tennent.'

His shirt was sticking to his back with perspiration. In the sanctuary of his office he closed the door, removed his jacket, then opened the window, letting in a faint hint of a breeze and the ever-present scent of cut grass. He checked his e-mail, then picked up the receiver to call Teresa Capstick, and then put it down again, not sure what he should say to her. Had word of the phone call from Amanda during his radio show reached her? He should tell her the truth.

Except that right now the truth wasn't looking good.

He rang her, and gave her part of the truth. He told her Amanda had called, that he was having the tape analysed and there was some evidence to indicate her voice had been a recording and not live. He promised to let her know as soon as he had more news, then pressed the intercom and told Thelma to send in Mrs Gordon.

For the first few minutes of the session, it was almost a relief to get back to the normality of work. He worked through Anne Gordon's litany of events in this past week of her sad life. In her mind she had been snubbed by a Safeways checkout girl, by a succession of telephone operators, a taxi driver, her next-door neighbour, and even by a caller for Christian Aid, who clearly did not think her contribution (five pounds) to have been enough.

Increasingly his mind kept returning to Amanda, and he began to watch the clock fiercely, willing those minutes away, desperate for the session to end so that he could check with Thelma to see if there had been any calls.

Anne Gordon noticed. 'You're not interested in me either, are you, Dr Tennent?'

The final ten minutes shot by as he struggled to extricate himself from that one.

'Are you familiar with the writings of Mahatma Gandhi, Dr Tennent?'

In contrast to Michael's ragged, perspiring state, Dr Goel leaned back on the sofa in a commanding pose, the picture of cool. Dressed in a lightweight black suit, collarless white shirt, black Nubuck loafers and immaculate hair, he looked like a hologram from a style magazine.

'I presume you are,' Michael replied, determined to dominate this session with this man. 'Tell me why.'

'Actually I prefer the writings of his son Arun. Mahatma wrote the *Seven Blunders of the World*. Wealth without work. Pleasure without conscience. Knowledge without character. Commerce without morality. Science without humanity. Worship without sacrifice. Politics without principle. But it was Arun who added the eighth, which is the greatest of them all: rights without responsibilities. Do you not believe this applies to psychiatrists, Dr Tennent? That you assume rights over people without any ultimate responsibility?'

'Tell me why you think that.' Michael watched him carefully. Goel seemed to be struggling with a deep inner anger, but his response came out in a measured, calm voice.

'Why do I think this? I don't think this, Dr Tennent, I *know* this.'

'Would you like to explain your feelings on this to me?'

'Come on, Dr Tennent. You sit arrogantly on your chair, telling people what's wrong with how they perceive the world, with the way they live their lives, and you gaily tell them what they should do about it. But they walk out of this office, and it doesn't matter to you what they do then, does it? You carry no responsibility for their actions once they're out of here. None. You can say what the hell you like and there's no comeback. I think that is *rights without responsibilities*. Don't you?'

Michael considered his reply. 'Psychiatrists are doctors of medicine, and we do the best we can for our patients. I think we take our work very seriously, and we are acutely aware of how what we say can affect our patients. I can't agree with you, but let's continue down your line. Tell me how you think psychiatrists should become more responsible.'

Thomas Lamark watched the man squirm in his chair, hot, uncomfortable, exhausted. 'Have you ever been in love and lost someone, Dr Tennent?'

Michael leaned forward, eyes on his patient's face. 'It sounds like you've had this experience yourself. What were the circumstances?'

'On a country road. I was driving with my wife and we hit a truck. She was killed.'

And suddenly, with utter clarity, it was all back in Michael's mind. That February Sunday morning. Rain tipping down. Late for a christening. Driving his red BMW M3 fast down a country road. Too fast. Katy sitting beside him, crying. He had told her the previous night that he no longer loved her, that he had been having an affair with another woman, a nurse called Nicola Royce, for three years. He was sorry. Their marriage had run its course, he was leaving her.

It wasn't Katy's fault, she had done nothing bad. It was just the way she was – a nice person, but cold, obsessed with her own work. They had grown apart. He had married her because he had been in love with her beauty and with her talent. They had made a glamorous partnership, the successful artist and the successful shrink. But they weren't a loving couple and never really had been, except perhaps in their earliest days. They had few things in common. She didn't enjoy sex, she was always too damned serious, obsessed with her looks, her health, her career.

Nicola, a nurse whom he had met at a party, gave him warmth. They had fun, terrific sex, got drunk together, she made him feel young – he'd even taken up motorcycling because Nicola loved bikes. Life with Nicola was a party for two. He adored her. They had planned their future life together.

That Sunday morning his mind hadn't been on the road. He was trying to explain his feelings to Katy. She told him to slow down, he was driving too fast, it was his fault they were late, they should have left earlier, he was trying to cover an hour's journey in forty minutes.

They were overtaking a lorry, Katy shouting at him

357

through her tears to slow down. Empty road ahead. Pulled in past the lorry. Coming up to the brow of a hill, a right-hand bend. Something was coming the other way, a yellow blur; a van losing it on this bend. Crossing onto their side. Coming straight at them.

Michael saw the replay in his mind now in slow motion. He swerved to the right, trying to angle in front of it, the van impacting on Katy's side, airbags exploding, a man in the passenger seat of the van bursting through the wind-screen, the glass shards looking like feathers from a ruptured pillow. The van bouncing back, the front pushed right in, the roof twisted, the driver through the open windscreen still behind his wheel but part of his skull had been sheared off.

Then he looked at Katy. Not a mark on her, but she was twisted round at an impossible angle, her head hanging slack like the airbag.

'I still cannot remember how the accident happened,' Terence Goel said.

Michael stared at his patient. He ignored him, held the image inside his head. The memory.

The guilt.

Nicola had come to see him in hospital. He had ended his relationship with her there, from his hospital bed.

It had felt then as though his whole life was finished.

Ten months later, he heard that she had married an eye surgeon in Sydney.

He stared at the picture of Katy on his desk; then he looked back at Dr Goel, aware that he was waiting for his response. 'Do you blame yourself?' he asked.

'They tell me it wasn't my fault.' Thomas leaned back further in the sofa. This was hitting home. Dr Tennent was looking distressed. Their eyes met again, and Thomas lowered his, not wanting to push his luck too far.

Michael tried hard to pull himself together, to put the crash from his mind. And yet . . . last week Goel had mentioned a car crash. Then on Tuesday, he had talked about a bird, the bower-bird, losing a loved one. It was uncanny. Too uncanny.

This man seemed to know something about his past.

'Tell me more about your wife,' Michael said.

The morning sun was coming in through the window now. The left side of his patient was in shadow, the right side brilliantly lit. It made him look even more unreal. He remained almost hypnotically calm as he spoke. 'I bought two birds, two white doves, after she died. They loved each other. I used to sit and watch them in their cage, and envy them so much. They used to nuzzle each other all the time, and made strange little sounds.' He paused, then he said, 'Have you ever envied something's happiness so much you wanted to destroy it, Dr Tennent?'

'Did you want to destroy your birds?'

'I took one out of the cage, and I put it in darkness, down in the cellar. Then I just sat, for days, watching its mate pine in its cage. It stopped eating, after a while it stopped calling for its mate. Its coat became matted and dirty.'

Like me. I'm pining like the dove, for Amanda.

'And the mate in the cellar?' he asked.

'I left it there.'

'To die?'

'It didn't. It kept on living, somehow. Eventually I killed it.'

The man's face was a mask of steel. He gave Michael the impression he was enjoying himself. Michael was curious about this, and wanted to draw him further.

'Tell me about how you felt when you were watching the dove in the cage. Did you feel powerful?'

'I always feel powerful, Dr Tennent.'

'Are you sure you always feel powerful, or are you just feeling powerful at the moment?'

For the first time, Michael detected a change in the man's body language. Terence Goel glanced down at the floor, and tightened in on himself. Defence. 'The past is –' He fell silent.

'The past is what?' Michael pushed him.

'Do you know your past, Dr Tennent? Do any of us know our past?'

Michael pursued his original question. 'Tell me what else you felt when you were watching the dove in the cage.'

'I despised it.'

'Why?'

'Because it was so weak, pathetic, helpless. Because it neglected itself, it allowed itself to get run down, malnourished. It did not portray any strength of character, Dr Tennent.'

'Was it the male or the female that you locked in the cellar?'

'The female.'

Did this man have Amanda locked in a cellar?

The thought was absurd, and yet Goel was looking at him as if he knew he had the upper hand. But *what* upper hand?

Michael, determined not to lose control of this session again, used the one weapon he knew he had.

Gently, he asked, 'I'd like to know something about your own past, Terence. Tell me about your mother and father.'

The effect was instant. Goel looked like a frightened child.

'I'm not sure I want to talk about them.'

'Are your parents alive?'

Goel was trembling. His eyes were shut. Several times he opened his mouth to speak but nothing came out. 'You know –' he said finally, then stopped.

'What do I know?' Michael kept his tone gentle and pleasant, easing the man through his distress.

Pushing his hands through his hair, Goel said, 'I – I don't think –' He fell silent again.

Michael allowed the silence to play for a while, then he said, 'You said you despised the bird. Do you think this might be some aspect of yourself that you are despising? Do you feel trapped by something?'

'You're missing the –' He stopped abruptly, clenching his fists.

'Point?' Michael suggested.

Goel shook his head angrily. 'We just need a bit of silence here, you're getting me confused, you are not helping me, OK?'

360

This man was in a worse state than he had previously suspected, Michael thought. On the verge of a breakdown. What the hell had been going on with his parents that he was unable to talk about? He waited for Goel to compose himself.

'Let's go back to the dove in the cage. Can you imagine what it feels like to love someone and then to lose them, Dr Tennent?'

'Did you feel that by tormenting your doves you were somehow compensating for the loss of your wife? That because she had died, no living thing had the right to happiness? I'm interested in how you reconcile that to Arun Gandhi's statement about rights without responsibilities.' Michael raised his eyebrows at the man. 'You are stronger than the dove, you can put it in the cellar, but what about the feelings of the dove in the cellar?'

'Fallout shelter,' Goel corrected.

Michael leaned forward. 'Fallout shelter?'

Thomas felt his face going red. He hadn't meant to say that, it had just come out. *Careful. Careful. Bugger, bugger, bugger.*

Michael watched Goel shaking, his knees banging together, as if he was close to having a fit. He was aware this was because the man was angry with himself. Why?

'It's – she's – it –' Thomas windmilled his hands. *Careful. Careful.* His face was burning, his voice seemed to jam in his throat. *Careful.* 'A joke – she – she used to – used to say it was a shelter.' He opened his hands out expansively. 'People do, don't they?'

'She?'

Goel rocked backwards and forwards for a moment. 'I think we need to return to the cellar here, Dr Tennent. I think we were doing better with the dove in the cellar.'

Michael decided to strike hard again, while the man was floundering. 'Tell me about your childhood. I'd like to know about your parents. Let's talk about your mother.'

Careful. Thomas closed his eyes, clenched his fists again. *Careful. Careful. Why are you asking about my mother? Are you trying to trick me?* 'You haven't answered my question about

361

the dove, Dr Tennent. Answer my question about the dove, for God's sake, will you?'

Michael noticed the anger in his outburst. Against what? What had this man's parents put him through?

'I really think it would be helpful to talk about your relationship with your parents. Tell me about your father – or your mother, if you prefer,' he said calmly.

Thomas got to his feet and paced up and down the room, agitatedly, trying to compose his thoughts, trying to connect back to the psychiatrist. Rage seethed in him. *You smug bastard, you killed my mother and now you want me to talk about her. You want to sit there and get some kind of sick, sadistic pleasure out of hearing about how much I loved her? I'm not going to give you that pleasure, Dr Michael Tennent.*

He went over to the window and looked at the cloudless sky. 'We'll talk about them but some other time, all right?'

'I'd like to know why you find it difficult to talk about them,' he heard the psychiatrist say.

Thomas marched over to the door. Then he turned towards Michael and said, 'We'll talk about her, I promise you. Some other time. We'll talk about her a great deal. We really will. I think our time is up now, isn't it?'

Michael looked at his watch. 'We have another ten minutes.'

Thomas nodded. He wanted to get out of here, he was scared that he had said too much already. It was dangerous to stay, Dr Tennent was outsmarting him, he was going to give too much away. 'You can have these ten minutes as a gift from me, Dr Tennent.' He smiled, some of his composure returning. 'Enjoy them. Use them well.'

He opened the door and was gone.

Michael turned to his computer, logged on to the Net, entered a search command for 'Dr Terence Goel'.

A website address appeared. Michael typed it in, then read it as it downloaded. It was a smart site, but a little showy, perhaps.

There was a colour photograph of the man, followed by his biography. Dr Terence Goel was cousin of the astronomer Sir Bernard Lovell. A member of the Scripps Research

Institute. A junior professor at MIT. A member of the Select Presidential Advisory Committee on the Search for Extraterrestrial Intelligence for Ronald Reagan.

Michael decided he would ask him about his work on that committee at their next session, he was interested in UFOs himself.

He looked at the man's list of hobbies. Food. Chess. He was a member of Mensa.

Dr Goel's credentials were extremely impressive.

Far more impressive, Michael thought, than the man himself.

Chapter Eighty-two

The actress, Natassja Kinski, breasts hanging free through her open négligée, was straddling her black lover, Wesley Snipes. They were both gasping, groaning, her lover was reaching up, holding those breasts, they were coming, they were both coming –

The television screen went blank.

'Why are you watching that, Tom-Tom?'

Staring at her holding the remote in her hand, his face flushed, he had no answer. Because. Because.

'She's so thin, Tom-Tom. A beautiful clothes-horse, but that's all. Skeletal. She reminds me of someone out of a concentration camp. Doesn't she remind you of that?'

Images of skeletal figures in Auschwitz came into his mind. Natassja Kinski's face transposed. Straddling him. He squirmed in revulsion. 'I – I –' he said. 'It was just on. I was watching the film, a preview.'

'My films were pure. We suggested, but we never showed. I could never have lowered myself. You understand just how low actresses have sunk, don't you?'

'Yes,' he said quietly, angry because she was right, angry because she had stopped him watching Natassja Kinski, angry because – because of the images she had put in his mind.

'Can you imagine how you would feel if you were watching me on the screen doing that, darling?'

He looked up at his mother, confused thoughts swirling around inside him. What would it be like with Sharon Stone? Or Kim Basinger? Sigourney Weaver? Would they be thin, too, like concentration-camp survivors? Would they laugh at him the way the nurse at medical school had laughed at him?

Then the guilt came up at him, like some dark shadow. His mother looked so beautiful; she was lovelier than any of those other famous actresses. Why was he thinking like this?

She would leave him if she knew he was thinking thoughts like this.

'I love you, Mummy,' he said.

Sternly. 'Are you sure?'

'Yes.'

She released the sash cord on her dressing gown. Her breasts, larger, whiter, less firm but so much larger, so much whiter and softer than Natassja Kinski's, fell free in front of him. 'Show me how much your choo-choo loves your mummy.'

He opened his trousers, lifted himself in his armchair and pulled them down, and then his boxer shorts.

She stood, staring at his erection. 'Dr Rennie tells me I spend too much time at home. Shall I do what he says, Tom-Tom? Shall I go out and do charity work for other people? Shall I leave you, like your daddy left you?'

He stammered, 'No, please, I don't want you to do that.'

'Is your choo-choo for me, Tom-Tom, or is it for Natassja Kinski?'

He hesitated, confused, he wasn't sure. He wanted to make love to Natassja Kinski but he did not want his mother to leave him, in case – in case –

Images of walking skeletons.

He hardened even more.

Images of walking skeletons.

'If you want to make love to Natassja Kinski you can't be my little boy any more. I'll discard you. No more treats, Tom-Tom. Other people might laugh at you, Tom-Tom. You remember how that girl you took out at medical school laughed at you?'

Lucy. The student nurse he had met in his second year at King's, who had been friendly to him. They had gone out for a drink a few times. He'd brought her to meet his mother, and his mother told him she was not good enough for him. He'd asked her when he drove her home after that meeting if she would like to play with his choo-choo. He could still remember her laugh, it was echoing in his head still, now, sitting in Terence Goel's Ford Mondeo in the car park below Dr Michael Tennent's office in the Sheen Park Hospital.

The way the prostitute, Divina, had laughed at him.

What is wrong with me?

He accelerated down the drive. Angry with himself. Angry with the psychiatrist. You think you're clever, Dr Michael Tennent.

Will you still feel clever when you find Amanda Capstick's breasts pushed through your letterbox packed in ice?

Chapter Eighty-three

Circadian cycles. The human body is out of sync with the rest of nature. Humans live a twenty-five-and-a-half-hour cycle. Experiments had been done by people spending months in total darkness down mine-shafts, with no watches. All of them calculated they had been down a shorter time than they actually had.

Amanda had read about this a long time back and she was thinking about it as she worked away monotonously in the dark, slowly twisting and interweaving the spring she had removed from the mattress around the belt buckle, trying to make it into a sturdy handle, hammering every fraction of an inch into shape with the sole of the loafer. It was ready to test now.

'Amanda darling, come here!'

Her mother's voice. She spun round. The darkness swirled as if she had disturbed it. She tracked the silence with her ears. Nothing. Just her imagination.

She doubled the mattress once more against the wall, climbed onto it, reached up, found the grille, located the rim, then the first screw. Then she dropped the screwdriver. It rolled with a clatter somewhere below her.

'Shit.'

Down on her knees, crawling forward, moving her hands in front of her like a swimmer. She collided with the latrine bucket.

Tears of frustration ran down her cheeks. *Sod you, damn you, fuck you, where are you?*

Pull yourself together, Amanda Capstick. Survivors stay calm. Your screwdriver is in here, somewhere. Just work your way across the floor and you'll find it.

Within a couple of minutes, she did.

Back on the mattress, taking it more slowly, she got the blade into the groove, then turned. Nothing. She cautiously applied more pressure. Still nothing. Wobbling on the mattress, it was hard to remain steady. She twisted harder still.

The screw turned.

It felt like a valve had opened inside her.

Upstairs, in his den, on the World Wide Web, Thomas Lamark was studying photographs of a mastectomy that had been carried out at St John's Hospital in Santa Monica. The pictures were good, but he needed more clarity.

Conveniently, there was a mastectomy being performed in the teaching theatre at London's King's College Hospital tomorrow afternoon. He had seen this on the list when he had dropped by there early this morning, to collect some things he needed from a store room to which he still had a key.

It would be good to attend this, he really wasn't at all familiar with this operation. And he wanted to get it right.

Chapter Eighty-four

After logging off from Dr Goel's website, Michael just had time to put a call into Maxine Bentham before his next patient arrived. But Amanda's therapist was able to shed no light on her disappearance.

She told Michael she did not consider Amanda to be depressive, and she thought it improbable that she would have disappeared like this of her own accord. She wasn't surprised to learn that Brian Trussler had another girl-friend, and from all that Amanda had told her about the man, she didn't feel he was likely either to have kidnapped Amanda or physically harmed her.

She asked Michael to keep her informed and he promised he would.

He sat through his next two sessions finding it difficult to concentrate on his patients. Terence Goel was drumming in his head. *The parallels*. The accident that had killed Katy. The dove separated from his mate.

During his session with Dr Goel he had dismissed these parallels as being connections made in his own fanciful mind, but now with Goel gone and time to reflect they weren't going away.

Goel could have found out about the car smash easily enough, it had made the national press at the time. But Amanda's disappearance? Could he know about that?

Michael churned over their session this morning. The dove pining for its mate. Again, he wondered, *Am I reading too much into this?*

The dove pining could apply as much to his grief after Katy's death as to his distress now over Amanda. It was just how he had felt after the accident. At times in a state of denial, unwilling to accept that she was really dead, convinced that somehow she would return.

His patient, Guy Rotheram, a seriously rich thirty-five-year-old packaging tycoon who was suffering from panic attacks, was sitting on the edge of the sofa describing the feeling he kept getting that he was outside his own body. The man worked sixteen hours a day, seven days a week, that was the main reason he was having panic attacks, but he couldn't accept this. He couldn't accept being beaten by his own body.

'Are you listening, Dr Tennent?' he asked suddenly.

Michael was aware that he was not giving Guy Rotheram his full concentration. But Guy Rotheram would be going home to his Chelsea home tonight to his beautiful wife and his adorable children. Guy Rotheram's panic attacks made life uncomfortable for him, but they would eventually stop. Guy's worries were big worries, but his own were even bigger right now. Today Guy Rotheram, along with the rest of his life, was on hold.

Who are you, Dr Terence Goel?
What is your real problem?
How much do you know about me?

As soon as Guy Rotheram left, Michael pulled out Terence Goel's file and took out the original letter of referral from Goel's GP, Dr Shyam Sundaralingham, bearing the address, 20 West Garden Crescent, Cheltenham.

He dialled the phone number. It was answered on the third ring by a middle-aged male voice with a pukka military clip. 'Dr Sundaralingham's surgery.'

Michael was surprised to hear a male voice. He assumed this was one of the increasingly common new breed of practice managers answering the phone. 'My name's Dr Tennent, I'm a psychiatrist. Dr Sundaralingham recently referred a patient to me, and I'd like to have a word with him about the patient.'

'I'm afraid Dr Sundaralingham's out at the moment. May I take your number and have him call you back?'

Michael gave it, then hung up. The sun had moved past

the window now, and he opened the Venetian blind to let more air into the stuffy room. His phone rang. It was Lulu.

He logged back onto the Internet to check his e-mail while they talked. Lulu had no news, and sounded relieved to hear that Roebuck was taking the tape of Amanda's call seriously.

'Four days now,' she said.

There was a disturbing finality in her voice. And there was a disturbing finality in the number, also, he thought. As if to go missing for one day, or two days, or even three days was somehow all right. But after four days . . .

Two hundred and fifty thousand missing persons a year. Roebuck hinted at a possible connection between Amanda's disappearance and that of Tina Mackay. The publisher had been missing for three weeks, and he got the distinct impression from the detective that the police hadn't yet found a single clue.

Now with the tape they had something for Amanda. And they had *hope*.

Amanda had spoken those words: there was no way of telling when, but there was a good chance she had been alive last night. He and Lulu had speculated on the way home from Beamish's house about the edited silences on the tape. Lulu was convinced the editing wasn't Amanda's work. If Amanda had wanted to pull a stunt on the phone to embarrass him, she'd have had the guts to do it live, she insisted.

Michael had agreed. And if it wasn't her phoning him, but someone else, they must have a reason. Kidnap? A ransom? *She must still be alive.*

'Where do we go from here?' Lulu asked. 'Are we going to wait to see what the police do?'

For three fruitless weeks, like Tina Mackay? Michael thought but did not say. 'No. We keep looking, we keep doing everything we can. I don't know how much the police are going to do – I don't know how much they *can* do.'

'And us? What more can we do?'

'I'm thinking. I'm not going to just sit and twiddle my thumbs. I can't do that, I need to keep looking.'

'That's how I feel.'

'Don't lose that feeling.'

He had a ton of correspondence and phone calls to deal with from his unscheduled day off yesterday. He suggested to Lulu they spoke at the end of the afternoon, hung up, then turned his attention to his e-mail.

There was one with an address he did not recognise, and which had a JPeg attachment, a photograph or an illustration titled, LAST PIC OF AC INTACT.

The e-mail message said, simply: 'Wish you were here.'

A burst of nerves confused his fingers. He struggled to move the mouse, to get the cursor on the attachment, then finally he succeeded and double clicked on it.

It took several agonisingly slow moments to open. Then he could see it was a photograph. Dark. A hazy, greenish hue. In the middle, cowering, in a grubby white T-shirt and blue jeans, staring in stark, eyes-wide-open terror at the camera was Amanda.

Thomas Lamark, at work in the garage, tackling the dismantling of the back axle assembly of Amanda Capstick's Alfa Romeo, heard Terence Goel's mobile phone ring. A few seconds later there were four short beeps from the machine, indicating that there was a message.

Peeling off his greasy surgical gloves, he entered Terence Goel's PIN and played the message back.

He recognised immediately the clipped military voice of Nicholas Lubbings, sole proprietor of the Cheltenham Business Communications Centre.

'Dr Goel, a Dr Michael Tennent just telephoned Dr Sundaralingham. He has – ah – left a message for the doctor to phone him about a patient he has referred.' Lubbings's voice was deadpan; if he had any curiosity about his clients' activities, he kept it well masked.

Thomas cursed. He had made mistakes with the psychiatrist this afternoon. Damage limitation was essential. He had not given Tennent sufficient for him to feel suspicious, but he needed to plan his next consultation with the man much more carefully.

Heading from the garage, through the garden, back to the house to fetch a glass of water, Thomas wondered whether Dr Sundaralingham should call Dr Tennent back, but he was wary of the psychiatrist, and did not want to risk being tricked into making another mistake. He decided to think about it for a while.

The Times lay on the kitchen table, open at the page on which was the announcement:

Cora Edwina Burstridge. Much-loved mother of Ellen and grandmother of Brittany. Funeral service on Friday 1 August at 10.30 a.m. at All Saints Church, Patcham, East Sussex, followed by private cremation. No flowers. Donations instead to the Actors Benevolent Fund and the Royal Variety Club.

The timing was good. He wanted to attend – his mother would be pleased to know he had watched Cora Burstridge being sent to the ovens. Afterwards, he would still have sufficient time to get to the mastectomy operation at King's College Hospital.

Perfect.

You won't be so cocky in our next consultation, Dr Michael Tennent.

Chapter Eighty-five

'She's in the same clothes she was wearing on Sunday,' Michael said, pointing at his laptop screen. 'You see – the white T-shirt, jeans, those were what she was wearing.'

They were in the small but immaculately tidy office of DC Roebuck's two senior officers, his detective sergeant and his detective inspector. Roebuck had introduced them, but Michael hadn't clocked their names properly. It was lunch-time, and he was back in Hampstead police station for the second time that day.

DC Roebuck had ascertained through a colleague that the e-mail with Amanda's photograph had been sent from the cybercafé Cyberia, off London's Tottenham Court Road. With hundreds of people paying cash to use their computer terminals to send e-mails every day, there was only a slim chance of getting any description of the person who had sent this one. But Roebuck was still going to try.

The detective inspector, a tall woman in her early forties, with tidy fair hair and an orderly manner, squinted at the screen. 'Can you put the brightness up a little?'

Michael increased it. The image was grainy, as if it had been taken through some kind of a mesh, Amanda's red eyes adding to the demonic quality of the photograph. Jesus Christ, she looked so damned scared. He found it hard to watch, his mind churning up wild, disturbing images, memories. He thought of the films, *Silence of the Lambs*, *The Collector*; he thought of all the dozens of beautiful, inno-cent women's faces that had stared from newspaper pages or television screens over the years. The stark words of those headlines that in the past had seemed so remote but now were frighteningly real. FOUND DISMEMBERED . . .

Michael could see Amanda standing on a floor, he could see a wall behind her and another to her left, and what looked like the edge of a mattress on the floor.

'Strong shadows,' said the detective sergeant, a solid-looking plodder.

'She could be in darkness,' the DCI said.

'Darkness?' Michael asked sharply.

The DCI touched the screen with a well-manicured finger and moved it around to illustrate her point. 'She had red eyes from the flash, and she's lit brightly on her upper body, but the brightness falls away rapidly down towards the bottom of her jeans – that indicates a flashgun aimed high. But we can barely make out anything else in the room apart from Miss Capstick. If there is a light on in the room, why can't we see anything?'

Michael nodded grimly. *Darkness. Oh, my God, you poor darling.*

'I'd like a copy of this picture on disk – we'll get it enhanced and see if anything else shows up on it,' she added. 'They have some very powerful new digital enhancers. If there are any clues on this, they'd have the best chance of finding them.'

The detective sergeant now touched the screen. 'Bare floor, some kind of hard surface, might be a cellar or a garage.'

'How long will it take you to get it tweaked up?' Michael asked.

The detective sergeant said, 'We'll have to get it to the photographic lab in Birmingham – we can get it overnighted.'

'Overnighted!' Michael exploded. 'Jesus! That means another twenty-four hours is going to go by – we don't even know that we *have* twenty-four hours. It's a two-hour drive, for God's sake! Give me the address and I'll take it up myself now, I'll –'

Roebuck interrupted, 'We can send it as an e-mail attachment. They'll have it instantly.'

The sergeant gave Roebuck the bewildered gaze of a man still not quite there with technology. The DCI looked at him approvingly. 'Good idea. You won't lose any picture quality?'

'None at all,' Roebuck said.

The inspector and the detective sergeant both handed Michael their cards and direct-line numbers. The DCI told him that they were going to print posters and put them up in petrol stations and other places along Amanda's likely route to London on Sunday night. They were also putting her name and picture out on the missing-person slots on regional and national television, and planning to interview everyone who lived in her building or close to it.

Michael headed back to the office. He'd let two patients down, but he might just make it back in time for the third.

She was being kept in darkness.

Some monster out there had Amanda, the lovely, beautiful, incredible Amanda.

He pulled over to the side, put on the handbrake and closed his eyes. *Amanda, darling, we've had so little time together. Please be all right. Be strong. I'm looking for you. I'm going to find you. You are going to be all right. You are going to be fine.*

At ten past five, just as Michael was about to see his last patient, Thelma told him that DC Roebuck was on the line.

The detective had a report from Birmingham. 'Dr Tennent, I don't know if any of this will help. The place Miss Capstick is in would seem to be some kind of underground chamber, or a vault, from the absence of any natural light. There's a mattress, and the edge of an orange bucket is visible. The floor and walls both appear to be made of concrete. The technician says that Miss Capstick's T-shirt looks dirty and her hair's matted.'

The detective held back that there were bloodstains on the T-shirt and that her jeans were torn.

'She's normally very neat,' Michael replied. 'Anything else?'

'No, I have the number of the technician, who'd be

happy to speak to you, and I'm having a print sent down here. We can meet at nine in the morning and take a look, see if there is anything you recognise. I'll bring it to you if it's not convenient for you to come here, and I'd like to take another statement from you.'

'Of course.' Michael wondered if he was still considered a suspect. If he was, he wanted to get that thought out of Roebuck's mind so that the police didn't waste any precious time on him. Could he account for his movements on Sunday night after he had left the track? He'd gone home, read the papers, worked on some notes for a talk he was giving in a fortnight, then gone to bed. No alibi. Anyhow, surely Amanda's call to the radio station was evidence enough?

He was so desperately tired it was hard to stop his brain from rambling. *Forget it, you're not a suspect. Concentrate! Concentrate on Amanda.*

After he had hung up, he sat, thinking. DC Roebuck said she appeared to be in an underground chamber or vault.

His mind flashed back to his session with Dr Terence Goel.

'You are stronger than the dove – you can put it in the cellar, but what about the feelings of the dove in the cellar?'

'Fallout shelter.'

Goel had fumbled after saying *fallout shelter*. As if he had let something slip.

Fallout shelters were made of concrete. Lead-lined concrete. Underground.

Ordinarily, he would not have had enough here to justify breaking the patient/client confidentiality code, but right now he didn't care about that. He wanted to explore every possible area, even if it meant being hauled over the coals by the British Medical Association Complaints Bureau.

He rang DC Roebuck back. 'I have a patient who is bothering me. It might be nothing, but there are things he said in a consultation with me this morning that tally a little with what you are describing in that photograph.'

'In what way exactly, sir?'

'This is a little delicate. He's an eminent scientist and

everything he has said to me is confidential, but I feel you should know. I'd be grateful if you could be very discreet – perhaps just check him out? I'm trying to get hold of the GP who referred him and I might get some more information from him.'

'Shall I wait until you've got that?'

'Sure.'

'Can I have his name and address? You know where he works?' Roebuck asked.

'His name is Dr Terence Goel.' Michael spelled it out. 'He works at GCHQ.'

'The government intelligence surveillance headquarters?'

'Yes.'

'He'd have gone through extensive positive vetting before getting a post there.'

'I know. But I'm not at all happy about him. Although this could just be me clutching at straws.'

Michael explained his concerns in more detail. Roebuck listened to him and then said, 'You're right to be concerned. It may well turn out to be nothing, but we should definitely take a closer look at this man. I'll go and have a word with him myself.'

'I don't want him to know that you're seeing him because of my concerns.'

'Don't worry, I'll find some excuse.' Good-humouredly he said, 'I'll tell him his car was in the vicinity of an accident and we're looking for witness statements, something like that.'

Michael gave him Dr Goel's address and mobile phone number, thanked him and hung up.

Dr Sundaralingham had not rung back. He dialled the doctor's number, and it was answered by the same man as before.

'He does have your message,' the man assured him. 'I spoke to him a short while ago, but he's busy. He asked if you have a home or mobile number he could call you on after office hours.'

Michael gave him both, and stressed that it was urgent

that he spoke to Dr Sundaralingham. The man promised to convey this to him.

Thelma buzzed to remind him that his patient had now been waiting for fifteen minutes.

Suddenly he had a thought. There *was* someone who might be able to help. A patient who had hinted he knew something. A total long shot, but it was worth a try. Hurriedly he opened a drawer in his filing cabinet and thumbed through the headings under the flagging 'D'.

Then he lifted out the file, opened it at the first page, and wrote down the address. A visit would get a better reaction than a phone call. He would go straight after his last patient.

Chapter Eighty-six

The tenth screw almost slipped from Amanda's fingers, but somehow she managed to grip it between whatever was left of her nails. A burst of light flashed in front of her eyes. The headlamps of a train coming out of a tunnel. Somewhere in the darkness around her she heard her mother call her name. Then she heard rising laughter as if she was walking past a crowded pub.

She swung her head, staring out: a spark like a firefly shot through the darkness and died. Then Lulu appeared and disappeared like a spectral figure on a ghost train. An oceanic swell of anxiety heaved up inside her chest then dropped away. More voices. Her mother again, now Lara.

Quiet, please leave me alone, not now, don't do this to me now. Darkness crashed over her, dragging her, like undertow, away from the wall. She leaned forward against it, the mattress tilting away beneath her feet, tried to steady herself.

She pocketed the screw then slid both hands up the wall to the edge of the grille and, using the blade of her screwdriver, pried the bottom surround of the grille away from the wall.

It was far heavier than she expected, and before she had a chance to do anything, she was overbalancing backwards under the weight.

She yelped as she crashed onto a bucket, and the grille fell beside her onto the concrete with a clatter like collapsing scaffolding. Slowly, she eased herself onto her side. The liquid was cold, soapy water; not the latrine bucket, she realised, with some small relief.

Back onto her knees, then she stood up. She found the

mattress, positioned it against the wall, stood on it and reached up. Her hands located the lip of the shaft. She pushed them as far inside as she could reach. There was no resistance, just soft fluff that felt like dust and harder stuff that was probably mouse or rat droppings. The shaft seemed to go horizontally. Good. Easier to get into.

Pressing down as hard as she could with her hands, and taking her full body weight with her arms, she heaved herself up, her legs kicking out against the bare stone wall for a purchase. But as she tried to push her head into where she thought the opening was, she cracked it painfully on the edge.

Dumb. Stupid. So dumb bloody stupid.

All she had thought about was getting the grille off. She hadn't considered how, without a decent foothold or handhold, she was going to be able to get up and into a space that was only two feet wide.

I need a fucking ladder.

She stood up, then staggered sideways, feeling sudden nausea from her splitting head. *Maybe I should ring room service for paracetamol.*

And a Bloody Mary.

And a ladder.

Her head felt like an axe blade was stuck in it.

Fuck you, Michael Tennent.

Fuck room service. Fuck you, fuck you, fuck you.

Get me out of here.

Calm down.

Think.

Improvise.

She didn't want to think about it too much, she didn't have the luxury of time or the guts to think about it. She got up, made her way carefully through into the next chamber, found the corpses, knelt down and put her hands around the dead woman's ankles. Gripping them tightly, and using all her strength, she hauled the corpse through into her own chamber and laid it against the wall beneath the shaft.

Then she repeated the process with the male corpse, and

hauled it on top of the woman, in reverse position so that her head was locked between his legs, and the stumps of his arms were interlocked with her thighs.

Close to exhaustion, she pulled the mattress up over the male corpse's back and tucked it firmly down the other side, making a bridge. Then she climbed carefully onto the mattress, feeling her way up the wall with her hands. It worked! Her face was now level with the shaft.

Reaching forward as far as she could, she explored the space with her hands. There was no resistance. Just more fluff and droppings. Her knees bashed against the sharp edge, her shoulders jammed against the sides, then she was inside the shaft.

Shaking. Heart punchballing her chest. Squeezed on both sides, her head rubbing the ceiling, her shoulders just able to make it along the sides. Breathing sharp, rapid gulps, the dry smell of dust in her nose, and another faintly sour, rancid smell with it, she felt her way forward, horizontally, with her hands.

Aching with hope, she inched onwards, one knee ahead, now the other knee, terrified that at any moment she was going to hear a voice, see a flashlight beam, feel a leg being pulled back. She had her right knee ahead again. Then the left. Her hands touched something metallic, like an exposed girder. She stopped and traced it up. It was like a porthole, several inches narrower than the shaft.

She felt through it, and on the far side, the shaft curved sharply upwards. Vertical!

She tried to put her head through it, but that did not work. She tried her right arm first, then her head. The metal pressed against her back, scraped down her T-shirt. Then she wedged, half in, half out.

Perspiration sloughed down her face and her body. She struggled, all the time wedging herself tighter.

She had no idea how long it would be before Michael came back down and saw the grille missing. She just had to keep going somehow.

Then suddenly she was free, through the hoop. She moved on forward, her waist going through, now her knees. As the shaft curved upwards, she started to stand. Her shoulders still wedged against the walls when she let herself expand. It was a vertical climb now. She pushed her shoulders out, her legs out, and managed to get some kind of a purchase on the coarse texture of the concrete.

Concentrating hard, desperate not to slip back, using every ounce of her strength she wormed her way several feet up the shaft. Her fingers touched something metallic.

Desperately, she eased her legs further up the wall, then raised her body. Now she could feel what this metal was more clearly.

It was one of the blades of a turbine. Part of an extraction system. The metal was as thick and heavy as the blades of an aircraft, and blocked the shaft above her.

Crying with frustration, she dropped back down until her feet were back on the level part. Then she stood in the blackness shaking with utter terror. It felt as if every bad fear she'd ever had in her life had been stored away in some compartment inside her, waiting for this moment to burst out and engulf her.

She now felt sure that she was going to die.

Chapter Eighty-seven

A grim South London high-rise, the lower floors daubed in graffiti. There might have been a front door once, but not any more.

Michael stood in the lobby, the beat of rap music resonating down the bare walls, and glanced at his Volvo parked out on the street, wondering, in this rough neighbourhood, how much of it would still be there when he came out.

He took a large lift up to the eighth floor and emerged into a narrow, dark, uncarpeted hallway that stank of boiled potatoes. Through a wall he could hear a baby crying and a demented-sounding woman screaming at it.

Flat 87 had a blue door, with a frosted-glass window, like all the rest, and a small plastic bell-push with no name. Music was playing inside. He pressed the bell and heard a feeble rasp. He rapped on the glass with his knuckles.

No response.

He rapped harder, then harder still, and suddenly his fist went clean through the glass.

For an instant he stood still, in shock. Then he felt the sting of the cut and saw a band of blood appear across the back of his hand. Carefully he withdrew it, picked out a shard embedded in the skin, then sucked the wound. The music was louder now. A woman singing, a tune familiar to him, but only a few words, then they repeated. She was singing English words in a German accent. She sounded like Marlene Dietrich.

No other doors opened. The mother and baby were still hammer and tongs at each other.

Shit.

Two youths came out of the fire exit at the end of the corridor, eyed him, then stopped nonchalantly outside a door and rapped on it. Michael continued to watch them. The door opened, they said something to the occupant and within seconds it was closed again. They moved to the next door, glanced at Michael again, then rapped. Both wore sneakers, one was in a shell suit, the other in jeans and a bomber jacket, carrying a hold-all.

Michael knew exactly what they were doing, and what would happen when they reached this door with no glass in the window and the occupant out.

'Falling in love a . . . falling in love a . . . falling in love a . . .'

The sound was scratchy. A record stuck in a groove? Michael pressed his face close to the gap in the broken pane and called out, gently at first and then more loudly, 'Mr Dortmund. Herr Dortmund!'

No answer.

He tugged free the remaining shards to avoid cutting his hand again, then reached in and groped for the door latch. He found it after a few seconds, a robust mortice, and gave it a tug.

The door opened.

He let himself in, calling loudly now, 'Mr Dortmund! Hallo! Herr Dortmund!'

The song continued.

Uneasy, he closed the door behind him. He was in a tiny hallway, barely larger than a cubicle, most of it taken up with a Victorian coat-stand, on which hung the elderly Nazi's herringbone tweed overcoat, mackintosh and brown trilby. The fine coat seemed oddly incongruous; it was too elegant for this poky space, and stood in stark contrast to the unremitting ugliness of the building beyond.

He walked a few feet down a passageway carpeted with a threadbare runner, past a couple of framed prints of rural Bavaria, and entered the sitting room.

And stopped in his tracks.

It was a sad little room, with net curtains obscuring a view of an identical tower block only yards away, and furnished like an impoverished student's lodging. Two beat-up armchairs, a meagre rug, an old radio and an even older hi-fi, on which a record was spinning, the arm of the stylus bobbing, a fan heater against the wall.

But it was none of this that he was taking in. It was the oil painting on the wall, in pride of place, presiding over the room, dominating it. A portrait of Adolf Hitler, in uniform, standing in front of a swastika, his arm raised in a salute.

Michael turned away, repulsed at the thought that his patient, who had come to him in search of redemption, was still under his idol's spell. He went back out into the passageway and called out again, 'Mr Dortmund? Hallo? Herr Dortmund?'

There were three further doors, one wide open, two ajar. He peered in through the first door, which opened into a bedroom. A stark, lonely-looking room with a narrow single bed, tidily made up, and which, like the rest of the flat, smelt of old age. Underwear was neatly folded on the one chair; carpet slippers beneath it.

He went to the next door, which opened into a tiny, old-fashioned kitchen, with a grimy gas cooker, and a small Formica-topped table on which lay a German newspaper.

Back in the passageway, he noticed an old, frayed flex, plugged into a wall socket, running into the end room. His unease deepening, he called out once more, 'Mr Dortmund?'

He waited. Knocked on the door, then pushed it open.

He'd been expecting something like this, but it was still a shock.

Herman Dortmund's pitifully emaciated body lay naked, motionless, partially immersed in water in his narrow green bathtub.

His eyes were wide open, staring unblinking ahead in an expression of surprise. His mouth was open also, his jaw jutting forward, his lips forming an almost perfect, agonised circle. Michael saw that his eyebrows were singed. And he saw, clutched between the German's bony hands, and submerged in the water between his splayed open thighs, an ancient electrical heater to which the flex was connected.

He stepped back out of the room, and jerked the plug out of the wall socket. Then he went back in and touched Dortmund's face. The flesh was cold, he had been dead for a while. Even so, he checked the man's pulse, but it was a formality. There was nothing he could do for him.

Leaving him as he was, he went back into the sitting room in search of a phone. Marlene Dietrich still sang the same words over and over on the turntable. He wondered whether to switch off the machine, but decided he should leave everything as he had found it.

Then his eyes fell on the only object of beauty in this room, a roll-top writing desk, on which, next to the telephone, four addressed envelopes were neatly laid out, almost as if they had been left on display.

He went over and glanced down at them out of curiosity. One, in shaky handwriting, was to a firm of solicitors in Croydon. One was to a woman in Bonn. The third was to a man in Stuttgart. The fourth letter was addressed to himself.

Probably paying his bill, Michael thought. But out of curiosity, he picked it up and opened it. There was a note inside, in the same neat, shaky handwriting. It said:

Dear Dr Tennent,

For me, the time has come to stop my pain and torment. For you, this torment called life must continue.

With reference to my concerns at our recent sessions, and these psychic abilities that are unwelcome to me, I have recently been receiving the name *Dr Goel* in connection with you.

Goel is a Jewish name. This man, Dr Goel, is a Jew. You would be advised to acquaint yourself with knowledge of Hebrew. Among the ancient Hebrews the *goel* was the next of kin whose duty it was to redeem wrongs done to a kinsman.

The *goel*, Dr Tennent, in Hebrew mythology, was the *Avenger of Blood*.

Chapter Eighty-eight

Glen Branson was melting in the heat. He was standing on a carpet that was sticky with spilt beer, in the packed upstairs room of a pub somewhere in North London – he wasn't sure where – surrounded by a hundred or so boisterous police officers, who were cheering loudly.

The object of their exultation was the retiring Detective Inspector Dick Bardolph, for whom this celebration was being held and who at this moment had his tie off, his shirt unbuttoned and his face buried between the naked breasts of a grossly well-endowed blonde stripagram girl.

Glen was leaning over the counter, trying to catch the eye of the solitary, harassed barman, carrying a list of eight drink orders in his head. He had seen enough demeaning behaviour to women in his night-club bouncer days. He didn't like stripagrams. He didn't like large crowds of drunken men. And he wasn't in a party mood tonight. He'd seen his share of dead bodies since he'd joined the force, but nothing had disturbed him as much as Cora Burstridge's last week and the one hauled out of Shoreham harbour this morning. The images of the skull sticking from the leather jacket and the bloated body, the terrible smell, were still with him now, and three pints of lager hadn't dimmed them. Nor had they dimmed his anxieties about Cora Burstridge.

It was her funeral tomorrow. There was a finality about that which scared him. Sure, there was still the inquest to come, but with her body cremated, if any new evidence did come to light, it was going to be even harder to get to the truth of what had happened to her.

Fleetingly Glen caught the barman's eye, but he turned

and served someone else. He wondered how long the evening would go on: there was talk of a Chinese meal after this, but he was tired. He would be happy to get home and not have too late a night.

Mike Harris, who had brought him up here, had been looking after him well, introducing him to several good Metropolitan Police contacts, but the noise level from the music and the general hubbub meant that all conversations had to be shouted. Still, he had collected a few impressive cards: a deputy chief constable, a chief superintendent, two detective chief inspectors were the prize trophies so far. As with any organisation, promotion in the police depended in part on whom you knew.

Someone was jostling Glen, trying to elbow his way up to the counter beside him. Glen moved over to make space and glanced round. He saw a huge bear of a man, with a bull neck showing through his open-throat shirt, a hefty rugger-player's frame and a baby face, his fair hair cropped to a fuzz. The man, who was sweating profusely, gave him a friendly nod, and shouted, 'Just got here, I need to catch up!'

The voice sounded vaguely familiar, but Glen couldn't immediately place it. 'One barman,' he replied. 'Crazy! They need three.'

Behind them was a roar of 'Get 'em off!'

Both men turned their heads, but could see nothing.

'Where you from?' Glen's new companion shouted to him.

'Sussex.'

'Whereabouts?'

'Hove.'

His companion nodded thoughtfully, then shouted, 'D'you know a DC there called Branson?'

Glen knew now why he recognised the man's voice. 'That's me!'

'You're Glen Branson?'

'Yup!'

The other man beamed warmly and held out his hand.

'What a coincidence! Simon Roebuck from Hampstead – we spoke on Monday.'

Glen shook it. 'Tina Mackay.'

'That's right!'

'You palmed me off with some of your donkey-work – checking up on a Robert Mason.'

Roebuck smiled. 'Any time I can reciprocate . . .' He raised his massive hands. 'What are you drinking?'

'My round, let me get you one.'

'Pint of bitter, thanks.'

Glen signalled at the barman once more, still without success. He turned back to Roebuck. 'Any progress with Tina Mackay?'

'Got another missing woman now. Similar age, build, successful career woman too. Left her sister in Sussex on Sunday evening, never arrived back in London. I was going to give you a call to see if you could check out a couple of people for me in Brighton.'

'No problem.'

The barman finally took his order. Roebuck helped Glen deliver the drinks through the crowd, then they returned to the bar. The roistering was still going on, and it was impossible to stand still without being jostled. Some of Glen's beer slopped over.

'I need some air,' Glen said, irritably.

'Me too.'

They took their glasses out onto the pavement. It was a sticky evening, only just growing dark now at half past nine. A bus blatted past. 'You think these two missing women are connected?' Glen asked.

'I have a hunch they are, yes. A lot of similarities.'

Glen sipped his lager; he felt an easy rapport with the London detective, as if they were friends of some standing rather than telephone acquaintances of a few days. Both men eyed two girls who strode past in skirts that were barely street-legal.

'The day I stop looking have me put down,' Roebuck said.

Glen grinned. 'How long have you been in the force?'

'Thirteen years. Nine in CID. You?'

391

'Four. Two in Sid. I'm just a new kid on the block.' He smiled. 'Tell me something, you just said you have a hunch – seems to me a lot of police work is about hunches. You agree?'

'*Hunches*?' Roebuck drank a gulp of beer and wiped his mouth with the back of his hand. Three youths in succession flashed past on trail bikes. Glen and Roebuck watched them, exchanged a glance. Roebuck went on, 'Yeah, I suppose, hunches . . . informed guesses . . . intuition . . .' He scratched the top of his head. 'I think good detectives are intuitive.' He fished a pack of cigarettes out of his pocket and offered one to Glen.

'Don't use them, thanks, I quit.'

Roebuck lit one. It smelt good to Glen, much sweeter than the fug of smoke inside. Glen said, 'Have you ever had a hunch – intuition, whatever, about something and not been able to do anything with it? Like, not being able to convince your senior officers that you should investigate further?'

'Yeah.' He drew deeply on the cigarette, then removed it from his lips with his forefinger and thumb. 'A few times.'

'And what did you do?'

Roebuck shrugged. 'Let it drop.'

'You never had anything that you just couldn't drop?'

'It doesn't work that way in the force. I don't have enough hours in the day to deal with everything the way I'd like to.'

'I have something I can't drop,' Glen said.

Roebuck gave him a strange look, part curious, part wary. 'What is it?'

'A sudden death I attended last week. Everyone else reckons it's suicide, but I don't.'

'Why not?'

Glen drank some more of his lager. 'OK. You know Cora Burstridge, the film star?'

'She died last week, great actress.'

'I found her in her flat, with a plastic bag over her head.'

Roebuck wrinkled his face. 'Sad way to end up. I've attended suicides like that. How long had she been there?'

'A couple of days.'

'Wait until you get someone who's been there a couple of weeks.'

Glen thought, queasily, about the body from Shoreham harbour. 'Thanks.'

'Don't mention it. What's your problem with her suicide?'

'Nothing I can convince my DCI on, but there are things that don't stack up for me. Anomalies. Why did she go out on the afternoon she died and buy an expensive Babygro suit for her grandchild in the US, but never send it? Why did she have an intruder in her flat, who was seen by a neighbour, who didn't take anything? Why would she kill herself less than forty-eight hours after being presented with a BAFTA Lifetime Achievement Award?'

Roebuck looked at him thoughtfully. 'There are probably good explanations. Is that all you have to go on?'

'Tell me, Simon, would you be concerned by that information, if you'd found her yourself?'

'Concerned by what you've told me?'

'Yes.'

'I'd want a post-mortem, and I'd have the flat dusted – I'd put SOCO in there for sure. Then I'd see what showed up. I think I would definitely want to satisfy myself that it was suicide.'

'I haven't told you the best bit. Cora had a rival years back, an actress called Gloria Lamark. Unless you're a movie buff, you probably won't remember her name.'

Lamark. It was ringing a bell but Simon Roebuck could not for the life of him think why. 'Lamark. How do you spell that?'

Glen spelled it for him, and noticed the pensive look on the detective's face. 'So, she has this rival, Gloria Lamark. In nineteen sixty-six they were both up for a role in a film called *Mirror to the Wall*. Cora Burstridge got the part, and an Academy Award nomination. I haven't seen the film in a while, but I managed to rent a copy last night and watch it through. Cora plays an actress in the film who gets horribly disfigured in a car accident, and one of her lines is, "I can no longer look at myself in the mirror.'' Those were the exact words used by Cora in her suicide note. That was *all* she wrote.'

Roebuck studied his face. 'Do you think Gloria Lamark might have done this?'

Glen shook his head. 'Gloria Lamark loathed Cora Burstridge but she certainly didn't kill her. She died three weeks ago, took an overdose. Odd coincidence, don't you think? That they died within three weeks of each other.'

Roebuck dragged again on his cigarette. *Lamark. Lamark.* He had a feeling he knew why the name sounded familiar to him, but he couldn't be sure. 'Are you on duty tomorrow, Glen?'

'Yes. I'm at Cora Burstridge's funeral at ten. Otherwise in the office. Why?'

'I'm tired and I want to go back to the office and take a look at something – sorry to be a party pooper. We'll talk in the morning. Good meeting you.'

'Good meeting you, too.'

Glen took both their glasses back inside and, wondering what the name Lamark had triggered off for his new friend, slowly and with more than a little reluctance, climbed the stairs back to the party.

Chapter Eighty-nine

Michael sat at his desk in the Sheen Park Hospital, with Dr Terence Goel's file open in front of him, and the telephone in his hand.

The voice-mail answered. 'Dr Sundaralingham can't come to the phone right now. Please leave a message and he'll get right back to you.'

He hung up without saying anything, surprised to get an answering-machine and not a human. Doctors normally had someone to cover when they were off-duty.

He rested his head in his hands.

Dr Terence Goel, you came into my office talking about the loss of loved ones, about a car smash that mirrored the one Katy died in, the dove in the cage, the cellar, the nuclear fallout shelter.

Your name means Avenger of Blood.

Are you just an innocent man with a whole heap of problems and some bizarre parallels with my own life?

Or is there a whole lot more to you that I should know about?

There was a message on the answering-machine from DC Roebuck, saying that he'd been to the cybercafé but, as he had suspected, it could have been any of a couple of hundred customers who had been in that day. If he had a photograph of a face to show, then he might have better luck.

Michael logged onto the Internet, went back to the address of Terence Goel's website and called it up. Then he copied Goel's photograph onto a separate file and e-mailed it to Roebuck.

As the e-mail was going through, he dialled Roebuck's

mobile phone, and got his voice-mail. He left a message telling him the latest information he had about Goel, from Dortmund, and that he had sent him a photograph of Goel for him to try out in the Cybercafé.

Then, something struck him. On his computer he called up the Alta Vista search engine and entered a search command for the name, 'Dr Terence Goel'.

As before, there was just one hit. The address of Goel's web page. Nothing else.

If Dr Goel was such an eminent man, why weren't there more mentions of him on the Internet? Why only one? Surely there would be links to other sites. Maybe not to the highly secretive GCHQ, but surely to *Nature* magazine? To the Scripps Institute? To USC? To MIT?

He entered a search command for *Nature* magazine. When the index came up, he typed a search command for Dr Terence Goel. Nothing appeared.

He repeated the process with the Scripps Institute website. Nothing there either. Nor could he find anything at the Massachusetts Institute of Technology.

He closed his eyes against a headache down the front of his forehead that was growing increasingly acute, then popped two paracetamol.

He dialled Directory Enquiries, and asked if there was a number for GCHQ. A little to his surprise, there was. But when he rang the number, he got a recorded voice telling him the office was closed until nine o'clock the following morning.

He checked his e-mail. The usual mountain of incoming messages, most of it to do with work, and one from his brother in Seattle telling him that he and the family were planning a visit – and was Michael aware that the year after next was their parents' golden wedding anniversary?

While he was logged on, another e-mail came through. It was a reminder about the tee-off time for his golf match on Saturday. Golf, he thought. How the hell was he going to be able to concentrate on a golf game?

He read through Dr Terence Goel's file again, word by word. The letter of referral from Dr Sundaralingham. The new patient form on which Goel had filled in only his name, address and cellphone number. He dialled it and instantly heard Goel's recorded voice.

'This is Dr Terence Goel. Please leave a message and I'll get back to you.'

Michael hung up, then dialled Directory Enquiries, gave the operator Goel's address and asked for his home number. She told him it was ex-directory.

Michael replaced the receiver, cradled his forehead in his hand, and squeezed his temples. Then he looked up. The sky was dark against the window. Twenty-five past ten.

He stared back at Goel's notes. *Fallout shelter.*

A cold flush of fear churned in his gut.

Fallout shelter.

. . . *some kind of chamber, maybe a vault.*

Fallout shelter?

He stood up, walked around his office, then he went outside and paced the empty corridor. Dr Goel was obsessing him.

The Avenger of Blood.

What was he avenging?

He looked at his watch again. Half past ten. Cheltenham was a good hour and a half's drive, he remembered, from the last time he'd been there a few years back to give a talk.

He went back into his office and looked at the man's address again. A flat. A flat with a cellar or a vault or a fallout shelter?

It was possible.

He closed Dr Terence Goel's file and slipped it into his briefcase. Ten minutes later he was in his Volvo, on the South Circular road, heading towards the M40 for Oxford and Cheltenham. His eyes hurt in the oncoming lights. He was dog-tired and the night air was stiflingly warm. This was madness. He should phone Roebuck, tell him his thoughts, then go home to bed. Instead he drove on.

An hour later he pulled into a motorway service station, bought himself a tired-looking burger, soggy fries and a beaker of coffee. He sat at a table by a window and stared out at the grey ghost in the glass that was staring back at him. The ghost's hair was dishevelled. Even through the oval tortoiseshell glasses he could see huge black rings around the ghost's eyes.

But from inside those rings determination stared back at him.

Chapter Ninety

A Mandelbrot Set screen saver was busily drawing crop circle designs, wiping each one when it was complete before moving on to the next. Complex fractals, concentric circles, linked star clusters. Simon Roebuck stood in the doorway of the Tina Mackay incident room on the second floor of Hampstead police station, watching a new design appear on the screen. A series of smaller hexagrams clustered around a larger central one, which in turn grew smaller hexagrams.

Patterns, he thought. If he hadn't gone into the force, he would have liked to have taught mathematics. Sometimes he envied the intellectual satisfaction that his fiancée, Briony, who taught maths and physics at a comprehensive, got from her work. He didn't find enough intellectual challenges in policing, not even in the CID. It was mostly steady plodding, using a mixture of bureaucracy, observation, common sense, intuition, perseverance and sheer hard slog.

Each small portion of a fractal is a reduced scale replica of the whole. There was an elegance about mathematics and about fractals that Simon Roebuck liked. Police work was rarely elegant. It was gutty. Grubbing around against the clock and the budget for clues, for tiny bits of a puzzle, and when you did find them, sometimes you had to bash them with a mental hammer to make them fit.

He was tired. It would be nice to go home now, have a cool shower, and curl up in bed with Briony and talk about his day and listen to hers, then make love to her, fall asleep in her arms, and start tomorrow fresh and alert.

Instead, at half past ten on this hot, sticky oven of a

night, he was back at the station, entering the incident room, hoping against hope he could do something for two women he had never met. Tina Mackay and Amanda Capstick. Hoping that, God forbid, if anything ever happened to his beloved Briony Donnelly, some other detective, in some other incident room in some other police station, would work just as hard for her.

The room had an abandoned feeling about it, as if it had been evacuated in a hurry. All six computer screens were still on, unfinished paperwork lay on the desks, a half-eaten Mars bar poked out of its torn wrapper on the top of one in-tray. One filing-cabinet drawer was half open. Busy. Bedlam. He doubted if any of the team had finished before ten tonight. They were a hard-working lot. Caring men and women. Caring desperately for two strangers.

Tina Mackay's disappearance had been featured on the national television programme, *Crimewatch*, earlier in the week and there had been hundreds of phone calls of possible sightings; there'd be another raft of them next week when Amanda Capstick's name was put out, if she hadn't turned up by then.

And she wasn't going to turn up, not of her own accord, he was pretty certain of that. She was going to have to be found. He just hoped she and Tina would be found alive. He hadn't told the women's relatives, or Amanda Capstick's psychiatrist boyfriend, but he didn't think the chances of finding either alive were good.

He walked across the room, and put the capped Styrofoam cup of sweet black coffee down on the desk he had allocated as his workspace up here, then glanced down at the list of actions completed today by the other five team members. Nothing new on either woman. The cap leaked, a dribble of coffee ran down the side of the cup; he caught it with his finger and sucked it. The sweetness tasted good. He turned pages of the report, touched his keyboard to bring the screen back to life, and the Mandelbrot Set disappeared. It was replaced by a list of cases around the country from the Holmes national crime system, in which attractive, successful career women, within Tina and Amanda's age

400

bracket, had disappeared during the past five years. Still no correlations with other case histories.

He listened again to Dr Tennent's message about Dr Goel on his mobile voice-mail, then sat in front of his computer screen and tried to open the photograph of Dr Goel that the psychiatrist had e-mailed him.

He failed.

He cursed the computer. Photographs were always a problem: the only person in here who had the knack was the systems manager – he'd get him to do it first thing in the morning.

Turning his attention back to his main reason for being here now, Simon Roebuck walked across to a stack of deep cardboard boxes piled against the far wall of the room, all containing files borrowed from Tina Mackay's office. Simon Roebuck examined their scrawled labels, and found the two boxes he wanted, one marked, REJECTION LETTERS, JAN–DEC 96, and the other, REJECTION LETTERS JAN–JUL 97. He heaved both of them back to his desk. Tina Mackay's secretary had told him a week back that they received over a hundred manuscripts a week, which meant some eight thousand letters in these boxes to go through.

He could have done with another pair of hands – and eyes – and debated whether to call one of the team back out, but thought better of it. They were all exhausted, they would work better after some rest. He was aware that he would also, but that wasn't an option. He'd already scanned through the entire lot once, some days back.

He popped the lid from his coffee. A phone rang and he answered it. 'Incident room, Simon Roebuck.'

It was a wrong number. Someone wanting a taxi. He hung up, selected the 1997 box first, and began working through it letter by letter, glancing at the name of the addressee, looking for just the one name blinking away inside his head.

He might be mistaken. The spelling might be different. His brain might be playing tricks. The letters were banded together in wodges of one hundred. He finished the first lot, placed them face down on the floor, then started on the

401

second bundle. Nothing. Nor the third bundle. A moth flew erratically around the room. Tiny black flies swarmed across the ceiling. A mosquito whined past him and he attempted to swat it, without success. Traffic passed outside.

He phoned Briony, told her he was going to be late and she said she'd wait up for him. He told her to go to bed, he had no idea how late he'd be, he might be all night. She told him she loved him and he told her he loved her too, more than anything in the world, and he did. Then he hung up and concentrated on the rejection letters.

The letters had a sadness about them. They contained bad news, most of them flat, bald statements with empty hope.

Dear Mr Witney,

Thank you for submitting your manuscript, *Twice Nightly*, to us. After careful reading, we regret we are unable to consider this for publication on our lists.

We hope you will be successful with it elsewhere.

Yours sincerely,

Tina Mackay, Editorial Director.

Months, years, maybe even a whole lifetime of work dismissed in three lines. Eight thousand possible suspects, double that if he went back a further year and a half. An impossible task to investigate them, to interview them all on just a long-shot hunch.

But whittle this lot down to just one, and that would be different.

A few had short, handwritten notes at the top, presumably by either Tina Mackay or one of her assistants. Some said the author was a friend or relative of so-and-so in the publishing house. Others were comments about the authors themselves, if they had been pushy, or it was suspected that the manuscript had been plagiarised from somewhere else, anything that might be useful for future reference. He was sure the one he was looking for now had a note at the top.

He flicked on through the names. Page after page of Pelham House Publishing Group headed notepaper. Word-processor typing. All kinds of names, male, female, British, foreign. Some titled names. Simon Roebuck dreamed of writing a book one day. He wondered if he, too, would get letters like this.

Then he stopped. He had found it.

Thomas Lamark,
47 Holland Park Villas,
London W14 8JJ
Dear Mr Lamark,
   Thank you for submitting your manuscript, *The Authorised Biography of Gloria Lamark*, to us. After careful reading, we regret we are unable to consider this for publication on our lists.
   We hope you will be successful with it elsewhere.
   Yours sincerely,
   Tina Mackay, Editorial Director.

At the top of the letter, in handwriting he presumed was that of Tina Mackay's secretary, were the words: 'Phoned several times, quite aggressive'.

The detective made a photocopy of the letter. He put the original back into the box. He folded the copy and slipped it into his jacket pocket.

Chapter Ninety-one

Headlights flared through the windscreen, momentarily dazzling Michael. Shadows leaped up at him as if they had torn free from the road. A car driving on full beam, thumping out a bass beat, turned across him then headed off up the wide Cheltenham avenue.

It was a quarter to one in the morning. The traffic light changed to green and Michael drove on, following the town-centre signs. The radio, badly tuned into a station it had found by itself, played hotel-foyer music. He pulled onto a garage forecourt to ask directions; the shop was locked and the attendant, seated behind a bullet-proof window with voice holes, was buried in a book propped against the window – Minette Walters' *The Echo* – and didn't notice Michael until he tapped on the glass.

With some reluctance he put down the book and produced a map from somewhere beneath him. 'Royal Court Walk?'

Michael nodded.

The attendant found it, gave him the directions then yawned and returned to his novel.

Michael drove for another mile, as he had been instructed, down a series of wide, almost deserted avenues with silhouettes of Georgian façades beyond their edges. Then he saw the landmark pub the attendant had mentioned and turned left.

The first road on the right was Royal Court Walk. He pulled the Volvo over to the kerb and switched on the map light to check the number: 97. Then he looked up at the elegant terraced houses. On the right he saw number 5. On the left number 4 and then number 6. Odd numbers on the right. He drove on: 17, 19. Further, then he looked again: 31 . . . 33 . . . 35. Further: 71 . . . 73 . . . Further, 91 . . . 93 . . . 95.

The street ended in a T-junction at 95. Puzzled, he did a U-turn. The last house on the opposite side was numbered 96. Then, just to make sure, he got out of the car and walked round the corner. Sometimes houses on a corner took the smarter address of their neighbouring street. But there was no 97 round the corner either.

Back in the car, he kept the driver's door open and under the interior light checked once more the number that was on the form. Clearly written. No possibility of either digit being mistaken for anything else. This was deliberate.

Dr Terence Goel had chosen this number because he knew it did not exist.

He switched off the interior light and sat in the shadowy glow of the street-lighting. Amanda had disappeared only days after Goel had first come to see him.

He was now even more convinced that Goel was involved. The man who could help him was here, in Cheltenham, a GP, a man who did not return phone calls.

He tried Directory Enquiries, to see if they had a home address listed for Dr Sundaralingham. They did, but it was ex-directory. Michael pleaded with the operator that he was a doctor and this was an emergency, but her only suggestion was for him to try the police.

He considered calling Roebuck, but it was now after one in the morning. He wasn't going to get the best out of Roebuck or Sundaralingham at this hour.

Ten minutes later, Michael drove into the tired-looking crescent where, according to the letterhead, Dr Sundaralingham's practice was located, and pulled up outside number 20.

There was a list of names on a brass panel beside the front door of the building, but no Dr Sundaralingham among them. Or any other doctor.

The crescent was quiet, no traffic, just the warm silence of the night. He took his mobile phone out of his car, walked up close to the building and dialled

Dr Sundaralingham's number. Moments later, somewhere up above him, he heard a phone ring. Four rings, and then the same recorded voice he'd heard before, through the receiver.

'Dr Sundaralingham can't come to the phone right now. Please leave a message and he'll get right back to you.'

He hung up, and to make sure, redialled the number. Again, after a few moments he heard ringing above him.

He tried each of the doorbells in turn, twice, but there was no response from any of them. He got back into his car, reversed a few feet until he had a clear view of the imposing columned steps that led up to the front door, then reclined his seat a little, and locked his doors. His body felt dog-tired but his brain was still churning. He would hear footsteps or a car. Anyone arriving here was going to wake him if he did doze off.

He closed his eyes to find his thoughts spinning in a whirlpool. Like a centrifuge, they held him, giddy and helpless, slowly drawing him down into the funnel of pure dark dread that was their centre.

There he slept.

Chapter Ninety-two

Beneath the Philippe Starck desk lamp, shadows from his fingers prowled over the keys.

Sometimes Thomas felt these were the keys of a Steinway piano, and that he was a great musician playing with all his soul, as he sat in his den, lost to the world, mesmerised by the glow of the monitor, the keys clicking under his fingers, his body swaying to the rhythm of the words that streamed across the screen.

Words that came out of the ether, pouring from his hands as if he was merely the conduit between the creator and the screen. *Surgeon's hands*, his mother had told him. Yes, slender hands, with long, beautiful fingers, the nails trim and spotless, the cuticles exquisitely manicured.

She had been sad when he left medical school. Sad and angry. *'You're not right in the head, you do know that, Tom-Tom, don't you?'*

Why had he left?

It was so far in the past, it was hard to remember any more. He was never exactly sure at the time. People at the school were angry with him, yes, but they were constantly angry with him over such petty stuff. Maybe it had been the bitch nurse he'd punched in the face when she'd laughed at him when he asked her to touch his choo-choo. There had been some big anger about that. His mother had been right about her. But was that the reason he'd had to leave? So much went clean out of his mind, and it seemed to be getting worse all the time. But not this morning. His memory was good this morning,

Powered up like a fully charged battery. Cool summer air bathed his body, which was naked beneath his silk dressing gown. Freshly bathed, shaved, cologned, ready. Busy day today. Cora Burstridge's funeral in Brighton. Then the mastectomy operation at King's. Then *he* would operate on Dr Michael Tennent's bit of fluff.

His supplies chest was light on anaesthetics; he'd used up most of his stock on Tina Mackay and the punky little newspaper reporter, Justin Flowering. Trying to keep them alive long enough to go on experiencing pain. He had forms printed in the name of Dr Sundaralingham but maybe they weren't necessary. Perhaps he could have more fun if Amanda Capstick remained awake.

Much more fun.

The cursor blinked on the screen in front of him as he sat in the darkness of drawn curtains in his den, responding to an e-mail that had arrived minutes ago from across the world.

Joe,
always quite magical to hear from you. I am coping well with my sad loss, thank you, it is kind of you to be so concerned. It was Gore Vidal, I believe, who said we are all fading to black at different speeds. How true! Bereavement is difficult – I cannot remember, did you tell me that you, too, had lost your dear mother? Too bad you couldn't make the funeral, it was quite something. We had to have a police presence to control the crowds. Understandable, of course, there was quite extraordinary love for my mother. It is hard to turn on the television at the moment without finding a Gloria Lamark retrospective of some kind, and I find these painful to watch.

The weather is hot here in London at the moment, yes, we are having a heatwave!!!! I know you think that we poor Londoners live permanently in fog and smog and drizzle, but really we are having an incredible heatwave. Hot also in Hong Kong, I expect?

What have you read about quantum vortexes? did you see the piece in *Nature*? I think the government are using these for mind control – electromagnetic influences on the brain, we talked about that. the US govt grid in Alaska using the power grid equivalent of ten major cities. Come on, what is this???

Stay in touch!

Your friend.

Thomas

The doorbell rang.

Thomas looked at his computer screen. Eight o'clock. The postman with a large quantity of fan mail? It was long overdue. Perhaps it had been piling up down at the sorting office. Maybe the world had finally realised.

Have I fed the thing? Last night, I took it down some food. Must not forget breakfast. I want it to keep its strength up today of all days. Yes, Amanda, the stronger you are the more pain you will tolerate!

He went into the hall. Eight o'clock in the morning. Yes, it must be the postman. Black slippers slapping on the grey flagstones, past the long-case clock, past the lacquered table, up to the door, he slid the top and bottom bolts, then peered through the spyhole. He saw a man he did not recognise, in a suit and tie, his face blubbery in the distorted fish-eye lens.

There was, of course, no need to open the door.

Thomas felt uncertain about this man: Jehovah's Witnesses and Mormons came in pairs. Postmen wore uniforms.

He listened. Positively no sounds from the thing down in the shelter beneath him.

Be careful.

He opened the door, relaxed, natural, the way any man in a Paisley silk dressing gown who is happy to be alive on such a fine morning might open his front door. 'Yes? Good morning?'

The stranger was a tall man with a hefty frame shoehorned into a cheap suit; the muscles of his bull neck bulged through his open-throat drip-dry yellow shirt. Alert grey eyes in a baby face beneath a crown of fair hair cropped to a fuzz.

409

'Mr Thomas Lamark?' The bland North London accent carried a certain authority.

'Yes,' Thomas continued his charm offensive, 'what can I do for you?'

'Detective Constable Roebuck from the Metropolitan Police.' He showed Thomas his identification. 'I apologise for coming by so early. I wonder if I could have a few minutes of your time, sir?'

The sharp bob of Thomas Lamark's Adam's apple gave DC Roebuck his first clue that he was facing an anxious man. But that wasn't anything to get lit up on; from experience he knew that many innocent people became nervous in the presence of policemen.

The man's voice remained calm. 'It's a little inconvenient, Officer. I have to go to a funeral.'

Instantly Thomas cursed himself. He hadn't meant to say that.

The detective looked suitably contrite. 'I'm sorry – someone close?'

'No, not really. I mean – you know how it is, one has obligations in life.' *What do you want?*

'Of course.'

They remained staring at each other, a silent freeze-frame on the top step.

'I really won't take up more than five minutes of your time,' Roebuck said.

There was an insistence in his voice that concerned Thomas. Eight o'clock. He had time. Half an hour maximum to deal with this man, to give the bit of fluff its breakfast, and to leave. He needed to find out what the man knew. 'Please come in. Would you care for coffee? Colombian roast? They are excellent beans, I can recommend them. Harder to come by than usual this year, because of coffee-rust disease, but well worth drinking, I can assure you.'

'Thank you, I'm fine.'

They entered the hall. Thomas saw the detective admire an oil painting of his mother stepping from a limousine in a blaze of flashguns.

'My mother, Gloria Lamark,' he said proudly. 'At the première of her film, *The Widow of Monaco*.'

'Ah, right. She died recently, I believe. I'm sorry. I gather she was quite famous, once.'

Thomas had difficulty containing the anger that erupted through him. *Once*!

With balled fists and white knuckles, he took the detective through into the grand drawing room and opened the curtains. Every inch of wall space was filled with photographs, paintings and framed photographs of Gloria Lamark. Thomas led him over to a photograph of his mother shaking hands with Lord Snowdon and Princess Margaret.

'A very beautiful lady,' Roebuck said.

'She was.' It came out like an explosion of air. Thomas's nerves were going haywire. He turned away from the policeman, taking deep breaths. This was not good. He needed to calm down, but the man was jangling him around inside his head. He led the detective to a sofa, then sat down on the edge of the one opposite, and tried to calm his mind again. But it was no good: his thoughts were jumping, his brainwaves a mess of spikes and troughs.

Roebuck pulled a notebook out of his pocket and opened it. The man was going to a funeral. He remembered the Sussex detective, Glen Branson, last night saying he was going to a funeral this morning. The same one? Unlikely.

He stared directly into Thomas's eyes. 'Mr Lamark, on March sixteenth of this year I understand you submitted a manuscript titled *The Authorised Biography of Gloria Lamark* to the publishers Pelham House. Is that correct?'

It was so unexpected that the words hit Thomas like a punch. And yet it *wasn't* unexpected. He had known that, sooner or later, someone would make this connection, that there would be a policeman coming round, making routine inquiries, and he had it all rehearsed, he knew exactly what he was going to say.

Except now he had forgotten.

'Yes.' He frowned, suddenly starting to feel calmer again. 'Yes, that was one of the firms I sent it to – I think.' That

411

came out well, confident. *Doing better now*. He managed a smile. 'I'm afraid I sent it to several publishers.'

'Did anyone accept it?'

'Not yet.'

'Were you a little surprised to get this kind of reaction?'

The detective's eyes were roaming. Up to the ceiling. Down to the floor. The man was fishing away. Thomas pressed his hands together. *Body language*. He leaned back more expansively on the sofa. *Maintain eye-contact*. He smiled, disarmingly.

'Officer, I think too many people today take Mr Warhol's dictum of fifteen minutes of fame a little too seriously. They find it hard to accept that true talent broaches all boundaries of time. The films that my mother made are as important to the world today as they always were. Some were so far ahead of their time that their true value is only just starting to be recognised. Naturally it is disappointing to be turned down. But I take solace from the knowledge that mediocrity recognises nothing higher than itself. Only *talent* recognises genius.'

The detective continued to watch him in silence. Then he said, 'I understand that you made several phone calls to Pelham House in connection with your manuscript. Can you remember the nature of those calls?'

Relaxing totally now, Thomas grinned broadly. 'Sure, I was pissed off. I didn't hear a word for two months after I sent them the manuscript. Not even a letter of acknowledgement.'

Roebuck said, 'I had a mate who wrote a book about a police officer – the first publisher he sent it to took over a year.' He raised his eyebrows then grinned. 'Pretty frustrating.'

Thomas grinned back, but let out no slack. This man was playing a game, trying to get some communality between them, trying to make him feel comfortable enough to drop his guard. 'Your friend was upset?'

'Yes, he was.' The detective nodded. Still smiling, he said, 'So is it your normal pattern to phone publishers up and be abusive to them?'

412

Thomas did not like this question. But he opened his arms and laughed. 'Do I look like a flake to you, DC Roebuck?'

The detective shook his head.

'I'm just a regular guy who wanted to do the right thing by his mother. She was a very great actress. She turned down hundreds of offers from people to write her biography because she didn't trust them to get it right. She went to court four times to stop unauthorised biographies. You know what the problem is? Today's publishing houses are filled with ignorant young people still in their shit-stained nappies who can't believe anyone older than the Spice Girls or younger than Darwin could possibly be of interest to the world!' Thomas slammed his fist furiously down on the side arm of the sofa.

Then he clocked the expression on the detective's face and knew that he was blowing it.

With his eyes locked on Thomas Lamark's, DC Roebuck said, 'I don't know if you have seen the news, sir, but Tina Mackay disappeared three weeks ago.'

And Thomas knew that DC Roebuck suspected him. He knew that DC Roebuck was intending to try to get a search warrant. A few bits of the Alfa Romeo were still in the garage. He wasn't ready to be searched yet. This was dangerous. This was a very bad situation.

Stupid.

Simon Roebuck watched Thomas Lamark stand up and say, 'Would you excuse me for one moment? I have to go to the bathroom.'

'Of course.'

He watched Lamark leave the room. Something felt wrong. He stood up and paced around the room, thinking. He stopped by the mantelpiece. Two invites stood there, both for previews at art galleries, both several months old. Strange, he thought, that a man in a house this grand, with a celebrity mother, did not have more invites.

And why the hell was Lamark so edgy? He was trying to

413

put on a calm, jovial, relaxed front, but that's what it was: a front.

Roebuck thought hard. He wanted to have a thorough look around here, but did he have enough evidence to convince a magistrate to grant a search warrant?

He walked over to the window and looked out into the garden. A beautiful garden, but in a state of neglect. No one had cut the grass in weeks. Why not? Perhaps Lamark was just in a bad way from his bereavement, but surely in a house this grand he would have staff. A gardener?

Thomas Lamark stood behind him.

'DC Roebuck, would you mind if we continued this conversation on another occasion?'

Roebuck turned round, startled. 'Er – no. When would be convenient for you, sir?'

'Later today, perhaps, after the funeral?'

'Shall we say five o'clock?' Roebuck's mind was racing now. *Was* he going to a funeral? Or to Amanda Capstick's hiding place? He decided to follow him.

'Five o'clock would be entirely convenient.'

They walked through into the hall. Thomas stretched out a hand. Roebuck shook it firmly. Then Thomas opened the door, glanced down at the palm of his left hand, then swung it forward.

As he stepped out into the porch, Simon Roebuck felt a prick in his backside, as if he had been stung by a wasp. But, unlike a sting, within seconds the pain had faded. He slapped his hand against his bum and turned round, but the front door was already closing on him.

He wondered if the dry cleaners had left in a safety pin, but he couldn't feel anything. And the pain was almost gone now.

A delivery van rumbled down the street, followed by a Range Rover loaded with small children. Roebuck had come straight from home in his own small Vauxhall, which he had parked on a meter around the corner. As he walked

414

the short distance down the street, he began to feel a little giddy.

Tiredness, he thought. He'd lain awake much of the night, unable to drift off in the muggy heat. He turned right, and saw his battered bright red car a hundred yards ahead. Suddenly, it felt like a hundred miles.

His legs were moving in slow motion. Then they started to fold up under him and he had to grip the front garden wall of a house to stay upright. He remained where he was for some moments, aware that he was sweating profusely, breathing in deep laboured gulps. He glanced up and down the street, but no one was around and he was glad – this was embarrassing.

More breaths and he began to feel better. Was he suffering anaphylactic shock from that sting on his bum? He remembered the symptoms from his first-aid courses: rapid pulse, sweating, collapse.

But he wasn't allergic to stings. Shit, he'd disturbed an entire wasps' nest in his loft last summer and been stung a dozen times with no big problem. Anyhow it was passing now, he was feeling a little better. It was just tiredness, the heat, no breakfast.

He found the strength to let go of the wall, and walked on up to his car. Unlocking it, he climbed in and sank with relief into the seat. He reached up, pulled down the belt, clicked it home, then started the car. *Have to follow Thomas Lamark. Drive round to his street, stay well back.* He pulled out and, feeling very disoriented now, drove to the end of the street. Floating, almost disembodied. Made a left turn. He was having to breathe harder, as if his lungs were shrinking. *Must radio in, ask for a second car.*

Coming down to a busy junction. Fighting for breath. Wheezing. High Street Kensington. The lights were red. He braked. But he wasn't stopping – his right foot wasn't obeying him. He reached for the handbrake, but he only reached it in his mind. His arm did not move.

There was a black cab dead ahead, waiting at the lights. The gap was closing. Closing too fast to stop.

He saw the jerk but felt nothing. Saw the front of his car

bounce back, the taxi catapult forwards and slew outwards into the road, and come to a halt, the back stoved in. He saw a man in an open short-sleeved shirt with a check pattern, and cream trousers, come running angrily up towards him. The man was shouting.

Simon Roebuck tried to reply, but his voice did not work now. A faint wheeze that dried up after a few seconds. His lungs had locked. No air went in or out of them. He stared at the angry man who was shouting at him, helplessly. 'Arsehole. You blind arsehole!' the man shouted.

Now the light was fading. The man was fading. Roebuck needed air in his lungs. He tried to suck it in, through his mouth, his nose. He was shaking with panic now. His whole body had shut down on him.

He screamed with his eyes for the man to help him.

Shaking now. Terrible pains racking his insides. The light was coming and going. Burst of brilliance, then darkness. An explosion like a firework inside his skull. The man in the check shirt mouthing at him, he had the door open, he wasn't angry any more.

Roebuck could see only a shadowy blur now.

The cab driver pulled open the Vauxhall's door. A woman in her late twenties, in jeans and a tank-top, came running up. 'I'm a nurse,' she said.

'He's having a heart attack or an epileptic fit,' the cabbie shouted.

'Get him out of the car,' the nurse said, fumbling for Roebuck's seat-belt buckle.

Together they levered him out and laid him on the pavement. The nurse crooked one of his arms under him and put him into the recovery position. She checked his airways, then pulse, then heart.

Nothing.

She pressed her mouth to his and blew hard and steadily. But the air would not go in. Desperately, she tilted back his head and tried again. Still the air would not go in.

'His airway,' she said. 'I think it's obstructed. He's choked on something.'

They sat him upright, oblivious to the crowd that was

gathering, and thumped his back. Still nothing. They hauled him to his feet and tried the Heimlich manoeuvre. Still no result.

Finally, in panic, using the cab driver's penknife and a hollow pen tube, the nurse performed an emergency tracheotomy.

Chapter Ninety-three

Urgent faces. Voices raised with advice. His mother. Father. Brother. Lulu. DC Roebuck. They were all in a room together, shouting at him, clamouring for his attention.

Then Amanda appeared. She was standing in the doorway with a bemused expression. 'I was waiting for you,' she said. 'Why didn't anyone come?'

'Amanda!' Michael yelled, and tried to wade through the crowd, but he couldn't move, they were all jam-packed together, no one could move. He pushed harder, tried to run, but it was like trying to run through water. Then, after an age – an eternity – he reached the doorway, but she was gone.

He stared down the empty hallway. Someone was patting him on the back. His father. 'You did what you could, old boy.'

Lulu said, 'I don't think that was really her, Michael.'

Footsteps. Running. The light was changing. Grey light. The dream dissolved into daylight that was flat and dull, like under-exposed film.

She was gone.

Early morning.

A jogger pounded by. Receding. Quiet again. The whir of a milk float somewhere close. Bottles clinking. Ratchet of a handbrake. From here, lying on the flattened-out seat-back, Michael could read the car clock. Six fifteen.

Drenched in sweat, he sat up, feeling a little chilly. He switched on the ignition and closed his window, checked that his phone was on, then pulled his jacket over his chest, like a blanket, and lay down again.

Sleep sucked him back under its surface.

When he next opened his eyes the daylight was much more vivid; there was a steady background roar of traffic; the town had come to life. The click of heels on the pavement, approaching, then stopping.

He jerked the seat-back upright. A young woman was entering the next-door building. Five past eight. He needed to piss. There was birdshit on his windscreen and on the bonnet. His back ached and his right thigh had gone numb. He massaged life back into it, then opened his door. The cool air beneath the cloudless dark blue sky held the promise of a warm day to come. Still stiff, he crossed over the road onto the pavement on the other side of the crescent, where there were wrought-iron railings in front of a small private garden. Here, in the bright sunlight, it already felt hot.

He stared up at the building, looking for signs of life in any of the windows. All were shut. The crescent was in decay; genteel shabbiness. Birdshit spattered steps up to the porch of number 20. Chunks missing from the columns. The green front door needed repainting. Sash windows in poor repair. There was a vile taste in his mouth, and he felt badly in need of a wash. He wiped his forehead with the back of his hand and felt a layer of grease. He raised an elbow and surreptitiously sniffed his armpit. Not great.

Badly needing to urinate now, he crossed his legs. It had been stupid to sleep in the car. What had he gained? He should have checked into a hotel, had a decent night's sleep and got up early. Now, tired, unshaven and grimy, he felt like a hobo.

He got back in the car, rummaged in the glove locker and found some Tic-Tac mints. He shook one into the palm of his hand and put it in his mouth. Someone was walking up the porch steps.

A woman, early fifties, matronly figure. She looked like a book-keeper. She let herself in with a key and the door closed behind her. Michael watched the windows carefully. After a couple of minutes his patience was rewarded when a sash opened a good eighteen inches on the first floor. He could just make her out before she retreated back into the gloom of the interior.

He dialled Dr Sundaralingham's number once more. Four rings, then the voice-mail kicked in. This woman didn't work for him.

Where do you take a piss in Cheltenham at ten past eight on a Friday morning?

His bladder was hurting so much it was hard to think straight. Public toilets; hotels; restaurants; offices. He started the car, drove out of the crescent and a short distance along the road, then saw a café in a parade of shops. It didn't look much of a place but it was open, that was all that mattered.

He went inside, ordered coffee, eggs and beans on toast, orange juice, then found the tiny washroom at the back. He urinated, then tugged off his shirt, washed his face, chest and arms, brushed his teeth with a soapy finger, and dried himself with paper towels.

Twenty minutes later he was back outside number 20 West Park Crescent, feeling a lot better. He dialled the number again. Once more, four rings then the machine. He ended the call and dialled Thelma's direct line at the Sheen Park Hospital. He told her to apologise to all his patients, and to arrange cover for his in-patients, but he wouldn't be in until late morning at the very earliest. She took it calmly and told him not to worry, she would do her best to explain the situation to them. And she would postpone a staff meeting he was chairing, set for eleven.

A small BMW pulled up and parked directly in front of him. Two men in their thirties climbed out, talking animatedly, and entered the building. He watched them while he was still talking to Thelma, and gave them five minutes to settle into their office, but could see no sign of any window opening. Maybe they had air-conditioning, or maybe their offices were at the rear. He dialled the number. Again four rings then the voice-mail. Neither of them was Dr Sundaralingham or any colleague of his.

Six more people arrived at the building during the next

twenty minutes. Each time he gave them five minutes then dialled. But still no luck.

He watched the postman arrive, ring a bell and enter. Then a couple of minutes later he saw a buffoonish-looking man in his late forties, ambling along the pavement. Heavily overweight, wearing a yachting blazer and grey slacks, clutching an ancient attaché case, he appeared to be conducting an invisible orchestra with his free hand, nodding in time to the music. He walked up the steps, glancing up at the building with a proprietorial air as if he owned the place, unlocked the door and went in.

Michael gave him his five minutes, then dialled. On the second ring, the phone was answered by the same clipped, military voice he remembered from yesterday. 'Dr Sundaralingham's surgery, can I help you?'

With a beat of excitement, Michael pressed END. He slipped the phone in his pocket, climbed out of the car and locked it. Then he walked up the porch steps and stared at the choice of bells. He pressed one at random. A woman answered. 'Hallo?'

'Special delivery!' Michael said. 'Two packages.'

'Two packages?' Surprise in her voice. Then the rasp of the door lock.

Michael pushed it open and went into a hallway that was as tired as the exterior. A staircase faced him and there was a lift to his right. On the opposite wall was a panel listing the occupants of the building. Chapel Music Ltd. Crossgates Financial Services. Nimbus Translation Ltd. Chiltern Associates. The Cheltenham Business Communications Centre.

No Dr Sundaralingham.

There was an assortment of post on a shelf below the panel and he sifted through it. Nothing addressed to any doctor. The place smelt musty.

The front door lock rasped again. He turned his head but no one was there. He dialled his mobile phone, then pressed it against his jacket to silence any sounds from it, and listened out for ringing in the building. He couldn't hear anything. Then he brought the phone to his ear and again heard the same voice answering as a few minutes ago.

'Hallo?' the voice said. 'Hallo? Dr Sundaralingham's surgery. Hallo?'

He pressed END, walked up to the first floor and rang the number again. This time he heard a phone ring above him, faintly. He hung up, ran the next flight, then stood in the corridor and dialled once more.

Two rings and then he ended the call before it was answered. He had heard those clearly, coming from along the corridor, on the right. He walked down and stopped outside the door bearing a smart brass panel marked, CHELTENHAM BUSINESS COMMUNICATIONS CENTRE.

He dialled the number again. Two rings and then the clipped, military voice once again, its patience a little strained this time. 'Dr Sundaralingham's surgery, can I help you?'

Michael could hear the voice coming from the other side of the wall.

Holding his phone firmly in his hand, he opened the door and walked in. The overweight buffoon in the navy blazer, whom he had seen entering the building a short while ago, was seated right in front of him at a bank of telephones, holding a receiver to his ear and staring at a computer screen. Close up he smelt of brandy and hair-cream, and looked unkempt. There was a button missing on his jacket cuff, scurf on his shoulders, and his shirt collar was scrunched up by his food-stained regimental tie.

Looking harassed, the man shot an unwelcoming glance at him.

'Yes,' Michael said. 'You *can* help me.'

The man covered the receiver. 'I'm on the phone, just a tick.'

Michael pointed at his mobile. 'I'm on the phone too.' He pushed the door shut behind him. 'I'm on the phone talking to you.' He swept the place with his eyes. A cheesy little office. An accommodation address, that's all this place was. He stuck the phone right under the man's face and pressed END. 'You can hang up, too. We're going to have a chat face to face.'

The man listened to the dead receiver briefly, then set it down, looking at Michael with a mixture of anger and concern. 'Who are you, please?' he barked, in that clipped, military voice that sounded too grand for his slovenly appearance.

Michael saw the sign on his desk, which said, Nicholas R. Lubbings, BA Com. MBA. There was a stack of business cards next to the sign: he picked one up and read it aloud. 'Nicholas R. Lubbings, BA Com. MBA. Director. The Chel- tenham Business Communications Centre.' I thought you were a doctor's surgery, Mr Lubbings. Am I mistaken?' Michael was seething with anger.

'We're a business centre and answering-service,' he said defensively. 'Would you kindly tell me who you are and what you want?'

'I want to see Dr Sundaralingham, right now.'

'I can leave a message for him.'

'He's not very good at returning his calls, Mr Lubbings. I'm glad I'm not one of his patients.'

'I'll do my best to get him to respond to you quickly.'

The phone rang. 'Excuse me.' Lubbings signalled with his finger, tapped his keyboard, checked the monitor then lifted the receiver. 'Cheltenham Sporting Saloons, good morning . . . No, I'm afraid none of our sales staff is available just at this moment. If you'll –'

Michael snatched the phone from his hand and hung it up. Then he grabbed Lubbings by the knot of his tie and hauled him half out of his chair, scattering a box of pens, a pile of correspondence and other oddments across his desk. 'I'm not pissing around with you, Lubbings. I want Sundar- alingham on the phone or in this office in the next *thirty seconds*, and I'm deadly fucking serious.' Michael shook him violently, then released his grip.

Lubbings sagged back into his chair, his eyes bulging. His face had gone puce and he was coughing. He looked terrified. 'I – I'm calling the police.'

'Go ahead, make my day,' Michael said, standing right

423

over him, his face right inside Lubbings' face. 'But you'd better read something first.'

The phone started ringing again. Wisely Lubbings ignored it. From his inside pocket, Michael produced Dr Sundaralingham's letter of referral for Dr Terence Goel, and slammed it down in front of him. 'Something look familiar about this letter to you, Mr Lubbings? Would the Cheltenham Chamber of Commerce be interested to see this letter?'

He watched the man's lips moving as he read the letter and saw his eyes dart nervously up to the address at the top. Then Lubbings looked back at him.

'I'm Dr Tennent, OK? This is a fake letter of referral. It's a criminal offence to impersonate a doctor, Mr Lubbings. You're allowing these premises to be used for criminal purposes. Go ahead, call the police.'

Lubbings' face was draining back to its pasty colour. 'I – I didn't – realise – that he – that –'

'Mr Lubbings, I'm interested in one thing right now, and one thing only. I don't give a shit who Dr Sundaralingham is. I need to know who his patient, Dr Terence Goel, is. Now either you are going to get Dr Sundaralingham on the phone, or take me to his house or his office, or I'm going to have the police come here right now and take this place apart. The woman I love has been kidnapped. There's a nationwide manhunt going on for her right now. She might even be dead, but there's a chance of saving her life. Your Dr Goel knows who's taken her. Understand how serious this is, Mr Lubbings?' Michael leaned across the desk, so that his face was inches from the other man's. 'Do you fucking understand?' he said, then he stood back.

Lubbings nodded like a trapped rat. 'They're the same person,' he said lamely. 'Dr Sundaralingham is Dr Goel.'

Michael absorbed this. 'The same person?'

'Yes.'

'What address do you have for Goel?'

Lubbings raised his arms. 'Here. This office. This is the only address.'

'What do you mean? You must have some other address?'

Lubbings' demeanour became increasingly helpful, as if by ingratiating himself with Michael he might be able to avoid trouble. 'I've only met him twice, once when he came and paid six months' fee in cash in advance for the address and services, and once when he came to collect a package. I – I have a phone number.'

'Gimme.'

Lubbings tapped a couple of keys, then wrote down a number off the computer screen onto a scrap of paper and handed it to Michael.

Michael recognised the number instantly. It was Terence Goel's Orange mobile number. He instantly dialled it on his own mobile, and once more got Goel's recorded voice. He killed the call. 'Jesus Christ.' His eyes drifted around the room. Squalid. Coffee mugs unwashed since yesterday. One wall lined with wooden pigeon-holes, some empty, some containing correspondence. A solitary golf club with most of the grip peeled away. Lubbings wasn't hiding anything any more: he could see from his face how concerned he was. Concerned for his own skin. Concerned not to have police rummaging through his books. He was going to co-operate.

'Mr Lubbings, please think really hard. What else do you know about this man?'

Lubbings shook his head pensively. 'Nothing. Nothing at all.'

'Do you know what he does? Where he works? Does he work for GCHQ?'

Lubbings hesitated. 'I – ah – have a chum there. I can find that out for you.'

'Can you do it now?'

Lubbings made a call, clearly to some old forces friend from the way he spoke. After a couple of minutes, he replaced the receiver. 'Definitely not. No one there by the name of Goel.'

'How long has he been using you?'

'Two or three weeks.' He tapped another key. 'Friday, July the eleventh. Three weeks, exactly.'

Michael sat down on a plastic chair. The phone was

ringing again. Lubbings tapped his keyboard then looked at his screen to check the caller. 'It's not Dr Goel.'

Michael nodded. The phone stopped ringing and the voice-mail took the call. 'Please think really hard, Mr Lubbings,' he said, more calmly now. 'Are there any details you can remember? Anything at all that struck you about Dr Goel?'

Lubbings scratched the end of his nose with a grubby finger. 'I can describe him, if that helps.'

'Uh-huh.'

'Very tall, about six foot six –'

Michael interrupted him. 'Good-looking? Striking-looking?'

'Yes – actually he reminds me of a film actor, the one who played Schindler in *Schindler's List*.'

'Liam Neeson?'

'That's him.'

Michael nodded. 'Anything else?'

Lubbings rummaged in a drawer and pulled out a packet of King Edward cigars. 'Do you mind if –?'

'Go ahead.'

Lubbings lit a stubby cigar with a book match, then waved away the smoke. 'One minor detail, if it's any help. The first time Dr Goel came to see me, he was wearing a black tie.'

'A dinner jacket?'

'No, not a bow-tie, an ordinary tie. He was wearing a dark lounge suit and a black tie. You know, as if he was in mourning.'

Michael stared back at him. 'Mourning?'

'Yes.'

'Did you ask him anything about that?'

'I'm discreet with all my – ah – clients, Mr – ah –' He glanced down at the letter. '*Dr* Tennent. I make a point of not asking questions. You get my drift? Run a tight ship here.'

Three weeks. Dr Goel in mourning. Michael's mind was churning over this information. Three weeks. *Mourning*.

Mourning whom?

He gave Lubbings his own numbers, pocketed one of the man's business cards and left.

Outside, in his car, he dialled DC Roebuck's direct line at Hampstead police station. He was told that the detective hadn't yet come in. Then he dialled Roebuck's mobile number and got Roebuck's voice-mail. He left a message, asking him to call him back, urgently, and also to contact the Orange phone company and see if he could find out anything about a Dr Terence Goel from the man's cell-phone registration details.

Then he sat and thought hard for some minutes. *Mourning. Fallout shelter.* For some reason, these two things connected together in his mind. For whom had Dr Goel been in mourning three weeks ago?

He powered up his Mac, went to his addresses section, and entered the name of an old friend, Richard Franklin, who headed a large architectural practice in the City. Then he dialled the number. Franklin's secretary told Michael he was in a meeting and couldn't be disturbed. Michael told her it was urgent. After a couple of minutes' wait, the architect was on the line.

He hadn't spoken to his friend for several months, but dispensed with pleasantries and went straight in. 'Richard, listen, I'm sorry to disturb you but I'm desperate. Is there a database anywhere that lists nuclear fallout shelters in England? Say, within Greater London?'

'The Cold War's over, Michael. I'd be more worried about germ –'

'Richard, please, forget my reasons. Just tell me if there would be any kind of database?'

'Do you mean military? Civil service? Private?'

'All of them.'

There was a silence. 'I'm sorry, Mike, you'll have to give me a moment to get my head round this one. You could try looking at planning permissions, but there wouldn't be any kind of database for them. There are specialist firms for this kind of construction. It's civil-engineering work. Structural engineers would be involved. I wouldn't think there is any one central database. You'd have to do a trawl through all the specialist firms and the structural engineers.' There was a brief silence. 'Even then, I would think a lot of these were built secretly. I think you'd have a problem getting a comprehensive list.'

'Who'd have a better chance of getting this list quickly? Me, you as an architect, or the police?'

'The police, I should think. Listen, how are you? Long time no hear.'

'I'll call you at the weekend, we'll talk, OK?'

'Sounds good.'

Michael ended the call. He leaned back in his seat, staring at the dial of his phone as if somehow, among its numbered keys, was the answer he searched for.

Three weeks ago, Dr Terence Goel was in mourning.

Three weeks ago, Dr Terence Goel went to a lot of trouble to get himself referred to him.

Who the hell was Dr Terence Goel mourning three weeks ago?

Who had died? Who? Who?

He dropped the phone as the thought hit him. Gloria Lamark had died just over three weeks ago.

Gloria Lamark?

Was there some connection between Dr Terence Goel and Gloria Lamark?

It was an absurd long shot, but right now he had no other ideas. Anything was worth a try. He dialled Richard Franklin's number again. The architect sounded less pleased to hear from him this time.

'Richard,' he said, 'one more question. If I wanted to find out whether one specific house has a nuclear fallout shelter beneath it, how would I go about that?'

Chapter Ninety-four

Cora Gertrude Burstridge. 15 August 1933 – 22 July 1997.

Someone, maybe Cora Burstridge or maybe her daughter, had chosen 'The Lord's My Shepherd' as the psalm. Glen Branson approved of that. And 1 Corinthians 13:12 for the first reading. 'Through a glass darkly'. He liked that passage in the Bible. 'Jerusalem' was the last hymn. 'And did those feet, in ancient times, Walk upon England's pastures green . . .'

Stirring, emotional stuff. A grand funeral for a grand lady.

He sat in his unmarked car with the order of service sheet in his lap, listening to the sound of the hymn playing now, the blast of the organ, the voices of two or three hundred people carrying out through the open church doors into the blazing mid-morning heat. He thought back to last Thursday. To Cora Burstridge's face inside the plastic bag.

He shuddered.

The narrow street, more like a lane, which climbed up past the lychgate was clogged with cars, vans, photographers, news cameras, sound booms, the press and the public jostling for position. Cora Burstridge's public, mostly middle-aged and elderly, had come either to pay their respects to an actress who was much loved, or to gawp at the celebrities.

The church was full of them. Actors and actresses, directors, producers, singers. It was rumoured that Vanessa Redgrave was in there, and Alan Rickman. Someone said Elton John had come, but Glen hadn't seen him, although he thought he had caught a glimpse of Sir Cliff Richard.

Glen wasn't here to pay his last respects, although he would like to have done; he wished he could have been in that church just so Cora would know he was close by, that he hadn't forgotten her, that he wasn't going to forget her. That he wasn't going to let go of her death until he was certain of the truth.

He was here, outside the church, to watch the crowd. To find a face, just one, that did not fit. But it was impossible in this extravaganza. Broad black hats, veils, black chiffon scarves, black silk dresses shimmering like water, this was a fashion event, a summer season photocall to rival Ascot. He thought he had parked sufficiently far back, but still people teemed around his car, blocking his view.

> Bring me my bow of burning gold!
> Bring me my arrows of desire!

Only one more verse after this. He started the engine. After the church service there was a private cremation, family only. He backed the car carefully through the crowd. They lined the street, as if they were waiting for royalty, all the way down to the bottom of the hill.

The gardens of the crematorium were orderly; too well laid out, too well tended, they felt like Toytown grounds.

Sprinklers tossed spray over impossibly green turf. Absurdly colourful blooms rose from dark chocolate soil. A Toytown waterfall tumbled down stepped rocks into a Toytown pond.

Glen drove down the winding drive towards the bland red-brick crematorium. A hearse was parked outside the doors, and two black Daimler limousines. On the opposite side were several cars. A service was in progress. These places were like factories. They ran to strict timetables. Cora Burstridge was next on the list to be processed.

Glen scanned the cars, driving slowly towards a space on the far side. Eight cars. Seven were parked front-in. One, a blue Ford Mondeo, was parked tail-in, giving the man sitting in the driving seat a clear view of the crematorium entrance.

Its engine was running, and the lightly tinted windows

were shut making it hard to see the occupant clearly. Glen wondered who he was, and why he wasn't inside the building. Someone's driver? Possibly. A member of Cora Burstridge's family, who had arrived early for the cremation? Also possible, but unlikely – he'd have gone to the church. A bereaved person just come to be near his loved one's remains?

Glen parked nose-in, facing the garden of remembrance, where two rows of flowers and wreaths were laid out, not wanting to look obvious, and angled his interior mirror to give him a view of the Mondeo. He was in the full heat of the sun and there were no shaded places to park.

The service was over. People were coming out of the side door. A group congregated in front of the entrance. Two tearful women in black, one holding a small child, walked through to the garden of remembrance and began looking at the floral tributes.

The man in the Mondeo stayed where he was, in the cool of his air-conditioned car.

More people came into the garden of remembrance. They peered closely at some of the bouquets, kneeling, reading the tags, commenting to each other, then dispersing.

The limousines were leaving now. They moved a short distance down the drive then stopped, to allow other mourners to form a convoy, presumably to the wake. Some of the cars were starting to roll. Soon all of them, except the Mondeo, were moving.

The convoy snaked slowly off up the drive. Mondeo man sat tight. Two men in grey suits and another in dungarees were hastily gathering up the floral tributes. Glen switched the volume of his personal radio right down, not wanting the crackle of static or the burble of voices to give away his identity, and climbed out of his car. Flashing a surreptitious glance at the Mondeo's number-plate, he walked over to the garden of remembrance, then sat on a bench shaded by a rose trellis, his back to a brick wall engraved with names and dates.

From here he had a clear view of the area. He jotted the Mondeo's number down in his notebook, then waited.

After about ten minutes a hearse, followed by a black Daimler limousine, came down the drive and halted outside the entrance to the building.

An elderly man came out of the limousine first. Then two boys in their teens, followed by a good-looking middle-aged couple. Then a glamorous-looking woman, whom Glen guessed was Cora Burstridge's daughter.

They filed inside, while the pallbearers struggled with the coffin. The men in grey suits reappeared, took flowers out of the hearse and carried them through to the garden of remembrance.

The man remained in the Mondeo. Glen took a stroll around the gardens. The service was brief. Ten minutes, and Cora Burstridge's close relatives were coming out. They spent just a short while looking at the flowers, then went back to the limousine. Glen could see that the daughter was crying.

The limousine drove off. When it had cleared the crematorium gates, the Mondeo reversed out of its parking space and headed off down the drive.

Glen returned to his own car, gave his call sign into his radio and asked for the vehicle police national computer. When an operator answered he gave his warrant number, followed by the Mondeo's registration number. Within seconds the operator came back to him.

'Are you looking at a blue Ford Mondeo?'

'Correct,' Glen replied.

'Registered owner from Cheltenham. Dr T – tango Terence G – golf Goel. Ninety-seven – nine-seven – Royal Court Walk, Cheltenham. No trace lost or stolen, no markers.'

Glen wrote down the details as she spoke and thanked her. Then he drummed his fingers on the wheel. *Dr Terence Goel, what is your interest in Cora Burstridge? What kind of a doctor are you? Why did you drive all the way from Cheltenham to Cora Burstridge's cremation but not get out of your car? Why didn't you go to the church?*

You're not making much sense to me, Dr Goel.

In fact, you're really bothering me.

He picked up his radio mouthpiece and asked the operator to put him through to the Divisional Intelligence room at Cheltenham police station.

A harassed sounding detective answered. Glen asked him if he had any details at all about a Dr Terence Goel of 97 Royal Court Walk.'

'How urgent? We're up to our necks.'

'It's urgent,' Glen said.

'Will an hour do?'

'An hour would be fine.'

He put the mouthpiece back on the rest and yawned. He'd got to bed after two this morning. Officially it should have been his day off today.

Closing his eyes, he allowed himself a five-minute cat-nap.

Chapter Ninety-five

At twelve fifty-five Michael sat in a tiny, stuffy, windowless microfiche booth in the Royal Borough of Kensington and Chelsea Planning Department offices, ending a call on his mobile phone.

Shocked, he put the phone down on the wooden work surface, scarcely able to believe the words of the detective at Hampstead police station, who had just given him the news that DC Roebuck had died earlier this morning, at the wheel of his car, from an apparent heart attack.

Bleakly, he stared at the pattern of holes in the pegboard wall in front of him. Roebuck had been his anchor, the man who cared, the man who had been trying his hardest for him.

The phone was hot and the right side of his head felt as if it was on fire. He'd had to call his architect friend Richard Franklin out of yet another meeting to pull strings to circumvent the three working days the clerk at the Planning Department had told him were required to retrieve a file from the archives.

So far the clerk had taken half an hour. He picked up the phone again, and rang Lubbings in Cheltenham to see if he had heard from Dr Goel. Lubbings, deeply deferential, assured Michael he hadn't. After Lubbings, he rang Thelma and blew out his afternoon appointments, then he rang Lulu. He'd already spoken to her earlier, on his way up to London and given her his findings about Lubbings and Dr Goel, but he called her again now because he preferred to keep busy, and told her the latest, about Roebuck.

'Do you think it's suspicious, Michael?' was her immediate response.

'I don't know. He was only in his thirties, but he was overweight, he'd been working around the clock, and this heat isn't clever for anyone with a heart condition. I don't have enough details. He came home late last night, left early this morning, and he apparently had a heart attack in his car in traffic this morning.'

'It doesn't strike you as odd?'

Her voice irritated him, as if she was accusing him of some deficiency. 'Lulu, I don't have enough information, OK? I don't know what's odd and what isn't odd any more. Everything's bloody odd.'

'I'm sorry,' she said gently. 'We're all stressed. Is there anything I can do to help you?'

A shadow fell over the desk. Michael looked up and saw the clerk standing right behind him, holding a microfiche film.

'I'll call you back in a while,' he said to her.

'Michael,' she said. 'I know you're doing your very best. I appreciate it, I really do. We all do.'

'I wish I was doing my best,' he replied. 'I feel I'm running around like a headless sodding chicken.'

He thanked the clerk, loaded the microfiche, which contained all the planning applications for the whole of Holland Park Avenue since the first Planning Act of 1953, and began to scroll through it.

He found Gloria Lamark's house. An application, in 1957, to build a double garage at the rear. Granted. An application in 1961 to widen the roof to create larger servants' quarters. This had been turned down. There was an appeal. All the objection letters were listed. The appeal was rejected on the grounds of it being out of character with the neighbourhood.

Then he found an application dated 7 October 1966.

APPLICATION TO EXTEND CELLAR FOR FINE WINE STORAGE PURPOSES.

Permission had been granted, but with strict provisos on structural work to shore up the foundations of the house, and elaborate drainage instructions.

As he studied the plans carefully, trying to get his

435

bearings on them, he began to grasp the reason for the provisos. The plans showed a cellar beneath part of the ground floor of the house. But instead of broadening it to extend under more rooms, they showed that the new cellar was to be dug underneath the existing one, making it thirty feet below the ground floor of the house. It was shown as having a ten-foot high ceiling. The existing cellar had only a seven-foot high ceiling. It was nine feet from the hall floor to the bottom of the existing cellar. The new plan showed a twenty-one-foot gap between the floor of the old cellar and the new one.

Michael was puzzled. If the new one was only ten foot high, that left eleven feet unaccounted for. He studied the plans more closely, and saw a different shading between the ceiling of the new cellar and the floor of the old. Then he found the key to the plans and saw what the shading indicated. Concrete. The new cellar had a concrete ceiling nine feet thick.

Next he looked at the walls: they were six feet thick.

This cellar hadn't been built to store wine. Wine needed to be kept at a steady temperature, but it didn't require six feet of concrete around it and nine above.

This was a nuclear fallout shelter.

He was shaking from tiredness, excitement, nerves.

Is this where you are, Amanda? Are you down here? Under nine feet of concrete?

But why? It still did not make any sense. *Why should Dr Terence Goel hold you prisoner in Gloria Lamark's cellar?* He closed his eyes, trying to think. If – *if* there was anything in this crazy idea then Dr Goel would have to be a close friend or relative of Gloria Lamark.

Or of her son.

He tried to think of anything Gloria had told him about her son that might give him some pointers, but he had been a taboo subject in their sessions, and despite all his many efforts at prising information from her over the years she had been his patient, she had always resolutely refused to talk about him. Michael had to think hard even to recall his name. Thomas, he thought. Yes. He had had a feeling the boy might be gay, but when he'd tried to broach this with Gloria, she had been furious. Anything that threatened the perfect fantasy world of Gloria Lamark provoked a rage in her.

Dr Goel had said he was a widower. But nothing he said could now be trusted. Could he be having a relationship with Thomas Lamark?

The plans showed that the shelter was divided into three chambers. There was an entrance directly at the foot of the stairs. This was a small, airlock chamber. A door led through to a second room, the size of a modest bedroom. Another door led through into the third chamber, which was the largest. All were served by an elaborate ventilation shaft system.

He put his Mac on the table and powered it up, then went to the photograph of Amanda. It was hard to look at her. Just seeing her face churned him up. His mouth dried and he swallowed, stared at the crazed red of her eyes, the terrible state of her hair, her clothes. The darkness all around her. *Are you here? Darling Amanda, is this where you are?*

He swigged from a bottle of mineral water he'd bought in a garage shop. There were psychics who could find people by dowsing. He'd read a piece on one a year or so back. Maybe he could take this photograph, a copy of these plans and have a psychic –

He sank his head into his hands and squeezed his temples with his thumbs. *You don't need a bloody psychic, you need to go to the police, tell them what you think, have them go and check out Gloria Lamark's house.*

He dialled the number of the new detective he had been given as his principal contact, DC Paul Stolland. The number was answered by a harassed-sounding woman.

'Incident room, DC Rhonda Griffiths.'

'Could I speak to DC Stolland?'

'I'm sorry, he's out of town. I'm not sure if he's going to be back today. Is it anything urgent or can you call him back tomorrow?'

'*Tomorrow?*' Michael shouted.

'Can I help you instead?' she asked.

'My name's Dr Tennent.'

Blank silence.

'I'm the one who reported Amanda Capstick missing.'

She sounded as if her mind was on something else entirely. 'Oh, yes, right, I'm sorry, Dr Tennent. I think you may have heard we're having some problems today.'

Michael started trying to explain his thoughts about Amanda's whereabouts, but after he was only a few seconds in she interrupted him to take another call. It was two minutes before she was back on the line again. 'What address was it you want us to check out, Dr Tennent?'

Michael gave her the details.

'And can you tell me exactly why you think Amanda Capstick may be at this address?'

Michael again started to tell her, but it came out clumsily and he could tell he wasn't convincing her.

'Dr Goel is a patient of yours, you say?'

'Yes.'

'And his own doctor doesn't exist?'

'Apparently not.'

'And this Dr Goel has given a false address?' She was sounding more interested now.

'Yes.'

'And he talked to you about a fallout shelter?'

'And about losing a loved one – he talked about keeping a dove in a cellar or a shelter,' Michael said.

'Excuse me if I'm sounding dim, sir,' she said, politely, 'I can't see how you've made the connection to the Lamarks' house.'

'It was a long-shot guess.'

'And you're suspicious because it has a fallout shelter?'

'It certainly looks like a fallout shelter from the plans.'

Her enthusiasm was waning. 'I'll get someone to stop by there, sir.'

'How soon?'

'As soon as I can.'

'That's not good enough. I want someone to go there *now*.'

'Sir, we have a reported sighting of a woman in a car outside Northampton, and we have a body of a woman in her late twenties who has just been found in Epping Forest. On top of that we've had another thirty calls logged today from the *Crimewatch* programme. I'll try to get someone there today. If not, it will be tomorrow.'

'What do you know about this sighting?'

'I'm sorry I can't tell you that.'

Desperately, he pleaded, 'Just tell me whether it's Amanda Capstick or Tina Mackay.'

'A dark-haired woman,' she said.

'And this body?'

'I can't give you more details.'

'Just one detail, please. Is this body fresh, or has it been there a while?'

Again a hesitation. 'I understand it's a few weeks old.'

Michael thanked her grimly and hung up. Neither sounded like Amanda, but the woman's words about the body in the woods were freaking him. If Amanda was dead –

He had to block that from his mind. He couldn't handle that right now. *She's alive. The photograph was sent because she's alive.*

Under Gloria Lamark's house?

The police weren't going to check it out probably until *tomorrow*.

Another twenty-four hours.

No way.

Chapter Ninety-six

friday, 1 august 1997
Three hundred and twenty-seven people came to make sure Cora Burstridge was dead this morning.

Most of them came just to be seen. Notice how few real stars were there – they were mostly second division, poseurs, has-beens, wannabes. Some had been hired to be there – you could tell by looking at them. That's pretty sad when you have to hire people to come to your own funeral.

We Lamarks are above tricks like that.

I forgot to give the thing any food today. In fact, when I arrived home after the funeral, I completely forgot it was down there! Easy to do that, because I've cleaned the bloodstains from the reporter off the sauna walls.

This forgetfulness is no laughing matter, actually. I'm getting more and more concerned about my erratic memory. Dr Goel must ask Dr Tennent about his erratic memory during his next consultation. I will be interested to learn if Dr Tennent thinks this is something to worry about.

In an hour I am going back to my old alma mater, King's College, to watch the medical lecture and operation. It will be strange, being back at school. My mother always told me I had the ability in me to be a really great surgeon. I have a passion for surgery.

All greatness stems from passion.

Curare is untraceable in a post-mortem unless you are specifically looking for it. When the pathologist examines DC Roebuck's body, he will conclude that cause of death was heart failure, probably caused by an unspecified allergic reaction. Sad.

Dr Michael Tennent has telephoned Dr Goel's mobile phone

number several times in the past twenty-four hours. I think he is really suffering now.

But he hasn't even begun to know what suffering really is.

Chapter Ninety-seven

Low tide. Midday. The pebble beaches a riot of colour, densely packed with sunbathers and kids. Beyond, acres of wet sand stretched out into the distant shallow waves, far beyond the end of the concrete groyne. This should have been his day off. He could have been down here on this beach with Sammy. Sammy liked to build things in the sand. Sammy was smart, he could figure things out. Puzzles. Computer games.

Glen sat on the end wall, his jacket slung over his shoulder, tie off, shirt open, eating a vanilla ice-cream and thinking about the man in the blue Mondeo. This was where he liked to come to work out his problems. Sometimes the movement of the sea got his brain going.

Who the hell turns up at a funeral and doesn't get out of their car? Someone who doesn't want to be seen? Why don't they want to be seen? Are they shy? Worried they will upset other relatives by their presence? Was this some secret lover of Cora Burstridge who didn't want to upset the family by showing up, but had to stay to the finish?

No. You'd have gone to the church.

If you cared about Cora Burstridge, you'd have gone to the church.

Glen licked the last traces of ice-cream off the inside of the wrapper, then balled it up tightly, glancing around for a waste bin. He couldn't see one and slipped it into his jacket pocket. Then he looked at his watch. One forty. Over an hour since he had spoken to the divisional intelligence room at Cheltenham police station. A light breeze off the sea cooled his face and flapped his jacket. Peaceful here. He could hear the shouts of kids on the beach, and the rasp of a distant speedboat, but he had this breakwater to himself, and he savoured that.

Then his radio crackled. He heard his call sign and answered. At the other end was a hesitant voice.

'DC Carpenter from Cheltenham. I have some information for you regarding Dr Terence Goel, ninety-seven Royal Court Walk, Cheltenham.'

'Thanks, go ahead.'

'That address is false. The numbers stop at ninety-six. I've been on to the local council tax office. They show a Dr Terence Goel as a ratepayer at this address. Their records show he is up to date with his rates payments and has lived there for five years.'

'Do you have any explanation for that?' Glen asked.

'They're doing further checks for me. He shows up on their current database, but not on their master database backup.'

'What does that mean?'

'It sounds like this character has hacked their computer and entered false data.'

'Shit.'

'I've run a check on him on the Police National Computer. There's a record that Dr Terence Goel was stopped for erratic driving in Tottenham Court Road, London, at eleven thirty p.m. last Saturday, July the twenty-sixth, and cautioned.'

'Anything else?'

'No. Do you want us to continue making local inquiries?'

'Yes, please. You said your name's DC Carpenter?'

'Andy Carpenter.'

'Andy, thanks. That's very helpful.'

Glen walked quickly, deep in thought, back to his car. He closed the door, opened the windows and switched on the engine to get the fan going. Then he radioed the local Police National Computer operator, to whom he gave the registration details of Goel's Mondeo, then said, 'I want this vehicle flagged to me personally, *DC Branson*, no one else. All sightings. I want no visible police interest in the vehicle. Can you make that very clear?'

'No visible police interest in the vehicle. All sightings reported to you personally.'

'Instantly. If anyone sees the car, they're to stay with it but keep out of sight. I want this vehicle kept under surveillance, all movements documented and description of the occupants.'

The operator repeated the instructions back to him. Glen thanked her, then drove straight to his office, his brain racing.

Dr Terence Goel, are you a doctor of medicine or do you hold a university doctorate? You exist on a computer file as a ratepayer at a non-existent address. You own a motor car. What else do you own in this name? I'm going to find out, I promise you that.

I'm in your face.

Glen's colleague, Mick Harris, was reading through a pile of documents, eating a sandwich out of a plastic lunch-box, when he arrived back.

Glen perched on the edge of his desk. 'Good sandwich?'

'Uh-huh.' The detective didn't look thrilled to see him.

'You've got a good wife, Ren feeds you properly.'

'Thought you were off today,' Mick said, through a mouthful of egg and cress.

'How's your hangover?'

'Very nice, thank you. How's yours?'

'I've had better ones. Tell me, a man creates a false identity, right? This man is smart, he can hack computers, he gives himself a false address, hacks the local council office computer system, puts himself on the electoral roll, gives himself a good-citizen history, rates always paid on time, that kind of shit. He has a car registered in his phoney name. I have an alert out for the car. What else do I look for?'

'Mobile phone.'

Glen nodded. 'Good one.'

'Get his call log, see who he's called. Yup?'

'Yup.'

'Do you know what he looks like?'

'No.'

'Geographical area where he might be?'

'Some idea.'

'Check with the CCTVs – the car will show up if he's out and about in it. And check the credit-card companies.'

'Yes, I'm about to get on to them.'

'You could also try drinking a cup of tea.'

'Huh?' Glen looked at him blankly.

'Drain it to the bottom, then read the formation of the leaves.'

For an instant, Glen took him seriously. Then he grinned. 'And I suppose I ought to sacrifice a chicken and read the entrails.'

'Always works a treat. Mind if I finish my lunch in peace now?'

Glen slipped off his desk. 'Sorry.'

'Start with what I've given you.'

'I will,' Glen said. 'I'm starting right now.'

Chapter Ninety-eight

Michael pulled up the Volvo on the opposite side of the road and observed Gloria Lamark's house through his open window. It was as grand as he had imagined it would be. And as cold-looking. And secretive. This was a London house where you really could be a recluse in style.

You could have all the secrets you wanted in this house.

He drove around the block, trying through his exhaustion to formulate a plan. He was travelling up a narrower, less impressive street now, along the rear of the houses, lined on both sides with garages, sheds and dustbins. He saw the double garage at the rear of the Lamark house, which had been on the 1957 planning application. It appeared in good condition, and had a modern up-and-over door. A high wall either side of it protected the privacy of the rear garden.

He found a meter bay in the quiet avenue at the top of the street and parked. From the glove-box he took a small torch he kept in the car, and he also took his phone. Then he walked back to Holland Park Avenue, and along towards Gloria Lamark's house. The street was sleepy, the traffic light. A gardener was weeding a flower-bed two houses up from Gloria Lamark's. Smart cars were parked in driveways; he could hear people splashing in a swimming pool close by. Birdsong.

The wrought-iron gates were shut, but he couldn't see a bell, and neither, to his surprise, was there any evident security system, no closed-circuit camera watching the gates, nor any sign of an alarm box on the house. Michael looked up at the windows: the curtains were drawn in some of the upstairs ones; the others yielded only darkness. A

Mercedes sports car, driven by a brunette, went past. Then a taxi, followed by a rattling van.

Michael pressed the latch handle on one gate, expecting it to be locked, but the gate swung open. He stood where he was. Was this a smart thing to do? What was he expecting to find?

Maybe he should turn back. If Amanda was here, all he was going to do was alert whoever had taken her and make the police's job even harder.

Leave her for another twenty-four hours?

He approached the house, gravel crackling under his shoes. The ground-floor windows were too high to see into – he could make out a rather ornate chandelier in one room but nothing else.

Close up, the house seemed even bigger, darker, more impenetrable. He took a deep breath, trying to calm his jangling nerves, as he climbed the sweeping steps, past two grandiose carved Egyptian lions, up to the front door. It was white, recently painted, and had a spyhole. He pressed the brass bellpush and heard the clear, strong ring inside.

A full minute passed. Something made him glance over his shoulder, but there was no one behind him. A cluster of cars drove along the street. He rang the bell again. A pulse nerve plucked at his throat. A bee flew around his face and he flapped it away. It came back and he ignored it. After another minute he rang the bell again.

In the burning heat, the door was releasing a strong smell of paint. Michael could also smell something sweet – perhaps honeysuckle, he wasn't sure. Katy had been the expert gardener.

No one answered the bell.

He pushed open the heavy brass flap of the letterbox and peered into the hall. He could see a long-case clock. Grey quarry tiles. The hall looked still. Complete silence in the house. Complete silence inside his head. The wail of a siren somewhere in the distance. The faint shout of a child.

He went back to the bottom of the steps, looked up at the windows, checking each one in turn, then walked round to the side, into the welcome cool of the shadow from the neighbouring house. No windows at ground-floor level down this side. Then he came into the back garden. He saw the handsome pond with its columned island, flower-beds badly in need of weeding, and grass gone wild from a month of neglect.

Maybe the son is away and the house is empty, he wondered. *The best hiding place is often the most obvious.*

He was rambling again, he realised. Why should this place be obvious?

Patio doors from the kitchen at the rear led out onto a small terrace. To their left, a metal fire escape rose the full three-storey height of the house. A dozen windows, all closed. A tortoiseshell butterfly jigged past him. He turned and looked at the neighbours' houses on either side. Could anyone see him? Not easily. Dense foliage protected him.

Anyhow, what the hell if the police did come? That was fine by him – that was what he wanted!

He climbed the steps onto the terrace and peered in through the patio doors at a rather dingy, old-fashioned kitchen. An empty pizza container sat on the table. Several flies buzzed around, and he could see why: there were some dirty plates on the draining board.

Someone had been here recently. Her son? Where was he now? Out shopping? Away? Left the clearing up to the staff. Housekeeper? Why were there no staff? Gloria had always talked about her staff, her *retainers*, she called them. Probably dancing on her bloody grave, he thought irreverently.

With trembling hands he tested the doors. They were locked.

Jesus, I could get struck off for this. Breaking and entering. The press would have a field day.

He examined each of the ground-floor windows in turn. They were all secured shut. Then he began to climb the fire escape. Struggling against a life-long fear of heights he kept going right to the narrow platform at the top. Gripping the handrail, he walked forward slowly and pressed his face against the glass of a sash window. Through it he could see what appeared to be a changing room.

Gingerly, he tried to raise the bottom half of the window. To his surprise, it shot up with well-oiled ease. This is madness. Turn round, go back down the fire escape, get in your car and go back to work, Michael Tennent. You haven't a shred of evidence to justify breaking into someone's house.

Very nervous now, he turned on the platform and looked around. He had a clear view down into the garden of the house on his right. It was empty. The cover lay in place over the pool; it seemed that the occupants were not there. The view into the house on the left was obstructed by a giant laburnum tree. Similarly, conifers at the end of the garden, some planted, he presumed, to block out the unsightly view of the garage, screened him from the houses behind.

He climbed over the sill and dropped down onto the thick pile of the wall-to-wall carpet. Then he held his breath and listened as carefully as he could, engulfed in the smell of leather and mothballs. Silence.

A thousand pairs of women's shoes were laid out in long, tidy rows in the room. Hat boxes were stacked on top of each other. Dresses in plastic dry-cleaning bags bulged out of the open sliding door of one fitted wardrobe. He trod lightly down the narrow pathway through the shoes to the door, gripped the handle, listened. As he opened it, a rubber draught excluder shuffled along the carpet but the hinges were mercifully silent.

He looked out onto a landing, eyes darting in every direction, ears tracking the silence in the house. Just the tick of a clock down below. Nothing else. His whole body was pulsing as he slipped quietly onto the landing, which was carpeted in the same grey as the dressing room, and glanced at the walls lined with framed publicity photographs of Gloria Lamark. There were several closed doors, a bronze bust of her on a pedestal, and a wide, handsomely carved staircase leading down.

One step at a time, keeping to the edge of the treads, testing each for a creak, he reached the next landing, stood still, listening, glancing warily at each of the closed doors, unsure what he was going to do if one opened suddenly.

Run, he supposed, either to the front door, or back up to the dressing room, whichever exit was clear. One door was open just a crack, but no light came from it. Probably one of the rooms with the curtains drawn.

He noticed a large Wedgwood vase on a plinth, filled with dead flowers. And on the floor, right beside his foot, was a coffee cup, half full, with a thick green crust of mould.

There isn't anyone here. The house is empty. It's been empty since her death. Where's her son? Away? Unable to bear being here on his own?

Making less effort to remain quiet now, he reached the hall. Images of Gloria Lamark covered every inch of wall space. There was a massive oil painting of her stepping out of a limousine, framed posters, production stills, framed press cuttings. The whole house was a shrine to her.

He wondered, absurdly, if she was looking at him right now, angry with him for what he had said to her in their last session. She had been a great beauty: these pictures told the story. Stunning. She had the looks to have been one of the greats, but she had not had the intelligence. People forgot that the most enduring actors and actresses had more than great looks: they had fine minds, too.

In the plans he had studied, the steps down to the cellar were from the kitchen. There was a passageway in front of him, which he presumed led to the kitchen, and he walked down it.

In the darkness of his den, Thomas Lamark stood by the door that was open just an inch, no more, listening to the psychiatrist's footsteps.

Took you long enough to get here, Dr Tennent. Dr Goel gave you enough hints in your office, surely to God? It just goes to confirm what I have always suspected about you. You think you're smart, but all you really do is cause pain and suffering to others. You're about to find out that you really are not at all smart. Enjoy!

He remained in his den. There was no hurry, no need to take unnecessary risks of being seen. There was still a full hour before he needed to leave in order not to miss the lecture at King's.

Michael saw the cellar door, secured by two bolts, as he entered the kitchen. First he went over to the table, waved away the flies from the pizza container and looked at it. Pizza San Marco, wood-smoked ham and mozzarella. He looked at the best before date and saw that it was still current.

He opened the fridge door. Two full bottles of milk, one half empty. He sniffed the half-empty one. It was still fresh.

Someone was either living here or coming here – they must have been here within the last few days. They could come back at any time.

He opened the cellar door, found the light switch and pressed it, then pulled the door shut behind him. At the bottom of the short flight of brick steps, past shelves stacked with empty glass storage jars, he found himself facing another door, locked with a heavy, old-fashioned key. He turned it, pushed it open and smelt new carpet.

He found a light switch, and when he pressed it, a whole battery of strip-lights flickered then came on. He was in an elaborate modern gymnasium. There was a running-machine complete with a huge video screen, a rowing-machine, weights, mats, parallel bars, and a sauna cabin. One of the lights was making a loud hum right above him.

According to the plans, the entrance down into the shelter should be directly in front of him. But all he could see in front of him was the sauna cabin. Puzzled, he looked carefully around the cellar. But there was no break in the matting that covered the floor, and no sign at all of a door. Just one recess, racked out for wine storage, and filled with several hundred dusty bottles.

His heart sank. Was he being really stupid? He'd seen the plans – had he jumped to an assumption? Sometimes people put forward plans, but then, for one reason or another – usually financial – never got round to carrying them out. Just because Gloria Lamark had obtained planning permission didn't necessarily mean she'd gone ahead and had the bloody thing built.

He banged his knuckles together. Stared at the sauna cabin. Thinking. The application had been for a wine cellar. Why a *wine* cellar and not a *fallout shelter*? Why had she wanted to keep it secret? Because if her neighbours knew about it she could find herself shut out of it – or even killed for it.

There was a creak above him. He froze. Tried to get his ears to tune out the blasted hum of the light, but he couldn't. He walked over to the light switch and snapped it off. Then he moved into the shadows, away from the throw of the single bulb over the stairs, and listened hard again.

Nothing.

The pulse was throbbing in his throat. Fearfully he watched the staircase. For a minute, maybe longer, he stayed like this. No further sounds above him. This was an old house; probably just the heat causing expansion; old houses moved around all the time.

All the same he kept the light off as he walked over to the sauna and opened the door. The strong scent of pine greeted him as he fumbled around for a light switch, then found it. He shot a glance behind him at the cellar steps, then looked around the interior of the cabin, casting his eyes over the stones in the grate of the electric fire. The empty water bucket. The tiered seats.

Look in the obvious place. He lifted up the slats of the first seat. Nothing below, just the concrete floor. Nor beneath the second slats, nor the third.

He examined the wall panels. They appeared to be fixed permanently and very securely.

Shit.

He stepped outside the cabin, looked up at the ceiling, then at the stairs. Stood still, listening.

Look in the obvious place..

The obvious place can be the most obvious – or the *least* obvious.

He went back into the cabin and looked at the grate. Both

452

it and the bucket stood on a wide strip of metal, which was not entirely flush with the rest of the floor. Then he noticed a tiny scrap of paper trapped under the metal strip.

Which meant the strip had been put down on top of it.

Which meant it had been moved. Recently.

He lifted away the water bucket. Then he gripped the grate with both hands, testing its weight. It was even heavier than it looked, too heavy to lift, all he could do was slide it. The flex trailed behind it.

When it was clear of the metal strip, he knelt, eased his fingers under the edge of the strip and lifted it up.

It came away easily, to reveal a steel trapdoor beneath.

He lifted the strip clear, set it down and stared at the trapdoor. Then he knelt and gripped the recessed handle and tried to lift it. The door wouldn't move. He tried again; then he realised the handle was a locking device and he rotated it several times, feeling the pressure easing with each turn. *If this is a fallout shelter, why is the handle on the outside? Surely it should be on the inside, to keep people out?*

He tried again. This time the door lifted. A blast of cool, dank air came up with it. Stone steps spiralled down beneath him into darkness.

He lowered himself through the hatch, planting his feet firmly on a step. Then, holding the frame of the trapdoor with both hands, he took a few tentative steps down. He found the light switch and turned it on. Complete and utter silence beneath him.

A squall of fear was blowing inside him as he descended, turning in a constant, giddying, clockwise direction. He had no idea what the hell he was going to find down here. He just prayed with every step he took that, if Amanda was down here, she was alive.

He reached the bottom. A small flat standing area, with steel vault door ahead, in the centre of which was a heavy four-pronged locking handle, of the kind that might be used to secure the waterproof hatch on a submarine.

He tested it, and the handle moved easily, as if it had been turned recently. He gave it two rotations, then stopped and listened. Silence above him. Six more turns and the handle was rotating without pressure. He gave the door a push, but nothing happened. Then he pulled and, with a deep sucking sound, it swung open slowly. He couldn't believe how thick it was. Over a foot thick and still opening. Two feet. Three feet. Almost four feet before a gap appeared between the door and the jamb. He carried on pulling, opening up a larger and larger gap into the pitch darkness beyond, a gap big enough for him to fit through.

No light switch in here. He pulled the torch out of his pocket and turned it on. The beam was weak – it had been sitting in the car for a couple of years, unused, and the battery was low. There was enough light to see that he was in a small chamber: this must be the airlock chamber he had seen on the plan. On his right was a long narrow metal table on wheels, which reminded him of a rather primitive hospital trolley. Next to it were what looked like drip stands, a stack of electrical equipment and a row of oxygen cylinders.

Ten feet in front of him was another vault door, with the same locking handle as on the one he had just opened.

Was she in there? The other side of the door?

He wanted to call out, but there was no chance she would hear him. Gripping the handle, he began to turn it swiftly, six full rotations. Then he pulled. Slowly the door moved outwards. He pulled even harder, and finally the gap into the darkness beyond appeared. And with it a powerful stench. Body odour, excrement and unwashed clothes; but stronger than these was an acrid smell, which he recognised instantly.

Formalin. Used in laboratories to preserve dead tissue and organs. At medical school, the cadavers for dissection in the department of anatomy had been preserved in formalin.

Oh, sweet Jesus Christ, what was in this chamber?

He shone the weak beam. Shadows jumped back at him. 'Amanda?' he called. 'Amanda?'

He took a step forward and then he saw the figure lying on the ground, motionless. *Oh, God, don't let it be Amanda.*

He walked over. It was a human body. 'Amanda? Amanda.'

Then he heard the rustle of clothes behind him. As he swung the torch, a gigantic shadow hurtled at him. He heard Amanda's voice, screaming, 'Fuck you, you bastard!'

Then he felt the agonising jarring pain on the back of his neck. An explosion of lights inside his skull.

He crashed to the ground.

Amanda, standing behind him, raised the heavy metal grille from the ventilation shaft over her head again, holding it there with every ounce of strength she possessed, ready to bring it swinging back down on him if he moved just one muscle, ready to pulp his skull into the concrete.

The torch had rolled to the side. In the glow she could see he was lying motionless, head twisted awkwardly to one side, blood pooling on the floor around him.

She stared down at him, barely able to trust her eyes, gulping air, until she was certain he wasn't about to get up and come after her. Then she put down the grille, grabbed the torch, and turned with desperation in her heart to run towards the open doorway he had come through.

She let out a whimper of terror.

The door was closed.

Chapter Ninety-nine

PC Tim Willis, who had stopped Dr Terence Goel's blue Ford Mondeo car in the Tottenham Court Road last Saturday night, was on the line.

'He was tall – about six foot six. Medium build. Slick dark hair, good-looking – *very* good-looking, if you know what I mean, movie star, matinée-idol looks, and he had an American accent.'

'Anything else you can remember?' Glen asked, seated at his desk, writing this down, trying to wring every last spark from the police constable's brain.

'He seemed agitated. He said he was going to Cheltenham and that he'd set out from visiting friends in Barnes – one hell of a detour.'

'Did he have an explanation?'

'Said he got lost in London very easily.'

'Did you search the car?'

'It was clean. And we breathalysed him. Negative.'

Glen thanked him and hung up, then looked back at the notes he had just written. Cheltenham made sense. He wondered about Barnes. Why *Barnes*?

Half an hour later, shortly after three o'clock, his direct line rang. It was a woman from the Orange phone company. They had a Dr Terence Goel as a customer. Glen's hopes rose, then immediately sank again when she gave him the address: 97 Royal Court Walk.

The address that didn't exist.

He asked if she could request a mapped log of all Goel's calls in the three and a half weeks since he had become a subscriber, which would show Glen the geographic location to the nearest cell where each call was made. In parts of central London that could narrow it down to within a few hundred yards. She rang him back ten minutes later to say she wouldn't be able to get the log for him until some time on Monday. She also had the name of the dealer in Cheltenham from whom Dr Goel had purchased the phone.

Glen wrote down the information and thanked her. Moments after he had hung up, the phone rang again. It was the closed-circuit television room for the South East Central Metropolitan London area. They had a positive ID on Dr Terence Goel's Ford Mondeo crossing Westminster Bridge, heading south, at 3.19 p.m.

The surveillance operator had calculated all possible major routes the car might have taken from there and asked patrols to keep a vigilant eye for it, but so far there had not been any further sighting.

Glen grabbed a map. South over Westminster Bridge. It only took him a few seconds to realise the hopelessness of trying to guess where he might be heading, except that it wasn't Barnes. Goel could have been heading anywhere in the entire south of England.

With a ruler and a pencil he drew a line from Tottenham Court Road to Barnes, from Barnes to Westminster Bridge, and from Westminster Bridge to the Tottenham Court Road. The area inside covered a big swathe of central London.

It told him nothing.

Although Goel was American, he checked with the British Medical Association and ascertained that they knew of no doctor called Terence Goel. He asked his own divisional intelligence unit to find any Dr Terence Goel on the Internet. When the printout of the man's web page was brought into him, one phone call to the MIT in Boston confirmed that no Dr Terence Goel had ever been a junior professor of astronomy – nor had they ever had a Terence Goel either as a teacher or student.

A movie called *Big Night* was showing at the Duke of York's at nine o'clock tonight, and Glen really wanted to see it. It was now ten to six. If he left right away, he'd have time to play with Sammy for an hour and read him a story, have supper with Grace, and then maybe she'd let him go out to see it, even though he'd been out last night. Hell, last night was *work*.

Most people had already gone home. The room was quiet. Outside, the air was cooling down, it was going to be a humdinger of a beautiful evening. Maybe he'd give the movie a miss, catch it on video in a few months' time, and instead fire up the barbecue, sit out in the garden, share the evening with Sammy and Grace. Open a cold bottle of rosé. He stood up, hitched his jacket off the back of his chair and slung it over his shoulder. A barbecue sounded good. And he was starving.

He was heading for the door, thinking about a spicy chicken marinade recipe, when his phone rang. He stepped back.

'Glen Branson,' he answered.

Crackle at the other end. Someone on a radio, patched through by a PNC operator. 'This is Charlie Delta Four-Two-Zero. I'm a uniform patrol car in Kensington and have your suspect vehicle Blue Ford Mondeo, Romeo Seven-Five-Nine Kilo Golf Charlie under observation. He is heading west along Kensington High Street.'

Trying to contain his excitement, Glen asked, 'Can he see you?'

'We're in dense traffic. I'm several vehicles behind, I'm being careful, I don't think he would have seen me.'

'Stay with him, but for God's sake don't let him see you. Is anyone travelling with him?'

'He appears to be alone.'

'Do you have any description of him?'

'I'm afraid I've only seen his car from behind so far.'

'Well done, well spotted. I'm very grateful. Do your best to stay with him. Have you called for back-up?'

'Yes. He's indicating right. He's making a right turn into Holland Road.'

Glen listened, tense.

'OK, we're moving up Holland Road. Approaching Shepherd's Bush roundabout. Heavy traffic, we're still well back.'

While the police officer was giving his commentary, Glen opened the map where he had earlier drawn his pencil lines. Goel was within the zone he had drawn, although that still did not tell him much.

He continued to listen, frightened that he was going to hear that they'd lost him. But instead, the officer raised his voice. 'He's turning into a drive! I'm stopping . . . waiting . . . OK, I'm going forward again. I'm passing now, got it! He's driving into a double garage, remote controlled up-and-over door, I'm going round again, get the address for you. This is the rear of the house, I'll check the front.'

Glen pressed the phone to his ear as if he were drawing lifeblood from it. Dr Goel . . . Dr Goel . . . Goel . . . you and I are going to have a cosy chat . . . you're going to tell me all about your interest in Cora Burstridge . . . and you are going to tell me what your real name is.

Crackle of static then the police officer's voice again. 'I have an address. Four-seven Holland Park Villas. London West one-four.'

Glen scrawled it down triumphantly. 'Can you keep it under surveillance without being observed?'

'No problem.'

'I'm on my way,' Glen said.

He tore the address from his message pad, then sprinted out of the office and down to the car port.

As he came out of the building, he saw a young uniformed police constable, Nick Goodwin, with whom he had worked before joining the CID, getting into a marked Vauxhall patrol car. He ran over to him.

'How long are you on duty for, Nick?'

'I'm lates, till midnight.'

'Fancy a fast drive to London? I could do with the twos and blues to get me through the rush-hour traffic. It's an emergency.'

The constable looked hesitant. 'I'm meant to be doing my beat.'

'I'll take responsibility,' Glen said. 'My neck on the block.'

Chapter One Hundred

Conserving what life remained in the battery as best she could, Amanda switched on the torch for just a few precious seconds at a time, to check on her prisoner.

He was still unconscious, but his breathing sounded a little stronger and that was good. She needed him to come round and tell her how to open the door.

She had bound his hands and legs with strips of fabric she had torn from the clothing of the cadavers, and she'd staunched the flow of blood from the deep gash in the back of his head with a strip of cloth she'd soaked in her wash bucket. The floor was awash with blood and she was scared he might have lost too much and wasn't going to survive.

Kneeling beside him, she shone the torch in his face and patted his cheeks. 'Michael?' she said, urgently. 'Michael, wake up.'

What the hell was the secret of this door? She'd searched his clothes and his wallet for some electronic gizmo that might do it, but had found nothing other than his mobile phone. She switched it on again now. It beeped reassuringly, then the same signal appeared in the window as appeared each time.

NO SERVICE.

She tried dialling anyway: 999 then SEND. Musical chimes followed.

No bloody signal.

With the torch, and the light from the dial of the phone, she had enough to tell the time by. It had been just past two when Michael had come in here. Now it was almost six. He'd been unconscious for four hours. And she knew the date now, from the tiny window on his watch.

Friday, 1 August.

She had gone to the stock-car racing with him on Sunday, 27 July.

Five days.

That was really scaring her. She knew it had been a long time, but not five days. And this meant that if people had been looking for her they hadn't found her in five days. Would they ever?

Maybe they would now that she had Michael Tennent down here. People would start to wonder where he was and would be looking for him.

Six p.m., Friday, 1 August.

The end of the week. Would Michael Tennent be missed over the weekend?

She patted his cheek harder. 'Michael! Michael, wake up!'

He grunted.

She snapped on the torch – the beam so weak now it didn't hurt her eyes – and shone it in his face. His eyelids were moving. One opened. She held the beam under her chin so he could see her face.

'Michael?'

Both eyes open now. Bewildered. Hard to gauge what he was registering. Even so, she remained wary. She glanced at the bonds holding his arms, checking they were secure.

'Michael, tell me how to get out of here. Just tell me how to open the door.'

He stared at her, saying nothing.

Shining the torch directly into his face she said, 'Michael? Can you hear me?' The faintest hint of a nod. 'Tell me how to get out of here.'

Michael felt as if he was staring through binoculars at the sun. His retinas were scalding; the inside of his skull was ablaze. Through it, Amanda's voice.

'Michael, for God's sake, tell me how to get out of here!'

Thomas Lamark, back now in the sanctuary of his den, switched on the speaker, and heard the thing saying, 'Michael, we are both going to die if you don't tell me how to open the door.'

461

Good, it hadn't killed him. He'd been afraid that it might have done: it had hit him so hard. He needed to remember its strength when he went down there.

He wound back the voice-activated tape-recorder to see what he had missed while he had been out. He pressed PLAY. Only the thing's voice. Then the masculine grunt. Good. Dr Michael Tennent was coming round. Impeccable timing! He needed to get started now because he was sure time was getting short.

A police car had been behind him along Kensington High Street. He'd caught glimpses of it in his rear-view mirror up Holland Road, and he had seen it again, some way behind him, just as he turned into his garage.

He needed to hurry, although once he got into the shelter he could disconnect all the exterior handles and lock the doors from the inside. It would take them hours to drill through and get them open – and that would only be after they had found the right equipment and got it into the house.

If he hurried, he would have more than enough time to remove the thing's breasts, using the brilliant surgical technique he had just witnessed, and allow Dr Michael Tennent the privilege of watching the whole procedure. Afterwards, he could watch the thing bleed to death.

And after that? After that Thomas would have achieved redemption. After that he could move forward once more with his mother's blessing. Get back to a normal life again. But that was way ahead, somewhere in the future. Right now, he must concentrate on the present.

Happy that you killed my mother, Dr Tennent? Happy now? Sleep easily in your bed at night, do you?

A groan through the speaker. Then the thing's voice again. 'Michael? Please, wake up! For God's sake, wake up!'

Dr Michael Tennent made an incomprehensible sound.

His voice was sounding stronger. This was good.

Thomas pulled the neck strap of his night-vision goggles over his head, and tugged on his radio headphones. Then, remaining tuned into the fallout shelter, he opened the drawer in the tallboy at the back of his den where he kept his surgical kit.

His knives gleamed out of their black felt cradles inside the hand-tooled leather box as brightly as when he had last used them, at college, thirteen years ago. He tested the blade of the scalpel against his index finger: just as keen as it had always been. He closed the lid and secured the clasp, removed also a fresh pack of hypodermic syringes, then carried them down to the kitchen and opened the fridge door.

From a plastic container marked SALAD CRISPER, he removed a small vial of curare and a larger one of adrenaline. The adrenaline would help the thing stay conscious during its operation. From the closet where spare light bulbs were stored, he took a roll of duct tape.

Then he went down into the cellar.

Amanda never heard the door open behind her. She was sitting in the darkness, right beside Dr Michael Tennent, listening to his breathing, coaxing him back into consciousness.

'Michael! Come on, Michael! Tell me about the door. Do you want me to hurt you? I don't mind hurting you, Michael. I'll hurt you as much as it takes to get you to tell me about the door. So you might as well tell me now.'

Michael, slow, confused, said, 'Door. What – what door do you mean?'

'The door to this room, Michael.'

Thomas watched them through his lenses. Dr Michael Tennent and his bit of fluff. The *thing*. A green figure hunched on a green floor. It moved forward, then suddenly the whole chamber exploded into brilliant light.

Thomas closed his eyes in shock, dazzled. The thing had a torch! He opened his eyes again, bracing himself. It switched off the torch. Back to cold green light again.

Relief.

Dr Michael Tennent must have brought the torch. He needed to move, now, while the torch was off, while he had surprise with him. He checked the palm of his hand. The needle was in place, held securely by the sticking plaster.

Stepping forward swiftly, noiselessly crossing the floor, until he was right behind it.

Amanda felt a sharp prick in her neck. And at the same time she heard a cheery voice.

'Pre-med!'

Chapter One Hundred and One

Glen, in the passenger seat, watched the road ahead. PC Nick Goodwin was driving at ten tenths, flat out, total concentration, in the fast lane of the M23, the speedometer needle jiggering over the 120 m.p.h. mark. Vehicles ahead moved sharply out of the way the moment they saw the blue flashing lights in their mirrors.

Glen liked Nick Goodwin. He was a quiet, serious man in his mid-twenties, good-looking, with neat dark hair and a tidy nature. Dependable. He rarely showed emotion.

The constable reached up and pressed the two-tone siren button to warn off a car that was weaving erratically, the driver probably trying to change a tape.

The traffic was thickening as he neared the M25 turn-off. Friday-night rush-hour hell. They were forced to slow down.

'How's your little one, Glen?'

'Sammy, yup, he's coming up to four. He's a good kid, love him to death.'

'Having any more?'

'Ari miscarried last year. But I hope so. Want lots of kids. You?'

'Any day now. Our first.'

'No kidding! Going to be at the birth?'

'Yes.'

'Magic,' Glen said. His personal radio crackled. He heard his call sign and responded. It was the PNC operator. 'We have the householder's name for four-seven Holland Park Villas. Gloria Lamark. Golf London Oscar Romeo India Alpha. London Alpha Mike Alpha Romeo Kilo.'

For several seconds, Glen was silent, absorbing this information.

Gloria Lamark.

Dr Terence Goel lived at Gloria Lamark's house? Or was he a frequent visitor?

Had the once great Gloria Lamark had a lover with a false name, a false address, an entire false identity? Had she known he was a fake?

Then he remembered, last night, Simon Roebuck had reacted strangely when he had mentioned Gloria Lamark's name. As if it had struck some chord with him. Why?

He tried to recall their conversation. Roebuck had been talking about a case he was working on of two missing women, Tina Mackay, which was a big news story, and another woman: he had thought there might be a connection between them. Had Roebuck made some connection between these women and Gloria Lamark?

A Dr Terence Goel connection?

Gloria Lamark dies. Then Cora Burstridge dies. A man who calls himself Dr Terence Goel, who seems to live at Gloria Lamark's address, gets stopped for driving erratically in London last Saturday night. He goes to Cora Burstridge's cremation but does not get out of the car.

Dr Terence Goel, you are really bothering me a lot.

He picked up his radio handset and requested to be patched through to DC Roebuck at Hampstead police station. He wanted to know exactly what the name Lamark had meant to him.

A gap was opening in the traffic ahead. Siren wailing, lights flashing, Goodwin bullied them through it.

Chapter One Hundred and Two

The lights were on now. Michael, muzzy and confused, could see that he was lying in a concrete walled chamber. Out of the corner of his eye he could make out a figure, someone with brown hair, lying on the floor, motionless. *Amanda had blonde hair.*

The figure was too motionless. Dead.

He tried to move, first his arms, then his legs, but could not. His head was pounding, he felt sick. He tried to speak but his mouth was clamped shut by something that smelt unpleasant, faintly oily, and he could only make incoherent sounds. If he threw up he would choke on the vomit.

Dr Goel, a strange pair of goggles hanging around his neck, was kneeling on the floor in front of him, holding a length of rope. 'You are going to enjoy the show, Dr Tennent. I've given you the best seat in the house. I shall look forward to your reaction. You might like to write a review afterwards. Perhaps for the *British Medical Journal*? If you wish to communicate with me, best to do it through your eyes.'

Suddenly Goel pulled hard on the rope. Michael's wrists shot up in the air, then a brutal jerk ripped his chest and shoulder muscles as his arms took the full weight of his body and he was hauled upwards until his feet were clear of the ground. He was left hanging.

Helplessly, he watched Goel leave the room. Then he tried to move his legs apart, but they were too tightly bound, as were his hands. His thinking was becoming clearer. Amanda waking him. Angry. Desperate. Threatening.

Where was she now?

What was Terence Goel doing here in Gloria Lamark's house?

He tried to struggle but the pain in his shoulders became worse. He bent his legs back until they touched something hard, the wall behind him. For an instant he got a purchase, a fraction of a second's relief on his arms, then they slipped and his arms and shoulders took his full weight again with an even more agonising jerk. It was hard to breathe like this and the pain from his shoulders was making it difficult to think clearly.

A clattering sound snapped his attention to the door. A metal table on wheels was coming in through it. Someone was strapped to the table; he saw white, bloodstained trainers, blue, bloodstained jeans, a white, bloodstained T-shirt. His throat tightened. Amanda: strapped down on that trolley, cords binding her legs, midriff, arms, a breathing tube in her mouth, eyes wide open, staring at him, being pushed in by a tall figure in green surgical scrubs. And in that instant a terrible, silent scream shook every cell in his body.

Amanda. No. Amanda. Oh, God, no, no, no, no, no.

Goel took his time, lining up the table squarely in front of him. Michael watched him, took in the tray of surgical instruments attached to the side of the table, the hideously calm way in which Goel checked Amanda's pulse, then her blood pressure. He twisted inside at the pitiful sound of the choked groans and grunts as she tried to speak. Tried to catch her eyes to give her some reassurance that whatever nightmare they were in, somehow they would find a way out of it.

But she did not once look at him.

Dr Goel went out of the chamber, then returned carrying a large radio cassette player. He set it down on the ground, switched it on, and Michael's voice boomed around the chamber.

'This is Dr Tennent speaking. Gloria, would you please give me a call as soon as you get this message. I'm afraid I upset you this morning. It might be helpful if we had a quick chat over the phone.'

468

Goel pressed STOP and stared up at Michael. Finally, Michael connected. Now he realised who Dr Terence Goel really was. And now he understood the chilling words of Dortmund.

Avenger of Blood.

In disbelief he stared back. Is this what it was all about? His error of judgement with Gloria Lamark?

Why was Amanda here, strapped to the trolley? There had to be something more complex going on. Was she a past girlfriend of this madman?

Thomas Lamark reached up and tore the duct tape from Michael's mouth. It felt to Michael as if half his face had been ripped away.

'Something you want to say, Dr Tennent?'

Screwing up his eyes from the pain, Michael gasped, 'This has nothing to do with Amanda. Let her go.'

Staring coldly at him, Thomas said, 'Gloria Lamark was my mother. She had beautiful breasts.'

Michael stared back at him, his wits dulled by the pain and his difficulty in breathing. He thought back to his sessions with this man in his consulting room. The deeply troubled unstable Dr Goel. Close to a breakdown. Filled with anger. A man who liked to play games. Intelligent. All the parallels. His dead wife. The dove in the cage separated from its mate. A control freak.

Fallout shelter.

'Terence,' he said, 'you should let Amanda go, please.'

Eyes flaring in anger, he said, 'My name is *Thomas*. Don't try to be smart.'

'I only know you as Terence. Dr *Terence* Goel.'

'This woman made love to you, Dr Tennent. She polluted her body with your filthy seed. She has inside her the seed of the man who murdered my mother. Were you ever breastfed, Dr Tennent?'

Michael tried to think what the best reply would be – the reply that this man wanted to hear. He hedged, 'I believe so. I don't remember.'

'You'd remember. You really would remember. My mother had such very beautiful breasts. She was famous for her looks, as I am sure you are aware. What I'm going to do, Dr Tennent, is to help you to take your mind back to your infancy. I'd like you to suck Amanda Capstick's breasts. But you stay where you are. I'll bring them over to you.'

Thomas Lamark picked up a scalpel, lifted the neck of Amanda's T-shirt, then cut it open all the way down and pulled the two flaps apart, exposing Amanda's breasts.

Amanda was writhing under her bonds.

Michael howled, 'For God's sake, Thomas, leave her alone!'

'Would you like duct tape over your mouth again, Dr Tennent? Or can I rely on you to remain quiet? You must understand, my need to concentrate during surgery will be crucial to the welfare of my patient.'

Desperation corkscrewed through Michael's utter helplessness. 'Operate on me, Thomas,' he gasped, imploringly. 'Cut me to pieces, just please don't hurt her.'

'Don't worry, Dr Tennent, you will get your turn. I intend to ensure you are never able to harm another patient, Dr Tennent. You have condemned me to twenty-five days of greater pain than it is possible for any human being to imagine. I'm intending to ensure that at least once, every day for the next twenty-five days, you will beg me to end your pain. And each time I will quote a line from Shakespeare's *King Lear* to you. "The worst is not, so long as we can say, 'This is the worst.'"'

He turned his attention to Amanda, who was thrashing even more desperately in her bonds, her eyes bulging in terror.

'Now, little thing, this wriggling around is no good!' He lifted a tiny glass vial from the instrument tray attached to the table, and held it in front of her. 'Are you familiar with the techniques of modern anaesthesia?'

She stared at him in abject suspense.

'We use a balance of three or four agents. One paralyses to produce complete muscle relaxation. The agent I favour is curare, an extract from a South American plant used in the tips of poison arrows – nice to be able to use natural medicines, don't you think? Natural curare is so much better for you than some horrible fabricated chemical concoction.'

He broke the seal on the vial, then tore a hypodermic syringe free of its pack. 'The second agent would cause the patient loss of consciousness, but I really would not want to deprive you of consciousness today. It would be too much of a wasted opportunity – I'm sure you understand even if you do not approve. And, similarly, the third agent, which will deaden any pain, will not be needed. But a fourth agent, which is adrenaline-based, will be helpful in constricting your blood vessels, to prevent excessive blood loss – and it will help prevent against your passing out in shock.'

'Thomas, please, listen to me,' Michael begged. 'Let's talk about this.'

Without turning round, Thomas felt in his pocket for the vial of adrenaline. It wasn't there. He rummaged around inside his scrubs, getting increasingly angry with himself. *Shit, shit, shit.*

He knew exactly what he had done. He had put the vial of adrenaline into his jacket pocket. When he had changed into his scrubs in the kitchen, he had hooked his jacket over the back of a kitchen chair.

Shit, shit, shit.

Dr Michael Tennent was saying something to him, but he tuned the man's voice out. He had more important things to think about right now than the whingeing psychiatrist.

Damn you, Dr Tennent, you made me forget the bloody adrenaline!

He stormed out of the chamber.

Michael heard the footsteps receding. Then the sound of the door opening. He was staring at Amanda, and finally she was staring back at him. Anger rose through the raging storm of fear inside him. Anger at his foolishness for getting himself – both of them – into this situation. *Oh, God, why the hell hadn't he let the police deal with this?*

'Amanda,' he gasped. Then his voice dried. *What could he say?* Lamark was out of the chamber. He needed these

471

precious moments to *think* not speak. There must be *something* he could do. He tried to drill the pain out of his mind. To clear everything out, to focus on one thing, this reality now, these few precious seconds.

Could he lure Thomas over to him, then lash out with his legs and knock him unconscious? He tried a kick now and it felt pathetic. Dangling like this he couldn't get any kind of power into his legs. He tried to get a purchase on the wall behind him, but that barely helped. Besides, even if he succeeded and got the man in the right place, under his jaw, and knocked him out, what then?

He was hanging as helplessly as a dead chicken, the cords cutting deep into his wrists. How the hell was he going to get down even with Thomas unconscious?

There had to be another way.

He stared at Amanda again. Searching for a signal in her eyes. But all he could see in them was his own helplessness mirrored back at him.

Chapter One Hundred and Three

The front doorbell rang assertively.

Thomas heard it as he hurried out through the sauna door. Then he heard it again as he reached the brick steps from the cellar gymnasium up to the kitchen.

Go to hell.

His jacket was hanging on the back of a chair at the kitchen table. Just a few steps away. Quickly, hand into the side pocket and there was the vial of adrenaline.

My bloody memory. Forgetting the adrenaline!

The doorbell rang again. Who *was* it? They were knocking as well now, solid insistent raps with the brass knocker.

His mother hated people who rang and knocked at the same time like this.

He turned towards the door and said, quietly, 'Do you think we're deaf or something?'

On tiptoe down the passageway, across the slate floor, up to the spy-hole. He looked out.

No one was there.

Gone.

Relief.

He walked quickly back along the passage, but as he entered the kitchen he stopped dead in his tracks.

A man outside was looking in through the window. A tall, bald, black man in a suit.

Thomas ducked back into the passageway, everything lopsided in his brain now. Had the man seen him?

There was rapping now on the patio door. Bare knuckles on glass. Thomas stayed in the shadow of the passageway, holding his breath, not daring to move. Who was this man? How dare he come prowling around the back of the house?

Could he be from the police? Thomas tried to think this through. If he was a police officer and he had seen him, what was he going to think if he didn't answer the door?

Was he following up from the detective this morning? Was he suspicious?

Let him in or ignore him?

If Thomas ignored him, what would the man do? Did he have a search warrant? Would he break in? Thomas realised he would be fretting about this while he was performing his surgery. He needed a steady hand, a steady mind. Best to open the door, find out who it was, what he wanted, deal with it. If necessary, he could buy enough time to get down into the cellar and conceal the entrance to the shelter. No one would find it.

Except, he wondered, how had Dr Michael Tennent found it?

The rapping had stopped. Had the man given up and gone away? Was he prowling around the outside, trying to look in more windows? The front doorbell rang again, followed moments later by another rat-tat-tat from the knocker.

'Coming!' he said quietly.

Then he remembered what he was wearing. Quickly he tugged the strap of his night-vision goggles over his neck, peeled off his surgical scrubs, balled the goggles up inside them, threw them into the broom closet beneath the stairs, then hurried through into the kitchen, grabbing his jacket off the chair back and tugging it on.

Need to look respectable. Calm!

Glen Branson, standing with Nick Goodwin outside the front door, was certain he had seen a figure moving inside the house when he had looked through the kitchen window just now. The London police constable who picked up and followed Dr Goel's Mondeo had called for assistance, and the house had been watched front and back for the hour and a half that it had taken Glen and Nick Goodwin to get here. Unless Goel had made off over a garden wall, he was still in here. And if Dr Goel was in here,

Glen wanted him to be under no illusions that if he ignored the bell the police would simply go away.

I'm missing out on one of the most beautiful evenings of the year, Dr Goel. I've missed out on playing with my son tonight. I've missed out on sitting in the garden eating a meal with my wife tonight, just so that I could have a chat with you. You are going to answer this doorbell, Dr Goel, I promise you, I'll drive you into dementia until you do.

He pressed the bell again. Rapped the knocker. Pressed the bell.

Suddenly, the door opened. A tall man, in a cream linen suit, beamed out at them, his face a picture of charm.

'So sorry to keep you,' he said, in a cultured English voice. 'You caught me short. I was having a pee.'

The man seemed normal, relaxed, good-natured. The description from PC Tim Willis, who had stopped Dr Terence Goel's car in Tottenham Court Road last Saturday night, was in the forefront of his mind.

'He was tall, about six foot six. Medium build. Slick dark hair, good-looking – very good-looking, if you know what I mean, movie star, matinée idol looks, and he had an American accent.'

This man was about six foot six. He was of medium build. He had slick dark hair, and he was *very* good-looking, no question, but his voice was public-school English, no trace of American. Was the accent an invention – like his address in Cheltenham?

Watching him closely, Glen asked, 'Dr Terence Goel?' He clocked genuine surprise in the man's eyes.

'Goel? Did you say *Goel?'*

'Dr Terence Goel.'

The man looked too at ease to be hiding anything and yet the description was perfect in every detail – except for that accent.

'I'm sorry, no, the name Terence Goel means nothing to me. I'm afraid I can't help you.' He took a step back.

To halt him, Glen held up his warrant card. 'I'm Detective Constable Branson from Sussex Police. This is PC Goodwin.'

Goodwin produced his warrant card and held it up.

Eyes scanning the body language of the man's hands for a brief instant – they were relaxed, gave nothing away – then back up to his face, Glen said, 'A Ford Mondeo motor car registered in the name of Dr Terence Goel was seen entering the garage at the rear of these premises, at approximately five past six this evening.'

Still totally at ease, the man said, 'Ah. My mother let the garage. This must be the tenant.'

'Dr Goel is your tenant?'

'My mother's. I really wouldn't know the name. I'm just keeping an eye on the house. You know what it's like when a celebrity dies – all the ghouls who want to break in and steal souvenirs.' He stared hard at Glen, as if for confirmation.

'I can imagine.'

'I haven't been able to bring myself to go through her papers yet. She died three weeks ago – Gloria Lamark, the actress, you would have heard the news.'

'Yes. I'm very sorry.'

'Thank you.'

'You're Gloria Lamark's son?'

'Yes, I'm Thomas Lamark.'

'I was a fan of hers.'

His face lit up. 'You were?'

'She was a truly wonderful actress. She was in some of my all-time favourite films.'

Almost bursting with excitement, Thomas said, 'Which ones?'

'*Wings of the Wild* and *Paris Romance*. I've seen them both several times.'

'*Wings of the Wild*? You really like that?'

'Uh-huh. That scene when Ben Gazzara's out on the wing of the plane with the gun, and she's flying it and trying to knock him off under the bridge – that's one of the greatest scenes in cinema, I think.'

'Me too,' Thomas said. This was good, he liked this man. He wished he could spend time with him talking about the films, but this was not the moment.

'Mr Lamark, these papers of your mother's, do you have

476

them in the house? The ones that might show the name of the tenant?'

Careful.

This man was pleasant but he had a quiet persistence that made Thomas uneasy. He needed to think this through.

'I – yes – possibly.'

'Would you mind taking a look while we wait?'

Thomas wanted to say a firm no. But then the detective added, 'I've seen every single film your mother has been in.'

There was such sincerity in the detective's face that Thomas was elated. 'I can't understand why she never won an Oscar.'

'Me neither. Any chance you could take a quick look for those papers?'

'Of course, come in.'

Thomas cursed himself. This was stupid. Dangerous. He should have told them it was inconvenient, to come back another time. Yet, perhaps, if he could keep up this pretence – this masterstroke, his mother's tenant – maybe he could buy some time. There was nothing in this house to link him to Dr Goel. Even the mobile phone was in the car. The garage was clear. Dr Goel's Mondeo and Dr Goel's white van. All traces of the Alfa gone now.

If he could just remain calm and convincing, he would fool the detective. Fool him enough to get rid of him for now – and that was all he needed. The future would take care of itself.

He stepped back, closed the front door behind the police officers and watched the detective immediately walk over to the painting of his mother stepping out of the limousine.

'The royal premiere of *The Widow of Monaco*,' Thomas said proudly.

'She was an incredibly beautiful woman,' Glen said. It felt strange to have been in the homes of two of his idols and within such a short space of each other. And it felt strange also, that Cora Burstridge, who had been so much bigger and more enduring a star, should have lived in a far less grand home than Gloria Lamark.

This man was strange, too. His mother had died three weeks ago, yet he seemed as if he didn't have a care in the world.

Was this English accent an act?

Thomas ushered the policemen into the drawing room. He was picking up bad vibes from the detective now, he could tell that he was suspicious. *Get them out of the house.*

Or kill them?

'Make yourself comfortable,' Thomas said. 'I'll go and have a look in her files.'

Glen, standing in front of one of the dozens of framed photographs on the wall, watched Thomas Lamark leave the room. He listened to the tramp of his feet receding up the stairs, all his instincts telling him he should not let this man out of his sight. Then he silently signalled to his colleague to stay down here.

In his den Thomas was losing his calm. He pulled open a drawer, rummaged around in it, slammed it shut, loudly, so the detective would hear him downstairs, would know that he was looking. He opened another drawer, rummaged in that, trying hard to think now of something convincing to say.

He slammed the drawer shut.

He opened a third drawer, then, from the corner of his eye, saw a shadow. It was the detective, standing outside his den; there was an expression on his face that Thomas did not trust.

'Beautiful house,' Glen Branson said.

'I'm having a problem,' Thomas said. 'I cannot find –'

He was cut short by a sharp crackle, followed by the sound of Dr Michael Tennent's gasping voice.

'Amanda – can you move? Can you move anything at all?'

Their eyes sprang towards each other and locked for one fleeting second, before Thomas lunged across the room and snapped off the loudspeaker. Turning back to the detective, he said, with a broad, edgy smile, 'The radio – I – was listening to a play –'

But Glen barely heard him. He was staring at something he had just noticed. A tiny rip, no more than half an inch long, on the right hand shoulder of Thomas Lamark's jacket. His mind hurtled straight into Cora Burstridge's loft. The strips of cream thread hanging there, high up, caught on a nail that was sticking out of a rafter.

The same cream; the same length.

Glen glanced away, but not quickly enough. The man had noticed. Their eyes locked again and this time the man's expression was that of a cornered animal.

Glen's brain was spinning with several different thoughts simultaneously. *Amanda*. The name of the woman who had gone missing this week. The name Simon Roebuck had said last night in the pub.

And today Simon Roebuck was dead.

The terrible bitterness between Gloria Lamark and Cora Burstridge. How much did Thomas Lamark share in this? Enough to go and gloat at the crematorium? Enough to have killed Cora Burstridge?

'*Amanda – can you move? Can you move anything at all?*'

And what play? It was a quarter past seven. Radio 4 was the channel for plays and *The Archers* was on now.

What the hell was going on here?

A voice was screaming in Glen's head to arrest this man. But on what charge?

The fist came like a missile from the dark, powering into Glen's face so fast that it wasn't until he was falling back against the door jamb that he even realised he'd been hit. He crashed down onto the floor, dazed and disoriented as if he had just dived into a murky pool and was still somewhere underwater.

A shadow passed over him; he reached up and grabbed, instinctively, felt something hard, shoe leather; holding on with all his old club brawl self-preservation, not sure what he had hold of, but it felt like a leg, and he pulled hard, wrenching it sideways at the same time. The floor shook with a crash and now he was up on his knees. Groggily, he saw Thomas Lamark pulling himself up from the landing floor. As Glen stood, Lamark launched himself at him; he

479

felt a winding blow in his belly, then another stupefying punch in his jaw and he was jerking up in the air, and falling over backwards.

He crashed to the floor with a jarring, winding thump; he lay for a few seconds, instincts screaming at him to keep moving. Somehow he found the energy to roll, then he got up on his hands, ready to turn, to dodge, looking for the enemy, trying to work out where he was coming from next, how to get an advantage. But Thomas Lamark had disappeared.

He staggered to his feet, pressed a hand to his face – it felt like half his jaw had been knocked off – then looked warily out through the doorway into the landing. Where the hell was the man?

Nick Goodwin came pounding up the stairs.

Glen stepped warily out onto the landing, heart thudding, listening hard. There were half a dozen doors, all shut; Lamark could be behind any of them. Or have gone up or downstairs. Was he making a run for it?

One floor up in his mother's bedroom, Thomas rummaged through piles of her silk scarves in a drawer. He *knew* it was somewhere here, in this drawer, where she always used to keep it, permanently loaded, for Armageddon. Then he found it, carefully wrapped inside a Cornelia James silk square. Just as heavy as he had always remembered.

She had smuggled the gun back from America and had shown it to him several times when he had been a child, taught him how to take the safety catch off, how to aim it. She said that when nuclear war broke out they might need this gun to stop other people getting into their shelter.

He was going to use it now to stop the policemen getting into the shelter.

'Did you see him?' Glen asked.

Goodwin shook his head.

'Cover the back of the house – I'll take the front.' Glen reached for his personal radio, and was about to press TRANSMIT, when there was a sharp crackle like an insect buzzing past him, a blast of air against his ear, then a startled look on Goodwin's face, his eyes bulging, his hair lifting up like a toupee, as a bullet tore out of his temple. A shower of blood and bone splinters sprayed hard in Glen's face, stinging his cheeks and eyes like grit, accompanied almost instantaneously by a throbbing shockwave and a deafening bang.

He dived onto the floor and rolled, and a chunk of polished oak board exploded inches in front of his face. As he rolled again he saw Lamark above and flame burst out of the muzzle of the gun he was holding. The next instant he was hurtled backwards by a thump in his chest like a massive kick.

He'd been shot, too, he realised, running on autopilot now. There was no pain. He just knew he had to get off this landing. Goodwin was down, dead, oh Christ, the poor bastard was dead. He saw another flash from the muzzle as he threw himself headfirst down the staircase, curling into a ball, head buried in his arms, thumping down the treads. He heard another bang as he rolled. Then he was at the bottom.

Still balled, he rolled twice along the floor, scrambled to his legs without looking up or behind him and ran forward, into a passageway, through it, along into a kitchen. Patio doors at the far end. He ran at them, tried to open them; they were locked, with the key removed.

Panicking now, he charged the glass with his shoulders, and bounced off it. Toughened glass; he wouldn't be able to throw a damned chair through it. He looked around, desperately, for a weapon or a shield. Then he could see Lamark lumbering down the passage. He saw the open door that went somewhere internally, probably to a cellar, didn't like it, but had no choice. He upended the kitchen table, pushing it in front of him, like a shield, ducked down behind it, then dived through the door and slammed it shut behind him, just as the gun fired again.

No damn key on this side.

He launched himself down the brick steps into the gymnasium. Running across it, towards the only solid

481

structure, the sauna, he scanned the keep-fit equipment looking for something to get behind. Another bang and a hole ripped in the green carpet right in front of him. He threw himself to the ground, praying silently, curled into a ball again, crashed in through the open door of the sauna, pulled it shut behind him, felt a hammer blow on it and saw wood splinter inwards, stinging shards striking him in the face and body.

Going to die in a goddamn sauna. Oh, God, no.

Sammy's face flashed in his eyes. Then Ari's.

Now he saw the blood all over his chest. But also he saw the hole in the floor, the steps spiralling down. Horribly aware that he was trapping himself, he found the strength to propel himself forward and down them.

Panting hard at the bottom, gulping air, he stared, in near blind panic, through the open door into the empty chamber ahead, and at the second open door on the far side that looked as if it led through into another. What was this place? Where the hell could he hide? He looked up, fearfully, expecting to hear the clatter of footsteps at any second, but instead there was silence.

He waited, watching for a shadow, in case Lamark was tiptoeing down. But nothing moved.

Glancing behind him, he wondered if there was another entrance to this place – and if so, another exit. With trembling fingers, he clicked on his radio but all he could hear was a solid crackle of static. No reception. He looked down at his chest again. Nick's startled expression flashed in front of him. The bullet tearing out of his temple. He was in shock; had to pull himself together

Not going to die down here, no goddamn way. I joined the police force to make you proud of me, Sammy. I didn't join it to bleed to death in a concrete vault.

He took a step back, eyes locked on the spiral staircase. Then another step. Another.

Inside the chamber now, staring at the massive door. Could he lock it from this side?

If he could buy time. The other police officers out on the street watching this place would get concerned when they didn't hear from him. All he had to do was sit tight. Wouldn't they have heard the gunshots – or were they too far away?

Help would come.

It took him all his strength to heave the door shut. Then he looked for bolts. He could see bolt holes, clearly drilled, top and bottom. But the bolts had been removed – and, from the freshness of the marks showing their positions, they had been removed recently.

Christ. His weight against Lamark's. Lamark was a huge, powerful guy. Glen looked down at his chest; his entire shirt front was sopping wet with blood, and he was wheezing horribly. And he could feel the pain, too, now; a fierce, intense pain, a blowtorch blazing inside his chest. He pressed all the weight he could against the door, not daring to leave it and risk exploring further.

Then he heard a male voice behind him, nervous, short of breath.

'Thomas, we need to talk about this.'

Glen spun round. The voice came through the open door behind him. He listened, but could see nothing. It had sounded as though the voice was addressing him.

Then the voice again, louder, more insistent; more desperate. 'Thomas, I know you're a caring man and you've been a wonderful son to your mother. Don't you want her to be proud of you?'

Glen called out, 'Who is that?'

There was a brief silence, then, filled with surprise, the voice came back, 'Michael Tennent. Who are you?'

'I'm a police officer.'

Glen was close to weeping at the emotion in the man's voice when he heard him again.

'Thank God! Oh, thank God! We're here, through here, in the back chamber! Thank God!'

Glen stayed where he was, weight against the door. Just what in God's name was going on down here?

Why hadn't Lamark come down the spiral stairs to finish him off? Had he run out of bullets? Had he fled?

483

He had to do something, fast: he was going to bleed to death if he didn't get medical help.

His heart in his mouth, he turned from the door and ran through into the second chamber, then the third. Then he stopped in his tracks. It felt as if he had entered some tableau in the Madame Tussaud's Chamber of Horrors.

Two bodies on the floor. A man in a bloodstained shirt, hanging from his arms. A woman, intubated through the mouth, in bloodstained clothes, strapped down to a wheeled operating table.

When Michael saw the tall, bald black man stumble into the room, his face scratched to shreds, blood gouting from his sodden shirt front, his elation fell away.

Then they were plunged into darkness.

Chapter One Hundred and Four

A trinity of green figures in front of him. He concentrated on the detective, who had positioned himself between Dr Michael Tennent and the bit of fluff. One hand on the end of the operating table. Staring this way, looking startled.

What can you see Detective Constable Branson? Darkness? Even darker darkness beyond that? Too bad we didn't get to talk more about my mother's films. I hope you understand that I'm getting no pleasure from killing you.

In the magazine of his gun he had three bullets left. Good that he had stopped to check. If necessary, one for each of them, but he hoped that would not be necessary. Bullets were for people who did not matter. Bullets were for people like Detective Constable Glen Branson.

Bullets were too quick.

We haven't come this far, Dr Michael Tennent, to end it all with a single headshot.

The doors were all secured from the inside now. No one was coming in without an invitation. There was no need for him to hurry. He could think everything through carefully. Take his time.

Enjoy!

Get rid of the detective and then resume. He patted his scrub suit pocket, checking that he now had the adrenaline. The vial was there. Perfection!

He sighted the gun on the detective who was now crouching down low – as if this would protect him! – but he was twenty feet away and there was a danger that if he missed from this angle, he would hit the psychiatrist. No need to take this chance. Shoot the detective point blank, put the gun against his temple.

Suddenly he heard the psychiatrist shout, 'He has night-vision goggles!'

Glen, in the giddying darkness, gripped the end of the metal table as if it were a life raft; so long as he was touching the table, he had his bearings.

He knew where the entrance to the chamber was, where the man hanging from his arms was, he could reach him in one step. He knew where the woman was. And the position of the tray attached to it containing sharp medical instruments, just a short distance along this same edge that his hand was gripping.

All his thoughts were focused on the two people in terrible trouble in this room. Somehow, in the pitch darkness, in a room where there was a man with night-vision goggles who had shot him once and was going to try to shoot him again, he had to protect these people.

The image of the two bodies on the floor flashed in his mind.

He was starting to feel dangerously weak and light-headed, and he had no idea how many minutes of consciousness remained to him. He had to keep focused on what he needed to get onto a level footing with the madman in this room.

Light. Weapon. Shielding.

There were surgical instruments on a tray attached to the trolley just in front of his hand. But where were the lights? Where the hell was the master switch?

Keep low, keep in a tight ball, keep moving.

Still holding the table, he skittered on his feet right, then left, bobbing, ducking, thinking. Thinking. Thinking.

Clearly and firmly, sounding a lot more confident than he felt, Glen said, 'Mr Lamark, there are police outside the house, at the front and rear. Turn the lights back on and put down your gun. Surrender peacefully. You don't want to make this any worse for yourself than it already is.'

Thomas Lamark used the time while the detective talked to move in on him. Now he was less than six feet away. Keeping his breathing down slow and calm, he raised the gun, holding the grip with both hands, angling the barrel

486

forward until he had the front sight lined up in the V-shaped nick in the rear sight. Hand guns tended to fire high from the kick, he had read this on the Internet. He needed to aim low, as he had before.

Both sights were lined up on the detective's chin now. Allowing for the kick, the bullet should go through one of his eyes or his forehead.

He could afford to get closer still, why not? Only three bullets left – why take any chances?

Conveniently, the detective spoke again. Thomas detected a tremor in his voice. Good. The detective was less confident than he was trying to sound.

No tricks, good.

'Mr Lamark, I know you can hear me. Let's deal with this in a sensible way. You're proud of your mother. Don't you want her to be proud of you?'

Thomas ignored him. Then he heard Dr Michael Tennent's voice cut through the darkness. 'Thomas,' he said, 'I'd like to talk about your mother.'

Thomas froze.

'Tell me about your mother, Thomas.'

He closed his eyes. *Shut up, Dr Michael Tennent!*

Michael persisted, 'Tell me about your mother, Thomas. You always seem to have a problem talking about your relationship with your mother.'

Thomas was quivering. He knew what the man was trying to do and he had to stop him.

Ignore him.

Close your ears.

Just get on with what you were doing. Don't let him get to you. He destroyed your mother, don't let him destroy you, too.

He was less than four feet away from the detective. But his hand was shaking too much now. Another two feet and he'd be point blank.

Point blank would be better. Gun right up against his temple. No missing.

'Tell me about your relationship with your mother, Thomas,' Dr Tennent said.

487

Thomas, in a haze of anger and confusion, took another step forward and as he did so, there was a loud crack under his foot, as he trod on something.

The sound told Glen his position. Ducking as low as he could behind the operating trolley, knowing the woman was strapped securely, he pushed it with all his force in the direction of the sound. It stopped, abruptly, with a jarring, clattering thud, accompanied by a pained grunt, followed by two bright sheets of flame in rapid succession, and gunshots that boomed through the chamber like thunder, accompanied by the banshee howl of ricocheting bullets.

Grimly, the dense reek of cordite in his nostrils, Glen yanked the trolley back, then hurled it forward again, with every ounce of muscle-power he had left in him. He felt it crash into its target and jar to a halt with a crunch of what might have been bone, followed almost instantaneously by a searing flash of flame, another explosion, and this time he felt the shock wave of the bullet as it cracked past his head.

No ricochet.

Christ, he hoped to hell the man hanging hadn't been hit.

Frantically pressing home his advantage for all he could, he yanked the trolley back and shoved it forward again with even more force. Again it jarred home. He heard an oath, presumably Lamark, and something clattering across the floor. The gun?

He jerked the trolley back and slammed it forward again.

'Fuck you, bastard.'

Lamark's voice, for sure.

Glen slammed the trolley forward again; then again, and again. Then he reached up, scrabbled for the instrument tray, found something long-handled, and launched himself around the side of the trolley into the darkness.

Almost instantly he stumbled over legs on the floor and fell on top of a writhing figure. Flailing for Lamark's gun-hand, he lunged down his instrument with his right hand, and heard the ping as it struck the bare concrete floor. Then he lunged again. This time it plunged into something soft and firm, and he heard a scream of agony.

He had a wrist in his left hand! Letting go of his weapon, he scrabbled frantically with his other hand for the man's face. He found the goggles! Ripped them up off Lamark's forehead. The strap was caught under something, maybe the man's neck. He pulled harder, heard a strangled gasp beneath him.

Then something slammed into his face; a fist or a gun butt or a bullet, he had no idea, he just knew he was falling backwards and crashed against something, almost splitting his head open.

Somehow he got back onto his knees. *Keep moving*. Crab-like to the left. His knee came down on something hard.

He felt. Broken plastic. It was a torch! *Careful*. Ready to dive left or right, he switched it on, thrusting it forward into the darkness like a dagger.

The beam wasn't great but it was enough. He could see everything in one sweep. The man hanging did not seem to have been hit; he couldn't see the woman. Thomas Lamark was three feet in front of him, crouched in an attack position, the handle of a scalpel sticking out of his thigh. The gun lay on the floor, six feet behind him.

Glen dived for it a fraction ahead of Lamark. Crashing down onto the concrete, he hauled himself forward. Grabbed it, scrabbled forward more, then turned, pointed it straight at Lamark, whose hand was gripping his ankle.

The beam of the torch was fading. Holding the gun steady on Lamark, he shook the torch. A flicker. The beam was stronger for a second then faded again.

Don't die on me, baby, please don't die on me.

He shook it again. Stronger beam now. Lamark was staring at him. Smiling. Totally unhinged.

'Put your hands on top of your head and stand up,' Glen gasped, the rattling wheeze in his chest startling him.

Thomas Lamark stayed where he was.

Close to panic at his own condition, Glen wheezed, as loudly as he could manage, 'Put your hands on top of your head, Mr Lamark, or I'll shoot.'

Sounding as charming as when he had opened the front door, Thomas said, 'I counted before I came in, Detective

Constable Branson. There were only three bullets left in the magazine, I'm afraid. You have an empty gun in your hand and you are bleeding to death. We can wait, I'm in no hurry and my friends here aren't going anywhere. I'm afraid I really don't have any alternative to suggest at this moment.'

'Thomas,' Michael Tennent said suddenly, again, 'I'd like you to tell me about your mother.'

With no last-minute warning flicker, Glen's torch went dead. Then out of the darkness, he sensed something coming at him. Pointing the gun dead ahead, no idea whether Lamark was bluffing or not, just sensing imminent danger, he pulled the trigger.

The muzzle flash, the numbing bang, the heavy kick of the weapon all took him as much by surprise as the terrible shrieking that followed. It was like some wild animal in mortal agony.

For some moments it was impossible to tell whose voice it was. Glen got to his feet. The howling continued, deep, gulping bellows of pitiful agony.

It was Lamark's voice.

'Help me, oh, help me, help me!'

Glen shook the torch again, slid the on-off switch back and forwards. A weak beam flickered on. Lamark was on the floor, writhing like a snake, his face contorted, screaming. Glen stood at a safe distance from him, not trusting him. Then he saw the bloodstained right leg of the cream linen suit and knew that he had shot Lamark through the kneecap.

The man looked up at him, begging, 'Get me something, oh, God, please get me something.'

Still wary, not knowing what strength the man had, Glen studied him for a few moments more, then in a swift movement, using almost his last reserves of strength, he knelt down, yanked Lamark's arm onto his stomach, ignoring his shrieks and clamped handcuffs on him.

Then he stood up, and staggered sideways, his legs starting to buckle. He gripped the side of the trolley and gave Amanda a reassuring smile. 'You're going to be all right, you're going to be fine, you're safe. I'll free up your friend, and we'll help you together. Don't worry about anything, we're going to make you fine.'

On the floor, Thomas Lamark screamed again. 'Do something for me! Oh, God, please, do something to stop – stop – stop – pain oh, please – please, somebody, do something!'

Glen looked down at him, and Thomas fell silent.

'I'm surprised at you, Mr Lamark,' Glen said, his breath shorter and raspier every moment. '"*There's always one bullet left in the chamber; never forget that one in the chamber.*" You didn't remember, did you? The last line of *Wings of the Wild?* Your mother's greatest film.'

Chapter One Hundred and Five

Amanda clung tightly to Michael in her sleep, shuddering, making little sounds every few minutes, tiny, frightened moans.

In the morning she would stare at him with wide eyes and say, in genuine innocence, 'I did it again, didn't I? I don't remember, I really don't remember!' Then she would kiss him and say, 'Poor darling, I woke you again, I'm not being fair to you.'

But she never woke him. He was always awake – like now, wide awake at three o'clock in the morning, exactly one year, four months and eleven days since that sweltering July Friday last year when he had entered the Lamarks' house.

Maybe one day, Nietzsche's dictum, 'That which does not kill me makes me stronger', would come true for him.

For them both.

In the meantime they slept every night with the light on. Amanda wanted it on and, silently, he was grateful. He wanted it on too, but to tell her would mean admitting his own fear to her, and in trying to make her strong again, he needed to pretend to be strong himself.

Churning it all over again and again inside his head. That last consultation with Gloria Lamark. Wondering, always wondering, whether five people, an editor called Tina Mackay, a junior newspaper reporter called Justin Flowering, two police constables called Nick Goodwin and Simon Roebuck, and the actress, Cora Burstridge, might still be alive today if he had handled that consultation differently.

Gently, trying not to disturb Amanda, he prised himself free of her arms and eased himself up in bed, as he did on so

492

many nights, and picked up his worn copy of the writings of the grand old father of medicine, Hippocrates. The book fell open at the passage he had read and reread so often in these past sixteen months.

Life is short, and the Art long; the occasion fleeting; experience fallacious, and judgement difficult. The physician must not only be prepared to do what is right himself, but also to make the patient, the attendants, and externals co-operate.

He moved on to the next passage, which also fell open to the touch.

Medicine is of all the arts the most noble; but, owing to the ignorance of those who practise it, and of those who, inconsiderately, form a judgement of them, it is at present far behind all the other arts. Their mistake appears to me to arise principally from this, that there is no punishment connected with the practice of medicine (and with it alone) except disgrace, and that does not hurt those who are familiar with it. Such persons are the figures which are introduced in tragedies, for as they have the shape, and dress, and personal appearance of an actor, but are not actors, so also physicians are many in title but very few in reality.

He put the book down on the bedside table. He liked the wisdom of the ancients. Sometimes, it showed how little humans had progressed between millennia in the areas that really mattered. We were better at easing pain than the ancients; we were better at dealing with diseases and with injuries. But we weren't a whole lot wiser.

He had given Gloria Lamark the advice that in his heart he had felt was the right advice. Events had proved otherwise. He felt deep sorrow for the victims, but no disgrace. He had done what he thought was best for his patient. And he knew that, for his own sanity, he had to go on believing that.

This was how he lived now, in a state of denial.

One day, perhaps, that might change. Maybe today. Or tomorrow. Or in a year, or ten years, or when he was old and infirm and thinking back over his life, thinking about regrets, thinking about what might have been. And maybe there was, in a parallel universe somewhere out there in another dimension, a psychiatrist called Dr Michael Tennent who had an ageing movie star called Gloria Lamark as a patient, and this Dr Tennent never told her to face the fact that she had lost her looks and had blown her career, and never told her to stop living in the past and go out and get a life. And this Gloria Lamark was still alive, and in this parallel universe, so were Tina Mackay and Justin Flowering and Cora Burstridge and the young policemen.

And in this parallel universe, Dr Michael Tennent was a lousy psychiatrist who hadn't the guts to tell his patients the truth about themselves.

Big day today.

A massive crowd of press and media were gathered early outside the Central Criminal Court at the Old Bailey. Many of the morning papers carried the story on their front pages.

Months back, Thomas Lamark's lawyer had failed in his efforts to have his client declared unfit to stand trial. The case had lasted for seven weeks and the jury had unanimously found Lamark guilty on five counts of murder, on one count of attempted murder of a police officer, and on four counts of kidnap.

The judge had delayed pronouncing sentence for two months, pending further psychiatric reports requested by Lamark's counsel.

Today he would announce whether Lamark went to prison or to a secure psychiatric hospital, and for how long.

Michael and Amanda climbed out of their taxi into the bright October sunshine, and ran the gauntlet of the barrage of flashlights and microphones, up the steps and in through the doors.

Through the mêlée of people in the foyer, one man made

his way across to them, smiling broadly, hand outstretched in greeting. He was a tall, bald, black man in a sharp brown suit, white shirt and sober tie.

'Good to see you two guys!' he said.

Michael pumped his hand warmly, and Amanda gave him a kiss on both cheeks.

'So!' Glen said. 'Congratulations are in order! I got your wedding invitation.'

'You're coming?' Michael asked.

'Try and keep me away!' His smile was tinged with sadness. There would always be a shadow in his life. The responsibility he carried in his soul for the death of Nick Goodwin.

Michael grinned and Amanda laughed. Then, out of the corner of her eye, she saw Lulu pushing her way over to them. Amanda was leaving 20–20 Vision to go freelance, so she could spend more time with Michael. Lulu was being promoted to her job.

The two women hugged. Then Amanda said, 'Lulu, let me introduce you to the man who . . .' She faltered. 'Who saved our lives. Detective Constable Glen Branson.'

Glen raised a finger, a feigned hurt expression on his face. 'You didn't hear?' Then with a proud beam, he said, 'I'm not a detective constable any more. I'm now a detective *sergeant*!'

Michael congratulated him warmly, so did Amanda. Then all four stood in awkward silence, as if suddenly they had become aware that their good news was tainted with the collective guilt they all carried. Guilt, because in some way all of them had gained from their encounter with the monster to whose house the press had given the soubriquet, 'Holland Park Chamber of Horror'.

As they shuffled forward towards the courtroom door, unsure quite why they had come today, Michael put one arm round Amanda the other round Lulu. He squeezed their shoulders. They hadn't come here to see a man sentenced. The sentence did not matter. That was a formality. A symbol. A marker. An end.

They had come because it was also a new beginning.

Epilogue

wednesday, 9 july 2000
I haven't decided whether I am going to tell Dr Michael Tennent. I have a lot on my mind right now.

There are some very weird people in here and, frankly, they irritate me.

It seems I am destined for ever to go on despising Dr Michael Tennent. He no longer appears to have the high public profile he used to; in fact, he seems to have gone into hiding. He doesn't write his newspaper column any more, and I don't hear him on the radio these days, although it is difficult tuning into that station on the one communal radio we have: all the idiots here can never decide what they want to hear, so usually we end up hearing nothing.

Instead, Dr Michael Tennent has taken to publishing serious papers in medical magazines. He seems quite obsessed with the responsibilities of psychiatrists and psychologists in our society. In the latest British Medical Journal *he was even having a go at the so-called media and celebrity shrinks – which he himself was, for God's sake! Sound-bite psychiatry, he calls it.*

I see my own name appears in two papers. He never asked my permission, and there is perhaps the question of royalties I should raise. However, I'm not about to seek revenge, I've learned to my cost that revenge is indeed its own executioner.

They don't even allow me a computer in my little padded cell. What do they think I'm going to do? Beat my brains out on the keyboard?

They really are idiots here. Last week, my mother's film, Wings of the Wild *was showing, but I didn't watch it. Too many memories. And you know something? Not one single colleague of mine in here said they had even heard of my mother.*

I will have to make an example of someone and punish them for this, but there is no hurry: looks like I'm going to be here for a while.

I really ought to write a book to set the record straight, but the thought of having to do it in longhand, with pen and paper, is really too degrading. And, besides, do I want Dr Michael Tennent to know the truth?

This is a question I have asked myself repeatedly over the last year and a half that I have been here. That old proverb, and the truth shall set you free.

Do I want to set you free, Dr Michael Tennent? Do I have any reason to? Do I owe you anything?

All I ever wanted was to be free. It's strange, how I didn't remember, because my memory is so much better these days – I think it must be the medication they're giving me. But honestly, I had no recollection then at all. I seemed to forget so much.

I forgot that afternoon, that Monday afternoon in July 1997, when my mother came home in such a bad mood after she had been to see you. She went up to bed and asked me to make her a large whisky. I didn't tell her about the message on the answering-machine you had left, because this was my own chance to be free.

I popped the blister packs and dissolved the Nembutal in her whisky. I poured in the liquid Valium also; and just to speed the process along, and to make sure, after she had drunk the drink and was fast asleep, I injected curare through her heel.

Funny how it has all come back to me now. And to think I blamed you for this, Dr Tennent! I really did, I was so angry with you. Perhaps what my mother said to me as a child was true all along. Perhaps I am not right in the head.

Although I really do feel fine now.

All I wanted was to be free. And now, in reaching for my freedom, I have committed myself to a lifetime in institutions for the criminally insane.

Huh!

I've been locked up and they've thrown away the key.

But you are locked up, also, aren't you, Dr Michael Tennent? In your own way, you are just as much a prisoner of your actions as I am.

But I at least have the power to set you free. I will deal with this the way I have dealt with so many decisions I've had to make in my life.

I will let the coin decide.

All Orion/Phoenix titles are available at your local bookshop or from the following address:

Mail Order Department
Littlehampton Book Services
FREEPOST BR535
Worthing, West Sussex, BN13 3BR
telephone 01903 828503, *facsimile* 01903 828802
e-mail MailOrders@lbsltd.co.uk
(Please ensure that you include full postal address details)

Payment can be made either by credit/debit card (Visa, Mastercard, Access and Switch accepted) or by sending a £ Sterling cheque or postal order made payable to *Littlehampton Book Services*.
DO NOT SEND CASH OR CURRENCY

Please add the following to cover postage and packing:

UK and BFPO:
£1.50 for the first book, and 50p for each additional book to a maximum of £3.50

Overseas and Eire:
£2.50 for the first book, plus £1.00 for the second book, and 50p for each additional book ordered

---

BLOCK CAPITALS PLEASE

name of cardholder ....

address of cardholder ....

....

....

postcode ....

delivery address
(if different from cardholder)

....

....

....

postcode ....

☐ I enclose my remittance for £....................................

☐ please debit my Mastercard/Visa/Access/Switch (delete as appropriate)

card number ☐☐☐☐☐☐☐☐☐☐☐☐☐☐☐☐☐

expiry date ☐☐☐☐   Switch issue no. ☐☐

signature ....

prices and availability are subject to change without notice